Berkley Titles by Samantha Vérant

The Secret French Recipes of Sophie Valroux

Sophie Valroux's Paris Stars

Praise for

the secret french recipes of sophie valroux

"Vérant transports us to the enchanting setting of Southern France and the magic of an exquisite French kitchen. This delectable novel is pure escapism through the delicious dishes made by chef Sophie's expert hands, the romance involving a childhood friend, and the splendor of France. Vérant's amazing recipes are included as the perfect companion to this tasty debut."

—Roselle Lim, author of *Natalie Tan's Book of Luck & Fortune*

"A passion for all things gourmet leaps off the page in Samantha Vérant's newest novel. Told from the perspective of a determined female chef, set amid a beautiful French backdrop, *The Secret French Recipes of Sophie Valroux* is a delicious tale of self-discovery. Thoroughly enjoyable!"

—Nicole Meier, author of *The Second Chance Supper Club*

"Indulge in the delicious story of a professional chef, spiced with a French château and sweetened with a love story. A charming read."

—Janice MacLeod, *New York Times* bestselling author of *Paris Letters* and *A Paris Year*

"Samantha Vérant brings her love of France and food to this vibrant, gratifying book. The recipes and characters leap off the page, and Vérant deftly appeals to all five senses, as well as the heart. A perfect novel for anyone who enjoys good food and a great tale."

—Michelle Gable, *New York Times* bestselling author of *A Paris Apartment* and *The Summer I Met Jack*

"Told with pep and so-vivid-you-can-taste-it food descriptions, *The Secret French Recipes of Sophie Valroux* is a sumptuous, transporting read from start to finish. What a pleasure to follow Sophie's journey, one of love, family, and confidence lost—and found—through food."

—Jessica Tom, author of *Food Whore: A Novel of Dining and Deceit*

"*The Secret French Recipes of Sophie Valroux* is a scrumptious novel about family, love, and food, layered like the very best dishes, each bite revealing another luscious note. If you love fiction and food, Samantha Vérant serves it up right."

—Amy E. Reichert, author of *The Coincidence of Coconut Cake*

"I savored every page of *The Secret French Recipes of Sophie Valroux.* Join a 'ruined' chef as she rebuilds her life at an ancestral château, rekindles an old romance, and, of course, labors in the grand kitchens where aspirations are fostered and dreams brought to fruition. With an ear for language, evocative sensory details, and delectable recipes, Samantha Vérant invites us to take our seat at the table and relish a delicious sojourn in the South of France. And just remember: Never trust a skinny chef."

—Juliet Blackwell, *New York Times* bestselling author of
The Vineyards of Champagne

"Featuring an ambitious young chef, an elegant château, and the enduring charm of the French countryside, *The Secret French Recipes of Sophie Valroux* is the perfect escape! Pour yourself a glass of wine, put on a Charles Trenet album, pick up this book, and you're there."

—Ann Mah, *USA Today* bestselling author of *The Lost Vintage*

"Vérant's sparkling debut novel [and] enticing culinary tale will appeal to romance fans and foodies alike." —*Publishers Weekly*

"Vérant immerses readers in the sounds, smells, and tastes of a professional kitchen, with a cast of sous chefs, old friends, and a gruff but handsome mushroom forager along for the ride. Francophiles and fans of Mary Simses and Roselle Lim will adore Sophie's journey." —*Booklist*

"A great story line, strong writing, plus a handsome French 'hero' and lovely descriptions of France make this debut women's fiction book a sure winner. . . . A charming, feel-good French romance that transports you out of your everyday life and into the heart of France—a delectable read."

—*The Good Life France*

sophie valroux's paris stars

Samantha Vérant

BERKLEY
New York

BERKLEY
An imprint of Penguin Random House LLC
penguinrandomhouse.com

Library of Congress Cataloging-in-Publication Data

Names: Vérant, Samantha, author.
Title: Sophie Valroux's Paris stars / Samantha Vérant.
Other titles: Paris stars
Description: First edition. | New York: Berkley, 2021.
Identifiers: LCCN 2020054999 (print) | LCCN 2020055000 (ebook) |
ISBN 9780593097748 (trade paperback) | ISBN 9780593097755 (ebook)
Classification: LCC PS3622.E7325 S67 2021 (print) | LCC PS3622.E7325 (ebook) |
DDC 813/.6—dc23
LC record available at https://lccn.loc.gov/2020054999
LC ebook record available at https://lccn.loc.gov/2020055000

First Edition: October 2021

Printed in the United States of America
1st Printing

Book design by Alison Cnockaert

This book is dedicated to all of the female chefs—
in professional kitchens and at home—who are setting the
cooking world on fire one glorious meal at a time.

Author's note: Champvert is a fictional village
inspired by my life in southwestern France.

I

spring

STRAWBERRY SOUP

I started writing poetry very young, when I was four years old. And you know, food is language, and when I express myself it is really to understand what the language is, and to try to extract the emotion out of it.

—DOMINIQUE CRENN, AUTHOR OF *REBEL CHEF* AND THE FIRST FEMALE CHEF WHOM MICHELIN AWARDED THREE STARS IN THE UNITED STATES

I

------ ❧ ------

falling headfirst into spring

FOR THE FIRST time since Grand-mère's funeral two short weeks ago, contentment, not grief, filled my heart. I sat in the window seat, gazing at the blue sky, reflecting on the changes in my life. My once-soiled reputation in New York had fully recovered and I was now Sophie Valroux, Grand Chef and *maîtresse de maison* of Château de Champvert in southwestern France, not the saboteur blamed for costing my former employer in New York a Michelin star. I had a new best friend in Phillipa, who kept me more or less balanced when I was feeling out of whack. And I had the love of Rémi, my childhood sweetheart. All amazing transformations in the state of my world—save for the fact that Grand-mère was gone.

To keep the occasional wave of remorse from pulling me under, I kept myself busy—planning menus and testing recipes. Rule number one: no crying in the kitchen, so that's where I placed my focus.

Cooking always helped me to sort out my thoughts and pull myself together. Making Grand-mère's recipes, like spring lamb with a fresh mint chutney, the aromas of freshness permeating my nostrils, brought a sense of closure, and I felt closer to her. Food brought on nostalgia, all the happy times I'd spent with her. I needed to move on from my grief, dry up those tears, and forge on. We were going to be extraordinarily busy.

In two days, we'd open the gates of Château de Champvert to the public. The guests would be arriving in swarms, just like the bees in the *ruches* at the far end of the property, and we were booked solid from the third of May to the end of October—almost filled to capacity until we closed for the season in mid-December. At the very least, Les Libellules (the Dragonflies)—the château's flagship restaurant, which I ran—closed its doors on Sundays and Mondays, so I would have a bit of time off. Sort of. I knew there would always be some kind of challenge to overcome. But I'd risen up from the ashes of destruction before, and spring was a chance for a new beginning.

A smile curved across my lips. My gaze shot from the window to Rémi.

He slept peacefully in my bed, his breath rising and falling in soft whooshes. I wore his button-down shirt and held the collar up to my nose, breathing in his clean, woodsy scent. His left hand patted down the bed as he blindly searched for me. I let out a soft laugh, and his long eyelashes fluttered. He propped himself up on his elbows, the sunlight highlighting his muscular arms.

"What are you doing way over there? Come back to bed," he said, squinting.

I swung one leg down from the ledge slowly and purposefully, swiped my long hair over my shoulder, and smiled. "But shouldn't you get back to Lola?"

Rémi glanced at his watch. "She won't be up for another half hour. Which gives us twenty minutes."

"To do what?" I asked, my heart thankful that Laetitia—Lola's grandmother—looked after his daughter when Rémi snuck out to spend quality time with me.

"Whatever we want," he said with a wicked grin. "Get over here, woman."

"Did you just call me 'woman'?"

"*Alors*, you are one, and very beautiful at that." He paused, eyeing me up and down. "My shirt looks good on you. Really good."

I jumped off the window seat, ran over to the bed, and threw my body onto his. One of Rémi's hands cupped the back of my neck, and the other grazed my hip with a soft touch. Our mouths molded together and our breaths became one—hotter and heavier, my legs enveloping his waist. Rémi's tongue became more courageous, and I sighed as he wrapped his hand around my hair, pulling it lightly and tilting my head back. I loved when he did that—a bit animalistic, but hot nevertheless.

Our feverish eyes met. His lips brushed against my collarbone. "Do you know how much I want you right now?"

I knew. "And I want you, too, but—"

"You still want to wait," he said, his eyes not leaving mine.

"I do."

Aside from passionate kisses and clinging to each other's bodies in extremely heated moments like horny teenagers, we hadn't moved our relationship to a truly physical level. Prior to Rémi, I'd had only one boyfriend, and we didn't exactly make love. Eric was more like a pile driver and didn't care about pleasuring me. Plus, he'd cheated on me numerous times, the reason we broke up. At the time, my culinary aspirations were more important to me than the state of my heart, but, looking back, I realized he'd hurt me, made me feel useless as a woman.

There was no denying the deliciously satisfying chemistry between Rémi and me, but like a chocolate soufflé, the timing needed to be perfect or it would collapse. Having been burnt by a previous relationship, I didn't want Rémi and me to break apart, and I needed to be ready to fully let myself go. But I adored being wrapped in his arms, and, damn, did I love his kisses.

"You're killing me, Sophie," said Rémi with an exaggerated groan.

I kissed him lightly on the lips and whispered, "I could think of worse ways to die."

He wrapped his arms around my waist and flipped me onto my back, straddling me. "Hmmm, slow, painful deaths," he said, his eyes glinting mischievously. "Burnt at the stake. Drowning. Buried alive—"

"See," I said, rubbing my hands across his muscled chest. "You've got it pretty good."

"I do." Rémi flopped down beside me and let out a frustrated sigh. "I should get back to Lola before I lose all control. I'll see you later?"

"Of course," I said. "The staff meeting is this morning."

"I'd say you could keep my shirt," he said. "But I really shouldn't walk around the property half-naked."

I slipped his shirt off and he kissed my shoulder. "*Je t'aime*, Sophie."

"*Je t'aime aussi.*"

Love. It felt so good to say it, to feel it. I'd never really experienced it before, not like this. With another heavy breath, Rémi scrambled out of bed, and I watched him dress, noting his V-shaped torso and six-pack abs, wondering how in the world I stayed in control.

I'd already showered and dressed when Phillipa tapped on my door with her signature rat-a-tat-tat woodpecker knock. "I saw Rémi heading over to his house. I figured the coast was clear."

"I was hoping for a little me time." I said with a sigh.

Phillipa blurted out a laugh as she cracked the door open. "You never have *you* time. And I've barely seen you in two weeks. You're always with *him*."

"Are you saying you miss me?"

"I am."

"You'll be sick of me soon," I said, thinking of how busy the kitchen was going to be. "I'd run while you can."

"I'd never get sick of you," Phillipa said, and ambled into my room, a cheery grin lighting her face. She wheeled in a cart with a tray of buttery croissants and coffee in a French press. "It's a beautiful day. There isn't a cloud in the sky. The sun is shining. The birds are chirping—"

"And you brought me breakfast. Thank you."

Phillipa winked. "And you're about to get a real jolt. The review in *World Gourmand Magazine* just released. I wanted to be the one to share it with you."

"What? When were they even here?"

"Apparently at the soft opening," she said.

A lump formed in my throat. I couldn't take any more bad news. I tried to recall what we'd prepared. The flames of drunken shrimp flambéed in cognac sparked in my memories, which, as I recalled, we served over a terrine of chopped tomatoes, avocado, and strawberries, along with a creamy Parmesan-lemon risotto. Had it been good enough? Or would I be skewered in a review? I didn't want to know, so I changed the subject.

I focused on my friend. She usually went au naturel. Today, she'd painted her lips bright pink, and thick mascara coated her lashes. "Phillipa, are you wearing makeup?" I asked.

"Er, yes," she said, scrunching her pixie-like nose. "I may be getting in touch with my feminine side."

"For somebody? Maybe?" I said, and wiggled my brows.

"Maybe," she said. "But I don't want to jinx it."

For once the conversation wasn't concentrated on château business, the passing away of my *grand-mère*, or the relationship between Rémi and me. It was nice changing the subject and focusing on something else. "I want details," I said.

"And you'll get them once I know what's going on. We've only had one date. I will tell you one thing, though: she's a supercute pastry chef."

"Ahhhh," I said, my interest piqued. "And how was it?"

"No more questions until I know if Marie—"

"Her name is Marie? Why am I just hearing about her now?"

Phillipa shrugged. "You've been a bit preoccupied."

"I know," I said, and a pinch of guilt tweaked at my heart.

Phillipa stood silently for a moment, blushing. "Anyway, we were talking about the review." She thrust a paper in front of my face. "Do you want to read it?"

"No, you do the honors," I said, slumping my shoulders. "Just do me a favor and spare me the sordid details."

Her English accent rose and fell with excitement. "'Once-maligned chef Sophie Valroux is making her mark in the culinary world, rising up like a perfect soufflé—'"

"*Putain*," I said, interrupting her and driving my fingernails into my palms. "Can I ever escape my past?"

"Oh, you have. And please don't say 'putain.' It's absolutely vulgar. Unless you're a simpleton," she said.

I grabbed a croissant from the tray, pulled a piece off, and stuffed it in my mouth. Crumbs flaked onto my T-shirt as I chewed. One thing I loved about France was the way the breads and *viennoiseries* melted on my tongue in buttery goodness. Add the cheese, and I was in heaven.

"It's the New Yorker in me. And you sound like Jane," I said, mouth full, referring to her polar-opposite twin sister. Sometimes I wondered if they were even related.

"Well, I'd suggest you leave the New Yorker in you behind, because you're here now. And here's the proof," said Phillipa, and she continued to read. "'The flavors of southwestern France have never come so alive, with flair, a nod to classic recipes, and innovation. This Grand Chef deserves her title. The groans of delight emanating from the patrons of this wonderful restaurant every time they take a bite of one of her marvelous creations proves this. Never have I tasted the complex yet simple layers of flavors that Grand Chef Sophie Valroux provides, each dish complementary and more succulent than the last.'"

"Well, that wasn't bad," I said, straightening my posture. My eyes widened, and I smiled. "In fact, it was really nice. And, you know, I couldn't have done this without you."

"Thanks," said Phillipa, nodding her head enthusiastically. "I've heard this critic is the toughest of them all." She tilted her head to the tray. "Up and at 'em, sunshine. Live in the glorious moment. It's the start of a beautiful season."

"You're not having a coffee with me?"

"Nah, I've got some things to do before the meeting," she said. "Breakfast was my excuse to share the review with you." She pivoted for the door and, before closing it, said, "See you in a few."

Coffee in hand, I sat in the window seat, fascinated by the puffy white clouds rolling in the sky, a melancholy sensation washing over me. I wished it were Grand-mère who'd knocked on the door to share the review and offer some kind of advice or guidance for my first season running the château as Grand Chef. I thought of the effortless way she'd danced around the kitchen, the way the names of foreign ingredients had rolled off her tongue as if she was fluent in another language. When I was a child, I'd sit on a wicker stool, the seat making indentations in my eight-year-old thighs, and sometimes she'd blindfold me and hold up spices to my nose.

"Sophie, *ma chérie*, smell this," she'd say. "What do you smell?"

"Nutmeg," I'd answer.

"And this?"

"Saffron."

After going through quite a few spices, my answers usually right, she'd whip off the blindfold and pinch my cheeks. "One day, you're going to be a great chef," she'd say, and I'd grin.

"*Merci*, Grand-mère," I'd respond. "One day I want to be just like you."

And perhaps I was. I'd taken over her life.

A few weeks ago, after La Société des Châteaux et Belles Demeures decorated me with the honor of Grand Chef, I'd raced up to Grand-mère's room, opened the door, and held out the plaque. Her eyes glistened with proud tears. "Ma chérie, I knew you could do it. You must have Rémi take my plaque down and put yours up at the front gate."

She was so proud of me, so supportive. But now she was gone, and nothing I could say or do would bring her back.

BEFORE I HEADED down the stairs to the staff meeting in Grand-mère's office, now painfully mine, I slinked up one floor to her suite and stood in front of the large wooden door carved with the fleur-de-lis, breathing heavily. Finally, I found the courage to open it, and it creaked eerily when I did. Like my room, her living quarters weren't renovated, and the decorations screamed classic French in shades of blue and white, whereas shades of green made up the color scheme of my room. Same layout. Same format. But there was one major difference, one making my head spin. I had to place my hands on the doorframe to keep my balance.

Grand-mère's scent of Chanel No. 5, lavender, nutmeg, and cinnamon lingered in the air, hitting my nostrils, so potent I slammed the door shut, not able to bring myself to step into her chambers. Instead, I made my way downstairs, heading into the oak-paneled office. As I traced the letters on Grand-mère's Grand Chef plaque, moved from the outer gates, mine replacing it, a cough interrupted my thoughts; Jane and Phillipa stood in the doorway.

Jane—manager of the château, our head gardener in our expansive greenhouse, and, oddly, beekeeper—was always poised and polished, kept her blond hair in a tight French twist, had a figure most women would kill for, and wore kitten heels, possibly even when beekeeping and gardening. "Ready for utter madness?" she asked.

"As I'll ever be," I said with a gulp.

"We've got this," said Phillipa. She held her hand up for a high five.

"I don't do that," I said, cringing.

She burst into laughter, sounding a bit like a donkey braying. "I know. I was just messing with you, Chef."

Jane grinned, and it kind of unnerved me. Previously, when Jane smiled, I always felt like something was off, as if she were up to something. But even though we'd had our differences in the past, I didn't know what I'd do without Jane.

Before I could ponder the friendships I'd created with Phillipa and Jane, the rest of the staff entered the room. First came Gustave, our pastry chef and the man responsible for lunches at our second restaurant, Le Papillon Sauvage (the Wild Butterfly). Although he always had a bottle of pastis in hand, he was a maestro in the kitchen, preparing the wildest of desserts in the evenings and the most succulent of roast chickens and wood-fired pizzas during the day. Our guests loved him. He was the epitome of a southwestern Frenchman, always using exaggerated hand gestures and larger-than-life mouth sounds. He was the reason Le Papillon Sauvage had received a Bib

Gourmand from Michelin. Not quite the same as gaining stars, this honor was reserved for restaurants serving exceptional meals for a moderate cost. One could eat at Le Papillon Sauvage for the price of twenty-nine euros, including wine from the château's vineyards, complete with Gustave's maniacal laughter.

He held out his bottle of pastis. "Does anybody want some?"

Sébastien, or Séb, our all-around guy in the kitchen and the youngest one on our crew, sauntered in just then, and his dark hazel eyes widened with disbelief. "It's only nine in the morning," he said.

"Bah," said Gustave, guzzling back a sip. "It's the breakfast of kings."

Séb winced and lifted his upper lip into a sneer.

The gray-haired granny brigade, comprised of *les dames* Truffaut, Bouchon, Pélissier, and Moreau, arrived next. I had no clue as to how four little ladies could handle so much, but they did. Per their usual ways, after exchanging the required *bises*, kissing everybody on their cheeks, they sat down on the couch and clucked away, smiling.

My grand-mère's best friend, Clothilde, clicked into the salon with her bouncing red curls and her ladybug-covered ballerina flats. She was a force in the kitchen, and worked with Phillipa, Séb, and me to create the meals for Les Libellules. She raced up to me, clasped my hands, and said, "We're going to be busier than usual this year, thanks to you, *ma petite puce*. I'm so proud of you."

My little flea. I loved when she used this term of endearment.

Clothilde's husband, Bernard, in charge of the château's winemaking facilities, ran up to me and swung me around. "We're all proud of you, Sophie, and we're going to have the best season. The vines are looking great, just beautiful."

"I'm glad," I said. "I can't wait to see the harvest."

My adoptive family chatted away, throwing accolades in my direction as the rest of the staff, namely housekeeping and servers, arrived. Rémi was the last to show up, flanked by his two portly black

Labrador retrievers, D'Artagnan and Aramis. They panted as they drooled and then wriggled around on the floor.

Jane glowered at Rémi. "No animals in the château."

He smirked. "They work here too. Or did you forget?"

"They do not work here."

"Yes, they most certainly do. They chase off the *sangliers* and hunt down the truffles. Maybe they should receive a salary?"

I don't know why Rémi got such a kick out of needling Jane, but he did. He was also right about the dogs and their task. The sangliers (wild boars) on the property scared the crap out of me, which was why I didn't wander the grounds alone at night. Rémi raised a defiant brow, and the housekeeping staff burst into laughter.

By his stoic expression and sarcastic response, Jane knew she wasn't going to win this argument. Instead, she rolled her eyes dramatically and launched into manager-of-the-château mode. "Ladies and gentlemen, thank you for joining us today. As you know, we have a very, very busy season ahead of us, and we all need to be on our A game. With the exception of the season's end, the château is fully booked from May third, which is in two days, until we close our doors in the winter." She eyed the housekeeping team and bared her teeth into an intimidating smile. "Ladies, I expect all of the guest rooms to be perfect, no detail left unturned."

They nodded. "Yes, madame."

Jane turned to me. "Anything you want to say to the brigade and servers?"

The kitchen was where I sorted out my feelings, where I'd found my passion, where I expressed myself. Out of my comfort zone, all eyes on me, I ended up repeating the words Phillipa had said earlier. "We've got this."

Jane nudged me in the ribs and whispered, "You can do better than that."

I sucked in a deep breath. "After all the press, after everything, like Jane said, we've got a reputation to uphold. Every meal has to be better than the last one. No detail can be overlooked, especially in our main dining room. I realize we're all under a lot of pressure. And we're all still grieving over the loss of Grand-mère Odette, but we can do this—as a family."

Before the staff broke down into tears, Jane cleared her throat. "Are we all ready to make this the best season that Château de Champvert has ever known? Are we all ready to get to work? Do our best?"

Applause. Smiles. Rémi mouthed, "I love you," and then left with the dogs.

"Then let's get to it. I, like Sophie, have faith in all of you. If there are any issues along the way, please see me immediately," said Jane.

The staff chatted among themselves and then slipped out the door, leaving Jane, Phillipa, and me alone in the office. "Well, what do we do now?" I asked.

"This season is going to be absolutely amazing," said Jane. "The château was always near full but never booked to capacity. But it is now, thanks to you and all the glowing press. It's a dream come true."

Phillipa squealed. "It is."

The girls stood in front of me, grinning, eyes wide, waiting for me to say something. I forced a smile. "Sure is," I said wistfully, wondering about my dreams. "We're going to have a fabulous season. And I'm so glad I have the two of you by my side."

Jane and Phillipa wrapped me in overexuberant hugs and then sashayed out of the room, Phillipa leaping a few times. After they left, I traced the raised bronze letters on my grand-mère's Grand Chef plaque, gnawing on the inside of my cheek.

Prior to Champvert, I only had one dream, and running a château in southwestern France was never a part of it. I wanted to be one of the rare female chefs Michelin decorated with its prestigious stars. Although gaining a star came with a lot of pressure, and I was already under enough as it was, I didn't want to give up on the only life goal I'd had, the one pushing me forward for so many years. Before she died, Grand-mère told me that I could achieve my aspirations here in Champvert. I wondered if what she'd said was true, because my past had left me feeling quite jaded, always waiting for the other shoe to drop. I knew I held all of the ingredients to carve out a perfect life, maybe write my own culinary narrative, but something was missing, and not just my grand-mère. A huge part of me felt like I'd woken up from a dream that was never mine, and that I was sleepwalking in a story I hadn't written.

2

father knows best

EVERYWHERE I TURNED, Grand-mère's spirit materialized in hazy recollections, singing to me through the trees, whispering from every nook and cranny of the château. In a way, this brought a strong sense of comfort—as if she wasn't *really* gone. My eyes darted to the château, with its iron balconies, the slate roof soaring into the cloudless cornflower-blue sky, and my gaze locked onto Grand-mère's room. I wished she were sitting in her window seat, smiling down upon me and waving. But, of course, she wasn't there.

Instead of wallowing in self-pity, I forced myself to put grief to the side and focus on all things positive. That was what Grand-mère would have wanted. It was what I wanted. If I tumbled down a rocky path, so would the château, and I could never let that happen. People—namely, the entire village of Champvert—depended on me for jobs and survival.

Before I fell knee-deep into the fiery wildness of kitchen life in two days, I wandered aimlessly around the property, reflecting on and appreciating this magnificent world my grand-mère created. I wanted to revel in the warmness of my first spring in Champvert and to breathe in the rare minutes of me time that remained.

Ranging in different shades of pink from pale to vibrant, the peonies seemed to burst open practically overnight, swarms of bees zipping from flower to flower. In the orchard, fluffy white flowers adorned the cherry trees. The lake glimmered in the distance, the strands of the weeping willows blowing in the warm spring breeze. I'd read somewhere that weeping willows represented strength and were able to withstand the greatest of challenges. I wanted to be the tree, perseverant and ready for anything, even a storm.

The air buzzed with life, dragonflies and butterflies dancing in the clear blue sky. Everything was blooming and thriving. Maybe even me. Surreal as it was, all of this—this land, this château—was mine. And I had a lot going on for me, which included Rémi.

We'd shared our first kiss the day before I'd left Champvert after one of my summer visits. I was thirteen and he was fifteen. I remembered the look in his caramel eyes—dreamy and mischievous, just like they were this morning. We'd just gone swimming in the lake and we were sprawled out under one of the willow trees, drying off. As I recalled, he'd had braces and cut my lip.

I closed my eyes, thinking about his body pressed against mine, his throaty laugh, and his wicked sense of humor. I knew he'd only brought the dogs to the meeting to get under Jane's skin. And the joke he'd made this morning about slow deaths brought a smile to my lips.

Rémi drove by on the mower, tending to the sprawling lawn of grass kissed by the morning dew. His Mediterranean complexion was already tanned the color of golden honey and made the smile he shot in my direction brighter, becoming more swoon-worthy when his adorable dimples puckered. His muscled arms glistened with a thin sheet of perspiration, and I wanted them wrapped around me, if only for a moment. But there was too much work to do before the guests arrived. In addition to mowing acres upon acres of rolling terrain, Rémi needed to trim the fleur-de-lis-shaped hedges, the gravel driveway was in desperate need of a raking, leaves and weeds had to be cleared—the list went on and on. Still, he pulled up to me and turned off the engine.

"I'd like to take you out tomorrow night. Are you free?" he asked with a sly smile.

"I'm always free," I said with a snort. "I'm American."

"That joke again? It's old. You're also French. And I'll rephrase my question," he said, squinting into the sun. "Are you available tomorrow night? I'd like to take you somewhere."

"Like a real date?" I asked. With my settling Grand-mère's affairs and preparing for the château's opening, we hadn't actually been on one yet.

He winked. "I've got something special planned for us in Toulouse."

I clasped my hands over my mouth. "Escape the château for a night before madness sets in? I'm all for it. What are we doing? Where are we going?"

"It's a surprise," he said. "I'll pick you up at seven."

"Okay," I said, wondering what he was up to. "Wait. What about tonight? I thought you were coming over."

"Laetitia has a hot date. She's been whistling and smiling all morning," he said. "She hasn't gone out in years, so I promised Lola we'd have a *papa-fille* night. We'll do fun things like dance around in tutus and have an imaginary tea party with her stuffed animals."

"Lucky little girl," I said, my heart swelling because he was such a good dad. I tilted my head to the side, an idea coming to mind. "Can I stop by to see Lola?"

"She'd love that," he said with a wide grin. "But you better bring the ingredients for *un chocolat chaud*."

"I guess I can do that," I said, blurting out a laugh.

Before he motored off, he handed over a bouquet of lilies of the valley, the small flowers bobbing in the breeze like little bells. I brought them to my nose, inhaling the fresh, sweet scents of spring. "What are these for?"

"It's the first of May—*la fête du travail*, or Labor Day, in France. It's a tradition to give *muguet* to those you love with a wish for a prosperous year and happiness." He paused and brushed his hair out of his eyes. "*Et je t'aime*, Sophie. *Très fort*."

"Merci, for the flowers," I said. "I love you too."

I stood there with a goofy grin until Rémi turned on the engine and drove away, his T-shirt clinging to his muscled back.

LEAVING RÉMI, I wandered down to the river, where the Eurasian magpies always *chac-chac-chac*ked with their loud and unruly ways. The birds, although annoying, were beautiful with their iridescent feathers, glimmering in black, white, and sapphire blue. I sat at the edge of the burbling river, trailing my hand in the cold water, watching the dragonflies skimming the surface.

This land was mine. And it was beautiful. More than beautiful; it was magical. But running a château with two restaurants was going to be draining—physically and emotionally. I closed my eyes and prayed I could keep it together. The last thing I needed was another emotional breakdown. Been there, done that before, and it had been a rough road, one I didn't want to travel on again. I eyed the bouquet of lilies of the valley, thinking about happiness and Rémi—gorgeous, romantic Rémi.

A rustle came from the bushes, the crunch of footsteps on leaves.

I looked over my shoulder, surprised to see my father ambling down the path. Jean-Marc wore khaki shorts and a black polo, and carried a rake and a bouquet of muguet. His smile widened when he saw me, making him appear to be years younger and not as withered as when I'd first met him two weeks ago. When I'd first noticed him at that Sunday lunch, I nudged Rémi. "Who is that man? The one staring at me? Clothilde and Bernard don't look like they are all too thrilled to see him."

"Oh," he'd said. "Him? That's Jean-Marc Bourret. I invited him."

"Wasn't meeting him supposed to be *my* decision?" I'd asked.

Of all the days Rémi invited Jean-Marc, it was when the château was under audit by La Société. Part of me was still irritated with Rémi, because meeting my father was supposed to be my decision, but the other part of me was grateful.

"I hope I'm not intruding," said Jean-Marc, his eyes bright.

"No, it's a nice intrusion," I said.

Jean-Marc handed me the flowers. "I see you already have some," he said. "But you can never have too much happiness."

Trying to capture and hold on to this elusive emotion, I smiled. If anything, I wanted to be happy, and seeing my father did bring me joy.

"Merci," I said. "I'm really glad to see you. With everything that's been going on, we haven't had much time to talk. What brings you to the château?"

"Rémi called. He needed an extra pair of hands to prepare for the opening." He held up the rake. "I'm clearing out some of the underbrush in the forest."

I hugged my knees to my chest, blinking back my surprise. Although seeing my father brightened my spirit, this was another thing Rémi had done without my knowledge. I shook off my annoyance.

"I hope he's paying you well," I said, and Jean-Marc flinched.

"Paying me?" he scoffed. "I'm doing this for free. I want to help you out any way I can." His posture crumbled. "I would never take one *centime* from you, Sophie. I want to make things up to you for not being there—"

I instantly regretted bringing up the subject of money. I knew he wasn't after money. He'd made that clear the first time I met him after he told me my grand-mère had paid him off to stay away from my mother. Although he'd cashed only one check in the hopes of taking care of me and my mom, my mother left him high and dry when she took off with me for New York. He, not born of noble blood, was not good enough for her, and she broke off all contact. Jean-Marc may not have been a father figure during my childhood years, but he stood in front of me now, giving me the opportunity to finish the puzzle of my life.

"You didn't exactly have a choice in the matter," I said. "And I meant what I said. I really want to get to know you. Perhaps it's a bit selfish of me, but you're the only real family I have left now."

Jean-Marc sat down next to me, his eyes glistening with tears. He took my hand, squeezing it gently. "You're the only family I have too. And you're not selfish. You've let me into your life, making me the happiest man in the world. But, Sophie, why are you sitting alone out here?"

"I'm just thinking," I said.

"About your grand-mère?"

"Yes," I said with a sigh. "And all of the stress of running the château without her. I think I might crack under the pressure."

"If there's anybody who can figure things out, it's you."

"I'm not so sure about that," I said.

"I am."

"Why?" I asked.

"Look what you've already accomplished here in a short time. You're a Grand Chef. All the news outlets are singing your praises—"

My back straightened and my eyes widened with surprise. "You've been keeping tabs on all that?"

"*Bien sûr*, I'm really proud of you." He pulled his cell phone out of his pocket. "I have your name on Google Alerts."

Thanks to our successful "soft" grand opening and to an article in the *New York Times*, among other press outlets that latched on to the fact that I led a primarily women-run kitchen and business, the château was front and center in a media frenzy. According to the press, I was gloriously rich, young, and a beautiful porcelain doll—one who rose from the flames of destruction and couldn't be shattered.

But even with all the glowing reviews, my confidence wavered. I hadn't worked for any of the accolades; they'd been fed to me with a silver spoon and, after my grandmother passed away, included a château. I still had to prove my worth.

"It's a lot to live up to," I said with a sigh, and picked at the flowers. "The pressure is building, and we haven't even opened our doors to the public yet."

Jean-Marc clasped my hand and stopped me from destroying the bouquets. "Et alors, Sophie, you're surrounded with people who care about you and your success. If the pressure becomes too much, just let us know. We're here for you. You don't have to take on this world by yourself. Ask us for help."

Light filtered through the leaves of the trees, illuminating our faces. Maybe Jean-Marc was right. I'd been independent for far too long, holding on to the idea that depending on others showed weakness and that I didn't need anybody to "complete" me. I didn't want to appear desperate or, heaven forbid, needy.

"I suppose you're right," I said. "But enough about me. I want to hear more about you."

He cleared his throat. "I'm afraid I'm not that interesting."

"You are to me," I said. "You're my papa. And I want to know everything about you."

Jean-Marc's shoulders quivered. "Did you just call me your papa?"

We really hadn't tackled this subject yet, and I wondered if I was being too forthright with my American brashness. But an apple was an apple, an orange was an orange, and he was my dad—even though I barely knew him. And I did want to get to know him. It wasn't his fault he wasn't in my life until now; it was Mother's.

I inhaled a breath of air, feeling my lungs expand, and let it out in a soft whoosh. "I did call you papa," I said. "Because that's what you are."

Although spring was a chance for both of us to start over with a clean slate, for a brief moment, my mind wandered to my old life in New York, where I didn't have a château to manage. O'Shea had offered me a chef de cuisine position at Cendrillon NY, something I wanted for years, but I turned him down. I wanted to tell my own story, reach for my own stars, maybe even here in Champvert. Plus, if I hadn't stayed in France, I'd never know my father, and I wanted—no, needed—to let him into my life.

"So, tell me more about yourself," I said.

Tears streamed down Jean-Marc's cheeks. He gulped. "Where do I begin?"

"At the beginning," I said, squeezing his hand and needing a fresh start.

AT AROUND FIVE thirty, I walked over to Rémi's place, which was located toward the end of the château's property. A rustic stone house two stories high, it felt more like a home than the massive château. I knocked on the door and Lola opened it. She wore a white T-shirt and a pink tulle tutu with rhinestones on it. Her *châtain* (dark blond with hints of brown) pigtails glimmered in the sunlight, making it appear golden. Her hazel eyes went wide. "*Tatie* Sophie," she squealed. "Un chocolat chaud?"

I laughed and tousled her head. "You'll have to ask your dad."

"You can have one," said Rémi from the kitchen. "If you promise to eat your broccoli tonight."

Lola's little nose pinched. "Ew."

"Sophie, don't just stand there," said Rémi. "Come on in. I'm finishing something up. I'll join you in a minute."

I did as I was told and closed the door. Lola took my hand with her little chubby one and led me to the couch. Rémi had remodeled his home a few years ago, opening up the living space to the kitchen—American-style. The walls, like the outside, were stone, and there was a large mahogany table in the dining area. Along with Rémi's dogs, toys and dolls decorated the floor, and I gingerly stepped over them. A picture of Anaïs, Lola's mother, sat on the mantel above the fireplace, and I thought of what Laetitia, Lola's grandmother, had shared with me.

"I told you way back when that Rémi barely smiled. And then you returned to Champvert. I've seen the two of you together. I believe he makes you smile too," she'd said. "I also believe I told you that Rémi and Anaïs didn't love one another, but they did the right thing by Lola."

Like Lola, I'd also lost my mother, but Anaïs died during childbirth, not by suicide. I shuddered off the painful memory of finding my mother as Rémi approached. He wore a tiny purple tutu over his jeans, and I blurted out a laugh.

He lifted his shoulders and eyed Lola. "What can I say? It's daddy-daughter dance day."

Lola scrambled around on the floor, gathering her dolls—so many loaded in her little arms I thought she'd fall down.

"I think it's sexy that you're an amazing papa," I said, and then my brows furrowed. "Speaking of fathers, I have a bone to pick with you."

"*J'ai mal compris.*" (I don't understand.) "Bone?"

I crossed my arms over my chest. "You invited my father here without telling me."

"I don't see the problem. I needed help with the grounds. I called him. He was available. It's no big deal."

I straightened my posture, lifting my shoulders.

"It *is* a big deal for me," I said, keeping my voice in a low register. "Next time you do something like that, could you tell me first?"

"*D'accord*" (okay), he said.

Lola interrupted the conversation and dropped her dolls at my feet. She held out a brush.

"Do you want me to brush their hair?" I asked, doing my best to sweep my irritation with Rémi to the side. Plus, with the way he was dressed, it was hard to stay annoyed with his meddling, especially after he did some strange pirouette, followed by a goofy leap. And I did like running into Jean-Marc. We'd had a great talk.

Lola shook her head no, pigtails bouncing. "*Non*, make me pretty like you. And then un chocolat chaud."

"Sure," I said, patting the spot beside me. "Sit right here." My eyes shot to Rémi's as Lola scrambled onto the couch and handed me the brush. "I may have forgotten to bring the chocolate. There's some in dry storage in my kitchen. Could you go get it?" I said as I released Lola's hair from her pigtails. "You know where it is."

He nodded. "You're okay with the munchkin?"

"I'm fine," I said. Even though I'd never been alone with her, I was fairly certain I could handle it. Plus, she was being so sweet, humming a children's song and giggling.

Still wearing the tutu, Rémi left, and after I brushed Lola's curls, she set to becoming my almost-three-year-old hairdresser, mumbling, "Pretty, pretty, pretty." Surprisingly, her strokes were gentle and she didn't pull at or tear my hair.

I tucked my chin down, thinking of how I'd had to take care of my mom, how I'd had to brush her hair, cook for her, and how when she'd brushed my hair she'd nearly ripped it off my scalp. What kind of mother would I be? Mine had set the absolute worst of examples. And I'd forgotten the chocolate.

Lola set the brush down and placed her chubby hands on my cheeks. "Pretty," she said with a big grin, and my heart almost burst.

"You're very pretty too," I said.

She scrambled onto my lap and I inhaled her strawberry scent.

Although Lola and I shared a sweet moment, I was twenty-seven years old, and becoming an instant mom figure scared the crap out of me. I only knew my way around the kitchen. I could slice like the best of them, but I'd never changed a diaper. As I held on to Lola, my eyes locked onto the photo of Anaïs, her dark eyes, and I thought of her, my mother, and Grand-mère. Sometimes people just disappeared. I swallowed back terrible thoughts. If I got close with her, became her replacement mother, and something happened to me, Lola's life would be shattered. Even worse—what if something happened to Rémi?

3

merry jane

SOMETIMES GRIEF SNUCK up on me, catching me off guard and making it difficult to function. The following day, Phillipa and I were in the process of planning the menus for the upcoming week and a pit formed in my stomach, so tight I lost my breath and almost dropped to my knees. Grand-mère's poppy-print apron hung on a hook in the kitchen as a shrine to her memory. I placed my hands on the prep table to keep my balance.

"Are you okay, Sophie?" asked Phillipa. "You're zoning out. And you have a knife in your hand."

"Yeah, I'm fine," I said, snapping to attention and forcing a smile. "Let's get back to testing that new recipe of ours. I want to change it up a bit."

Phillipa nodded, maybe a little too enthusiastically. "Got it. She taught me that lesson well. Recipes are only guidelines. How were you thinking of changing the lemon chicken tajine?"

Hope fluttered in my chest. I had a chance to write my own culinary story, but I'd start off slow, one ingredient and one word at a time. Until I found my footing in this kitchen, it was all I could manage.

"We're not going to change Grand-mère's recipe too much," I said, eyeing the apron. "In addition to the parsley and garlic, I was thinking of adding in some of that Hungarian paprika we ordered, for a little heat. And maybe something else?"

"I'm already hungry," she said, licking her lips. "Too bad cèpes aren't in season. They would have been a killer addition."

It was the beginning of May. Cèpes, the wonderful mushrooms we were lucky enough to forage on the property, wouldn't be available until the end of August. We ran a garden-to-table outfit, serving only fresh ingredients that were in season or could be grown in the greenhouse—my sanctuary, the place where I oftentimes rebooted, smelling the tomato plants on my hands and collecting my thoughts, which were usually interrupted by some issue or another.

"What about leeks?" suggested Phillipa. "There are tons. And, yeah, yeah, yeah, I know it's May, and their season supposedly ends in April, but they are practically coming out of our ears and they are available year-round at the market." She paused. "They'll add flavor and bite, subtle and sweet."

"Phenomenal idea," I said. "I love it. Plus, you are so right; we need to use them before they expire. No waste, not on this land, not in this kitchen."

My eyes flickered toward the kitchen window. There she was, a large blue dragonfly (*une libellule*), zipping around in the blue sky, soaring and diving, never crashing down. These beautiful insects were the reason my grand-mère named the restaurant Les Libellules. I knew she wasn't the same one my grand-mère had discovered when she'd found her inspiration, but part of me wanted to believe that this marvelous creature, its iridescent wings sparkling in the sunlight, embodied her spirit, and the crazy notion that she was checking in on me bolstered my confidence.

Phillipa nudged my shoulder. "Sophie, you're spacing out again."

I pointed to the window. "She's here."

"I see her too," said Phillipa.

"So I'm not crazy?"

Phillipa laughed. "Maybe a little bit. But it's a good kind of crazy. Most of the time."

"Haha," I said, holding up my knife and raising a brow.

I was back to slicing tomatoes, zucchini, and eggplants, prepping my version of a *Provençal tian* (which people often confused with ratatouille, thanks to the movie with the rat), when Jane sashayed into the kitchen, looking all prim, proper, and gorgeous, even while wearing her beekeeper threads. But as she took her hat off and set it down on the prep table, I saw her hair was a mess. She wore many hats—none of which would ever fit me—and it was nice seeing her like this. Real. From her wicker basket, she pulled out bottles of vodka and vermouth, followed by a shaker, placing them on the counter.

"Would you mind zesting?" she said with a wink, nodding to a basket of lemons, and set to mixing martinis.

"Jane, it's only one p.m.," I said. "Are you channeling Gustave?"

She handed me a lemon. "You know, the smell of lemons is really quite therapeutic. And we're going to be busy. Might as well seize every moment while we can."

"I may need some therapy," I said, zesting and thinking about the upcoming stress of cooking nonstop. Jane handed Phillipa and me glasses, and I plunked in the curled rinds. "But this will work for now."

I lifted my martini, and the three of us toasted. Jane set her glass down and placed her hands on her knees. I was puzzled. "Jane, what is it? You're acting, um, bizarre, out of character from proper Jane," I said.

She inhaled a deep breath. "Yes, I know. I'm a bloody mess. Do you want the good news or the bad news first?"

I sighed. I should have expected this. Every time something good happened, there was always something malevolent lurking in the corner ready to smack me down. "Bad news first."

"There is a problem with the septic system," she said, her nose scrunching with disgust. "It's fine for now, but . . ."

"But?"

"It's going to cost fifty thousand euros to fix."

"I don't see the problem. We have the funds from my inheritance. Do it."

Along with the château, I'd inherited over fifteen million euros. Yes, I supposed I was an ingrate, but money meant nothing to me; along with cooking and creating amazing meals, people mattered. None of this, except for my newly formed friendships and Rémi, truly felt like mine.

"We can't," said Jane. "Because we won't have the funds from your inheritance for three and a half months, maybe longer."

"The château must have a savings account," I said.

"It does," said Jane. "But it's been frozen. We're only allowed to use the money coming in after your grand-mère's passing. Everything prior to that is considered hers until it's yours."

I snapped my head to face her. "I don't understand."

"French laws," she said. "People have four months to argue their case."

My grand-mère had enlightened me on the laws when she'd told me I'd inherit Château de Champvert, how they protected the children, how she'd done her best to build and protect my rights. But she hadn't prepared me for this.

"This is so messed up," I said, and then gnawed on the inside of my cheek.

"It is," Jane said. "But with all the guests and reservations, we have enough to cover the operational costs of the château. Sort of."

I gasped and jumped off my stool, knocking it over. It clattered on the ground. I picked it up with shaky hands, steadying it. "What do you mean 'sort of'?"

"Do you want to know about the finances of this place, how much it costs to run things?"

Not really, I thought. But this was my life now. I was in charge. "Lay it on me," I said.

"You better sit down," she said, and I did.

Jane pulled up a stool and sat next to me. She leaned forward. "Promise me you won't flip out."

"Please, just rip the Band-Aid off already and tell me how bad it is."

As I slumped lower and lower, Jane sat up straighter than I'd ever seen her, if that was possible. She let out a breath. "Along with the staff's wages, the utilities, the food deliveries, and everything else, we dole out around fifty thousand euros a month."

I sucked in my breath. "And how much will we pull in? With all of our guests? With both of the restaurants?"

"Until things are up and running, we'll barely break even."

My face found a life of its own. My chin quivered. My eyebrows felt like they were going to leap off my face. My shoulders shook. It took everything for me to keep from vomiting. "We won't break even?"

"I'm sorry, Sophie," said Jane. "But there is good news. I talked to the bank about getting a loan. They've agreed."

I placed my fingers to my temples. "We can't have toilets backing up."

Jane's eyes went wide. "Don't pay me my salary, not one centime, until your inheritance comes through. I know you're good for it. And when Christmas rolls around, I'll be expecting a big fat bonus."

"Me too. Just feed me. Let me work," said Phillipa. "We're in this together."

I bit down on my bottom lip, trying to think of a better solution, coming up with nothing.

"Now for the amazing news," said Jane, clearing her throat. She broke out into a wide grin. "I was looking over the reservations, and a very important VIP will be staying with us in a few weeks—a member of one of the most illustrious families in France."

"Who?" I asked, still reeling in shock over the bad news.

Jane leaned forward as if she were telling a salacious secret. "Nicolas de la Barguelonne. Can you believe it?"

"I can't," I said, throwing my hands up. "I don't even know who he is."

"The de la Barguelonnes, or rather the monsieur, his father, owns La Maison de la Barguelonne, all those emerging luxury fashion brands like Roux and Madeleine Bouchard, the cosmetic empire Déesse et Dieux, the jewelry line of Câlins de Luxe, the champagnes of Petit Fleur—"

I didn't see what the hoopla was all about and didn't connect with her excitement. I was still thinking about *merde*. "And?"

"And? Sophie, don't you see? One positive word from them, and all of Paris's elite will be knocking down our door."

She poured herself another martini and then looked up, holding her index finger and thumb an inch apart. "There's just one tiny issue."

Of course there was. She refilled my glass. I slammed back my martini, bracing myself.

"Monsieur de la Barguelonne is insisting on the bridal suite because it's the best room in the house. But we're booked to capacity and we're short one room."

"I suppose you have a solution," I said, shaking my head with disbelief and slouching lower.

"I do," said Jane. "And you're not going to like it."

"Jane, just tell me."

She glanced at the apron. "We have one available suite—"

I knew exactly what suite she was talking about.

"No way in hell," I said, my eyes bulging out of their sockets. "A complete stranger is not staying in Grand-mère's room, no matter how important they are. I can't believe you're even proposing this insanity."

"Sophie, we need all the press we can get. It needs to be continuous unless you want to be a flash in the pan. Right now Twitter is on fire with people talking about you and what an amazing chef you are. We've got to keep the momentum going." She paused. "What if you stay with Rémi? We'd use your suite? Would you be okay with that?"

Not really. My room held all of my childhood memories. The first time I met my grandmother, I was seven, and I spent the best summers of my life in Champvert until I was thirteen. Swimming in the lake with Rémi. Cooking with Grand-mère, learning from her. Escaping my mother.

Grand-mère and my mom were more than estranged, didn't talk, didn't write. When my mom left France, she didn't even look back. At least they'd made a deal: I'd spend my summers in Champvert so I could connect to my French roots. My mom was more than happy to get rid of me.

My trips ended when my mother spiraled into a well of depression and I had to stay home to take care of her. Prior to five months ago, I hadn't been back to Champvert for thirteen years. I'd been too focused on avoiding the pain associated with my mother, taking care of her, then her death, and I'd focused on my career, the kitchen a healing component, my only escape.

I guarded my summers with Grand-mère and the time I'd recently spent with her like the most sparkling of jewels. Grand-mère and I reconnected after I had nowhere to turn, after my career had erupted like an active volcano, leaving me in the wake of its destruction. I felt like a wounded stray cat. She was sick and took me in; I took care of her. We bonded over the past, sharing our joys and mistakes, most of which had to do with Mother. With so many memories swirling in my mind like a blender set to high, I needed to get out of this crazed plan of Jane's. I rubbed my eyes with the tips of my fingers, trying to come up with an excuse, my head pounding.

"I don't know about any of this," I said. "I'm not sure Rémi would want me staying at his house. And Lola would really be confused."

If I stayed with Rémi, I'd be closer with Lola. And, for now, I kind of wanted to keep myself at an arm's distance until I settled into this life more. I suppose I had severe abandonment issues, and two weeks wasn't enough time to heal a heart.

"Why? What's the problem? You're a couple," said Jane. "He stays with you all the time."

"Yeah, but she's not shagging him," Phillipa blurted out, and I shot her a glare.

"Oh," said Jane, her eyes widening with surprise. "That's a bit odd."

"I don't want to talk about my sex life, Jane," I said with a growl. "And, by your look, I know you're going to force me into this."

"That's the spirit. We're creating an empire here. Together," said Jane. "Fight the good fight."

"This quiet French countryside life isn't so quiet. I just want to sleep," I said.

"You can hibernate in the winter," said Phillipa, pumping her fist. "Until then, *vive le château*."

Jane clapped her hands together. "So, it's settled, then? We have a plan?"

I grunted. "Fine. But we're moving all of my stuff into Grand-mère's suite. I don't want a stranger rifling through my personal affairs."

"This is so exciting," said Jane, clapping her hands together with glee. "I'm going to order new staff uniforms."

"With what money?" I asked with a sigh.

"Mine," she said, lifting up her chin. "And no arguments. And no paying me back. I want to do this. Everything has to be perfect for a de la Barguelonne. This is of utmost importance. They could make or break us."

Who were these people if they wielded so much power? I didn't know if I even wanted them here, "gracing" us with their presence. I had enough going on in my head—the wavering grief, the pressures of the kitchen, and fitting into this life. Add the stress of kissing the asses of people who probably thought they were gods for the good of the château, and I'd snap. Plus, knowing this family could crush my dream with a mighty hand if they didn't like the château experience didn't bode well for me.

"I'd get on that septic system problem," I said, my stomach roiling. "Because I feel like I want to throw up, and it may be continuous."

Jane wrapped me in a tight hug, her violet perfume powerful and dizzying. "Thank you, Sophie. It's the best thing for the château."

"Yeah, yeah, yeah," I said. "But just so you know, I'm really not happy about this."

"I know," she said. "Which was the reason I brought the martinis to loosen you up." She shot me a wicked grin. "Do you want another one?"

"Hell yes," I said, needing to unwind and forget about all the looming stress.

After downing my martini, I headed into the walk-in and pulled out a leg of lamb (*un gigot d'agneau*) from the cooler. It was going to be one of the evening's specials, and I was going traditional with the recipe, using my grand-mère's kitchen notebooks—mostly because I was missing her and her guidance. I set to cutting up the garlic in thick slices and chopping the rosemary, the pungent aromas waking me up. I pulled out a meat tenderizer, swiftly slamming it onto the lamb over and over again. Then I stabbed the gigot with my knife and stuffed the garlic into the slits to flavor it.

Phillipa walked up to me, peeking over my shoulder. "I'd hate to be on the receiving end of that. But it looks like an excellent way to get your frustrations out."

Admittedly, this almost barbaric action felt really, really good. But then I dropped the knife and it clattered on the prep table. Hunching over, I placed my hands on my knees.

Jane caught my eye and dashed over. "What's wrong with you? You look constipated or something. Are you feeling okay?"

"I can't bring myself to enter her room," I said with a wheeze. "I—I tried this morning. And I couldn't."

"I miss her, too, but you need to do this. You, me, and Phillipa will do it together," said Jane, placing a tender hand on my shoulder.

THE PROBLEM WITH letting go was that you just had to do it, no matter how torn up inside you were. The three of us stood in front of Grand-mère's suite, sharing nervous glances. With my friends by my side, I didn't have to face this challenge alone. Hesitantly, I opened the door. Grand-mère's scent, which I'd thought I'd imagined before, hit all of us. Jane was the first to notice.

"Oh my goodness," she said. "It's like she was just here, Chanel No. 5, nutmeg, cinnamon, and lavender."

"You smell it?" I asked.

"Yes," she said, her voice low in register.

"Me too," said Phillipa. "And it's even stronger than before."

A dragonfly, large and blue with shimmering wings, flew over our heads, right into her chambers. It landed on a picture of my grand-mère and me.

"This can't be happening," said Jane with a gasp. "I think we should close the door right now."

"No," I said. "It's a sign. I'm going in. I have to."

Although eerie, the dragonfly's presence urged me on. Grand-mère was here. With me. I took in a deep breath, garnering up my courage. I walked in with purpose and opened the windows to air out the room. The dragonfly soared into the blue sky. I let out the breath I'd been holding.

"So we're doing this?" asked Phillipa.

"We are," I said.

"Are you ready?" asked Jane.

"Not exactly," I said.

For the next few hours, we went through my grandmother's personal effects, setting things to the side to sell when we could, deciding what we should junk and what we should keep. We looked through albums, and more than a few photos of Rémi and me as kids made me smile with sweet remembrance.

Jane spilled out the contents of Grand-mère's jewelry box on the bed, the pieces sparkling in the sunlight. Rubies, sapphires, emeralds, and diamonds, oh my.

"Putain," said Jane, eyeing each piece. Her mouth dropped. "Bulgari, Cartier, oh, for shit's sake, just name every high-end jewelry designer on the planet."

"Jane, did you just swear?" I asked.

"You have to have good reason to use a *gros mot*, and I have one."

I sucked in my breath, wondering if my mother's jewels were real too. I recalled the words she used to say: *"If you want to be a star, you have to look, act, and dress like a star—diamonds, rubies, sapphires, and emeralds included."* Maybe she wasn't a fake. And maybe her jewelry wasn't either. One thing I knew for certain was that my friendships were real. As I fingered through the pieces, I looked up to Phillipa and Jane. "Both of you choose something."

"Wait, what?" asked Phillipa.

"Just do it now before I change my mind," I said. "Think of it as an early bonus. And, considering you both offered to work for free until my inheritance comes through, which I may take you up on, and you've always been there for me, I want to do this."

In fact, Jane and Phillipa were more than friends; I'd become their third sister. Phillipa stood by my side in all my freak-outs and tough moments. Jane had gone above and beyond, teaching me everything there was to know about the château before the La Société des Châteaux et Belles Demeures audit. I couldn't have carved out this life without either of them. Plus, I was a chef and my tastes were simple. Where in the world would I wear the glitz?

"This is part of your inheritance—" began Jane, tears rolling down her cheeks. "I can't."

"Oh, but you can, and I insist. It's what she would have wanted. You were there for her when I wasn't," I said, guilt tweaking my gut. I'd stayed away from Champvert far too long. And for what? A career that had blown up in my face? But I was here now and I could make amends with the past.

"No," said Jane.

"Fine, then I'm choosing for you." I ran my hand through the pieces, finding a beautiful sapphire-and-diamond necklace, sweet and simple, not too fancy. "Phillipa, this one is for you. It matches your beautiful eyes."

Her hands shook when I handed it over. "Sophie, really, it's too much."

"No, it isn't. And you can't tell anybody I'm giving you this," I said. "Not until the château is out of probate. Until then, I'm just sharing my wealth, things I didn't truly earn, with the people I love."

"You do realize this is the first time I've heard you use the word 'love,'" said Phillipa, batting her eyelashes.

Funny, I'd only said those words to Rémi. But what I'd figured out about love so far was that it meant accepting people for who and what they were and supporting them when they were going through a tough time. These two had been there for me.

"It's because I mean it." I looked down at the pile of jewels, trying to figure out what would be stunning on Jane. And I found the perfect piece, or rather pieces: a set of ruby earrings with a matching bracelet, embellished with diamonds. I picked them up and placed them in her hands. "Jane, you are full of fire. And I love you too."

She cried, "Jesus Christ, Sophie, you're going to give me a breakdown."

Before she burst out into tears, there was more I wanted to do. "So are we ready to head back into the closet? Tons of Chanel, most of which won't fit me, but there are perfect things for you two," I said. "I'll race you."

"No, don't," said Phillipa. "You *will* fall."

"It will be worth it," I said, not able to live my klutziness down.

When I'd arrived in Champvert five months ago, I'd had a flip-out moment because I'd been expected to take over the château while Grand-mère was in the hospital. Still reeling from being fired in New York, I hadn't been sure if I'd be able to cook again. I'd run out of the kitchen, heading for my room, and ended up tumbling down the stairs in the servants' stairwell. It had taken a few weeks for me to get back on track, thanks to Grand-mère and Phillipa urging me on.

Honestly, going through Grand-mère's belongings was truly cathartic and lifted a dead weight off my soul. I would always grieve for my grand-mère and there would also be a piece of my heart missing, but the blood in my veins pumped, full of newfound power and purpose.

After Phillipa and Jane left loaded with a few Chanel skirt suits in their arms, I sat on the floor of Grand-mère's closet, tracing the plank with the knot where she'd hidden her journal—just like her kitchen notebooks. She'd been raised during the war, and her parents had taught her to hide anything of value where people wouldn't think to look. Old habits died hard. I lifted the slab of wood, placing it by my side, pulled out the book, rubbing my fingers across the leather before opening it, and then searched for the tearstained letter my mother had written Grand-mère before she took her own life. My eyes locked onto the words:

I should have never taken her from Champvert.
Something is wrong with me and I can't fix it.
Please take care of Sophie; she deserves better.

Through this letter, I'd finally come to terms with my mother's death and knew it wasn't my fault, that she loved me. I flipped through the pages of the journal, finding the photos of my mother dancing with wild abandonment in the garden and eating strawberries. The photo made me smile, because my mother had been happy once. I scanned the accompanying entry, written by Grand-mère, and let out a gasp.

Such freedom is a feeling I've never experienced, the way you're
blowing with the wind, your arms swaying in the breeze.
Sometimes I feel enchained. But this is the life I chose. Or perhaps
this life chose me. Or maybe I wasn't given a choice? But on days
like today, just watching you, I realize what a wonderful life

I have. And, Céleste, I want you to have choices—the choices I've never had.

I set the journal down, one of the last conversations I'd had with Grand-mère pecking at my brain like an overzealous chicken searching for bugs after a rainstorm.

"I did grow to love Pierre, but our marriage was arranged. I was born into a powerful shipping family in Bordeaux. He was a noble here in Champvert, and the selection of proper females from the right families was limited. He fell in love with me, and I accepted my fate in life," she'd said.

"Grand-mère, did you ever get a chance to follow your own dreams?" I'd asked.

Her eyes had brightened. "Why, yes. After your *grand-père* died, I bought the pied-à-terre in Paris and I attended Le Cordon Bleu. Like you, ma chérie, I found my heart in the kitchen. But it's my desire for you to know much more than that."

I sighed. What did I truly want?

Over the years, Grand-mère had kept so many secrets from me, and I wondered if there were more. Surely I didn't know everything about her life—just the things she shared with me through the letter and her journal. I searched the floor and every dark corner in the closet for another concealed hiding place, but my efforts didn't yield any results.

After reading her words one more time, I placed the journal under the floorboard, wondering if I'd actually chosen this life, deserved it, or if, like Grand-mère, it had been forced on me.

A strong feeling of dread washed over me, giving me the chills. Although she'd quoted Édith Piaf and had said, "*Non, je ne regrette rien*" (No, I regret nothing), I don't think Grand-mère truly followed her heart, which made mine beat all the faster with anxiety. Although running a château would be a dream for most people, I didn't want to just accept my fate in life like Grand-mère had done; I wanted to create my own destiny. Questions made my head spin, making me feel dizzy. Was I making decisions for myself or going through the motions because people, including Rémi, held very high expectations of me? Or did I want this life? Could I grow to love Champvert as much as Grand-mère had?

4

date night

BEFORE MY BIG date with Rémi, I stood outside on the front landing. Looming over me, four stories high, the château itself sprawled at over twenty-four thousand square feet with twenty-eight bedrooms, most of them soon to be occupied by strangers—one in my room. My gaze swept to the long gravel driveway, flanked by plane trees standing at attention like soldiers, to the high walls surrounding the grounds and the iron gate with the dragonfly motif in the center. Although nervous for the château's grand opening with me at the helm, I was excited to escape this world for one night, maybe get my thoughts together, because they were scattered all over the place.

I had no clue what Rémi had planned for us, so I wore a black sheath that hit above the knee, kitten heels, and a strand of Grand-mère's pearls—simple, not too fancy, yet elegant. As I reassessed my outfit, wondering if I'd gone overboard, I turned around and ran smack into Rémi. My eyes widened with a bit of surprise, but then he smiled, his dimple forming on his left cheek, and my heart melted like fondue.

"What are you doing out here?" he asked.

"I needed to get some air," I said, giving him the once-over.

I'd forgotten how well he cleaned up when he was out of his gardening or hunting clothes—not that he ever looked bad. Freshly shaven and model handsome, he wore slim black slacks offset by an Hermès belt with a silver *H*, a crisp white shirt with the sleeves rolled up to his elbows, and my grand-père's Rolex. He even made the watch look sexy.

"You're beautiful," he said.

"So are you," I said, my cheeks growing warm.

Rémi pulled me in for a kiss, his hands around my waist. First our lips met, then our tongues. One of his hands clasped the back of my neck, and the warmth of his mouth exploring mine sent wild tremors down my spine, making me feel faint. I stumbled backward from his embrace.

"Maybe we should stay in?" he said with a sexy growl.

Staying in held too much temptation. "And miss our only chance to leave the château?" I asked, my lips still tingling.

"Then we better go," he said.

"Where are we going?" I asked.

"You'll see," he said. He pulled out a black silk scarf from his pocket and waved it in front of my face. "Or maybe you won't."

I stared at the sash, mortified. His laughter started soft and then boomed. "I'm only going to blindfold you."

"Maybe I like being able to see," I said. "In fact, I'm a chef. I like having all of my senses."

"Lose one for a little while," he said. "Or you'll ruin my surprise."

"Maybe I don't like surprises."

"You'll like this one," he said as he tied the sash around my eyes. He gripped my hand and led me to his car.

Once he settled me in the passenger seat, I said, "I'm really not liking this."

"You will," he said, and started the engine.

I gulped. "How can you be so sure?"

"Trust me, Sophie." He gripped my hand, stroking it with his thumb. "I know you."

But did he? Sometimes I wondered if I even knew or trusted myself. In the past, I'd made some very bad decisions, and I didn't want to make them again. For now, though, I was just going to go with the flow. I couldn't see, but I could feel my heart beating, hear it, and I could still taste Rémi's minty kiss on my lips.

Forty-five minutes of Rémi teasing me about the blindfold later, he stopped the car. "We're here," he said as he scrambled over to the passenger door and opened it. His hand latched onto my arm, and he guided me out of the seat.

"No peeking," he said.

A door opened. People chattered softly, and forks and knives clinked on plates. The aromas of various spices hit my nostrils. At least I knew we were at a restaurant and not some weird Marquis de Sade bondage dungeon. But which restaurant? Rémi finally undid the sash. I blinked, the light blinding. Everything—the tables, the linens, and the bar—glowed white. A maître d' dressed in a tuxedo made his approach.

"Welcome to Blanc," he said. "Your table is ready, Monsieur Dupont. Follow me."

My jaw unhinged and I turned to Rémi. "Blanc? As in Georgette Blanc? The two-starred Michelin chef famous for molecular gastronomy?"

"The very one," he said.

One of the rare female chefs decorated by Michelin, Georgette

Blanc had done it, whereas I hadn't. A big part of me still wanted my stars, and not the little diamond ones hanging off the necklace Rémi had given me on my birthday.

Rémi flashed a self-satisfied smile. "Told you it was a surprise."

"H-h-how in the world did you get a reservation?" I stuttered.

"I have my ways," he said. "And I might have name-dropped the Valroux de la Tour de Champvert name." He linked his arm with mine. "Come, let's eat and see what all the molecular fuss is about."

The maître d' pulled out my chair and I sat. Rémi took his place across from me. "I've already ordered in advance for us. We're both having the surprise degustation menu. An amuse-bouche, followed by four *plats*, a cheese course, and dessert. I've asked the sommelier to match our wine selections. I hope that's okay with you."

It was more than okay with me. I was tired of making decisions. "It's great."

Rémi leaned forward. "What's wrong, Sophie? You're smiling with your mouth, but not your eyes. Do you not like it here?"

I sucked in a breath. "I'm just a little worried."

"About what?"

I took a sip of water and cleared my throat. "The château has a septic issue, and our inheritance hasn't gone through." I paused. "They're fixing it tomorrow, before the guests arrive. I don't know how I'll pay for it."

"Why didn't you tell me of this?"

"Because it's not your problem, and I'll handle it."

"Sophie, we are a couple. We're supposed to share things—both the good and the bad. If you keep things from me, I can't help you."

"I'm not a damsel in distress," I said with a squint.

Rémi went silent as a server delivered an odd-looking amuse-bouche to our table and poured a glass of champagne. "May I present you with an oyster in a spiced Lambrusco sauce along with a molecular Caprese salad."

"Merci. It looks interesting," I said, and the waiter walked away. I poked the ball with my fork and it wiggled. "Rémi, the Caprese salad looks like a mutated, gelatinous jellyfish."

"I'm sure it tastes better than it looks," said Rémi, taking a bite. "It's, uh, it's different, but not bad." He swallowed and then his eyes locked onto mine. "Back to the subject. I know you, of all people, don't need saving," he said. "But sometimes it's okay to ask for help when you need it."

I shrugged, deciding to try the amuse-bouche. It tasted worse than it looked. I choked back a laugh. "I do need your help. Will you eat the rest of my Caprese? I'm not into the texture. At all."

"Sophie, I'm being serious."

I raised a brow. "So am I."

Rémi batted his long eyelashes and let out a laugh. He stuck his fork into the wiggling ball, brought it to his mouth, and chewed. When finished, he said, "I'm glad you stick to the classics. And I'm serious about helping you when you need it. I have quite the savings myself—from my own inheritance. We're partners in this. All you need to do is ask."

"It's fine," I said. "Everything is sorted out."

His eyes locked onto the necklace hanging around my neck, the one with the engagement ring hanging off it. "Not everything is sorted. Even Grand-mère Odette thinks rings should be worn on fingers."

"What? You're speaking for her now?"

"No, these were her words. She told me this when she gave me the ring to propose," he said.

A few weeks prior, my answer to his proposal had made his smile wither like a crêpe falling onto a burner after a pan-flip accident: *"Can we just be engaged to be engaged?"* And then, after asking if we could take our time, I'd said, *"The château is booked solid and there won't be any breaks until after Christmas."*

Rémi shook his head as if to clear it. "Will you just put the ring on your finger? I don't want to be your *almost* fiancé. It's ridiculous."

Maybe. But I had my reasons.

"Rémi, sometimes if things are built too quickly, they fall apart. And I don't want that to happen." I bit down on my lip. "Why can't you just be happy with how things are for now?"

His eyebrows furrowed. He rubbed his temples. He placed his elbows on the table and leaned forward. "Honestly, I'm just scared."

"Of what?" I asked.

"Losing you," he said. "We've both lost so much already. You lost your mother and grand-mère. I lost my parents. Lola lost her mother." He cleared his throat. "Sometimes when everything falls apart, you need to look at all of the scattered pieces to figure out what's missing, to make the world fall into place. And what's missing from my life is you. I want a family. And I want to give you everything I have."

A long silence passed. His eyes met mine, pleading.

"So, tell me, Sophie, what are you so afraid of?"

"Nothing," I said out loud. "And everything," I said in my head. But things were changing for me, and I realized Rémi was scared of losing me too. He wouldn't purposely leave me. Perhaps I could get over my fears of truly committing to this life and leap into unchartered waters. I did love him—truly, madly, deeply—and Lola was as sweet as cherry clafoutis. But until I wrapped my head around motherhood and the château, all those lingering doubts, we'd have a very long engagement.

"Fine, you win," I said, and unlatched the necklace from my neck. I placed the ring on the table and raised a brow. "Are you going to do the honors?"

Rémi's smile widened. He picked up the ring and then stood up, dropping down on one knee. "Sophie Valroux, je t'aime," he said. "And I can't wait to start my life with you."

Tears formed in my eyes as he placed the ring on my finger, the five-carat yellow canary diamond glistening like clarified butter. As Rémi stood up and placed a delicious kiss on my lips, his hands caressing my face, the patrons of the restaurant clinked their glasses, shouts of felicitations coming from every corner.

"I love you, Rémi Dupont," I said as he took his seat. "The kitchen was my first love. But you've opened up my heart to the real thing."

He gripped my hands, circling his thumbs on my skin. "I want to give you so much more. I want to open you up to everything." His eyes darkened—intense, lust filled.

I picked up on the double entendre. "On that," I said, a warmness heating my cheeks and my inner thighs. "I still want to wait—just a little bit longer—"

He puffed out his lip in a mock pout. "I figured as much. But you can't hold it against me for trying. I'll be ready when you are." He sat back in his chair, crossed his arms over his chest, and grinned as the server set down our second course—a beet foam in a spoon. Once the waiter sauntered off, he said, "Sophie, if this is a Michelin restaurant, the stars you once desired aren't worth it."

I clamped my lips together. "I still want them, you know."

"Mais pourquoi?"

"Why? It was the only dream I'd ever had," I said, taken aback. "I don't want to give up on it."

"Dreams don't have to stay the same," he said, clasping his hands around mine. "Look at everything you have. Open your eyes up to the possibilities, to love."

"My eyes are open," I said, my shoulders rigid.

As course after inedible course arrived at our table, a big question weighed down on my mind, making it swirl. Would Rémi hold me back from achieving the stars I once craved and still desperately wanted, or would he be supportive of my dream? I was a woman. I was a chef. I'd made a promise to myself to have love *and* success on my own terms.

Arm in arm, we left the restaurant, me gazing up at the night sky. Rémi stopped suddenly and pulled me in for a kiss. He took a step back, his eyes meeting mine. "When do you want to set the date?"

I shrugged. "I don't know. Maybe next spring, when the château has closed its doors to the public?"

"I was thinking sooner," he said, wiggling his brows. "Maybe we can elope?"

Point taken. I knew what he was driving at. If we eloped, we'd definitely move our sexual relationship to the next level sooner rather than later. And I wouldn't have a good excuse to put him off any longer. But sex could lead to babies—condoms did break, and I'd surely forget to take a pill—and I definitely wasn't ready for this kind of big life change. Perhaps it was selfish, but I was young, and I wanted to follow my own dreams first. Grand-mère didn't have a choice; I did.

I clasped his hands in mine. "Rémi, we don't need to rush. I'm yours. Let's just see how the season goes and we'll take it from there. I mean, it hasn't even started yet."

We'd had this conversation before when he first proposed.

He blew out the air between his lips. "*Pfff.* You and your schedules," he said. "Just be sure to make some time for me and Lola."

My stomach twisted into knots. I didn't even know how much time I'd have for myself, if any. "I promise," I said. "And don't forget, you're going to be very busy too. We're both under a lot of stress."

"I like pressure. And I'm thinking you do too." He wrapped his hands around my waist and pulled me in close, his kiss—hungry and passionate—sending tingles down my spine. Lost in his embrace, I didn't have a care in the world, didn't think about my career, and I succumbed to the delicate force of his tongue and his lips, my knees going weak. My head and my heart played a strange game of tug-of-war, my former dream screaming to be heard. When we pulled away, I thought of the stars and if Rémi would take my dream seriously, because, although bringing me to the restaurant seemed well intended, it was almost as if he'd thrown it into my face.

5

kitchen confidence

GUESTS ROAMED ALL over the château grounds like frantic and excited ants on a luxurious picnic adventure—experiencing wine tastings with Bernard; cooking demonstrations with Clothilde; gardening in the greenhouse with Jane; skeet shooting with Rémi; or hanging out by the pool or the lake or relaxing in the hammam spa. I did my best to avoid them: I really wasn't up for socializing, because I was just getting into the swing of things. For the most part, I kept myself busy in the kitchen, trying to cook up the best meals I could muster and stealing the occasional heated kiss in the servants' entrance with Rémi.

Jane wandered into the kitchen. I hugged her. "I forgot to thank you for taking care of the septic issue," I said. "How did the château pay for it? The bank loan?"

She blinked. "The château didn't need to borrow money," she said. "Rémi took care of it. Did he not tell you?"

"No," I said, my voice catching. "He didn't."

Again, he'd gone and done something behind my back without telling me. I'd asked him to let me know about important matters so

I wasn't blindsided. I clenched my hands and my spine went rigid, bothered with his caveman "I do what I want" mentality. But I'd have to talk with him later. I went back to prepping, chopping up dill for the salmon, the grassy scent filling the kitchen.

"Did you want to do the speech tonight?" asked Jane.

"Nah," I said. "But I'll make my obligatory appearance."

Jane, bless her heart, took care of everything—welcoming the guests and giving the famous speech, the one I was supposed to be responsible for—"We are a family at the château and we are deeply rooted to our terroir" and how all of our produce was grown right on the grounds, how all our fishes and meats came from France. All I had to do was enter the dining room every night, wave, take a bow, and leave to applause. With the stress I'd put on myself, it was all I could handle, though the accolades did make my heart beat just a little bit faster, because I remembered why I loved being a chef.

For me, cooking was the way I expressed myself, each dish a balance of flavors and ingredients representing my emotions. I hoped our guests were eating not sadness or bitterness, which was the way I was feeling sometimes, but happiness. At any rate, so far nobody had cried over their porridge, and they licked their lips with delight, so I was doing something right.

IN ADDITION TO the river, my other escape from insanity and stress was the greenhouse, a true garden of heavenly delights. It shimmered in the early-morning sunlight, beckoning to me the following morning. It was early, around eight, so the guests would be at breakfast at Le Papillon Sauvage, eating buttery, flaky croissants and homemade yogurts and compotes, along with an assortment of pastries the granny brigade made. The château served up quite the spread. I figured I was safe, so I commandeered a wicker basket and headed over to my sanctuary of natural goodness.

It was no ordinary greenhouse, and the back wall soared thirty feet high with every herb imaginable. Placed in pots hanging off a trellis—basil, thyme, mint, coriander, parsley, oregano, dill, rosemary, lavender, and more—the choices were limitless. Vegetables of almost every variety erupted in every square inch of the room in vivid reds, dark purples, yellows, and greens. I opened the door and let out a breath, and then I inhaled deeply. This was my paradise.

I walked in and closed my eyes as I ran my hands over the leaves of the tomato plants. I brought my fingers to my nose, breathing in the grassy, earthy freshness. It was no wonder the French cosmetic brand L'Occitane en Provence had found a way to capture this aroma in one of their hand creams.

After pulling out my clippers, I gathered some tomatoes; some fresh herbs like tarragon, thyme, and rosemary; and a bunch of lemons, placing them in my basket. For some reason, the aromas emanating from this bounty of delights reminded me of the freshness of Rémi's scent—clean and delicious and oh so tempting to bite right into. Too tired after the frenetic dinner services from this first week, I hadn't spent much quality time with Rémi, as I was falling asleep almost immediately.

My cell buzzed. I pulled it out of my pocket, eyeing the caller ID. Walter. If there was anybody I needed to talk to, it was my best friend from New York. Like Phillipa, he must have had a sixth sense. I dropped my basket to the ground, lemons spilling and rolling in the dirt.

"Walter," I said. "Oh my god. I miss you so much. I've been meaning to call you, but—"

"Yeah, yeah, yeah, I know," he said with excitement. "You've been busy setting fire to the cooking world. We've been reading all about your success. Robert and I are so very proud of you." He paused. "How are you holding up?"

It hadn't been the best of circumstances, but Walter and Robert had come to Grand-mère's funeral, and he knew how important she was to me. He knew everything about me. I went silent for a moment and grabbed a handful of tomato leaves, bringing them up to my nose, the scent calming down the wave of pain. I let out a breath.

"Sophie? You there?"

"I'm here. I'm fine, I guess. You know how it is. The grief comes and goes—but life is good, tiring but good."

"I understand. Same thing happened when my father died. I was like a Dr. Jekyll–Mr. Hyde of emotions." He sucked in a breath. "Anyway, I don't want to talk about misery—the past is the past. And I have some news that may cheer you up," he said. "Because you don't sound too happy."

I could never get anything by Walter. Aside from Phillipa, he knew me inside and out. I had, after all, been his fake fiancée for three years until he came out to his mother. And he was my best friend.

"Spill," I said. "You're right. I do need to hear something good."

"Remember when you said Robert and I could get married at the château? That you wouldn't expect us to get married anywhere else?" he said breathlessly. "Well, we have to get married here in New York, a damn civil ceremony, but we'd like to celebrate after with you and our closest friends in France."

I squealed, needing a break from the château. "Did you want me to come to the ceremony? Be your best woman?"

"Sophie, I know you're busy and won't be able to leave France.

And the civil ceremony is just a formality. That's why we want to take you up on your offer. If the mountain won't come to Muhammad—"

"Then Muhammad must go to the mountain," I said, completing his idiom with a soft laugh. "When were you thinking?"

"We're not picky. Whatever's good for you."

I pinched my lips together in thought. "The château closes mid-December. And we always have a huge party on Christmas Eve. Why don't we make it an epic celebration?"

"I love it! Robert will too." He paused. "Give me an estimate for the costs."

As a friend and my roommate, as well as my fake fiancé, he'd gone above and beyond for me, especially after I'd been fired in New York and had spiraled into depression. He'd pulled me out of my slump, brought me back to reality. Plus, I'd lived with him rent-free for years in his gorgeous loft. I owed him.

"No, Walter. Consider this my wedding gift to you. You were always there for me."

"Sophie, no—"

"Seriously, Walter. I want to do this for you."

"I know better than to argue with you. We'll discuss this later. In the meantime, tell me what's going on with you. How's Rémi?"

"He's great. Everything's great," I said with a gulp. "And I formally accepted his proposal."

Walter chortled. "Maybe we should have a double wedding? You in? Could be fun."

My eyebrows knitted together. I paced in the greenhouse, crushing a lemon in the process. "I don't think so. I don't want to rush into a marriage." I let out a deep breath. I could be honest with Walter. "Look, we've never even taken a vacation together. We've only been on one real date. And we haven't even slept together."

"Wait. What?" he asked, and blurted out a laugh. "Take a vacation. Go on more dates. And jump into the sack with him. Test the waters."

I lifted my free arm in surrender. "When? When do I have the time? Look at everything that's going on. We're booked solid until December."

This was only part of the truth. But, after seeing the château, he'd just think I was crazy. Who wouldn't want this life?

"Sophie," said Walter. "You're not telling me everything. I know you."

Busted.

I slumped to the ground, preparing myself to tell the whole truth and nothing but the truth. "I think I still want my dream. I didn't work for any of this. And I don't want to feel chained to the château like my grandmother."

As I ran dirt through my fingers with my free hand, I listened to the sound of his breathing. Finally, Walter spoke. "Soph, I want you to fight for your stars, but I also don't want you to go crazy striving for them. You can make this new life whatever you want it to be. Unchain yourself." He cleared his throat. "But that's not the only thing bothering you."

"You're right," I said. "So here I go. I'm scared shitless of motherhood. You met Lola. She's the sweetest little girl, but look at the way I was raised. My grand-mère didn't choose her life; it chose her. And that's the way I feel."

Silence.

"Look, I saw how happy you were in Champvert, even at the worst of times. I saw how Rémi looked at you, the ways his eyes lit up when he saw you, the way your eyes lit up, too, and I met your new friends. Robert is still talking about how much he loves Phillipa. Jane, not so much, but whatever. You are thriving, you are living the dream. And I understand you still want to fight for yours. You can do it."

I gulped and gripped the ground, dirt crumbling in my fingers, and tried to find an emotional equilibrium. "What if I'm not ready to take all of this on at once? I'm still healing. From everything."

"But to truly heal, you need to commit to life one hundred percent," he said, and then laughed. "So, how about that double wedding?"

Walter, my Yoda, gave good advice. But what was supposed to be a pep talk had my mind spinning. I slumped against the tomato plants. Settling into life at the château was hard enough without adding motherhood and marriage into the equation. My head simply wasn't in the right place. One of Walter's proverbs sprung into my mind: "How do you eat an elephant?" The answer: "One bite at a time."

"Look, Walter, I can't take everything on all at once—the elephant rule," I said, and he laughed. "Plus, I don't want to hijack your day. But I'll let Jane know of our plans. She's on the ball."

"I'll send you our itineraries when we have them," he said, knowing not to push. "I'm so excited. And think about what I said. If you need me, you know I'm just a phone call away. But I'll let you go. You're probably cooking up a storm."

Yeah, I thought as we hung up—a storm of wavering emotions. Until it settled down, I'd cook and try to get some shut-eye.

For the next few days, after every service, I slinked up to my room without Rémi, explaining exhaustion had caught up to me. Although disappointed, he understood and gave me my space. But sleep eluded me and I tossed and turned alone in my bed, thinking about what was truly holding me back from committing to my life here, coming up with one excuse after the other, Grand-mère's journal haunting my every thought.

PER THE USUAL daily grind, I was busy planning the evening's menu with Phillipa, cooking and chopping, slicing and dicing, and doing my best to keep my head in the game. Tonight's meal was the most important because it was Saturday night, the meal the guests would remember most when they checked out of the château. True, I was only working with potatoes and didn't quite know what I wanted to do with them just yet, but I'd found some kind of rhythm and it did feel good. Maybe I'd just needed to get back into the kitchen to sort out my thoughts about Rémi and life at the château. Or maybe I was moving on autopilot. I crashed into Phillipa.

"Whoa, there," said Phillipa, balancing me by my shoulders. "Are you okay?"

I blurted out, "Walter and Robert want to have a wedding celebration here on Christmas Eve. I'm telling you and Jane. But if you tell Rémi, I'll kill you."

"I'm happy for them. It's exciting," she said. "But why don't you want Rémi to know?"

"He wants me to set a firm date for our marriage," I said with a huff. "He'll put more pressure on me. And I'm under too much as it is. There's too much going on, and I have a business to run. Promise me you won't tell him."

I raised my knife, shaking it in warning. Phillipa raised her hands in mock surrender and took a step back.

"Fine. I promise. I know you've got a lot on your plate. And, don't forget, I saw you stabbing the meat the other day." She winked and I flinched. "I get it. No more pushing. I'll go grab the leeks." Before she headed out the back door, she paused. "We should also think about the duckless option for the side course."

Lately, we'd been getting more vegetarian requests in the reservation system. Some of our guests wanted the flavors of the South of France . . . without the duck, duck, or the goose. France, even in the southwest, was embracing the vegan movement. More organic stores and vegetarian restaurants popped up left and right, and the traditionalists' jaws were dropping. All the changes in taste made planning the menus a bit of a challenge, but we aimed to please. Plus, the guests paid well over three hundred euros a night, and the customer was always right.

"What about *mille-feuilles de pommes de terre*? I dream about them in my sleep," said Phillipa.

"Good idea," I said.

"I'll grab the herbs," she said.

She smiled, and her thin green-bean frame glided out of the kitchen, wicker basket in hand. I pulled out a chopping block and slammed a potato with my knife. After taking my frustrations out on my vegetable victim, I felt better. Then, I commandeered Grandmère's notebooks from their hiding spot in the floor, thumbed through them, and stepped up to the board to plan tonight's dinner. By the time Phillipa returned to the kitchen, I'd finished.

MENU

AMUSE-BOUCHE
Biscotte with a Caviar of Tomatoes and Strawberries

ENTRÉES
Chilled Zucchini Basil and Mint Velouté

OU

Pan-Seared Foie Gras served on Toast with
Grilled Strawberries

PLAT PRINCIPAL
Gigot d'agneau, carved tableside

*Served with your choice of Pommes de Terre Sarladaise or
Mille-Feuilles de Pommes de Terre*

*Served with Greens and Lemon Garlic Shallot Vinaigrette and
Multicolored Braised Baby Carrots*

OU

Lemon Chicken Tajine with Almonds and Prunes

Served with Couscous and Seasonal Vegetables

OU

Panko-Encrusted Filet de Limande

Served with Wild Rice and Grilled Seasonal Vegetables

OU

Quinoa, Avocado, and Sweet Potato Timbale (vegan)

Served with Rosemary Potatoes

CHEESE COURSE
A selection of the château's cheeses

DESSERT
Gustave's Strawberry Surprise

Phillipa tapped me on the shoulder. "I think somebody has found their inspiration."

I turned to face her while dusting the chalk off on my chef's coat. "I'm so tired. I don't even know where it's coming from."

She smiled. "I do. Cooking is in your soul," she said. "And before you argue with me, tell me, which dish am I responsible for?"

"Whichever one you want—although the gigots have already been taken care of. They just need to roast."

"I'll tackle the fish dish," she said. "You taught me so well with the *daurade*."

"I have faith in you," I said.

"Right back at you, Chef."

The rest of our brigade ambled into the kitchen and murmured out their approval. Clothilde grabbed my hand, hers shaking. "Ma petite puce, your grand-mère would be so proud."

"Merci, Clothilde," I said. "You know, I am just as close to you as I was to her."

She pinched my cheeks. "I know, and I feel the same way. I love you as if you were my own *petite-fille*."

Gustave interrupted our moment of bonding and raised his bottle of pastis. "What about dessert? What should I make?"

"We're a team here. And you're the magician of magical creations. Do whatever you'd like with strawberries," I said, pointing to the full baskets Phillipa had gathered earlier.

"Anything?" he asked, his wild eyes sparking to life.

"Just not too much alcohol," I said. "And tell me what you're planning on making so Jane can print up the menus."

"When's the family dinner?" asked Gustave. "I'm starving."

"When everybody prepares a tasting of their courses," I said. "Clothilde, if you handle the vegan dish, that would be fabulous, and I'll get on the lemon chicken tajine. Okay, people. Let's do this."

"Yes, Chef."

A tingle shimmied down my spine.

We set to work. By five thirty everybody had prepped their ingredients, the *apéro* for the wine tasting was set, and each of the courses, enough for twenty or so of us, had been prepared. We all sat down on stools with anticipation of tasting the menu. The waitstaff and housekeepers and Jane, Bernard, and Rémi joined us. Soon, it was time for me to present the main courses. I pulled out one of the gigots from the oven, and everybody sighed as the aromas of savory goodness hit the room. I placed it on the table.

"Tonight, as you may have noticed, will be a bit different than what we're used to. The gigot will be carved tableside," I said. "So, to our stellar team of servers, this is on you."

As I turned to place the limande and chicken on the table, Rémi locked his gaze onto mine. "I don't know about the rest of you, but I've fallen in love with the chef who mastered this," he said, batting his eyelashes. "Now, if only my beautiful and talented fiancée would set a date."

I slammed the dish on the table and glared at him. I'd set a date when I was good and ready. And that day wasn't today. He was forcing his hand in front of the brigade, my staff. Not cool. When Gustave sucked in his breath and said, "Whoa! Trouble in paradise," and the rest of the brigade's jaws dropped, I knew this wasn't the time or place for a lovers' spat. I lifted my brows and cleared my throat. "Everybody dig in."

Rémi stood up and ushered me over to the servants' stairwell. I crossed my arms over my chest. "What is your problem?" he asked.

"You didn't tell me you handled the septic issue," I said. "And I had to find out from Jane."

"Because I knew you'd say no, and it needed to be taken care of."

"I told you I'm not a damsel in distress," I said with a wheeze. "The next time you do something for the château, I'd appreciate if you told me about it first. Oh, like asking Jean-Marc to help out. Can you find some boundaries? Because you're constantly overstepping them."

"I will," he said. "But the next time something serious happens, I want you to ask for help. You can't do everything on your own."

"I've been doing fine for twenty-seven years," I said, mostly trying to convince myself.

"And now you have other people to consider. Grand-mère, although not a blood relative, took me in when I lost my parents. Don't forget, I own fifteen percent of the château, so it's just as important to me as it is to you," he said, and I hung my head. He lifted up my chin and chuckled. "Do you realize we're arguing about merde?"

He was right. And I'd been acting like an utter ass. Still, I didn't find him going behind my back funny at all. I turned on my heel, about to head back to the kitchen.

"Wait, Sophie," he said, his hand clasping my shoulder.

I turned to face him, my head tilted.

"Look, I know you're mad at me. And that's okay. We may not be the perfect couple, but we are perfectly imperfect, and that's what life is all about—finding the beauty and the love in all the imperfections. And I love you, Sophie, with all of my heart," he said. "I also know it's a struggle for you, settling into this life. I'll give you your space. Just know that I'm here for you."

Guilt set in. I'd completely overreacted, realizing Rémi had only been looking out for my best interests, for the château. I placed my hands on his shoulders. "Why?" I asked. "Why do you love me?"

"Because you accept me. And I accept you, even when you're driving me insane. I think that's what love is all about. Accepting each other's faults and relishing in each other's positive traits."

"What are mine?" I asked, scrunching my nose.

He went silent, and my eyes went wide. "Well, for one thing, you don't put up with my merde. I remember when we were kids and you dunked me in the lake. You're obstinate."

"And that's a good thing?"

"It is," he said, his eyes twinkling. "And I know you have work to do. As much as I want to ravage you right now, I'll let you get to it."

After we shared a passionate kiss, I headed back into the kitchen.

AT SIX P.M. sharp, Jane, Bernard, and Rémi left to set up for the wine tasting in the salon. Finished with their tasks, les dames also exited the kitchen, leaving me with the remainder of my motley brigade, Séb, Phillipa, Clothilde, and Gustave.

It was go time.

Since we'd all worked together before, we'd already established a rhythm much like a ballroom dance. There were no mistakes. No spills. No falls. No overseasoning. Everything was orchestrated to perfection. Cooking, I realized, always brought me back to life, put me back in my element. I hadn't been this busy or inspired since our soft opening.

When Gustave placed an artful dish of strawberry crêpes before me, I gasped. Simple yet beautiful, it was the perfect complement to the meal. Buttery crêpes stuffed with cognac-infused (of course) strawberries, drizzled with a chocolate sauce, sprinkled with powdered sugar, served with a cloudlike whipped cream, and garnished with edible flowers. Perhaps his friend pastis inspired his creations. And they were always amazing, never a disappointment.

"Heaven on a plate," I said. "But you realize you have to stick around tonight? This dessert needs special care, especially since you're flambéing the strawberries."

Gustave usually prepared his desserts and left.

"Bah, tomorrow is the Sunday lunch, and les dames look after Le Papillon Sauvage in the morning," he said, raising the bottle of cognac. "I'll be fine."

AFTER A FRANTIC service, and making my obligatory appearance in the dining room, I headed up to my room in a melancholy mood. A time capsule from the past, this room harked back to the familiar, the memories I'd had as a child. Unlike the other rooms in the château, my bedroom—a large suite comprising a salon with a fireplace, a children's nursery, a bedroom, and a bathroom—hadn't been remodeled by my grand-mère. I regarded the same faded damask wallpaper, the same queen-sized wooden bed with the green jacquard comforter, the faded milky Aubusson carpet with floral patterns, my stuffed animal, *Bear*nard, and the photos on my dresser of Grand-mère and me.

Buzzed from the nonstop activity, I wasn't quite tired yet, so I sat in the window seat, gazing at the stars. The last time I'd wished on one, I'd wondered if my mother was looking down on me, if she was happy with my achievements. My hand flew to my neck. I touched the three pavé diamond stars dangling off the necklace Rémi had given me for my birthday, reminding me of the dream I wanted to fight for.

6

black sheep

A FEW WEEKS LATER, right before our VIPs were due to arrive, we found ourselves facing a major conundrum: Gustave didn't show up for work. I tried calling his cell phone, but it just rang and rang, and then went straight to voice mail. The guests in Le Papillon Sauvage were getting impatient, wanting their lunches, and, according to Clothilde, some of them were getting rather unruly, practically banging their forks and knives on the tables. One of the servers did her best to hold the diners at bay, serving up wine and drink orders along with bread and snacks, but she couldn't hold them off for much longer. At the very least, the granny brigade had turned on the rotisserie in the morning, so the chickens were roasted and ready. Unfortunately, not everybody wanted roast chicken.

Jane, in an un-Jane-like manner, skidded into the kitchen. "Gustave is missing," she said, her fingers unraveling her tight French twist. "He's not at Le Papillon Sauvage. He's nowhere."

"I know," I said with frustration. "I'm trying to figure out what to do. I guess I'll have to do lunch service."

"And how will we manage tonight's dinner?" she asked. "You can't do both. You have to prep."

The disappearance of Gustave quickly turned into an impossible nightmare, one I wanted to wake up from. Part of me hoped he'd lumber into the kitchen with his bottle of pastis, explain why he was late, and set to work. That didn't happen. As Jane paced, my eyes leapt to the window, searching for Grand-mère's spirit insect to tell me what to do. Instead of locking on to a dragonfly, my gaze latched on to Rémi as he tended to the grounds, riding a mower. I knew he could cook. He'd grown up with Grand-mère, and his skills in the kitchen almost matched mine—almost. I remembered the roast beef dinner he'd cooked for me—simple and succulent, perfect for Le Papillon Sauvage. And I knew he would do this for me, or at least for the château. I raced out the back door, leaving Jane in her panicked state.

I tried to get Rémi's attention, but he had earbuds in, probably listening to heavy metal. He loved AC/DC and Metallica. I ran toward him, waving my hands frantically. He didn't take notice of me. So I jumped right in front of the mower. He stopped.

"What are you doing? I could have killed you!" he exclaimed.

My voice came out in panicked wheezes. "I need you, quickly."

His lips twisted into an impish smile. "You need me? Right now?"

I wanted to laugh but couldn't. This was a five-alarm emergency and there was no time to spare, not even for a stolen kiss, no matter the temptation. "Not like that. Gustave is missing."

He hopped off the machine. "What do you mean?"

"He's not here, and he's not answering his phone. And people are heading to lunch. They're practically banging their knives and forks on tables. And I've got to plan and prep the dinner service. And I can't run both restaurants. I'm flipping out. So is Jane."

He squeezed my shoulders. "I've got this, Sophie. Don't worry, let me help you." He kissed me on the forehead. "I'll see you at the family dinner. Unless you want some afternoon delight," he said, with a raised eyebrow and a smirk.

I punched him lightly on the arm and then pointed. "Go."

"Anything for you, princess," he said, and bolted, leaving me in front of the machine.

"Don't call me that," I said, yelling after him. "I'm not a freaking princess."

He stopped running and turned around. "Yes, you are."

I shot him a mock glare. He bowed and then ran into Le Papillon Sauvage. I watched him hightail it into the restaurant. If anything, our female guests would be happy with our temporary chef. And I did have to ask for help after all. For me, this was progress.

PHILLIPA, JANE, AND I were trying to figure out the Gustave conundrum when Clothilde raced in, breathless, her chili-pepper-red curls falling across her face. She pushed her hair aside and hunched over, her hands on her knees.

"Oh, oh, oh, this is bad," she said. "I just spoke with Gustave's wife—"

"Gustave has a wife?" the twins and I asked in unison, shocked.

"Why, yes," said Clothilde. "Ines is not a fan of the château, never has been. It's all way too much for her." She took in a deep, shaky breath. "Alors, Gustave was in an accident last night. Good news, the gendarmes won't be pressing charges against him because he was on a bicycle and the sheep he hit will be okay." She let out a throaty laugh. "I really don't know how that damn sheep escapes his pasture. I've talked with monsieur time and time again."

I'd seen that sheep. The one with the cross of l'Occitanie emblazoned on his rear. The one Clothilde almost flattened into a giant fluffy filet with her rickety orange Deux Chevaux my first day coming back to Champvert from New York.

"Is Gustave okay?" I asked.

Clothilde's lips pinched together. "He will be, but I'm sorry to say that when he fell, he broke both of his arms." She paused. "The sheep has bike tire tracks on his fleece. Aside from that, he's fine and will be escaping his pasture again in no time."

"Was Gustave drunk?" asked Phillipa.

"What do you think? He's constantly drunk. I really don't how he manages to create such amazing desserts, but he does," said Jane, shaking her head. "Look, we all care about Gustave, and Rémi is looking after Le Papillon Sauvage, but what are we going to do about dessert? I don't mean to sound cruel. I care. I really do. But we're kind of in a pickle."

A heavy silence lingered, the only sound our panicked breaths. Finally, Phillipa spoke up, her eyes widening. "I'll call Marie. She's a pastry chef," she exclaimed.

"Is she any good?" I asked, hopeful.

"I think so," said Phillipa. "They don't let her experiment much at the pâtisserie. But the desserts she creates on her time off are to die for."

I gnawed on the inside of my cheek. This was a viable solution and also the only one we had.

"Do it," I said. "We need reinforcements."

As Phillipa pulled out her phone, I watched her pacing and talking until she hung up. Phillipa stood in front of us for a moment, her mouth twisting into a smile.

"Well?" I said.

"She'll do it. Tonight will be the test. After that, if you like what she's created, she'd be happy to take over the dessert service until Gustave is better."

"Deal," I said. "Tell her to get here as fast as she can."

"She's finishing up something and will be on her way," said Phillipa. "And she's crazy excited."

I placed my hands on the prep table and sighed before looking back up at Phillipa, Jane, and Clothilde. "It's a relief that we'll have dessert tonight, but Gustave is family and I need to check in on him."

"I'll drive you," said Clothilde, nodding, her red curls bobbing.

"When are you ever going to get your driver's license, Sophie?" asked Phillipa.

As a former New Yorker who took taxis and the subway, I didn't know my way behind the wheel and had to rely on people to shuttle me around, unless I cruised the grounds of the château on one of the ATVs—no permit required.

"When I have time," I said with a sigh. Still, I was working toward this elusive goal, taking expensive lessons at a local school in the morning and studying for the code. "I'm just not ready yet."

Phillipa laughed. "Yeah, I heard the gears grinding the other day. I think all of Champvert did."

"Not funny." I narrowed my eyes into a mock glare. "Phillipa, can you hold down the fort? Maybe start prepping?"

"What about the menu?" asked Phillipa. "You haven't written it down yet."

Damn it. This day was deteriorating.

"Jane?" I said, turning to face her. "Do we have any repeat guests?"

"Not that I'm aware of," she said.

"Pick out your favorite do-overs, Phillipa," I said.

"Yes, Chef!" said Phillipa, raising her hand into a salute. "You can count on me."

"I know I can," I said.

ALTHOUGH A BIT banged up, Gustave was in high spirits, mostly because somebody had snuck his bottle of pastis into the hospital. Both of his arms were wrapped up in plaster, and his eyes were encircled in a purplish black, which made him look even more like a madman.

He let out a boisterous laugh. "That damn sheep may think he got the better of me, but I'm plotting my revenge." He paused. "One word: *méchoui*."

I snorted back a laugh and Clothilde nudged me. "He kind of has a sick sense of humor," she said.

"I may be banged up, but I'm not deaf," he said, taking a swig out of his sippy cup. "Ahhhh, just what the doctor ordered. Can you pour some more in? My wife was a little light-handed."

I hadn't met this elusive woman yet and could only imagine what she was like if she put up with Gustave's shenanigans. Gustave tilted his head. "The bottle is under my bed."

"No, absolutely not," said Clothilde.

"Bah," he said. "They're releasing me this afternoon. I'll try and come by the château for the Sunday lunch if my wife, that horrible wretch of a woman, will drive me." His eyes went wild. "You know, I work so much at the château so I don't have to deal with her." He shivered with faux fear. "And now I'm stuck."

"Pardon?" came a voice from the doorway. "Did you just call me a horrible wretch of a woman?"

Clothilde and I turned to see a petite woman with bobbed gray hair and a big smile. She wore a tailored skirt, flats, and a perfectly pressed white blouse, not one crease on it. This was Gustave's wife? Not what I'd expected. "I'm Ines, or the horrid wretch," she said.

"But you're *my* horrid wretch," said Gustave. "And I've loved you since the day I met you."

She smiled at Gustave, and I saw sparks of love flashing in their eyes. "Don't forget. I've tolerated you for over forty years, you old, stupid drunk cow," she said with a laugh. She turned her attention to me. "You must be the enigmatic Sophie," she said, and I nodded. "And it's always nice to see you, Clothilde."

"Likewise," said Clothilde, and they swapped les bises.

"As you can see, Gustave is in no shape to work," Ines continued. "And he'll be retiring effective immediately. I'm sorry if this poses a problem for you."

"It's true," said Gustave, pouting like a child. "Ines and I are going to do some traveling, see the world."

"After he dries up in a rehabilitation center," she said, and Gustave snarled.

She leaned forward and planted a kiss on his lips, a bit too passionately. There were a lot of sucking sounds. And their motions and movements were getting heated. That ended any rumors that the French were more reserved than their American counterparts.

Clothilde nudged me and whispered, "I think we should leave."

Slowly, we backed away, right out of the room, tripping over our feet. Once out of earshot in the hallway, we erupted into laughter.

"I don't think I'll ever be able to unsee that," I said.

"Or unhear it," she responded.

I eyed my watch. "*Punaise!* It's almost one. We've got to get back to the kitchen."

We raced to the parking lot and jumped into Clothilde's banged-up orange Deux Chevaux. On the ride back to the château, we passed the rogue sheep, Clothilde swerving her car to the side and stopping it before we collided with him. For a second, we both sat breathless. The sheep let out a pissed-off *baa*. Along with the black cross of l'Occitanie branded on his rear, tire tracks marked his behind. The sheep walked down the road and headed into some bushes, which, for some reason, set us off in a full-blown giggle fit.

"Ah, life in southwestern France," I said. "It's full of surprises."

"Some good, some bad, and some just plain strange," said Clothilde.

Once our laughter settled down, I squeezed my eyes shut. I really hoped Marie and her desserts would be a wonderful surprise. I couldn't take any more bad ones. I crossed my fingers and prayed to the elusive cooking gods: *Please let her be phenomenal, and while you're at it, give me a break from all this stress.*

They'd ignored my pleas before, and I wasn't expecting an answer. For now, I had to believe in my own abilities to pull the evening off. And, having learned that being completely self-reliant was overrated, I had to lean on the people who cared about me for help.

My cell rang. I pulled it out of my pocket, expecting to see Walter on the caller ID, considering he was the only person who ever called me, and I was shocked to see the name Monica. I huffed and let the call go straight to voice mail.

I hadn't heard from Monica since O'Shea had fired me from Cendrillon NY. That day, Michelin had decorated her restaurant, El Colibrí, on the rising stars list and I'd called her, panicked, thinking my one friend from the Culinary Institute of America might possibly help out a sister in distress. She'd said, "I can put you in touch with chefs, chefs doing wonderful things," and "*Mi casa, tu casa,*" before brushing me off. After that, she hadn't answered one of my texts, responded to one of my calls, and it hurt me deeply, as though she'd held a knife to my neck.

My phone buzzed to life again. Monica. Then again. And then again.

"Who in the world is calling you?" asked Clothilde.

"Nobody," I lied. "Probably a telemarketer."

Instinct told me Monica probably wanted something from me.

After rumbling up the long driveway of the château, Clothilde pulled into a parking spot and jumped out of the car. Frantic, she said, "I have to tell Bernard about Gustave. I'll meet you in the kitchen, ma puce."

I nodded my agreement, watched her rush off to the guesthouse, where she and Bernard lived, and listened to the voice mails.

"Sophie, please call me back. Esteban and I are getting divorced and he's taking over the restaurant. He just used me for all of my recipes. I don't know what to do."

"Please, call me back. I know I was a shit and I should have reached out to you. I didn't."

"Sophie, I was a terrible friend. If you can ever find it in your heart to forgive me, please call me back. My life is a shitstorm and I don't have anybody else to turn to. And by nobody, I mean nobody."

I put my phone in my pocket, steaming. She hadn't been there for me when I'd needed her; she'd gutted me, leaving me out in the hot sun like a rotting fish. I could have been the bigger person, but this time, bygones weren't bygones. The bitter taste of anger filled my mouth.

7

new hires, stoked fires

W HEN I FINALLY ambled into the kitchen, Phillipa placed her arm around a woman who must have been Marie, hugging her closely. "Here she is, raring to go."

A red leopard-print bandanna knotted in a bow held back Marie's blue-streaked jet-black hair, her bangs curled and short. Retro tattoos of barn swallows and pinup girls in vibrant colors covered her arms, one smack in the middle of her neck. Her lips were painted a dark, scarlet red, and her bright blue eyes were outlined in black— true cat eyes. Even her eyebrows were perfectly manicured and drawn in with so much effort it must have taken hours.

I stood silent, still irritated with Monica's messages, and hoping this wild girl's sweets could offset the bad taste I tried to swallow down.

Marie must have felt me assessing her because she said, "I'm obsessed with rockabilly and burlesque. *C'est mon truc*" (It's my thing), she said, smacking the pink bubble gum in her mouth. "Aside from pastry, of course."

"Sorry I wasn't here to welcome you," I said, clearing my thoughts. "We had a bit of an emergency. I'm a bit shell-shocked."

"So I heard," said Marie. She stuck out her hand and I took it. "It's wonderful to meet you, Chef Sophie."

"I can't wait to see what you can do," I said, meaning it. "And sorry for staring at you."

"I'm used to being stared at," she said. "This is southwestern France. I, uh, don't quite fit into the norm." She laughed. "Unless you compare me to those old ladies with purple or red-chili-pepper hair. I think their hairdressers mess with them because they can't see."

Clothilde clicked into the kitchen with her ladybug-covered flats and coughed. She fluffed up her curls. "I like my hair color. It makes me unique and fiery. And you and your blue-streaked hair have to prove yourself."

Oh boy. Clothilde was as feisty as Grand-mère. While I adored Marie's exotic look and sense of self-expression, a seventy-year-old woman might have a difference of opinion. "You kind of remind me of a modern-day Bettie Page," I said, trying to lighten up the mood.

"Bettie Page is one of her idols," said Phillipa. "You've made her day."

Marie nodded, eyes wide. "I'm head over heels for her and Dita Von Teese," she said. "You've just paid me the highest of compliments. Merci."

A vision of my mother infiltrated my memories. Although she did land some bit parts in a few films, playing the unnamed French maid or waitress, her acting career never took off, no matter how hard she tried, and she'd worked at a burlesque club with the hopes of being discovered.

Hidden in the curtains, I'd watch my mother as she sang Édith

Piaf's "La Vie en rose" while bathing and splashing about in an oversized champagne glass. When I was five, I thought she was beautiful and exotic, prettier than the other women, especially when she wore her sequin dresses and feather boas.

"My mom worked at a burlesque club in New York," I said, my voice a whisper.

"Really? That's so cool," said Marie. "I'd love to meet her. Maybe she could teach me some moves."

Clothilde gripped my hand. My eyes darkened. My heart raced. I cleared my throat. "I'm afraid that's not possible. Unfortunately, she's not with us anymore."

"Oh," said Marie, jaw slack. "I'm so sorry. I have this awful habit of putting my foot in my mouth sometimes. It's a real problem."

I forced a smile, pushing the memory of finding my mother in the bathtub when I was eighteen into the back of my mind.

"Don't worry about it. You didn't know," I said, straightening my shoulders. "And Phillipa has a knack for shoving both her feet into her mouth too. So do I. Anyway, the past is the past, and I, for one, am looking forward to the future." I clasped my shaky hands, willing myself to keep it together. "Show me what you've got."

Marie's smile lit up her angelic, although heavily painted, face. She had the cutest space in between her two front teeth. *Les dents du bonheur.* (Happy teeth.) She pointed to the prep table, where four covered dishes sat. We gathered around her, my nose twitching with sugary anticipation. Even before I'd seen her desserts, every cooking fiber in me had been awakened with my keen sense of smell. I licked my lips.

"My specialty is the Trianon Royal, but I can make anything. I brought one for you to taste, but there are a few experiments I've been working on—they look a bit different from what you'd usually see—and I'd like to show them to you first," she said, her voice catching. "That's if you want to? I mean, I can do traditional."

"They're quite beautiful," said Phillipa. "While we were waiting for you, she gave me a sneak peek."

"You've had them before," said Marie.

"Yes, but every time I see them they're amazing!" exclaimed Phillipa.

With a shaky hand, Marie lifted up one of the lids, and my eyes nearly popped out of my head. Her eccentric spirit already intrigued me, but the sheer artistry she'd just unveiled almost knocked me over. This was no ordinary cake but a galactic fantasy resembling a starry night in various shades of blues and purples, with smatterings of white, the frosting reflecting and glimmering.

"*Et voilà*," she said. "I hope it's not too much. I, er, kind of like to break tradition. I can't help it." She curtsied. "As you may have gathered by my appearance. The inside is a dark chocolate mousse, but I can make any kind of mousse—caramel, white chocolate, raspberry— you name it. I can do whole cakes or individual portions. And I've been playing around with all sorts of colors and patterns, sometimes even adding edible gold."

This mirror cake was magic on a plate, fantastical, and a true dream. I prayed it would taste as miraculous as it looked. Clothilde gasped. I was rendered speechless.

"It's too crazy for you," said Marie, her shoulders slumping. "I can tone my ideas down if you give me a chance."

"Don't change anything," I said once I found my voice.

"Non, not a thing," said Clothilde.

Clothilde wrapped her arms around Marie. And I thought this was probably the strangest interview the girl had ever had, especially after Clothilde pinched her cheeks. "I think I misjudged you. You are magic," said Clothilde, turning her attention to me. "What do you think, Sophie?"

"I've never seen anything more beautiful in my life."

"I told you she was good," said Phillipa.

Marie's chin lifted with nervous pride. She lifted up another lid. "This is one of my hand-painted cakes."

This chalky white masterpiece held three layers of gorgeousness—painted with wild red poppies nestled in delicate green leaves and curved stems. "Phillipa told me you loved *coquelicots*," she said, eyeing Grand-mère's apron.

"I do," I said.

"I painted this one quickly with my 3D printer before I bolted over here," she said.

"You have a 3D food printer?" I asked.

She nodded. "I've been saving up for one for years. It arrived last week. And I've been going crazy learning about everything it does. The inside of the cake is raspberry mousse. It's not perfect, but I thought maybe you'd like it."

"If that isn't perfect, I don't know what is," I said, and Marie swooned, fanning her face. "What planet are you from? These are absolutely amazing. You've knocked me speechless."

"Wait until you actually taste her creations," said Phillipa. "Then you'll really be speechless."

"I'm dying to," I said.

"*Moi aussi*," said Clothilde.

Marie lifted up another lid. "If your needs are more traditional, here's the Trianon Royal." She blurted out a laugh. "Of course, this one isn't *exactly* traditional. Three layers of mousse—white, milk, and dark chocolate."

Shards of chocolate and crushed pralines decorated this cake. She lifted up the last lid, revealing smaller individual portions of each of her creations. "These are for you to taste." She winked. "I thought we'd save the big ones for tonight's service." She paused, handing me a fork. "That's if you're happy with what I've prepared. I'm a bit overzealous. I know."

A pinch of jealously tweaked at my gut. I could never make desserts as extraordinary as hers. I also wondered why she wasn't already working with one of the top chefs in the world. I stabbed my fork into the starry night cake and brought the morsel to my lips with anticipation, the sweet scents of chocolate permeating my nostrils. And, oh my god, Marie's desserts were foodgasmic, the best I'd ever tasted or seen or experienced. This girl's talent rivaled that of the best pastry chefs.

"I can do anything with fruit too," said Marie, a worried look sparking in her big eyes. "I mean, if you don't like these. Are they too sweet? Is something wrong?"

"Wrong?" I asked. "Are you crazy? Your creations are out of this world!"

Clothilde dug her fork into Marie's dessert. "I'm on another planet." She paused and then said, mouth full, "Delicious."

Marie let out a sigh of relief. It was then that I finally realized how nervous she'd been, how, like the glazed frosting, she wore colors and lacquer as a shell. More importantly, I realized how perfectly she'd fit right into this motley brigade of ours.

I locked eyes with Clothilde. "What would Grand-mère do?"

"She'd hire her," she said. We watched on as Clothilde shoved another forkful of cake into her eager mouth.

Marie clasped her hand onto Phillipa's. Phillipa's hopeful eyes blazed onto mine.

"It appears our dessert chef is retiring. Would you be interested in working here full-time?"

"Would I?" she asked. "You bet. I mean, if it's okay with Phillipa."

"Of course," said Phillipa. "Kind of my evil plan."

"So when can you start?" I asked.

"Are these okay for tonight's service?" she asked, pointing, and I nodded. "Then I believe I've already started. How many more do you need? And of which one? Or do you want individual servings?"

She spoke a mile a minute, her positivity, eagerness, and creativity infectious. I really liked her. She reminded me of Phillipa. They made a cute couple.

It was now just after two in the afternoon. "Do you have time to make individual servings? Dessert is usually served around eleven p.m., sometimes sooner."

"Sure, of the hand-painted ones," she said. "If that's okay. All of my supplies are in my car. I brought everything I need—including my printer." She paused and bit down on her bottom lip. "I hope I wasn't being too presumptuous, but I like coming prepared."

"It's perfect," I said. "I'll have Jane draw up your contract."

"Really?" she asked, jumping up and down.

"Yes, really," I said.

"Phew," said Marie. "I really hate working at the pâtisserie. They don't let me experiment. I'll give my notice and work for them in the mornings if they want me to. I can't leave them high and dry." She clamped her full lips together, her eyes darting toward Phillipa's, and Phillipa nodded. "One more thing," she continued. "I'm kind of in between apartments right now, couch surfing at my friends', and Gaillac is a bit far—"

"And I may have mentioned there was a room in the clock tower," said Phillipa.

"There is," I said. "And you can move into it whenever you'd like. No rent for château employees."

Marie hopped to attention. "This is the best day of my life," she said. "Merci. Merci beaucoup, Sophie. I mean, Chef Sophie."

"Just call me Sophie, Marie," I said, grinning. Relief washed over me. She'd saved the day. "Do you need help unloading your things?"

"Yes," she said. "Definitely. Especially with the printer. It's kind of heavy. And I may have every tool a pastry chef needs—"

"I understand," I said. "A good chef never leaves her tools behind. I would never depart without my knives." I tilted my head toward her station. "You can set up everything over there."

The granny brigade and Séb ambled into the kitchen, all of them eyeing this colorful girl with curiosity, and then the artful masterpieces on the prep table. Marie spun around in a circle and then did a fist pump. She put the "happy" in "happy dance."

"Gustave got into a drunk bicycle accident with a sheep, and, apparently, he'll be retiring. I'd like for everybody to meet our latest brigade member," I said, nodding in Marie's direction. "This is Marie and she's our new dessert chef."

Shocked gasps echoed in the room. Their eyes locked on to Marie, then me.

"Is Gustave okay?" everybody asked.

"I visited him in the hospital, and, aside from breaking both of his arms, he'll be recovered in no time," I said. "The sheep he ran over is fine too. And, although we all care about Gustave, the show must go on. You can visit him during your free time. I'm sure he'd love it." I paused. "Right now, we've got work to do. Please take the time to welcome Marie, and then let's get moving. Séb? Can you help Marie unload her equipment?"

"Yes, Chef."

After the introductions, the granny brigade pointed to the board, as there was nothing written on it. "Oh, right," I said. "Now, don't be shocked, but because things have been a little nuts today, I didn't have time to plan anything. But Phillipa did."

"The *poissonnier* delivered *noix de Saint-Jacques* as well as *morue*," said Phillipa. "Maybe we can change the menu up a bit? I had a few ideas but wanted to run them by you first."

"Okay," I said. "I'm ready when you are."

Phillipa ran to get her notebook. Then, hunched over at the prep table, we tweaked some of her ideas and got down to it. Thanks to Marie's divine creativity, inspiration hit. In a few short minutes, she'd motivated me to really get inventive, to make art. She'd won over my cooking heart, and I could feel it beating fiercely. This was why I loved the kitchen. And it was time to start telling my story. Phillipa and I walked up to the board to finalize the meal, whispering and writing.

Séb and Marie raced out to her car, returning with a huge wheeled suitcase filled with her supplies. She whipped out mixing bowls, hummed some old French song, and the kitchen sparked to life.

I turned to Phillipa. "Let's get on that *barigoule* of artichoke, asparagus with seared scallops, and clams. It's a recipe Grand-mère picked up on a trip to Provence, but we're going to change it a bit, because it's usually only made with artichokes." I paused. "Plus, I'm going to show you how to make the perfect scallop. They can be tricky."

"I know," said Phillipa. "I screw them up all the time and they're too chewy."

"Not with this technique," I said. "You probably cook them for too long."

"I'll go grab some," said Phillipa. "Teach me, Chef!"

SAVE FOR RÉMI, soon we were all seated for the family dinner, all of the attention focused on Marie and her incredibly delicious and beautiful masterpieces. I don't know when she'd found the time, but she'd also made little *verrines* (small cups) of strawberry soup for us and for the guests.

"It's a palate cleanser," she said. "Before the dessert is served. Nice and clean and refreshing. It was one of my grand-mère's recipes."

"Really?" I asked, needing a cleanser myself after listening to Monica's voice mails again when I'd taken a break. I brushed the thoughts of her away, shook my head to clear it. "Did your grand-mère hand a lot of recipes down to you?"

"Yes," she said. "She wrote them down in leather-bound note-books."

"Mine did too," I said, hopping off my stool. I headed to the knotty plank and pulled out Grand-mère's notebooks, rubbing my hands across the grainy leather. I placed the stack in front of Marie. "If you ever need inspiration—"

Just then, Rémi sauntered in. Marie jumped off her stool and ran toward the doorway, right into his muscled arms. "Rémi? Rémi Dupont? I can't believe it's you. It's been what? Three years?"

He picked Marie up and spun her around. His eyes brightened, and he smiled his dimpled smile, the one he usually reserved for me. For the second time that day, Marie had rendered me speechless. Phillipa and Jane blasted me with looks of surprise.

"You know him?" asked Phillipa, stealing the words right out of my mouth.

"Marie was a friend of Anaïs's," said Rémi, referring to Lola's mother. "They were attached at the hip in Gaillac. No bar was safe."

"Her best friend," said Marie. "And it's true. We did get into a lot of trouble together. I miss her every day."

"What in the world are you doing here?" asked Rémi, turning his attention to Marie.

Phillipa and I watched this exchange with our mouths hanging open.

Marie grinned. "You are now looking at Château de Champvert's newest dessert chef. Chef Sophie hired me this afternoon. And get this: I'm moving into the clock tower."

"That's amazing news," said Rémi. "We'll have a chance to catch up."

"Is Laetitia here?"

Rémi nodded. "Lola, my daughter, too."

"Oh my gosh, I'd love to see Laetitia and meet Lola. I was supposed to be Lola's fairy godmother, you know."

"Sure, stop by my house anytime," he said. "I know Laetitia would love to see you. And you are Lola's *marraine*"—(godmother)—"as far as I'm concerned. I know Anaïs wanted that."

Still speechless, I got up and plated the dish Phillipa and I had concocted, first placing the braised artichokes, then the asparagus, followed by the seared scallops and steamed clams, and finishing up with the garnish of toasted baguette slices infused with rosemary and lemon butter. Phillipa joined me.

"I had no clue she knew Rémi," she said in a whisper.

"It's kind of blowing my mind," I said.

Before Phillipa could respond, Marie peeked over our shoulders. "I can't believe this. I haven't seen Rémi in years."

"Why didn't you keep in touch with him?" I asked, shell-shocked.

"It's my fault. After Anaïs died, I shut myself away," she said. Her eyes glistened with tears. "I suppose everybody has their own way of grieving, and mine wasn't especially healthy."

That they did. I knew the process.

"But now I can make amends to him and Lola, thanks to you," she said. "Anyway, such a small world."

This small world had shrunk in size, making my heart tighten. Granted, everybody had a past, including me, but I didn't know much about Rémi's life. I knew he was a good dad. I knew he could be gruff but could also be kind and sensitive and truly romantic.

Although I wanted to ponder the subject, maybe ask questions, now wasn't the time to think of me, Rémi, or anything else, not when I had meals to prepare. I clapped my hands together and put my game face on. "Okay, people, the reunion is over. We have work to do."

"This is so crazy," said Marie.

"Believe me, things are going to get a hell of a lot crazier. You sure you want to stick around?" I asked, part of me dropping a hint.

"I called the pâtisserie after I unpacked my tools. They called me a traitor and don't want me back. I'm yours—free and clear," she said. "And I'm all for crazy."

"I can't promise you that it will all be good," I said.

"Who can?" she asked. "But I'll embrace the positive and shrug off the negative. On that, I better get on finishing up those desserts. Life with a little sugar can be sweet."

Maybe. But I was more of a savory girl.

8

---

real or surreal

A FEW DAYS LATER, after cooking nonstop and trying to keep my wits about me, I met with Séb, Jane, Phillipa, and Marie for pregame planning in the early morning. Jane was all dolled up in a gray skirt with kick pleats and a crisp white shirt with a small embroidered silver dragonfly on the upper left corner. A silky gray scarf looped around her neck. To top off her look, she'd put on so much makeup you'd need a spackle knife to scrape it off. She twirled and then curtsied. "The uniforms arrived today," she said. "And they are stunning. Look at my skirt."

"I'm trying to," said Phillipa. "But your face is really shiny and distracting. If I were you, I'd tone down the shimmer."

Jane ignored Phillipa's quip. "Today's the big day. Our VIPs, the de la Barguelonne fellow and his guest, are set to check in at five. I've already made the prototypes for the floral arrangements, and housekeeping is finishing them up." She took in a deep breath. "On that, everything needs to be perfect." She held up a finger. "I'll be right back."

Phillipa shrugged as Jane raced out of the kitchen. "She's really excited about this."

"About what?" I asked.

"You'll see."

A couple of minutes later, Jane wheeled in a garment rack and handed out new chef coats to Séb, Marie, Phillipa, and me. As Marie eagerly put hers on, I stared at mine. Of course, I'd seen it before; Jane had gifted me one for my birthday a few months prior. She'd had the seamstress embroider poppies around the cuffs, and it was a modern version of my grandmother's apron.

"You realize she's with us in spirit, smiling down on us," said Phillipa.

"I know," I said, eyeing the poppy-print apron hanging in the corner. Still, it wasn't the same.

Jane held up a crisp white shirt. "The tailor has made three sets of everything for the entire staff. Look how beautiful the dragonfly emblem came out. Isn't it to die for? And wait until you see the butterflies for Le Papillon Sauvage."

"Jane, you've outdone yourself," I said, jaw dropped. "The silver stitchery is incredible. How much did this set you back? I'd like to reimburse you."

"Don't worry about it," she said. "I've lived here rent-free for six years. It was the least I could do." She clapped her hands together. "I, for one, am very excited for the next few days. It will be exhausting, but I know we can do it. Right?"

"If you say so," I said.

She pushed me lightly. "We're in this to win it," she said.

Jane did not talk like this. Ever. "Who in the world are you?" I asked.

"Why, bonjour, I'm the new Jane, who has never been more inspired by this beautiful world we're creating and our fantastic chef. And I've never been happier in all of my life." She unraveled her tight French twist. "What? Don't look at me like that! Sometimes we all need to let our hair down."

"Where is this coming from?" I asked. "You've changed. You've done a complete one-eighty."

"Yes," she said. "And, whether you realize it or not, so have you. I guess we misjudged one another. So get ready for the future."

When I'd first arrived in Champvert, Jane and I were at odds. She thought I was the prodigal granddaughter returning to claim a world I didn't deserve; I thought she was a snobby twit who wanted my life. After a lot of strife, we'd made amends. We both wanted the same thing—making sure the château forged on, which is why I gave up my damn bedroom.

"I misjudged you too," I said.

"And now look at us. We're like sisters," she said with a wink. "Tonight is going to be amazing. You can do this."

"Thanks," I said. "I hope so. But I'll need all the support I can get."

"You have us and Rémi," she said with a frown.

"Is something going on?"

Jane let out a sigh. "I've been trying to get out there to meet men, and it isn't exactly going as planned." She paused and shook her head with indignation. "I can't believe Loïc had the audacity to ask me out on a date. Can you imagine? *Me* with the fish vendor?"

"Why not? I mean, he is kind of cute, and he has a nice laugh," I said.

"I could never." Her nose scrunched. "He smells like fish."

"You haven't changed," I said, raising my brows.

"Yes, I have," she said with a boisterous laugh. "I mean, I'll consider going out with Loïc, I suppose. But I just need to see if there are other fish in the sea first. Plus, he really doesn't smell like fish, he smells like lemons. And you know how I feel about lemons and martinis. Look, I'm no longer judging people on first impressions, thanks to you."

As Jane sauntered out of the kitchen with a bounce in her step, although I was happy for the changes she was making, growing pressures gnawed at my brain. If this de la Barguelonne family could make or break the château, they also held the power to stop me from achieving my dream, leaving my reputation gutted. Everything had to be perfect.

THE BRIGADE ASSEMBLED earlier than usual. Marie tapped me on the shoulder as I was writing the meal down on the blackboard. "Which dessert do you want me to make?" she asked.

I was over the shock that she'd known Rémi in the past. It wasn't her fault that I had absolutely zero knowledge of Rémi's friendship with her, and not much more of his past. And her desserts were phenomenal. We both avoided the subject of Anaïs because Marie got all teary-eyed. But what did make her happy was that she was now officially Lola's marraine—her fairy godmother. It was nice to think Lola would have another person in her life, one who could tell her about her mom when she was older.

"Whichever one you want," I said, trying to remain cool, calm, and collected for the service. "Maybe the galaxy, individual servings if they're doable."

"They sure are," said Marie.

It was time to launch into Chef Sophie mode, whoever she was. A whirling dervish? Somebody who could snap on a moment's notice? Or somebody who could take charge, who remembered her love of cooking? Yeah, the last one had to be me for the next few days and the rest of the season, me time a fantasy just out of reach.

"Nicolas de la Barguelonne's guest has special requests for her meal. Apparently, she's a vegetarian," I said. "So, in addition to the duck, lamb, and fish dishes, we have to come up with something else."

"What are you thinking?" asked Phillipa.

"Maybe a pasta dish? Something with all those beautiful wild artichokes growing in the garden? What about the truffles? What did you do with them?"

Her eyes lit up. "I preserved them. Which means they'd be perfect for a sauce."

"The vegetarian *plat principal* is set. I can whip up homemade gnocchi with a truffle sauce, served with spring artichokes and pan-fried prawns for those who eat prawns. The amuse-bouche? Maybe beet carpaccio with Parmesan? As for the entrée, an artichoke velouté. A spring salad followed by the cheese course," I said, knowing exactly what we had on hand. But there was something I needed to complete this last-minute addition. "Do we have a potato ricer?"

Phillipa scrambled around, opening up drawers and cabinets. "Right here! I've got it!" She waved the ricer triumphantly. "How's that for team spirit?"

"We'll need a lot of it tonight," I said, holding up my hand for a high five. Phillipa smacked it with hers.

"I can't believe you just did that," she said.

"It just felt right," I said.

AFTER BERNARD'S WINE tasting ended, it was time for service. Beads of sweat covered my forehead and my neck. Jane entered the kitchen. It was go time. Tonight, because of our special VIP guests, we'd decided it would be best if I gave the welcoming speech.

"Okay," said Jane. "The de la Barguelonne couple is seated at the table by the fireplace. And they like attention." She linked her arm with mine. "Ready?"

"Do I have a choice?" I asked.

"No," said Jane.

We entered the dining room—an immense salon with an ornate tin silver ceiling embossed with fleurs-de-lis, the cornices with an elegant ropelike pattern; sparkling chandeliers dripping with crystals; oak herringbone parquet floors; and a massive marble fireplace I could walk into. Jane's floral arrangements of white roses and wild red poppies astounded me. The sound of applause rang in my ears, so loud it was deafening.

Jane nudged my ribs lightly.

I could do this. I'd done it before. I'd been planning on spewing out my canned speech, but, at the last minute, I decided to change it, to be me.

"Merci. Merci beaucoup," I said with a gentle smile and locked my eyes onto the de la Barguelonne table. "I'm so very thrilled to welcome you to Château de Champvert and our flagship restaurant, Les Libellules. I hope your experience will meet all of your expectations and more." I let out a breath. "Honestly, I wasn't expecting any of this, this rise to culinary glory after I had a major fall. But I picked myself up, I proved myself, and here I am. Truth be told, I'm quite shy, and I've spent my life corralled in the kitchen." A flash from somebody's camera. "Normally, I like to stick to the sidelines, but something tells me I should get used to all of this attention. That is, if you enjoy our creations."

More flashes exploded from cameras, nearly blinding me. Although I tried to blink away the dotty halo of lights and focus, my eyes betrayed me. In this haze, I could see that our special guest was everything one expected a powerful man with money to be—dressed to the nines, on the younger side, a gorgeous model with long, shimmering blond hair by his side. But I couldn't see much more or make out his features, just movements.

The de la Barguelonne fellow indicated with a flick of his wrist for me to carry on instead of staring at their table. I cleared my throat.

"I cook from the heart, a lesson I learned from my grand-mère, and I wouldn't be standing in front of you if it weren't for her and her teachings."

I took a deep breath, the remaining part of my speech rehearsed.

"We are a garden-to-table outfit, the produce grown right here on the property. All of our meats and fishes are sourced in France. A lovely team of women makes all of our cheeses. We support our neighbors, who are family. With that said, I'd like to welcome you, dear guests, to our family, and it's my greatest hope you enjoy the meals we've planned for you during your stay. Merci. Merci beaucoup."

Jane took me by the hand, and we exited the dining room to thunderous applause. Relief flooded my core. I'd pulled the evening off. I hoped the next few days would play out the same way—for my sanity and for the château. In the interim, I just wanted time to breathe and fall asleep in Rémi's arms. Instead, as in previous weeks, I tossed and turned in bed alone, feeling overwhelmed and wondering if I had any control over my life, that gnawing feeling twisting my gut.

FINALLY, THE SUNDAY lunch rolled around. Now dressed in one of Grand-mère's tweed cream Chanel skirt suits, I told the girls I'd meet up with them in a few minutes. I sat in the window seat, just like Grand-mère, breathing in the moment and watching the guests and villagers gather. After touching up my lipstick and smoothing my hair, I slinked down the stairs and headed out the back door off the kitchen.

Toward the back of the terrace, Rémi manned the méchoui, a full lamb on the barbecue stuffed with couscous, Gustave standing next to him. Somebody had wrapped up Gustave's arms strangely like a mummy, and he sipped a drink from a straw, the cup tethered to his chest. He smiled a crazy smile as I made my approach, and we exchanged les bises.

"Gustave, you're here. What a nice surprise," I said. "But I thought you were supposed to be in rehab?"

"Bah," he said. "I didn't last three hours at the godforsaken place, and I came back home."

"Why?" I said.

He let out a strange cackle. "They wouldn't let me drink there. Can you believe it?"

Rémi rolled his eyes and shot me one of his delicious smiles before responding to Gustave. "Isn't that the point?"

"*Eh ben*, I'm seventy-six years old and I can do whatever I damn well please. Merci beaucoup," Gustave said, blinking wildly and shaking his head with defiance. "I'm going to live out the rest of my days as I want to. And I don't care what that wretched hag, my wife, has to say about it."

Ines's ears must have been buzzing. She barreled over to us. "Gustave, if you call me a wretched hag one more time, I'll castrate you."

His lips puckered into a kiss. "But you're my wretched hag," he said. "Et alors, je t'aime."

"Je t'aime aussi, you crotchety old drunk." Ines kissed Gustave on the cheek and then exchanged les bises with Rémi and me.

What a strange relationship. But whatever, it worked.

"Ines, so nice to see you at the château," I said. "I know you're not the biggest fan of coming here."

"Alors, look at the old coot. He can't drive or ride his busted-up bike, and he insisted," she said, shaking her head. "It was either come here or listen to him moan and groan and whine all day long."

She kissed Gustave fiercely. It was time to leave. The sucking sounds were too much to take. And I'd seen and heard this before.

"Well, I'm glad you're here," I said. "But duty calls. Please excuse me."

Before I left, I gave Rémi a peck on the cheek. He wrapped his arm around me and pulled me in close for a quick, but satisfying, kiss. I breathed in his woodsy scent, the aroma calming. How I wished we could escape and just swim in the lake or hang out under one of the willow trees like we did when we were kids.

Just as I turned to head into the crowd, Nicolas de la Barguelonne waved me over. He stood next to his blonde, who was holding a glass of the château's sparkling wine and wearing a slinky bronze summer dress that was right off the runway. Nicolas wore khaki linen pants and a white Façonnable button-down shirt with a brown Hermès belt. I only knew of these last two luxury brands because they were what my best friends, Walter and Robert, wore all the time.

I made my approach, careful not to trip over my klutzy feet, putting one foot in front of the other.

"Mademoiselle Valroux," he said. His scent, so much sweet cologne, too sugary and strong, infiltrated my nostrils. Did the guy bathe in it?

"Please call me Sophie," I said, extending my hand. Nicolas took it, his grip tight. "I do hope you've enjoyed your stay here, Monsieur de la Barguelonne."

He threw his head back with laughter. "Call me Nicolas. You come from noble blood. That makes us equals. Your full last name, as I recall, is Valroux de la Tour de Champvert and your *arrière-arrière-grand-père* was a *comte*."

I stood silent, thinking about my first trip to Champvert at the age of seven, when I'd asked my grand-mère if it was true what my mother had said, if we came from a noble lineage.

"We are the Valroux de la Tour de Champvert, but titles in this day and age are silly, pretentious, and don't mean a thing," she'd said.

"Am I a princess?" I'd asked.

She'd kissed me on the cheek. "You are *ma princesse*."

NICOLAS GRABBED A glass of sparkling wine off one of the servers' trays, the movement bringing me back to the present. At over six feet tall, he towered over me, intimidating. His perfectly disheveled chestnut hair blew in the breeze, as if he'd just rolled out of the sack with the blonde. His eyes bored into mine, dark blue with a devilish twinkle. His trimmed beard highlighted a chiseled jawline. By the way his chin lifted, he knew he was good-looking and he appreciated being looked at. But I didn't like the way he was looking at me—like a meal he wanted to devour.

He raised his glass and said, "I'm thoroughly enchanted to meet the world's most beautiful cooking face."

Wrong thing to say. My spine went rigid. "Believe me, I can carry my own pots and pans. Merci beaucoup."

"But you look so sweet and delicate," he said, eyeing me up and down.

I don't know if it was my imagination working in overdrive, but his eyes seemed to hold a certain lascivious quality. Whether it was rude or not, I turned on my heel to walk away. "It was lovely to meet you. I have to mingle with the other guests."

Before I could scurry off, Nicolas's hand clasped my wrist. "I've been wanting to speak with you but held off until we'd seen—and tasted—what you can do. I was quite impressed with your meals and the château experience."

"Now, don't go falling in love with her," said the blonde with a twitter. She gave me the once-over. "We both know the way to your heart is through your stomach." She winked. "He has an insatiable appetite."

I just stood there, supremely confused and slightly pissed off.

"Sophie," said Nicolas. "I want to invite you to cook at an event I'm hosting. You've certainly proven your worth."

"Where is this event, and when?" I asked, blinking rapidly. He put the "creep" in "creepster," the way he stared at me, not breaking eye contact.

"Paris, at the Musée d'Orsay, in mid-September," he responded. "The Museum of Modern Art in New York is loaning Vincent van Gogh's *The Starry Night* to the museum, and I'm planning a gala for Paris's elite to unveil this marvelous painting before the general public even glances one eye on it." He paused. "The event is called *Sous les étoiles.*"

Under the stars.

I almost fainted.

My dreams.

"I'd like more female representation," Nicolas continued. "You'd be cooking alongside my stepmother, Amélie Durand. Perhaps you've heard of her restaurant in Paris?"

Heard of Durand Paris? I'd studied it. Cyberstalked it. Dreamed of meeting her one day. She was one of the nine or so female chefs in France to gain three—yes, three—Michelin stars. My jaw dropped and my hands flew to my mouth.

"I think she's heard of her," said the model with another little twitter, her bronze dress blowing in the breeze, revealing perfect, mile-long legs.

I couldn't find my thoughts. I stood there for a moment, babbling like an idiot, my first impression of Nicolas evaporating like a puddle of water in a hot desert. "Oh my god," I said. "Amélie is one of my cooking idols. Aside from my grand-mère, she was one of the reasons I wanted to become a chef. She's an inspiration to female chefs. I have every one of her cookbooks." I paused. "When I was in New

York, I used to dream about being one of the only female chefs running a three-starred restaurant. But she did it. And not only does she run Durand Paris, she owns it."

"No, actually, my father does." Nicolas shrugged and sneered ever so slightly. "Anyway, I'm assuming you need some time to think about my offer, but I'll need an answer within a week, along with a proposed plat principal and four hors d'oeuvres. There will be a private sit-down dinner for one hundred and fifty guests and a more public offering for four hundred—an *apéro dînatoire*."

I didn't say a word. I couldn't. My mouth and my brain wouldn't work together.

Nicolas glanced at my unsteady hands. "You can bring along one sous chef; the rest of the kitchen will be staffed by students and former students from Le Cordon Bleu. Can you handle that?"

His offer rendered me speechless. To cook alongside one of my cooking idols? To escape the never-ending pressures of the château for a few days? Of course I could handle it. The question was how? How could I pull this off when people needed me here in Champvert? I'd have to do the one thing I was most uncomfortable with—ask for help. I could get over this weakness. I wanted to do this. This was *my* decision.

"I'll send you my ideas as soon as I formulate them. Thank you so much for this opportunity," I said, lifting my shoulders proudly. "Merci."

"Non, merci to you, Sophie." Nicolas swapped les bises with me, his kisses landing on my cheeks. "Your manager, Jane, has my contact information."

Nicolas eyed his extravagant watch and then slapped the model on the ass. "We have to go. The plane is waiting. We're off to the Loire Valley. I own a château there." He paused, lifting his chin. "Welcome to the family."

I don't know if I imagined this, but his tone carried a Mafia-like threat, and I blanched as he and his model sauntered up the steps.

I remained immobile, wondering what had just happened. It didn't seem real.

Honestly, I didn't know what I was feeling. Perhaps shock.

I should have mingled with the other guests or greeted the granny brigade. Or run into the gardens to join Laetitia, Jean-Marc, and Lola. But my feet were planted, and I couldn't move. Jane dashed over to where I stood, a crazed curiosity lighting her eyes.

"What was that all about? With Nicolas de la Barguelonne?" asked Jane. "Was he happy with the château experience?"

"He was more than happy," I said. "He invited me to cook at a private event in Paris."

Jane squeezed my tense shoulders. "This is the best news. Ever. Do you know what this means?"

"Yep," I said. "If the event is a success, all of Paris's elite will be busting down our doors."

"You've got that right. We've made it. Really made it."

Frankly, I wasn't quite sure how I felt about that, especially the way Nicolas had looked at me. Still, Paris offered a chance for escape, and I wouldn't be on the proposed menu.

9

planning for paris

ALTHOUGH IT WAS technically our day off, a joke between all of us, I called in Phillipa, Jane, and Rémi for an emergency meeting. The salon was empty of guests, so we met there, as it was more comfortable sitting on settees rather than breaking our backs on the kitchen stools. Once we were settled in, I spoke. "Yesterday, Nicolas de la Barguelonne invited me to cook at a very exclusive event at the Musée d'Orsay in Paris. I'm allowed to bring one sous chef along—"

Phillipa hopped up and down in her seat, waving her hands. "Moi! Moi! Moi!"

My heart broke. I wanted her to accompany me, but she couldn't. I had to let her down easy. "As much as I'd love to bring you, I can't. You have to run the kitchen with Clothilde during my absence, planning the menus and cooking them. And I'm counting on you both."

Phillipa sighed. "One can dream," she said. "I'm here for you, Soph, but who were you thinking of bringing?"

"Séb," I said. "He works hard and he knows how to work with me and, more importantly, around me. Which leaves us with a conundrum. We'll be short two chefs and we're fully booked."

"Which means you can't go to Paris. All the politics with those people, all the drama, all the backstabbing. And that Nicolas de la Barguelonne fellow was a jerk. I didn't like the way he looked at you," said Rémi, lifting a brow. "Voilà. Problem solved."

After a shudder, I shook my head. "I'm going. I have to."

"I'm not okay with this," said Rémi, his chin raised in defiance.

My eyes darted to Jane's, pleading *Help me out of this* in silence. She picked up on the situation immediately.

"Sophie has to go," said Jane pointedly. "If she said no to a de la Barguelonne, it would crush us. They could squash the reputation of the château with one swift nod of their heads. Nobody says no to that family." She turned toward me. "Do you have any ideas on what we can do, Sophie?"

I did. I'd thought about it all night.

"Monica. I went to school with her at the CIA, and she's a Michelin-starred chef. She's a workhorse in the kitchen and can take the place of three chefs. She's going through some serious issues right now and looking for any solution."

Phillipa raised her hand as if she were in a classroom and I was the teacher. "Wait. Monica, that friend of yours who left you high and dry when you needed her? I don't know about this. She doesn't know what loyalty is."

"She may have been a shitty friend, but she's one fine chef. And she'd work under you, Phillipa. The kitchen would be yours to run as the château's chef de cuisine."

Phillipa's hand shot up again. "Does this mean I get a promotion?"

"Yes," I said. "I suppose it does—at least in title."

Phillipa smiled at that statement and then said, "Ace brill."

"Has Monica agreed to come here?" asked Jane.

"No, with the time change, I wasn't able to connect with her, but I'll try her again now," I said, pulling out my phone and dialing.

Monica answered on the first ring. "How would you feel about coming to France for a couple of months and working for me?" I asked.

She screeched so loud, I almost dropped my phone. "Sophie, are you serious? You can't be serious," she said.

"I'm very, very serious," I said. Then I explained what was going down.

"I'll book my ticket the moment we hang up," she said. "I'll do everything in my power to make things up to you. You have to understand, one week after El Colibrí received its star, Esteban started divorce proceedings. And my life turned inside out. I'd signed a prenup and he got everything. I'm so, so stupid. And I'm so, so sorry—"

"Don't apologize," I said, feeling bad for her. I knew what it was like to lose your dream and to be betrayed by a man.

"When do you want me to come?"

"As soon as you can get here," I said. "You'll need to understand the workings of the château, how we do things here, meet the brigade, and settle in."

I gripped the phone, waiting for her answer, part of me hopeful, the other part dreading it. She'd really pulled a number on me, and I wasn't exactly over it even though I understood her situation. But, first priorities, I needed to look after the château, because nothing would stop me from going to Paris.

"How about tomorrow?" she said, her voice shaking. "By the way, I'm not only Mexican, I'm half-Portuguese, my mom's side, and I have EU status because I was born in Lisbon, so hiring me long term could be an option."

"Perfect," I said, perhaps a bit too coldly. I wasn't thinking about long-term anything. I was only thinking about the here and now.

"Sophie," she said with a sob. "Thank you. I never truly knew what you were going through until I went through it myself. More than anything, I need to get away. Thank you."

I needed an escape, too, to maybe find out if I was truly following my own path or if I was forced onto a road I didn't want to be on. I also needed to get away from Rémi's glare.

"Thank you, Monica," I said, turning my back on him.

"No, thank you," she said, and the line clicked to a close.

I set the phone down on the coffee table and brushed my hands together. "Well, that settles that. She's in." My eyes locked onto Jane's. "Could you do me a huge favor and look into hotels for me in Paris? I'm terrible with those kinds of things."

"Why in the world would you want to stay in a ghastly hotel when you have Grand-mère's gorgeous pied-à-terre to stay in?" Jane demanded. "I'll call up the Parisian housekeeper and have her get things in order."

I'd forgotten that along with the château, I'd inherited a Parisian apartment, one I'd never stepped one foot into. "Is it nice?" I asked.

Jane snorted and eyed the salon. "What do you think?"

"It's not a pied-à-terre, is it?" I asked.

Jane let out one of Phillipa's weird donkey-like laughs. "Well, if you compare it to the château, yes, it is. Four bedrooms in l'Île Saint-Louis. You and Séb can both stay there comfortably. It's so big you might not even see one another."

"Perfect. And wow," I said, my mind spinning. My grand-mère had really created the craziest of empires. I gathered my thoughts and faced Rémi. "As for other hires, are you happy cooking at Le Papillon Sauvage?"

"Why? Do you care?" he asked.

"I do," I said, a bit taken aback.

"Then I'm quite happy there," he said. "I'm just not happy about *other* things."

Phillipa and Jane shared a surprised look. Before Rémi launched into not being happy with me not asking his permission to go to

Paris, I changed the subject. This was, after all, a staff meeting, and not the time or place to air our dirty lingerie.

"The grounds need tending to. And I was thinking of hiring Jean-Marc to take over Rémi's duties. Jean-Marc's here all the time, things have been slow at his shop, and I believe there are two open rooms in the clock tower—one for Monica, one for Jean-Marc."

"Your father stayed at my house last night," said Rémi with a huff.

"Really? Why is he there?" I asked.

"Maybe he's been hanging out with Laetitia," he said smugly.

"I didn't know that," I said.

He glared at me. "And I didn't know about other things."

We stood in silence for a moment, Rémi's eyes blazing into mine. Jane jumped up from her seat and blocked his view before he set me on fire. I'd never seen him look so angry.

"I think hiring Jean-Marc is a brilliant idea," said Jane. "Do it."

I rubbed my hands together. "So we have a solid plan?"

"We do," said Phillipa.

"Do we?" asked Rémi.

Phillipa and Jane scrambled out of the salon, leaving me with Rémi. His breath was ragged. Angry. Then he collected himself and finally spoke. "Sophie, Paris is not a good idea," he said, huffing out his words. "You can't go."

I straightened my posture and puffed out my chest. He couldn't tell me what to do. I was a grown woman who could make her own decisions. "I'm going."

He brushed back his hair and looked me dead in the eyes. "I don't think you know what you want, Sophie."

"Yes, I do," I said, clenching my hands. "I want everything. I want love. I want success. And I want to go to Paris. And I don't want anybody to come between me and my dreams."

"Well, don't let me stand in the way," he said.

I didn't have it in me to argue with him. I just stood with my teeth and hands clenched. He shook his head with disappointment and shuffled out of the salon.

AFTER TAKING CARE of some château business with Jane, a few hours later, I made my way over to Rémi's place, using one of the château's ATVs, which I didn't need a license for and was fairly easy to drive. I knew Rémi had to prepare the lunch at Le Papillon Sauvage, so he wouldn't be home, but I was hoping Jean-Marc would be there. The wheels of the ATV spun out on the gravel. I hopped off and ran up to the door, knocking on it briskly. Nothing. I knocked again. I was about to turn around when Laetitia opened the door, her chestnut-colored hair a disheveled mess, her chocolate-brown eyes wild.

"Oh, Sophie," she said, placing her hand on her neck. "I wasn't expecting anybody."

That I gathered. "Sorry to bother you, but is Jean-Marc here? I'd really like to speak with him if he is," I said.

"Yes, yes, yes," she said. "He'll be right down. Come in." She eyed the clock. It was almost noon. "Would you like a coffee . . . or perhaps some wine?"

"Wine, please," I said, wanting to settle my boiled nerves. Damn Rémi. What a man-child.

Laetitia wiped her brow. "Exactly what I was thinking. White, red, or a rosé?"

"Rosé," I said. "Merci."

I settled on the couch as Laetitia grabbed glasses and opened a bottle. "Where's Lola?" I asked.

"At her music class," said Laetitia. "One of her friends' mothers is dropping her off a bit later—after a playdate." She handed me a glass. "We can take advantage of some quiet time."

Jean-Marc skipped down the steps, whistling. Somebody was happy. His eyes brightened when he noticed me. He grinned. "Well, I suppose there's no time like the present. And we wanted to tell you in person."

"Tell me what?"

"Your father and I are dating," said Laetitia, a blush creeping across her cheeks. "We met at the first Sunday lunch and, alors, we clicked. He's the sweetest man I've ever met."

"Laetitia is the first woman I've fallen for since your mother," said Jean-Marc, and Laetitia clasped her hand onto his.

Oh, so that was Laetitia's secret date. The promise of love sparked between them, the way they smiled at one another, the way their bodies mirrored each other. My heart fluttered. Love filtered through the air, making me think of Rémi and my feelings for him. I did have them. But, currently, anger topped the list.

"I'm happy for the two of you. Really, I am," I said, leaving out the fact that I was less than thrilled with Rémi. My relationship with him wasn't their problem; it was mine. "Rémi told me you were here, and I stopped by to talk to you, Jean-Marc."

"About what?" he questioned, eyeing Laetitia. He sat down, and Laetitia poured him a glass of wine.

I cleared my throat. "I was wondering how you'd feel about working at the château, tending the grounds, doing general handiwork. You've helped Rémi out before, and he's super busy at Le Papillon Sauvage." I paused. "You could also move into one of the rooms in the clock tower if you wanted to."

"Anything," he said, his eyes tearing up. "Anything for you, Sophie. Oh, to be closer to the people I love and to work outside with my hands. It's a dream come true. I'll get started today. I've always wanted to ride on one of those mowers."

"What kind of salary would you be looking for?" I asked.

"Salary," he harrumphed. "I'd do this for free."

"*Hors de question*," I said. (Out of the question.) I raised my glass. "Shall we toast?"

RÉMI SKULKED INTO the kitchen while I made notes for the Paris event. He brushed his hair back with both of his hands. "I'm sorry for leaving earlier," he said. "The Paris news hit me, and I lost my temper."

When he stood calm and kind, regarding me with love, I wanted him. I wanted his arms around me, his lips pressed against mine. Instead, I curbed my enthusiasm and lifted a brow.

"Look, I'm really happy you hired Jean-Marc to take over the grounds," he continued. "With Le Papillon Sauvage, it really was too much for me. But just hear me out. I'm really thinking Paris isn't a good idea."

"Paris is *always* a good idea," I said, my neck flaming hot. "And, as Jane said, I have to go. This is *my* decision. Why are you so against it?"

Rémi rubbed the back of his neck and shuffled his feet. "Because I'm afraid you'll go to Paris, become swept up by high-society life, and won't want to come back to Champvert. I'm just the farm boy from next door, and you were born with noble blood," he said, his eyes not meeting mine. "You'll find somebody else more worthy of your stature. Somebody like that Nicolas."

My breath froze in my throat. We faced one another in a moment of awkward silence. His words sideswiped me, leaving me stunned. It never dawned on me that masculine Rémi could be jealous or insecure. But I'd told him about my mother, how she'd left Jean-Marc for New York with the hopes of chasing her dreams and had never come back. I hopped off my stool and grabbed his hands.

"Rémi, none of that matters to me—money, titles. I didn't grow up with a life of privilege, and I find Nicolas repulsive. Titles in this day and age—like Grand-mère always said—are silly and don't mean a thing." I placed my hands on his cheeks. "And, believe me, I'm nothing like my mother."

"I believe you," he said, his caramel-colored eyes glistening with tears. He straightened his posture. "You really found him repulsive?"

"I did. Completely disgusting," I said with a shudder. "And you have nothing to worry about. I'm only cooking at the event, then I'm coming back."

He looked up toward the ceiling and took in a deep breath. "I'm not thrilled with your decision, but I can live with it if you make me a promise."

"What's that?"

He squeezed my hands. "When you come back from Paris, we'll set a date. I know you're under a lot of stress with the château, and I promise to give you your space until then."

My heart beat furiously, as if it had been wrapped tightly in plastic and placed in a pressure cooker, where it could explode any second. He didn't understand this was putting me under a completely different kind of stress. But my time in Paris did give me a chance to sort my feelings out. I held out my hand. "Deal," I said. "And, just so you know, I have been thinking about it."

"That's all I needed to know. And what's up with you and hand-shakes?" he said. His eyes twinkled like stars, and he pulled me in for a passionate kiss. In his embrace, I forgot about my previous frustration with him and focused on the warmth of his tongue and his lips, the physical passion between us knocking me near senseless.

When we pulled apart, he said, "By the way, Jane received an email from your friend Monica. She arrives at ten tomorrow. Did you want me to pick her up?"

"No," I said, willing the heat firing up my body to cool down. "We're too busy at the château, fully booked. She can take a taxi."

"Okay, Chef," he said. "Or should I call you boss?"

"I'm happy with both," I said. I tilted my head to the side coyly, flirtatiously. "Since I'm the boss, you have to do what I say. Kiss me again."

The dimple flashed on his cheek. He growled, "Okay, boss. I guess I can do that, since we've made up after our first argument."

"First argument?" I said with a snort. "Are you forgetting about when I first arrived in Champvert? And what about the septic issue? I think this could be our fourth, or maybe the fifth?"

JANE ALERTED ME when Monica's taxi pulled up, and I met her out front. She jumped out of the back seat, her dark eyes wide and her figure shorter and chubbier than I recalled. Her long black hair was tied back in a tight ponytail. She'd brought along three superlarge suitcases, which made me wonder if she thought she was here for good.

"Aye, yai, yai," she said, her mouth agape. "You live here? You run this place? I mean, I've seen pictures of it in the press, but I wasn't quite prepared for this." She wrapped me in a tight hug. "Thank you, Sophie. Thank you for forgiving me."

"Forgiveness, like trust, is earned," I mumbled.

"I know, babe," she said glumly. "I know I was a shit. But now I have a chance to make it up to you."

"Come on," I said, grabbing the handle of one of her suitcases and making my way to the clock tower. "I'll show you to your room."

She pointed to the château. "I'm not staying in there?"

"No," I said. "Aside from my room and my grand-mère's, all of the rooms in the château are for our guests. You'll be staying in the clock tower with Phillipa, Jane, Marie, and my father."

"Oh," she said, her tone peppered with disappointment. "Will I have my own room at least? And is there housekeeping?"

"Yes," I said, a bit annoyed with her assumptions. "Follow me."

"Wait," she said, pointing to two of her suitcases. "Those are filled with my spices, tools, and ingredients. They're for the kitchen."

I clenched my teeth together. Perhaps bringing Monica to the château was an impulsive and very bad idea. If she thought she'd be creating her dishes here, she'd be dead wrong. "I'll have somebody fetch them," I said. "And I hope you realize we cook mostly traditional dishes from southwestern France here."

"Yeah, yeah, babe, I know," she said, making me realize how much I hated being called "babe." "I brought them along just in case. I read the article about you when you said recipes are only guidelines. I thought, maybe, you might want to kick things up."

She got me with my own words. "Maybe," I said. "Let's get you settled in. I have to start prepping soon."

"I'll help," she said, raring to go.

We made our way to the clock tower. I opened the door, and we entered the gorgeous space with its pink-hued brick walls, reeking of rustic country charm. The ground floor hosted a small kitchen with a powder-blue Lacanche stove and a beautiful white porcelain sink, along with all the necessary equipment needs, including stunning copper pots. Like Rémi's home, the downstairs had been renovated American-style—the kitchen open to the living room and dining area, complete with a fireplace.

"Oh, babe," said Monica, reminding me she was there. "This place is amazing. So comfy and homey. I think I'm really going to like living here."

Stop calling me "babe" and we'll see how long you last, I thought.

Phillipa ambled down the steps. She looked at me with my lips pinched, and then her gaze shot to Monica, who smiled like a toothy horse. "You must be Monica," she said. "I'm Phillipa, Sophie's chef de cuisine. And I'll show you to your room." She paused. "The clock tower has three bathrooms. Jean-Marc, being the only male and Sophie's dad, gets his own. I share mine with Marie. You and my sister, Jane, will share the other one."

"Wait," said Monica. "I won't have my own bathroom?"

Phillipa lifted her chin. "We're not guests of the château. We work here. And, about that, you'll be reporting to me," she said. "Sophie, we'll meet you in the kitchen in a few. I'll show Monica to her room and then give her a tour of the château."

They clomped up the steps, Monica dragging her suitcase, panting heavily. I didn't know Phillipa had so much piss and vinegar in her. Perhaps she'd picked up these ingredients from me. If anything, Phillipa had proved her loyalty to the château and to me time and time again. Now, it was Monica's turn.

AFTER I INTRODUCED Monica to the brigade, Rémi, and Jane, I clapped my hands together. "Are we ready?"

"Babe," said Monica, "this kitchen, this château, is full-on amazing."

Phillipa tapped her on the shoulder. "*Babe*," she said, "in this kitchen we show respect. In this kitchen, our Grand Chef is referred to as Chef. And when she's not here, as chef de cuisine, that title is reserved for me. Got it?"

Looking extremely uncomfortable, Monica said, "Yes, Chef."

"You'll help me prep tonight," said Phillipa, jutting out her chin. A sigh. "Yes, Chef."

In a way, one part of me felt bad for Monica. She'd been a starred chef who had just lost everything, including her man, but she hadn't been there for me when I needed her. When my career had been eviscerated and I had nothing. I'd had to build up my reputation from ground zero. I'd had to prove my worth.

Then again, I didn't feel that bad. I'd come through for her, even though she hadn't done the same when I needed her. Whatever the case, Phillipa would make sure Monica knew where her place was in our kitchen. As I've said, forgiveness and trust were earned. And so was loyalty.

10

cherry pits

PHILLIPA AND I sat in the kitchen, brainstorming the week's menus, as well as what I could prepare for the Sous les étoiles gala.

"Since the theme is 'Under the Stars,' I'd like to do something interesting with that," I said.

Phillipa drummed the prep table with her fingers, squinting in concentration. Her eyes popped open wide. "Borage as a garnish!" she exclaimed.

"Borage?"

"They're edible flowers in the shape of stars, have a bit of a cucumber-like taste," she said. "My mum used to grow them in Bibury, and Jane has planted a ton of them here because they attract bees."

"Show them to me," I said, jumping off my stool.

We raced out of the kitchen, onto the terrace, and into the gardens, passing by Jean-Marc on the mower, his expression filled with contentment. He waved and chugged along, whistling. Phillipa grabbed me by the wrist, and we continued toward the back of the property to the ruches, or hives. Bees buzzed loudly, zipping around a sea of brilliant blue starlike flowers with fuzzy green stems—around two or three feet high.

Phillipa pointed and then walked, or, in this case, bounced up to the plants with her clippers. "Here they are, and there are a lot of them."

"Aren't you afraid of being stung?" I asked, backing away.

"Nah," she said as she cut two flowers. "Bees won't bother you unless you bother them. They're busy bees."

She returned to where I stood, and handed over a flower. I inspected the borage, holding it up like a culinary scientist, noting the blue petals, offset by white stamens, and a raised white ball-like structure in the center, decorated with a purplish-blue pattern with hints of red that resembled a planet or a galactic moon. My heart skipped a beat. Aside from Marie's desserts, I'd never seen anything so beautiful.

"This flower is mystical and magical," I said. "Did fairies or aliens create them?"

"I'd go with fairies. The thought of aliens flips me out. Eat it," she said, and I did.

The flavors of this edible flower rolled on my tongue in waves. A crunch. A bitterness. And sweetness. I closed my eyes, reveling in the magic, the flavor, thinking about what we could do with this. I met her gaze.

"Oh my god. You're so right. They taste like cucumbers," I said, licking my lips. "How long do they flower for?"

"Here? Until mid-September, I think. You'll have to ask Jane."

"They're perfect," I said, feeling inspired. "I know what to do with them. But we have to figure out how to get them to Paris." I smiled. "Are you ready to test my idea out? Or do you want time off?"

Phillipa jumped and turned to face me. "Time off? No way. I can't wait to see what you have planned."

"Let's head to the kitchen," I said. "We're going to create art—with food, of course."

"Should I pick more?"

"Yep, a bunch of them. This idea of yours has given me divine inspiration," I said. "We're going to re-create Marie's galaxy cakes with seafood and these flowers. We are going to make a starry night."

"Sounds awesome."

"It might be strange or weird, but I want to take a risk."

"Weird is good," said Phillipa. "Look at me."

I clasped her hand. "You're right, normal is boring."

Phillipa pulled me in for a tight hug. "This is why I love you, Sophie. You are real. I can't wait to see, taste, smell—whatever it is you're cooking up in your head," she said, and pulled away. She clipped a bunch of flowers. "We are going to make magic."

"We are," I said with a wink. "For the love of cooking."

"I can already smell and taste the meal, and I don't even know what it is."

She shot me a look. And we raced back to the château, inspired and full of crazy ideas.

A FEW GUESTS meandered around the grounds, and Rémi and I decided to take advantage of the empty pool to teach Lola to swim after Le Papillon Sauvage had closed its doors for lunch service. After Gustave's unfortunate accident, Rémi had been manning that ship, and our female guests were more than happy to watch him cook. Sometimes I'd peek in, just watching him chop or place a wood-fired pizza into the oven, his movements both graceful and masculine. I overheard one woman ask her friend, "Is he on the menu?" and then she fanned her face as she wiggled her brows and eyed his tight ass. Funny, I found myself staring at it too.

Laetitia and Jean-Marc were moving their budding relationship to the next level. Hand in hand, they'd scurried off for the day to visit Sarlat-la-Canéda, a medieval village in the Dordogne region of France. Jane had taken to using Tinder and bounced off to meet a hot day-date in Gaillac. I was happy for all of them and feeling really good about life. I settled in my sun lounger and took in a deep breath.

My gaze swept to the orchard. It was mid-June, and cherries were finally in season, the trees laden with dark red beauties nestled in green leaves. I squeezed my eyes shut. Cherries. Oh, sweet, heavenly cherries, how they reminded me of Grand-mère and how much I missed her.

Before I moved to France permanently, my annual visits coincided with cherry season, when Grand-mère Odette always made sure a bowl of plump black cherries sat in front of me, and I'd stuff one after the other into my eager mouth. I licked my lips, almost tasting the tart sweetness, but Lola's laughter broke the spell of remembrance.

My focus turned from the orchard to Lola's chubby body, ensconced in a pink bathing suit and water wings, her legs hanging like little plump sausages, to Rémi's tight muscles as he lifted her up and dunked her in the pool.

Just then, Marie wiggled onto the terrace, wearing a cherry-print high-waisted bikini, straight out of the fifties. Her ample cleavage bounced in the sunlight, her figure voluptuous and womanly. I regarded my own flat chest. She stretched out on the sun lounger next to me. Unlike Marie, I didn't have an hourglass and motherly figure with childbearing hips; my body was stick-ruler straight like a twelve-year-old's.

"*Coucou*," she said. (Hey, you.)

"Where's Phillipa?" I asked, slightly aghast.

"She's taking a nap," said Marie with a yawn. "This kitchen life of yours is exhausting. Not that I'm not loving every moment, but thank God for Mondays."

"Yeah," I said.

"Tatie Marie," squealed Lola. She wriggled out of Rémi's arms, bounded up the steps, and threw her arms around Marie's neck. When Lola released her, Marie's body sparkled with water droplets, making her look even more fairylike. She took off Lola's water wings and rubbed her shivering body down with a towel, tucking her in. Marie obviously had natural maternal instincts, whereas mine were lacking.

"Marie, you're still joining us tonight, right?" asked Rémi.

She propped herself up on her elbows. "Of course, I've already made the little munchkin's birthday cake," she said.

"*Impeccable*," said Rémi.

I cleared my throat and eyed Marie surreptitiously as I slathered on more sunscreen. I'd forgotten it was Lola's birthday. Heavy insecurities set in. I'd make one shitty mom.

"Can I borrow some of that when you're done?" asked Marie.

"Sure," I said, handing over the bottle. I wanted to get away from this perfect baker with motherly instincts, so I got up and dove into the pool. Maybe the jealousy pricking my brain would cool off.

I found, as many of our American guests had complained, that the water was beyond freezing. Lola and Rémi didn't seem to mind the chill. "I thought the water was heated," I said when I emerged. "When is the pool going to be warm enough for humans, not polar bears?"

"It is heated," said Rémi, his muscles glistening. "But it will take about a week for it to get up to speed." His eyes turned mischievous when he noticed my chattering teeth. "If you're cold, I can warm you up." His strong hands gripped my waist and he pulled me close. He nibbled on my earlobe, his breath sending shivers down my spine. "I can put Lola down for a nap," he whispered. "A few stolen kisses?"

"Not now," I said, eyeing Lola as she curled up to Marie. I had a plan. I could be fun, couldn't I? I hopped out of the pool and pointed to the orchard. "They're ready. Last one there is a rotten egg."

By Rémi's confused expression, I was pretty sure this idiom didn't translate well. He got the gist of it, though, when I quickly dried off, threw on my sundress, grabbed my big straw bag, and bolted toward the orchard. I stopped for a second, looking over my shoulder.

Rémi picked up Lola, placing her on his shoulders. She bounced with the movement of Rémi's pace, her giggles echoing in my ears. We raced to the orchard, soft blades of freshly mowed grass sticking to my feet. Breathless, I fell down, and Lola and Rémi got to the tree first.

"*On a gagné*"—(We won)—"Papa," said Lola.

"So what do you want as your prize?" I asked, propping myself up on my elbows.

She shrugged.

"*Un bisou?*" (A kiss?), I asked, and her nostrils pinched together.

"You're always giving me les bisous. That's not a *real* prize."

"You want a real prize?" I asked, and her head bobbled up and down. "After we pick the cherries, how about I make ma grand-mère's famed clafoutis? Would you like that?"

"Clafoutis?" she asked. "*C'est quoi ça?*"

She was in for a treat. I smiled. "A dessert made with yummy cherries."

Lola's smile stretched across her face.

And so we gathered cherries, Rémi lifting Lola up toward the powder-blue sky, her eager hands latching onto the bright beauties and dropping them into my basket. It felt like I was playing a role in some kind of picture-perfect Norman Rockwell postcard fantasy—until I stepped onto a boulder by the tree and reached up to pick cherries on a higher branch. My foot slipped on the green moss and I tumbled down to the ground, hitting my forehead on a rock. I rolled over onto the grass, blades pricking my skin. Rémi raced over to me as I blinked in pain.

"Are you okay? You're bleeding," he said, wiping my head. "Do we need to take you to the hospital?"

I tried to focus on Rémi but couldn't, the sun and nauseating dizziness blinding. I shook my head to clear it. "I'll be fine," I said. "Just give me a minute."

Lola stood over me and handed me a cherry, her tiny lips pinched with concern. "Tatie, eat this." She nodded her head, as if the fruit would make the soreness better.

I took the cherry from Lola with a quivering smile. "Merci."

She gave me a kiss on the cheek and nodded, her eyes wide. I'd expected to smell her strawberry-scented hair as she leaned over me. I didn't.

When I bit into the cherry, I didn't taste sweetness or tartness. I tasted acid. I spit the seed out onto the lawn and grabbed another one as Rémi said, "I think these are the best cherries we've ever had—so delicious and juicy."

"Really?" I questioned.

Lola nodded. *"Miam-miam."*

"They don't taste like acid?" I asked, wiping my mouth.

"Non," said Rémi. "They taste like summer."

Panic rose in my chest to my pounding head. Rivulets of sweat pooled on my back. I did my best to shrug off the pain, my worries, and smiled at Rémi and Lola. "Do you mind if we make the clafoutis later?" I asked. "I think I need to rest for a moment. The sun is so hot."

I couldn't cook, not now. Something wasn't right. I could feel it in my bones. But I didn't want to cry in front of Lola or anyone else. I had to keep it together.

Rémi gave me the once-over. He frowned with concern. "I really think I should take you to a doctor," he said, wiping away the drop of blood that was about to make its way into my eye.

"Believe me," I said, standing up, feeling a bit woozy. I straightened my posture. "Honestly, I'm okay. 'Tis only a flesh wound. There's a first aid kit in the kitchen. I'll grab it and then take a shower."

"Do you need help?"

He knew I never asked for help. This was a trap.

"With what?" I asked.

"Either-or," he said, his eyes glinting mischievously. "Playing doctor or helping you shower."

My eyes darted to Lola, who was pushing one cherry after the other into her mouth, juices dribbling off her chin. "I believe you have a little girl to attend to," I said. I gave Lola a kiss on the cheek, Rémi a quick kiss on his lips, and grabbed the basket of cherries, making my way toward the château. I looked over my shoulder, knowing Rémi would still be concerned. "Don't worry, I'm feeling okay. Really. I just need to clean myself up."

"Are you sure?" Rémi asked.

I nodded. "I'm sure. And I'll see you later. Sorry about the clafoutis. We'll make one tomorrow."

"Is that a promise?" he asked.

I nodded and turned for the château, picking up my pace so Rémi couldn't see how I really felt. I wasn't fine, far from it. But I needed to do things on my own—like figuring out why the cherry tasted like acid. I raced to the kitchen, throwing the basket of cherries onto the floor. They scattered everywhere like a strange Calder mobile, moving in a haze. I steadied my hands on the prep table and, once I regained my balance, rushed to dry storage.

The first thing I went for was salt. I tasted nothing. Monica's hot sauce. I drank a huge gulp that should have set my mouth on fire. Not hot. Not anything. My heart raced. Why did my taste buds take off on vacation? I brought some lavender to my nose, expecting the healing qualities to calm me down. But I didn't smell anything. Losing my senses of taste and smell? This was the worst thing ever imaginable for a chef. No, this could not be happening. No, not now. Not ever.

In my gut, I knew I should get to a doctor. But I hated doctors and hospitals, and, quite honestly, I didn't want to face reality. What if my senses were lost for good? What would I do then? Surely, I convinced myself, this weirdness would pass, and I brushed off this momentary sensory loss as the consequence of the fall and stress.

A few hours later of me trying to eat and smell anything, I was sucking on a lemon when Marie burst into the kitchen. She stopped mid-track. "What are you doing? And what happened to your head?"

My hand grazed my forehead, where an egg-sized lump was already forming. I made a mental note to *not* look in the mirror. What was I doing? Trying to taste anything. Smell anything. But Marie couldn't know that. I had to lie. "I'm whitening my teeth naturally," I said after spitting the rind on the counter. "And I may have collided with a rock while picking cherries."

"Oh my goodness," she said. "Are you okay?"

"I'm fine. Good as gold," I said with a weird smile. I knew it was odd, because my lips twitched.

"If you say so," said Marie with concern.

"Did you want something?" I asked.

"Sophie, you seemed irritated with me at the pool," said Marie. "Was it because Rémi asked me to make Lola's cake?"

I cringed. I didn't say anything, mostly because I felt terrible.

"Are you mad at me?" she asked, her bottom lip quivering. "I'm always overstepping boundaries."

"No, Marie, you're the queen of desserts *and* you're her godmother. I'm just her fake tatie," I said, thinking Rémi was the one who constantly overstepped boundaries, not Marie. "Plus, I'd forgotten it was Lola's birthday and you have great motherly instincts, whereas, obviously, I have none."

Marie's eyes went wide. She placed a pensive finger to her lips and then said, "That's because I have five little brothers and sisters. The youngest is five, and, well, he was a surprise. I know, crazy, right? Big Catholic family. My parents obviously didn't use protection," she said with a nonchalant lift of her shoulders. "You'll get the hang of things. And I'm sorry if I encroached on your private time at the pool. I should have left, but I wanted to unwind."

"Don't apologize," I said, my shoulders tensing. "You have every right to relax."

"So we're good?" she asked.

"We're always good," I said.

She blinked and then laughed. We were good. But I still felt like utter merde. "Seriously, I'm going to be the world's shittiest mother. Mine didn't set the best of examples."

"You have to remember, Sophie, that Lola is only three and can be a handful, but she idolizes you," said Marie. "I know being patient with kids is hard. Believe me. You should see what my baby brother does."

"Patience isn't one of my strongest virtues," I said as Phillipa sauntered in with a basket of herbs I usually could pinpoint.

"Yes, it is. You are extremely patient," said Phillipa. "You haven't done the deed with Rémi yet."

As Marie's manicured eyebrows shot up, I glared at Phillipa. "Change of subject?"

Phillipa raised her hands in mock surrender. Marie bounced up and down with excitement. "Okay, so I have a supercool idea for the Paris event. Do you want to hear it, Grand Chef?"

"More like grand asshole," I said, and Phillipa laughed. Both of their sunny dispositions killed me sometimes. I hoped their light and airy ways would rub off on me. I tried my best to put my worries to the side. "I'm all ears."

Marie took in an excited breath and then twirled. When she faced me, she said, "Savory stars made with the 3D printer for the canapé courses. This machine is killer. It works with anything that is puréed—dough, frosting, chocolate." She paused, and her big Cleopatra-lined eyes opened wider. "I came up with a design. All we need to do is make the dough, set the design, and then bake them."

"I love this idea," I said, wanting anything to get my mind off motherhood and my problems. "Let's try it out."

"I have to grab my computer. It's in the clock tower." Marie wiggled her butt. "I'll be back in two shakes of a lamb's tail." She jumped into the *Pulp Fiction* dance, sweeping her fingers over her eyes. "I love me some Mia Wallace."

A FEW HOURS later, Rémi found me in the greenhouse. I was in a panicked mode of trying to taste or smell anything. And I didn't want anybody to know what I was doing or why. I also wanted to avoid Rémi because he'd pick up on the fact that I was out of sorts, but he stood in front of the door, blocking my path.

"What are you doing?" he asked.

I shrugged. "Looking for inspiration."

"I know you're scared about becoming Lola's mom," he said, his eyes scanning mine.

That wasn't all I was scared about. Still, the conversation he wanted to have would be so much easier than what was weighing my heart down. "How?"

"I may have been in dry storage gathering ingredients for tomorrow's lunch service," he said, raising a brow. "And I may have overheard your conversation with Phillipa and Marie."

My hands raised in involuntarily resignation. "You were spying on me?"

He grinned, his dimple puckering. "I wasn't spying. I just didn't want to interrupt you. But what I'd like to know is why. Why didn't you tell me of your fears?"

I squeezed my eyes shut. He certainly didn't know all of them. Like my biggest one at the moment: I couldn't even smell his woodsy, clean scent even though he stood right in front of me. I wanted to tell him about my problem. But if I said it aloud, it would mean it was true, and I could say goodbye to my cooking career. I turned my back to him and picked some herbs.

"Rémi, you know what a mess my mom was. As a kid, I had to take care of her. And then, well, you know what she did."

Rémi placed his hands on my shoulders and spun me around to face him. "Didn't you tell me you weren't your mother?"

I nodded. For most of my life, it was my mission to not be anything like her.

"Do you know how many times I flipped out as a single dad? A lot. Thankfully, I had Laetitia's help. I know Lola can be a handful sometimes, and motherhood is a lot to take on. But if anybody can do it, it's you. And we're a two-for-one package."

"You know me and asking for help," I said, cringing. "It's kind of outside my arsenal of capabilities. But I'm getting better." I pinched my fingers together. "Just a little bit."

"We can do anything together," he said.

"Are you so sure about that?"

"I am," he said. "Sophie, have you forgotten that I lost my parents at a very young age too? And then your grand-mère took me in, changed me and my entire outlook on life." He lifted a brow. "I didn't turn out so bad, did I?"

"No," I said. "You're near perfect—aside from your bossiness. And overstepping—"

He gripped my hands and laughed. "You really are like your grand-mère."

I lifted my chin. "You know what? Maybe I am."

The thought made me wince. I'd taken over her life, and I still wasn't sure how I felt about that. Because it was a lot to take on. I knew withholding information was almost as bad as lying, but I could tell him the truth about Lola. So that was where I placed my focus. "You're right. I should have talked with you about my fears of motherhood. Now you know," I said, looking at my feet and wanting to change the subject. "Since we're talking, is there anything you haven't told me?"

"What can I say, Sophie? I'm an open book. What you see is what you get. I'm not hiding anything from you. I'm still Rémi the farm boy who lost his parents at a young age. I made some mistakes when I was younger, hanging out with the wrong crowd. Your grand-mère saved me from destruction when she took me in. All you really need to know is that you are the only woman I want to be with." His thumbs circled my hands. "Look, I'll give you the time you need to wrap your head around becoming Lola's mom. I know you, Sophie, and the troubles you've had in the past. I'll be patient. We'll talk more, d'accord? And if problems arise, we'll face them together."

He'd said the words I needed to hear. "Patient?"

"Well, not *that* patient," he said, puffing out his bottom lip. "I really want to kiss you now."

Rémi pulled me toward him, his hands on my waist. He just held me there for a moment before he kissed me, so passionately I almost fell down.

His kiss started slow with a little bit of force, and then it turned hungrier and hungrier, our mouths becoming one. I let out a moan. But I couldn't taste the minty freshness of his mouth. My hand latched onto a tomato and I squeezed it hard, the juices running down my fingers.

The sound of people chattering outside the greenhouse had us at attention in seconds. We managed to pull apart right in the nick of time. Clothilde opened the door, ushering a few of our guests in. I knew my cheeks were flushed, because they were hot to the touch as I brought them to my normally pale face. Rémi grabbed my basket.

I threw the tomato to the ground and said, "Well, that one was too ripe."

"Where would you like this, Chef?" he said with an awkward wink and a laugh.

"In the kitchen," I said, wiping off my sticky hands on my skirt. "Merci, Rémi."

He chuckled and exited the greenhouse, leaving me standing there under the curious gazes of ten guests, all of them women. Clothilde, oblivious to our shenanigans, introduced me to the group.

"Sophie," she said. "Would you like to join us with today's cooking demonstration? I'm sure everybody here would love to have a Grand Chef like you showing them your masterful techniques."

Oh, I was pretty sure she didn't know all of my techniques. Like that I could crush a tomato in a single bound. And I was caught red-handed. Literally.

I was stuck, cornered. Nowhere to run. Nowhere to hide. I pasted on the best smile I could, my knees still quivering from Rémi's kiss. "Would any of you like to help prep tomorrow night's meal?"

I knew the answer before anybody responded or uttered a breath. It was part of the château experience; people paid us to become a part of something, wanting to learn, and sometimes, but not all of the time, did the work. Odd, yes. But it was what they wanted. Who was I to argue? Plus, I needed their taste buds.

Murmurs of excitement reverberated off the glass walls.

"Grab your baskets, fill them up, and then meet me in the kitchen," I said.

A woman with a thick New York accent and curly black hair tapped me on the arm. "Do you have a planned menu? Should we be searching out specific ingredients?"

"No, I haven't planned the menu yet," I said, eyeing the eager faces in the crowd. "We're going to do it together. Pick out what you'd like. And we'll see what our vendors delivered."

"Really?" she exclaimed. "Planning a menu with a Grand Chef. This is my dream come true."

Duty called. I loved sharing my knowledge with others, and this welcome diversion would be soul satisfying. And, right about now, more than anything, I needed a distraction.

II

summer

❦

GETTING FIGGY WITH IT

*If you're not in a good mood, the only thing
you should make is a reservation.*

—CARLA HALL, CELEBRITY CHEF ON BRAVO AND
FOOD NETWORK

11

fake it until you make it

PHILLIPA AND I spent whatever free time we had testing recipes for the gala while Marie experimented with her 3D food
printer. June turned into July, July into August. A revolving door of
never-ending guests. Cooking nonstop. The heat of the summer.
Sweat coating our foreheads. Sharing hot kisses with Rémi. Swimming and laughing with Lola. Getting to know my father. Me cooking on autopilot and putting more pressure on Phillipa to taste all of
the meals before service, which she loved, as she thought I was giving her more responsibilities. Of course, I worried about myself and
had many sleepless nights, but I had other people to think of first.
Forget about me and my issues. It was like the movie *Groundhog Day*.
Press repeat.

Day after day, change whipped in the air, whisking me into the
world of Champvert, and I realized just how good I had it. Life at the
château didn't seem as overwhelming. I had wonderful friends. I had
my own kitchen. And I had Rémi. Although I hadn't caved in to full-
throttle lust yet, my body and my head still playing a strange game
of tug-of-war, Rémi was more than patient with me and slept over,

rubbing my back or my feet when exhaustion knocked me down for the count. Faking being a chef was more than exhausting, but I pulled it off. Nobody knew about my difficulties. And I wanted to keep it that way until my issue was resolved.

Only one other major problem reared its malevolent head.

Sometime in August, Jane, Phillipa, Marie, and I were hanging out in the pool when Phillipa nudged me. "While we're all together, and since she's not here, can we talk about Monica?"

"What about her?" I asked.

"She's been crying herself to sleep every night. She's probably in her room crying now. None of us can rest with all the moaning and sniffling," she said, and Jane and Marie nodded. "I can't take it anymore. We need to do something about it. And sooner rather than later."

I let out a groan. I knew how Monica was feeling. I knew she needed to feel appreciated, to get her cooking mojo back. "Maybe we've all been a little too hard on her," I said.

"I can't help it," said Phillipa. "After what she did to you. She just makes me angry. You didn't deserve that kind of treatment."

"You're right, but I'm going to be the bigger person." I paused in thought. "She needs to experiment more in the kitchen. We'll give that to her."

"What if her experiments suck?" asked Marie.

"Trust me, they won't," I said. "We went to the CIA together. She knows what she's doing."

Marie's Cleopatra-lined eyes widened. "You were in the CIA? I didn't know you were a spy. That is beyond cool."

I splashed her. "I wasn't a spy. The Culinary Institute of America is the States equivalent of Le Cordon Bleu, silly. CIA—it's an acronym."

Marie let out a wild laugh. "I feel so, so stupid right now."

"Don't. It was an honest mistake," I said, holding back a giggle. "So, we're all in agreement? We'll let her get a little bit loose?"

"Whatever you say, Sophie. You're the boss," said Phillipa. "If you think she's a good chef, I trust you. And so far she hasn't set fire to anything. Yet."

WHILE PREPPING IN the kitchen, Monica turned to me and said, "Figs are in season. Do you want to get figgy with it?"

This was the perfect chance to talk and connect. Until the girls had told me about Monica, I hadn't picked up on her unhappiness. With a smile, I said, "I sure do."

We grabbed baskets and headed to the orchard. On the way, she stopped mid-track. "I have a crazy idea for your event," she said. "For the apéro. A little something extra you could bring with you and knock their socks right off their feet."

"I'm listening," I said. "Tell me about it."

"Figs stuffed with a chipotle pepper, maybe drizzled with a cocoa-balsamic glaze," she said with trepidation, her hands clasped together. "You know? To change things up. Maybe? I mean, if you're into it?"

I'd forgotten what a culinary alchemist she was. I wanted to give her a chance to let her cooking flag fly. Just one problem. "I don't have chipotle peppers, and I have no clue as to where I'd get them," I said. "But we can come up with another concept."

"I have some. A lot of them," she said with excitement. "Remember those other suitcases I brought?"

"Yes," I said.

"Where are they?"

"In dry storage," I said.

Her lips curved into a wild smile. "So let's get figgy with it and test this sucker out!"

"Sure thing," I said, tilting my head to the side. "Can I ask you a serious question?"

"What?"

"Are you happy here?"

She exhaled. "Most of the time, yes, especially today," she said. "But sometimes no. I feel out of place here. I don't speak a lick of French, and I really miss home. I miss city life." She paused. "Don't worry. I'm here for as long as you need me. And, again, thank you for being here for me when I wasn't there for you. The guilt crushes me every day."

I hugged her. "Bygones are bygones," I said with a smile. "It's time to get figgy."

Back in the kitchen, we tested her idea with the cocoa-balsamic drizzle. When I bit into the fig, a sweetness should have hit my tongue first, followed by the heat of the chipotle pepper . . . It should've been sweet and hot. Sour and bitter. The flavors combined like a Kama Sutra of great sex. But I tasted nothing. "Paris isn't going to know what happened to it," I said, trying to keep up my front.

"You're going to bring them?" she asked.

"I'd be crazy if I didn't," I said, squeezing my eyes shut and imagining how the flavors would come together.

She did a little jump and clapped her hands together with glee. Her smile widened. "But, although it's almost absolute perfection, I think the recipe may be missing something," she said. Monica pursed her lips together, eyes squinting in thought. She licked her lips and then ate another fig. "It needs something."

I drummed my fingers on the prep table. When my eyes popped open, they landed on a mason jar filled with *fleur de sel*, sea salt, but I knew that would be too much. "Maybe something with a little salt?" I asked.

At the same time, we both said, "*Jambon sec.*" (Dried ham.)

We hugged each other.

"Thanks, Monica," I said. "Great minds think alike."

"Don't thank me, *babe*," she said. "Thank you. I think I've finally got my cooking spirit back, thanks to you."

I grimaced. I had my cooking spirit. I just needed my senses back.

Monica threw her head back in laughter. "And you've just reminded me of the old days at CIA and when we first became friends." She paused. "Your upper lip always curled when I called you 'babe.' It made me laugh, which was the reason I did it."

"Do you remember Professor Thomas?"

"That old bitch," said Monica, mimicking her. "'First, you have to crack the egg in the bowl, whisk it, then you add the flour ever so gently, folding it in . . .'"

"That was the best impression," I said.

"She thought she was Julia Child."

"I'm sure she nipped from the bottle in between classes," I said.

Monica and I sank to the floor, laughing our asses off, recounting the good old days when we were students. We wheezed until our stomachs couldn't take it anymore. Tears streamed down our cheeks. Our shoulders shook. We tried to stop, but the moment we looked at one another, we started up again. Once I gained an ounce of self-control, I said, "Monica, I really hope you'll stick around. I missed this."

She closed her eyes. "I missed this too," she said. "And who knows? I might get used to life in France. If you'll have me."

Oh, I needed her now more than I'd ever needed anybody. I wanted to tell her about my dilemma, but the words wouldn't form on my lips. What would I say? "By the way, I'm a fake chef. I can't taste anything. When I do, everything tastes like acid or bad eggs. Oh, and I can't really smell, either—the only odor is burnt."

No, I couldn't confide in Monica before Rémi. And I hadn't been busted yet. Everything at the château was fine.

"Consider yourself hired. Full-time," I said, and Monica wrapped me in a tight hug.

"You are one amazing chef," she said. "But you're a better friend."

Jane, Marie, and Phillipa interrupted our catch-up and bounded into the kitchen. Monica and I scrambled to our feet. I shoved a chipotle-stuffed fig in front of Jane's mouth. "Eat this."

Jane did as instructed. Her eyes went wide. Mouth full, she said, "What in the world is this amazing creation? I think I just had a foodgasm."

"I want a foodgasm too," said Phillipa, taking a fig.

"Me too." Marie bit into one, and, mouth full, she said, "Whoa, this is incredible. The way the flavors come together. You're a cooking goddess!"

I nodded my head toward Monica. "It was all her doing. And I'm bringing them to Paris."

Phillipa nodded. "Props to you," she said to Monica. She placed her hands on her hips. "Are you in this? With us?"

Monica looked down at her feet. "I am."

"Then I'm sorry for being so cold to you," said Phillipa. "Teach me what you know."

"I will," she said. "And you weren't cold. Just a bit standoffish. Maybe a little bit bossy."

Phillipa blurted out one of her braying donkey laughs.

"Does this mean you're sticking around?" I asked.

Monica winked. She'd proven herself to the rest of the staff and to me. My eyes shot to Jane. She wore the goofiest expression on her face, all dreamy.

"How was your date with Loïc?" I asked.

"It was great. I think I'm his girlfriend. Whatever. Things are moving along." She squinted at me. "I know what you're thinking. And no fish jokes. Would you stop blinking at me like that? Because we come bearing news."

I eyed Jane's hands—she didn't have the ingredients for martinis.

"There's more press for the château," said Phillipa, and I winced. "Don't worry, it's good."

She handed me a printout. The title of the article: FAIRY TALE OR FANTASY: THIS FEARLESS FEMALE CHEF IS ONE TO WATCH. I glanced at the picture of me giving my speech in the dining room, a bit shocked by the words and the accompanying image.

"No wonder I was always jealous of you," said Monica, peering over my shoulder. "Damn, girl, even your chef's coat, you put supermodels to shame. And you can cook like a motherfucker."

"I don't usually swear," said Jane. "But, putain, she's right."

Phillipa giggled. "Jane, you've been swearing a lot lately."

"Merde," I said, my mouth dropped open, my shoulders tensing. "Did you see this?"

I pointed to a photo of me with Nicolas de la Barguelonne talking at the Sunday lunch. Underneath this picture, the caption read: "Ms. Valroux has been enlisted by the famed de la Barguelonne family to prepare a few signature dishes for a private event at the Musée d'Orsay in Paris. This event could make or break her. We're rooting for our fearless female chef."

"Yikes," said Marie, pointing at the photo. "Talk about pressure."

Immobile, I stared at the words "This event could make or break her."

Fear coursed through my veins. I had to make sure everything was on point in Paris . . . or the media would press the blade against my neck. And poof. Along with my senses of taste and smell, I could kiss my dream of achieving the stars goodbye.

LATER THAT DAY, Jane called Phillipa, Marie, and me into Grand-mère's office. She took her cool-girl reading glasses off, placing them on the oak desk.

"I didn't know you wore glasses," I said.

"Only when I'm in front of the computer," she said. "And never in front of anybody. I look ridiculous in them." She smiled. "Do you want the good news or the strange news?"

"I'm all up for strange," said Marie. "C'est mon truc."

"Good," said Jane. "Because it applies to you."

"Uh, d'accord?" Marie said. "Bring it on."

Jane's back straightened. "I just received an email from Nicolas de la Barguelonne. I'll lay out the good news first," she said, turning her attention on me. "Sophie, he's approved your menu choices, thinks they are absolutely fabulous, right on target with what he was thinking." She paused. "And here comes the strange news. He said he couldn't stop thinking about Marie's galaxy cakes."

"And?" I asked, leaning forward. "Does he want to poach Marie? And we can't say no?"

"I wouldn't leave you, Sophie," said Marie. "Or Phillipa. Not for him. I'm happy here. They could offer me a billion euros and I wouldn't leave." She scrunched her nose. "Well, there's that, and I hate Paris."

Phillipa clasped her hand. "Thank god," she said. "I kind of like you."

"Right back at you," said Marie, leaning into Phillipa's shoulder.

Jane coughed. "Enough with the lovey-dovey tangent. Can we please get back on track?"

"Yes, ma'am," said Phillipa with a giggle. "We're all ears."

"Nicolas would like Marie to make the desserts for the gala. Two hundred of them. He thinks they fit into his 'Sous les étoiles' theme perfectly."

"Oh," said Marie with a shudder. "Does that mean they want me to go to Paris with Sophie?"

"No," said Jane. "He's sending a private plane to pick Sophie, Séb, and the desserts up."

Marie blew out a sigh of relief. For a moment, excitement lit up my face. A private plane? Whoa, what a strange life I was leading.

"Well, there's one problem solved," said Phillipa, her blue eyes sparkling. "Now we know how we can get the borage flowers to Paris for Sophie's courses." She held up her hand to me for a high five. I just looked at it. "What? You did it once."

"Once was enough," I said.

Jane slapped her hand on the desk. "Ladies, can we please keep our focus?" Her eyes bored into Marie's wide Cleopatra-lined ones. "Are you up for making these desserts in your spare time?"

"Sure," she said. "Everybody knows you don't say no to them." She sliced her finger across her throat. "Or else."

"Good," said Jane. "He'll pay you twenty euros per cake."

Marie blinked. "How much is that?"

"Around four thousand," said Jane. "How much do they cost you to make?"

"A hell of a lot less than that," said Marie with a wide grin.

Jane clapped her hands together. "It's settled, then. I'll let him know." She took in a breath. "He also sent me your schedule along with some requests, Sophie." She placed a printout in front of me.

I read with Phillipa and Marie looking over my shoulder.

Note: Please send me a full list of needed ingredients for your plat principal and apéro offerings. My staff will order them for

you. I'd suggest preparing whatever you can in advance, if it will
keep in coolers, and you will be reimbursed for your expenses.
As this is a black-tie event, along with your chef's coat, please
bring a ball gown. All chefs are expected to mingle with the
guests after the dinner service and apéro dînatoire. I hope you
have something appropriate. Chanel, lovely as it is, simply
won't do.

My heart raced. I looked up from the page, meeting Jane's eyes.
"Jane, we have a problem," I said. "A huge one."

"What?"

"I don't have a ball gown."

She winked. "I'll take your measurements and have something
perfect made for you. In fact, I'll design the dress myself."

I sucked in a breath, worried about money.

"Don't worry, I'll work within a reasonable budget," she said as if
reading my mind. "And we have a running account with the tailor.
They want our business. And they know you're good for it."

As there were no dress shops in Champvert, it was the only option, and Jane had good taste, always pulled through.

I let out a mumble. "Thanks, I really don't know what I'd do
without you."

Phillipa pointed to the printout, tapping it. "This is so not a break,"
she said. "You'll only have one day to dip your feet into Paris."

I scanned the list.

1) Wednesday, September 15
A van will pick you up at the château at nine a.m. sharp, taking
you to the aerodrome for a ten a.m. flight. Do not worry about
the desserts or any special ingredients you may want to bring
along with you. My father fitted the plane with a walk-in cooler,

as we entertain in air. My staff will deliver your goods to the museum, taking great care.

2) Thursday, September 16

All chefs will meet at the Musée d'Orsay at ten a.m. to get to know the lay of the land, the kitchens, and to meet the brigade members from Le Cordon Bleu. Any last-minute requests for ingredients or changes will be shared on this day.

3) Friday, September 17

All chefs will meet at the Musée d'Orsay at ten a.m. to prepare dishes or to prep additional ingredients that can be made in advance.

4) Saturday, September 18

All chefs will meet at the Musée d'Orsay at ten a.m. The gala will begin at seven p.m., the private dinner starting at eight p.m., ending at midnight for cocktails and dancing. Ball gown required.

5) Sunday, September 19

Chef's table. Dinner at Durand Paris. (Sous chefs are not invited.) A car will pick you up at your residence and bring you to us.

6) Monday, September 20

A driver will pick you up at nine a.m. and take you to the aerodrome for your flight home.

If you have any questions or concerns, please let me know at your earliest convenience. As for the chefs participating in this illustrious event, here's the list of who they are and the countries and restaurants they represent:

Amélie Durand (France) *Durand Paris*

Sophie Valroux de la Tour de Champvert (US/France) *Les Libellules*

Jean-Jacques Gaston (US/France) *Le Homard*

Dan O'Shea (US) *Cendrillon NY*

Cordialement,

Nicolas de la Barguelonne

My hands shook as I set the paper down. All of the chefs were starred. All of them but *me*. What did I rope myself into? And why hadn't Nicolas told me O'Shea and Gaston would be cooking alongside me? Granted, I was excited to see my old boss and meet his mentor, but not under these conditions. Rémi might have been right about Paris, because I felt like a lamb being led to the slaughter.

RIGHT AFTER THE family meal, Phillipa raced up to me as I was making final preparations for the evening's service. "Sophie, the tajine. What did you put in it? The entire brigade's mouths are on fire. And the grannies—"

I raced over to my station and picked up the spices, quickly realizing I'd used a hot *piment* instead of paprika. And I'd just made the same mistake I'd made when O'Shea fired me from Cendrillon. I hadn't tasted the meal. Because I couldn't. Some chef. The shame of my error rocked my head, making it pound. The tajine needed to slow cook for two hours, and I didn't have time to remake it. Plus, I'd used all of the preserved lemons.

My eyes met Phillipa's as the New York nightmare flashed in my brain. I didn't think I'd ever get over what happened. I still saw orange potimarron soup dripping down the walls after O'Shea threw it and fired me, still felt the rain freezing my body as I walked home like a wet rat. I couldn't face my problem, and it would be easier to blame somebody else. "Do you think somebody is out to sabotage me?"

"Oh, yeah, the granny brigade is so after you. Maybe even Clothilde. Or me," she said, placing her hands on her hips. "No, I think you just made a mistake. Don't beat yourself up. I have a plan."

My shoulders slumped. "Throw me to the wild boars?"

"No, we'll just redo it using the pressure cookers," she said, looking at the clock. "We have the time." She clapped her hands and yelled, "All hands on deck. We have another meal to prep. And quickly."

A meal I might mess up. Shame flooded my system. "Maybe I should leave?"

"To do what? Give up? So not the new you." She gripped my shoulders. "Mistakes happen. And we're going to fix it."

"What about the preserved lemons?" I asked, on the verge of tears. "I used them all."

"It's happened before. Grand-mère taught me a hack for the recipe," she said. "Nobody will know the difference."

I couldn't imagine Grand-mère ever making a single mistake. This proved she was human. Like me. Nobody was perfect all of the time. More than anything, I'd needed to hear this. I lifted up my chin and nodded.

"That's right. Pull yourself together, Chef, and let's get to it," said Phillipa.

Easier said than done. But I was going to try my best. My mind had catapulted into a dark place, and I wasn't going to bring everybody else down with me. I had two rules: no crying in the kitchen, and *always* taste. I'd broken both rules. Still, I had to set things right. I straightened my shoulders. "Let's do this."

Phillipa squeezed my hand. "Are you okay, Sophie? Don't get me wrong, but you've kind of been acting strange lately."

Now was not the time to unload my problems on my friend.

I lifted a brow. "I'm fine. And we have work to do."

"Yes, Chef," she said, eyeing me warily.

I wondered how long I could live this lie, how long I could keep up the front.

12

l'héritage

THE CHÂTEAU'S ORCHARDS burst in a sunset of oranges, thanks to a plethora of apricots and peaches. No matter how hard I tried, I couldn't snap out of a strange funk and really enjoy the fruits of my labor. I'd thought Paris was a good idea to get my head together, but it just brought along more stress. And I didn't want to admit to Rémi that he might have been right.

"We need to do something with all these peaches before they go bad," said Phillipa as she struggled into the kitchen with a large basket. "Any ideas?"

"You mean aside from the *confitures* the granny brigade has been making?" I asked.

"Yeah," she said. "They're exploding out of dry storage. We don't have any more room."

I pursed my lips together, not feeling so peachy. "We've done the grilled tomato and peach pizza at Le Papillon Sauvage. We've served the beet and peach soup. And the peach and cucumber salsa over the chicken. The tarts. The cobblers. The homemade ice cream. I don't know. I'm tapped out for ideas."

Phillipa rolled a peach on a cutting board, massaging it. "Pork," she said. "Peaches and pork would taste amazing together. Or pan-seared foie gras? What do you think?"

"If you can come up with something interesting, I'm all for it."

"Me?" she asked. "But you're the chef. And I want to be inspired by you."

"That makes two of us," I said.

"You're doing amazing things." Phillipa halved a peach, cut into it, and then handed over a slice. "Eat this, savor it. Find your inspiration!" she said, and as I bit into it, I tried, able to focus only on the texture.

As the juices from the slice ran across my tongue and down my throat, the sensation transported me to my childhood, to the teachings of my grand-mère in this kitchen, and her recipe for a peach crumble. The way she taught me to knead the flour, butter, and sugar into flaky crumbs, working her gentle hands with mine. I could almost feel her next to me, smell her cinnamon and nutmeg scent. And then, as quickly as the flavors flooded my memories, they disappeared like a dandelion seed blowing in the air. I wanted to catch the fluffy puff as it floated away from my grasp and make a wish.

Whoever is listening: *Bring my senses back.*

When I was a child, I didn't have a care in the world—no financial pressures, nobody depending on me. But I was all grown up now, and I had duties to fulfill. I ate another peach slice, and inspiration hit me like a warm ray of sunshine. I jumped off my stool and clapped my hands together.

"*Dos de cabillaud*" (cod filet), I said, recalling one of Grand-mère's specialties. "With a peach and almond crumble. We'll do your pork idea too."

Phillipa eyed me curiously. "That sounds amazing," she said. "I can almost taste the flavors."

"I wish I could," I said, but she didn't hear me. I threw the pit in the garbage can.

Phillipa locked her gaze onto mine, her look serious. "I know why you're acting so strange. I know you're worried about this Paris event. Sophie, you're scared."

"I am," I said, my mouth twisting. "Yeah, you're right. I'm scared shitless."

"You shouldn't be."

Phillipa pulled a printout from her back pocket, handing it over. My eyes scanned the page as I read another glorious review about the château experience and the meals we created. I never knew when reviewers were even eating or staying with us—probably a good thing, because it would just bring on more stress and I'd lose focus.

"You know," said Phillipa, "you really should keep up with all of this goodness. Because you're shaking up the foodie world."

My mind rocked. Something was definitely wrong with me. But ignoring reality meant I didn't have to face it. I straightened my shoulders and set to prepping.

TWO DAYS BEFORE I set off for Paris, the *notaire* called Rémi and me to his office. I sat in front of Monsieur Beaumont, focusing on his wrinkled hands as he shuffled papers, my heart beating. Rémi remained calm, but I was a shaky bundle of nerves. Finally, Monsieur Beaumont looked up and peered over his wire-rimmed glasses. He didn't smile.

"After digging into Mademoiselle Valroux de la Tour de Champvert's family history, I am happy to say your inheritance is in the clear," he said.

Rémi clasped my hand.

"So there are no wayward relatives who can stake a claim?" I asked, blowing out a sigh of relief.

"Non," said Monsieur Beaumont. "Your grand-père was an only child, as was your grand-mère. The inheritance is rightfully yours, and the bank accounts and all properties will be released to you." He placed a stack of documents in front of us, flipped through the pages, and said, "Sign here." Flip. "Sign here." Flip. "And here."

The pen shook in my hands, and the whole process took about ten minutes.

Rémi cleared his throat. "I floated funds, around one hundred thousand euros, to keep the château's business alive while we waited for the inheritance to come through. Are we entitled to a reimbursement?"

"Oui, if you kept receipts and proof of expenditures, it won't be a problem."

My mouth unhinged and my eyes snapped to Rémi's. "Rémi, what? Why didn't you tell me how much?"

"Because I didn't want you to argue with me," he said. "Voilà. I did what needed to be done—not for you, but for the château."

I crossed my arms over my chest, not sure if I should be thankful or angry. Then again, I hadn't exactly been keeping up with the business end of the château. I'd been busy enough for two people in the kitchen. Jane handled everything else, and, apparently, Rémi did too. "Merci, Rémi," I said. "I appreciate it."

Rémi shot me an inquisitive look. He was probably expecting me to flip out. But no. That was the old me, the one who lashed out.

"We're partners," I said with a shrug.

The notaire cleared his throat. "During our research, we found out something about your family history, Mademoiselle Valroux de la Tour de Champvert," he started.

"Please call me Sophie," I said.

"Alors, Sophie, we've never had a woman who comes from triple noble roots grace our presence."

"I'm sorry. I don't understand," I said, blinking back my surprise.

"I told you you were a princess," said Rémi. "Ma princesse."

I blurted out a laugh. "Some princess," I said.

"Your arrière-arrière-grand-mère is from the de la Roche de Saint-Émilion family," continued Monsieur Beaumont. "My curiosity was piqued, so I investigated some more. Although the vineyard and château they owned are not in working order, it's now apparently owned by a wealthy American through a trust. I was unable to find their name. None of the de la Roche de Saint-Émilions can be traced. Rumors in the wine world circulated about Hénri relocating to the United States, but nothing was proven." He popped his lips. "*Pffff.* It's as if this side of your family has all but disappeared."

His words blew my mind. There was so much about my family's history I didn't know. I knew a little about Grand-mère's life and a few things about my grandfather, but I knew zilch when it came to any other relatives. I felt terrible for not asking Grand-mère about her mother and grandmother. I took in a breath. "Are you saying I may have distant relatives somewhere in the world?"

"It's a possibility, yes," he said. "Regardless, even if they exist, none of these relations would have any right to your stake."

I turned to Rémi, blinking. "Do you know anything about Grand-mère's family?"

He shrugged. "You knew Grand-mère. She didn't like speaking of her past." He paused. "But she did mention one thing. After I told her about Anaïs becoming pregnant with Lola, she told me that her grandmother was estranged from her sister. Something about not following the Christian path and having loose morals. And that I had to do right by Anaïs."

"That sounds like Grand-mère," I said.

My head spun with the information I'd just learned. I needed more time, needed to do my own research. But, for now, my heart ached to complete the family tree with the one blood relation I was sure of.

"I know who my father is," I said breathlessly. "It's Jean-Marc Bourret."

"If he wants to claim you as his daughter, he can do so at the *mairie*" (mayor's office), said Monsieur Beaumont.

"I want his name to be associated with mine," I said.

"I think Jean-Marc would love that," said Rémi.

"Merci, Monsieur Beaumont," I said, standing up and shaking his hand, and Rémi followed suit. "You've certainly opened my eyes to my family's roots. Thank you for your time. I'm sorry to say we have to leave, but we both appreciate your help."

"It was my pleasure," he said.

Rémi and I left the stuffy office and headed back to the château, my head swimming with names. I was antsy for more information, but my curiosity would have to wait. We had a full house, and duty called, including a last-minute staff meeting that I hadn't prepared for.

MARIE WALKED INTO the salon with Lola, both of their faces smeared with makeup so horrific it would scare a clown. Red lipstick as eye shadow, blue eye shadow for blush, and I didn't know what shade of green was smeared across their lips. Marie twirled. "Do you like my makeover?"

"You look frighteningly beautiful," I said. "And I'd like to emphasize the word 'frightening.'"

"I did it, Tatie Sophie," said Lola. "I made Marie and me into mermaids."

I'd learn from Marie. When it came to kids, she could teach me a thing or two outside of the kitchen.

"Oh, you did, ma puce?" I asked with mock surprise, and Marie laughed. "You are a true artist."

"Picasso has nothing on her," said Marie.

Lola smiled proudly, nodding her head.

"Where's Rémi?" I asked.

"He's finishing up the lunch service at Le Papillon Sauvage," she said. "Laetitia had some errands to run, so I offered to watch the little makeup munchkin."

The rest of the staff trickled into the salon, eyeing Marie and Lola curiously, Jane gasping, "*Quelle horreur.*" The granny brigade clucked away on one of the settees, pointing at Lola with shaky hands. Phillipa threw her head back and laughed. Rémi finally walked in. He took one look at Lola and then focused his attention on Marie. "What in the world did you do to my daughter?"

Lola unlatched Marie's hand and ran to Rémi. He scooped her up. "I'm a mermaid, Papa," she said. "Like Ariel."

He tickled her belly and met Marie's smiling face with a scowl. "This better wash off," he said.

"Don't worry," she said. "It will."

Once everybody settled down, I spoke. "As you know, Séb and I are taking off for the City of Light in two days. Before we leave you, I have some news to share." I paused, meeting the staff's eager faces. "My inheritance finally came through. It took a bit longer than expected, but the good news is that I don't have any wayward relatives who blocked the funds or tried to take the château away from me and Rémi."

Jane let out an uncharacteristic woot-woot and pumped her fist. The housekeeping team exchanged curious glances, not quite used to this new unbridled Jane. I wanted to tease her, but not in front of the staff. Instead, I turned my attention to the brigade. "Phillipa,

Monica, Clothilde, and les dames, I'm sure you'll have everything in the kitchen under control. Phillipa and I have planned all the menus during my absence. And, Marie, your mirrored galaxy cakes are to die for. Paris is going to be eating them up. Thanks for your hard work."

"*Pas de problème*," she said, her green lips twisting like the Joker's. "He paid me a lot. And it was fun."

Her mermaid makeup distracted me from my thoughts. I just blinked.

"Don't worry. I'll wash my face," she said, as if reading my mind. "I wouldn't want to scare the guests."

The staff laughed. I placed my hand on my heart, thankful for all the people in my world.

"As you know, I won't be joining you for tomorrow night's service, but I'll be around if needed," I continued. "If any of you run into any problems, we'll sort them out before I take off. Otherwise, it's business as usual."

My heartbeat accelerated. For me, leaving the château was like leaving my baby for the first time—not that I knew anything about motherhood. Although I knew the château would be in capable hands, and I'd only be in Paris for six days, the thought that I'd have no control if something happened made me extremely nervous. After all, when it came down to it, this place and these people were my responsibility. And, whether I liked this side of my stubborn personality or not, I was a bona fide control freak.

I took in a breath and met my father's proud eyes. "The grounds look absolutely beautiful, thanks to Jean-Marc. Also, thank you for potting the borage plants so we can take them to Paris without them wilting."

"Anything for you, ma chérie," he said, and my heart sparked.

"Finally, I'll make an appearance in the dining room tomorrow night for the opening speech," I said. "Jane and Phillipa will handle the other evenings. Jane, it might be a good idea if you introduce Phillipa as the château's chef de cuisine."

Phillipa leapt out of her seat and threw her arms around me. I squeezed her shoulders. "I'm counting on you, Chef."

"We've got this," she said with one of her wide grins.

I clapped my hands together, signaling the end of the meeting. *"Merci à tous, et bon courage."* I tilted my head toward Séb. "Ready for the City of Light?"

"Yes, Chef!" he said, leaping off his seat. "You know, I'm really excited to visit Paris. I've never been there."

"Neither have I," I said.

He raised his hands, palms up. "What?"

"Aside from Champvert and the surrounding areas, I haven't experienced much of la France," I said. "So, yeah, I'm a little pumped too. Ready to get on those crab cakes?"

"Yes, Chef," said Séb.

The kitchen of Les Libellules was closed on Mondays, so we were going to take advantage of the empty and well-equipped space. As my grand-mère had taught me and as Nicolas had instructed: if it will keep, prepare what you can in advance. We had our work cut out for us. I had no idea how long it would take to make over eight hundred fresh crab cakes with my version of a rémoulade, adding Hungarian paprika and truffle oil, from memory. Even before we cracked one crab, I could *almost* taste the recipe.

"I'm going to lend a hand," said Phillipa.

"Me too," said Marie.

"And me," said Monica.

"No. It's your day off. Go relax. Take a swim in the pool," I said. "Really, I don't need your help."

"Yes, you do," said Phillipa. "You just don't want to ask for it."

She got me.

My three friends crossed their arms over their chests and lifted their chins with defiance. I knew I wouldn't win this argument. And I really needed their taste buds. "Fine," I said, and we shuffled to the kitchen.

"Where do we start?" asked Marie.

I gave everybody their duties.

Séb pulled out the crabs from the walk-in while Phillipa gathered the ingredients. We were using every burner—first to boil the crabs and then to deep-fry the cakes in oil. Marie commandeered every large pot we had, and we set to work. Monica mixed up the spices— red pepper flakes, whole white peppercorns, and *herbes de Provence*.

Phillipa lifted her eyebrows. "You better come back from Paris, or I'll hunt you down and drag you back by your hair."

"Why wouldn't I come back?" I asked.

"O'Shea is going to be there," she said, pouting. "He might try to tempt you with New York again."

As I whisked the base for the cakes—mayo, egg yolks, lime and lemon juice—I realized I was really happy with my motley brigade, and, now that I'd fully gotten the hang of things, thrilled with my château life.

"Not going to happen," I said. "My life is here now."

"Promise?" asked Phillipa, her eyebrows lifted.

I shook the whisk at her. "Have I ever broken one yet?"

Her eyes darted back and forth in thought. "No, I suppose not. And you're smiling again. With your eyes. So I believe you."

I set to cracking the crab and picking the meat. With five of us moving in tune, what should have taken eight hours to prepare took three. Cast-iron skillets bubbled with butter, onions, diced celery, and black pepper. After combining all the ingredients, the patties were set and deep-fried until golden brown. After the crab cakes cooled, Phillipa and Séb placed them in the walk-in.

"Phew," I said. "We did it. Thank you."

"Pool?" asked Marie, and Phillipa, Séb, and Monica sighed in agreement.

"I'll meet you in a bit," I said.

"Take a break," said Phillipa. "You deserve it."

"I will," I said. "But first, there's something I need to do."

"What?" asked Phillipa.

"Château business," I said, and raced to Grand-mère's office to Google sensory impairment and the causes. I'd been avoiding the subject, hoping I'd be miraculously healed.

The moment I brought up a browser and frantically tapped at the keys, disappointment set in. I didn't have Alzheimer's. I didn't smoke. I didn't have a dry mouth or dry eyes. Oral hygiene? I followed the rules, brushing my teeth for two minutes and flossing. Maybe I just had a sinus infection? Brain trauma. Maybe. But with this last search there was the possibility I'd never get my senses back. And I didn't want to believe that. I couldn't. No, I was a chef.

Shaken, I closed out of the medical site, thinking it was quite possible I had a vitamin B_{12} deficiency. That was it. I made a mental note to go to the pharmacy.

While I was on the computer, I searched Nicolas de la Barguelonne, only coming up with business ventures and pictures of him with one of his models of the day. Nothing unsavory, save for the fact that he was clearly a player. Still, something in this family didn't sit right. They were too rich, too powerful. I ran a couple more searches.

When I pulled up his photo, I remembered the way Nicolas stared at me with his cold blue eyes. I shuddered and brushed off the feeling as paranoia. He wasn't after me, just my food.

13

off to the city of light

A S I MADE final preparations for the event, I tried to put any fears that were smacking my confidence down regarding my impairment on the back burner and focus. When I'd proposed Monica's concept for the hors d'oeuvre we'd created, Nicolas had said it sounded interesting and couldn't wait to sink his teeth into them. I hoped he didn't want to sink his teeth into me. Paranoia. I had to push this out of my head. He wasn't out to get me. Nicolas was giving me a break.

Séb and I packed up most everything we needed for the event—including our knives, because a chef never enters any kitchen without his or her own knives. Then, wicker baskets in hand, we headed to the orchard to pick the purple and green figs.

The September sun beat down on our backs. Sweat trickled down our foreheads and necks. Soon, we had three full baskets of globe-shaped figs for the apéro dînatoire—at least five hundred of them. Séb wiped the perspiration from his brow and let out a sigh. He pointed toward the far side of the orchard. "The olives will be ready soon. I'll help with the harvest. I love olives."

"Thanks," I said, noting Séb's loyalty to the château. "Jean-Marc would probably love any help he can get."

Séb nodded. "*Chouette*" (cool), he said.

Over the past few months, I'd really connected with my dad. He was kind, gave good advice, and looked at me almost as adoringly as I looked at him. I smiled at Séb and then nodded to the baskets. "Why don't we pack up these figs in the coolers? And then take a break," I suggested, eyeing the lake. "The guests are most likely at the pool, and it's freaking hot."

"I didn't bring my bathing suit," he said with frustration.

"You can borrow one of Rémi's. He won't mind," I said, and we headed back to the kitchen.

Under Phillipa's guidance, the brigade had launched into full-on prep mode. I didn't want to disturb them or have them think I was checking up on them, so I just saluted and Phillipa shot me the thumbs-up. Séb pulled out coolers and we gingerly packed the figs, placing them in the cold storage walk-in.

By the time five o'clock rolled around, Séb and I had cooled off, and with all of our Paris-bound goodies gingerly arranged, we made our way to the family dinner. I still had to pack my suitcase, but I had plenty of time to get everything together this evening. Phillipa fluttered around the kitchen like a trapped, nervous bird as I took my place on a stool next to Rémi. He squeezed my hand and was about to lean over to plant a kiss on my lips when I caved in my back, my shoulders hunching, pulling away from him.

"Not in front of the staff," I said.

He scoffed. "Why? Everybody knows we are a couple."

"We are a couple *outside* of work," I said, scrunching my nose. "When we're working, we are business partners. We have to keep this professional."

He winked, his caramel eyes glistening with desire. Under the table, he ran his hand underneath my skirt and caressed my bare thigh. "What time do you get off work, boss?"

I removed his hand and whispered, "Meet me in my room tonight."

"D'accord, boss," he said with a smirk.

I slugged him lightly on the arm. "Not funny."

Phillipa stood at attention. "Sophie, do you want to do the honors of presenting the menu to the staff?"

"No, Chef," I said. "That honor is yours for the next week."

Maybe forever, I thought.

She grinned. "Okay, then. Tonight, along with the usual offerings, we've prepared everything that Sophie and Séb will be serving at the Sous les étoiles gala—the main course, the apéros, and the dessert for the family dinner." Her shoulders slumped. "Chef, I hope I don't let you down. I re-created the dish as best I could. I—"

I stopped her from blathering on; I'd already lived through the same thing. More than once. Plus, I'd seen and experienced the culinary talents she possessed. It was my turn to support her the way she'd supported me. "Phillipa, you won't disappoint. Straighten your shoulders. Live in the moment. Show us what you've got. We all believe in you."

When the rest of the staff applauded, she stuck out her chin proudly, smiled a toothy smile, and snorted.

"Right," she said, turning. "I'll get to it."

Phillipa placed one tray of appetizers after the other on the table—the jambon sec–wrapped chipotle figs with the cocoa-balsamic glaze; the crab cakes with the rémoulade dipping sauce; the varying star-shaped canapés, the bottoms buttery, toasted bread topped with different ingredients and garnished with chopped fresh herbs; the verrines filled with *bœuf bourguignon* and baby carrots; and the smoked salmon, beet carpaccio, and mascarpone bites served on homemade biscuits and sprinkled with capers.

Everybody dug in, oohing and aahing.

"I don't know which one I like best," exclaimed Marie, licking her lips. "They're all so delicious. I can't choose a favorite child."

Phillipa winked. "Just wait until you see and taste Sophie's plat principal," she said, turning on her heel. She returned with a large pressure cooker, placing it on the table. She lifted the lid, and everybody breathed in the aromas, noses sniffing with anticipation. "This is Sophie's version of *pot-au-feu de la mer*, but with grilled lobster, crab, abalone, mussels, and large shrimp, along with a variety of root and fresh vegetables, a ginger-lemongrass-infused sauce, and garnished with borage, or starflowers, a smattering of sea salt, a dash of crème fraîche, fresh herbs, and ground pepper."

As Phillipa commandeered the grilled shellfish, I scrambled off my stool to gather the bowls, returning with a stack. I handed her one with a wink.

She ladled the seafood soup into the bowl, propped up the shellfish in the center, and then placed it on the table. She added a drop of blue food coloring to the base, made from the petals of the borage, and then added cream. She gave the mixture a gentle swirl. Finally, she placed three borage flowers on the top, sprinkled a little fresh thyme and rosemary, and twisted in the fresh ground pepper. She presented the dish.

For a moment, nobody spoke.

"I hope it tastes as magical as it looks," said Clothilde.

I hoped so too.

"It looks like a painting," said Marie. "A beautiful painting of the Milky Way."

"It is," said Phillipa. "Sophie's inspiration came from Vincent van

Gogh's *The Starry Night*, which is the focus of the gala and why it's called Sous les étoiles." She paused. "You also inspired her, Marie."

"I did?" Marie asked, her hands fluttering to her neck.

"Yes," I said. "You reminded me of how good it feels to be creative in the kitchen and to break the rules."

She laughed. "I *am* a rule breaker."

"Can we eat it now?" asked a member of our waitstaff. "That's simply beautiful and it smells so good. Plus, I'm starving."

Phillipa nodded and filled up the bowls, garnished them, and handed them out to very impatient faces. Once everybody had been served, she said, "Dig in."

Aside from mumbles and murmurs of pure delight, there were no other sounds. Just heads tilted back. Breaths of joy. Eyes closed. Smiles of ecstasy. After watching my staff's expressions, I finally tasted this creation again. A symphony of textures exploded on my tongue, and I knew I'd created something truly special, a dish that would measure up to the other chefs I'd be up against. I was cooking from my heart. And, as they've said, love always won in the end.

Or so I hoped.

RÉMI KNOCKED ON my door around nine thirty.

"Come in," I said.

"You wanted to see me, boss?" he asked, and entered my room.

"Would you please stop calling me that?" I said with frustration. "Honestly, it's really beginning to grate on my nerves."

"I thought it was our inside joke," he said.

"I don't find it funny anymore," I said, throwing my clothes into a suitcase, taking great care of the gorgeous dress Jane the fashionista had designed.

It was made of green silk, the color she'd picked to match my eyes. Ruched in the bodice with a black sequin detail at the bust, the layers of fabric hugged my body, flowing down to my feet and draping midway down my back. It was absolutely gorgeous, like it had been made for me, which it had. Jane had suggested I pull my hair into a half French twist instead of my usual braid. I'd agreed.

"Where's your sense of humor?" asked Rémi as he helped me zip up the case.

I stood up, shaking my head. "Sorry, I'm a little nervous about the event."

He spun me around to face him, an intensity in his eyes. "Then don't go."

Every time I thought of Nicolas or making a fool of myself because my meals may be off, the thought of not going crossed my mind, but I'd committed to the event, and I never broke a promise.

"I have to," I said, flinching ever so slightly. "And when I'm in Paris, I really need to prove myself. And I won't have much time. Can you give me that?"

"You don't want me calling you every second of the day and checking up on you," he said with a grin. "To make sure that Nicolas fellow doesn't want to eat you for dinner?"

"Exactly. And you have to trust me," I said, my eyes meeting his.

"I can do that," he said, pulling me toward him. His clean, woodsy scent should have calmed my frazzled nerves, but I couldn't smell him. My heart raced.

"Can you just hold me tonight?"

"I can do that too," he said, and kissed my nose. "In fact, I want to hold you forever."

We undressed and settled into bed—me the sleepless little spoon as Rémi drifted off into slumberland, his arm slung over my waist.

Paris might turn out to be a nightmare. Still, I needed to get away from the château; to take a moment to press the reset button; to maybe find out more about my family, my grandmother, and figure out what was holding me back from fully committing to this life. I was eighty, maybe ninety, percent there. Why not one hundred percent? As I tossed and turned, I prayed to the ever-elusive cooking gods and to Grand-mère.

THE VAN THAT the de la Barguelonnes sent for us showed up promptly at nine a.m.—one driver, and one assistant, Nadeem, young with a golden complexion and intelligent, dark eyes. Séb joined me on the driveway, bouncing around excitedly like he had ants in his pants. Jane sauntered out of the château's front door, handing me instructions on how to get into Grand-mère's pied-à-terre along with the address.

"Everything's taken care of," she said. "Break a leg. And call me anytime, day or night, if you need anything."

I kissed her on the cheek. "Thanks, Jane. But you know me and my klutzy feet. Can we come up with another expression?"

"Sure," she said. "Knock their socks off."

"Mademoiselle Valroux de la Tour de Champvert," began Nadeem.

"Please call me Sophie," I said.

He seemed ruffled with me being so informal. But he hadn't dealt with the likes of me, probably used to Nicolas and his rudeness. At least Nadeem didn't have to deal with his creepy looks and sexual innuendos. I shuddered.

"Er, Sophie," he said. "I'm here to take you all the way through to Paris. I understand we are taking things along with us on the trip? Could you show me where they are, and we'll load them into the van?"

"Sure," I said, pointing to the borage plants. "Start with those. And thanks. We've got a shitload of stuff in my walk-in too."

Nadeem flinched ever so slightly when I said "shitload." Séb stifled a laugh.

"Okay," said Nadeem, looking at his watch. "We're on the de la Barguelonnes' schedule now. And we don't want to mess it up." He mumbled, "Believe me."

A half hour later, everything was packed into the van, including us. We were about to drive off when, out of the corner of my eye, I noticed Rémi racing out of the château. I had the driver stop the van and I jumped out, although Rémi and I had already said goodbye in the morning.

He pulled me into his arms and kissed me passionately, making my already shaky knees quiver. He looked me dead straight in the eyes. "Remember your promise," he said.

"I will," I said.

SOON, SÉB AND I were seated on the de la Barguelonnes' ridiculously gold-decorated private plane, a converted 777, all our goods locked and loaded in the cold storage walk-in, a flight attendant serving us champagne and caviar. We were off to Paris in the lap of luxury, comfort, and style. Séb wandered around the cabin with a shit-eating grin on his face, eyeing the chandeliers, the full bar, and the dining room table set up with crystal glasses and porcelain plates. Dazed, I just sat on the couch in the lounge, facing a big-screen television set, completely zoning out.

"You won't believe it," said Séb. "There's a bedroom suite with a full bathroom and shower. This is amazing." He took a seat on one of the recliners. "I've never flown before. Is this what all planes are like?"

"Uh, no," I said. "It's much less glamorous, especially if you fly economy. The airlines pack you in like sardines."

Damn. I frowned. I couldn't even taste the saltiness of sardines. I shook the thought off. I had to be on my A game.

"Oh," he said, sipping on his champagne. "I could get used to this."

"You'll have to become a billionaire. Or marry one," I said, cringing as I thought of Nicolas.

Certainly, there was a price for all of this. The question was: Who was going to pay? I couldn't help but think of Nadeem's statement about not messing with the de la Barguelonnes' time or schedule. I set my champagne glass down on the crystal table and gripped the seat of the couch tightly as the plane took off.

This supposedly fearless woman was a bona fide wreck.

14

───◦❦◦───

the not-quite pied-à-terre

ORTY-FIVE MINUTES LATER, the plane touched down at a private aerodrome just outside Paris. Nadeem entered the lounge. Séb and I straightened up in our seats. Nerves set in. In a few days, I'd be cooking for Paris's elite—politicians, fashionistas, millionaires, billionaires, and well-heeled trendsetters—people who were used to flying private and eating at the best establishments in the world.

"A car will take you to your residence," said Nadeem. "A van will take your supplies to the Musée d'Orsay, storing them appropriately. Do you have any specific instructions?"

"Aside from the black case with our tools and our suitcases with our personal belongings, everything else, including the flowers, should be placed in a cold storage walk-in," I said.

"As you wish." He nodded and held out his hand to shake ours. "It was lovely meeting you, Sophie and Séb."

"Same to you, Nadeem," I said, a tad confused. "You're not going with us?"

"No," he said. "We're off to pick up the East Coast chefs for the gala."

"Chefs O'Shea and Gaston?" I asked, and he nodded. I was looking forward to seeing my mentor and meeting his. "Wow, Nicolas is really rolling out the red carpet for this event."

"It's the de la Barguelonne way," said Nadeem with a slight lift of his shoulders. "I'll have your suitcases and tools placed in the car. Just head down those steps."

A black Mercedes waited on the runway, a uniformed driver by its side. He tilted his cap and opened the doors for us. Séb and I sank into the back seat. A few minutes later, the trunk slammed to a close and we whipped down the roads to Paris.

"This is so cool," said Séb. "Thanks for bringing me along."

Drops of perspiration dripped down my neck, pooling in the small of my back.

"Sure," I said with a slight wince, and then I smiled, wanting to bring on a positive vibe to this trip. Séb's legs jimmied with excitement, and I didn't want to bring him down. "And, you're right, this is kind of cool."

The Paris skyline came into view, stretching out before us. Séb and I drew in our breaths as the Eiffel Tower gleamed in the distance. We passed by Nôtre-Dame, still under construction after an electrical fire nearly destroyed it, its rose windows covered with a tarp. I let out a sad sigh. The magnificent structure had survived centuries, wars, and then some idiot didn't do the wiring right. The driver took a right, heading over an ornate stone bridge. After a sharp left, me bumping shoulders with Séb, and then another right, he rolled down the privacy window.

"Welcome to l'Île Saint-Louis," he said. "Do you need help with your bags?"

"Non, merci," said Séb with a shrug. "I can manage."

The driver hopped out of the car and placed our suitcases on the sidewalk. I reached into my purse, fumbling for my wallet.

"That won't be necessary, mademoiselle," he said. "Monsieur de la Barguelonne has taken care of everything."

Of course he had.

"I'll pick you up at nine tomorrow morning," said the driver, and tilted his cap. *"Bonne journée."*

Séb and I stood on a narrow, cobbled street lined with beautiful stone buildings decorated with wrought iron balconies. We faced a set of two massive, intricately carved wooden doors with lion knockers, all painted an elegant grayish blue and set into a tall limestone archway. Before we left, Jane told me the neighborhood dated back to the seventeenth century and hosted many celebrated inhabitants, including famed former president Georges Pompidou. I'd expected Paris to be a lot busier with people bustling around, and I'm sure in most areas it was, but this neighborhood exuded a quiet tranquility. After taking in my surroundings, I pressed the buzzer.

"Mademoiselle Valroux de la Tour de Champvert, I'll be right down," said a woman's voice.

A few moments later, the massive wooden doors opened, revealing a petite woman, about forty-five years old with a smooth bob and a charcoal-gray pantsuit, standing in a courtyard with paved bricks of various hues of browns and filled with flowers, trees, and potted topiary plants. I gasped, not expecting this hidden oasis of privacy. The woman stepped forward, regarding our suitcases, and spoke quick French into a walkie-talkie.

"Forgive me," she said with an apologetic smile. "I'm Marianne, in charge of all the residences here. Claude, my husband, will be right down to carry your bags to the apartment, which, after a bit of dusting and cleaning, is ready for you." She paused. "I've also stocked the refrigerator and cupboards with everything you'll need for your stay."

"Merci," I said. "And please call me Sophie."

She tilted her head to the side. "Granted, she didn't come here very often, but I see so much of your grand-mère in you. *Toutes mes condoléances*," she said sincerely. "She was a wonderful woman with a heart of gold. In fact, she was the one who convinced all of the members in the association to hire me over twenty-five years ago. We all miss her dearly."

"I miss her too," I said, swallowing back a lump of pain.

Before I lost it, a burly man with disheveled, graying hair barreled up to us with gardening clippers in hand. He said a quick bonjour, set his clippers on a clay pot, and grabbed our bags. Marianne shrugged. "Claude's a bit of a brute, but, alas, he's mine. Come on. Follow me. I'll show you to the apartment."

With that, she made her way to the left side of the courtyard. She grabbed a set of keys and opened another grayish-blue, carved wood door, similar to the one in the entry but a lot smaller. We entered the foyer. "There are two apartments on the rez-de-chaussée and the second floor," she said, heading up marble steps. "Your apartment is located on the top three floors."

As we made our way up two flights, Claude bounded down the steps, passing us with a quick "bonne journée."

The door to Grand-mère's apartment remained open. There was no sign of our suitcases. "I'll give you a quick tour, and then I'll be on my way to let you settle in. Claude has put your suitcases in your room," said Marianne, clearly noting my confusion.

Séb and I followed her into a stylish living room, bathed in light, and painted white with high ceilings and a fireplace, the floors inlaid with parquet. The white couches and chairs were of classic design, plush, and more modern than the château. Vases of white roses adorned the tables, impressionist paintings reminiscent of Monet's water lilies on the walls.

Leave it to my grand-mère to let me discover yet another aspect of her personality, her life, when I didn't have her by my side. A feeling of longing, the grief, hit me in those waves, thrashing and yawing. It took great effort to keep my feelings inside as Marianne continued the tour, leading us through a dining room with a rustic, country French table and white linen chairs, to the state-of-the-art kitchen, complete with a white Lacanche four-burner stove.

Dumbfounded and awestruck, I locked my eyes onto a piece of fabric patterned with wild red poppies hanging in the corner. It couldn't be. It had to be. I raced over to the cloth to find an exact replica of the apron hanging on the hook in the kitchen of Champvert. I brought it to my nose, wishing to inhale her signature scent of Chanel No. 5, lavender, nutmeg, and cinnamon. I squeezed my eyes shut. Memories of Grand-mère teaching me to cook when I was a child flashed in my mind, one after the other after the other.

"Are you okay, Sophie?" asked Marianne.

"I'm fine," I said, coming back from the past to the present. I held out the apron. "Can I keep this?"

Marianne eyed me like I was from another planet. "Of course," she said. "Everything in this apartment is yours."

Right. Mine.

"Let me show you to your rooms," she said.

In a daze, I nodded and grabbed the apron off its hook, carrying it like a child with her favorite blanket.

A staircase with a carved wooden railing led to the second floor, housing three expansive bedrooms. Marianne ushered Séb into the largest one of them, although, after peeking in, they were near to identical—painted white with soaring ceilings, beautiful cornices, and wooden beams. Grand-mère had decorated all of the rooms with wrought iron poster beds, white wood side tables, and a white dresser—every design element pristine and elegant.

"I hope you'll be comfortable here," said Marianne, nodding to Séb. "This is the finest of the guest suites."

Séb smiled and dove onto the plush bed decorated in pale blue linen. "It's perfect. The nicest room I've ever seen in my entire life."

"But you can't be that old," said Marianne with a humored tsk.

"I'm nineteen," said Séb. He kicked his shoes off. "I'm old enough."

Marianne let out a chortle. "You're just a baby," she said. "Come along, Sophie, I'll show you to your suite."

I nodded and followed her one flight up, gobsmacked. Grand-mère's suite took up the entire top floor. Although enormous, the master bedroom was cozy and similar to the one Séb would be staying in, but also had a fireplace and a newer Aubusson carpet, the pattern white and green, decorating the floor. This apartment seemed like another world from life at the château.

An orange cat scurried out from under the bed and proceeded to snake around my ankles, purring loudly. One eye rested shut, as if it were krazy-glued to a close, and her fur was mottled. Marianne scooped her up. "*Sac à puces*" (Fleabag), she said. "This stray is a devious one, always sneaking into the apartments. I don't know how she gets in. I'll have to warn Claude to stop feeding her tuna."

I scratched under the cat's chin, staring into her good eye—a kaleidoscope of greens and yellows. "She's sweet," I said.

"She's filthy," said Marianne, tucking the cat under her arm. "I'll leave you to settle in. The keys are on the kitchen counter along with the code for the front door, the Wi-Fi password, and my cell phone number." She smiled. "If you need anything, anything at all, don't hesitate to call. I'll do errands for you, laundry, whatever you need, and I'm happy to do it." With her free hand, she pointed to a stair-case. "That leads to the private roof garden. The views are simply magnificent."

"Merci, Marianne," I said.

"It was wonderful to meet you, Sophie. I hope we'll be seeing a lot more of you." She turned to leave but stopped. "Oh, one more *petit truc*." She pulled a package out of her purse and handed it over. "This arrived for you today. It looks important. Regal."

With that said, she rotated on her heel and left me to my own devices.

Wrapped in a sparkling midnight-blue wired ribbon, the small silk box, also midnight blue, shook in my hands. Immediately I knew who had sent it, thanks to the note written on postcard-sized ivory stationery with his initials.

Sophie,

I thought you would like to see the invitations we sent out to our esteemed guests for the private dining event. More than half of them have requested your plat principal. I suppose they want to see what this rising star in the culinary world can do. You'll have eighty meals to prepare along with the offerings for the apéro dînatoire. I know you can handle the pressure. Your brigade will help you see this through.

Cordialement,
Nicolas

PS I hope you brought something appropriate to wear for the gala.

The ribbon on the box fell to the floor as I untied it. Although I was going to be working with Séb, I didn't know this team from Adam. Or Eve, for that matter. Admittedly, the enclosed papers were beautiful and reminiscent of a wedding invitation, not a private party. Set in silver tissue, midnight-blue cards with elegant silver lettering listed the date and the title of the gala, Sous les étoiles, along with the names of the chefs, including mine, and the dishes we'd prepare, complete with an RSVP with boxes to check for the meal choices.

My throat tightened. Amélie's plat principal of filet of daurade seemed oddly familiar to one I'd created—the one putting me on the map, the one Eric had stolen from under me. I shrugged off the paranoia. She was a three-starred chef and didn't need to poach recipes from the likes of me. Her dish had to be different. Still, why had Nicolas really chosen me? He'd said it was because he wanted more representation from female chefs making their mark in the culinary world. But he'd peppered this note with a threat, with pressure. I thought coming to Paris was an opportunity, a chance to escape. Something deep in my gut told me I was dead wrong.

I hung up the beautiful green dress Jane had designed, smoothing out the flowing fabric, followed by my chef's coat. After unpacking, I explored the room, noting the photos on the dresser, including a picture of my mother when she was young, vibrant, and full of life. My grand-mère hadn't displayed any photos of my mom at the château, the only ones hidden away in her journal. I wondered why she kept them out here. Maybe because she didn't spend much time in Paris? I hugged the photo to my chest, my heartbeat slowing down and feeling in tune with my mother's spirit when she was happy.

One day, she'd told me that I was her everything. I'd tucked her into bed after preparing one of my meals to nourish her soul. I now knew what she'd said was true—even on her bad days, when her eyes glazed over from popping too many pills. Before I lost it, I set the photo down, examining the others, some of Rémi and me, our lips stained with the juice of cherries.

My heart sparked. It dawned on me: I missed him. I missed the way he looked at me under those long lashes of his. I missed his caveman-like mentality. I missed his warm body curled up against mine. The way he made me laugh. The fear of failure—not life at the château, I realized—still wrapped its chains around my mind, and I needed to set myself free, trust in other people, and believe in myself and my decisions.

A cough came from the doorway, and I turned to find Séb shuffling his feet.

"Sorry, Chef, I hope I'm not interrupting, but my stomach is speaking to me in hunger Morse code," said Séb. "We're going to be cooking like fiends the next few days. Do you want to head out and explore the neighborhood with me, grab something to eat while we have the chance?" He cleared his throat. "As mentioned, I've never been to Paris, never taken a flight. You've given this to me. You've given me everything. A chance to follow my dreams." He looked down toward the floor. "I kind of want to share it with you. If I'm not being out of line." His voice wavered ever so slightly. "I really hope I'm not being out of line. You're my boss."

I held up a finger and he froze. "Two seconds. We'll explore Paris together. Don't forget, I've never been here before either. But do you want to check out the roof garden with me first?" I pointed. "It's just up those steps."

Séb's jaw dropped. "A roof terrace? This is like a dream!"

"Yeah. And I really hope it doesn't turn into a nightmare," I mumbled. Thankfully, he didn't hear me. I wasn't about to be the kind of person who crushed optimism, not when I was fighting for it myself. "Let's head up."

Séb followed me up the iron staircase. We opened the door, stepped onto the terrace, and all of Paris spread out before us—the sparkling Seine, the old stone bridges, Nôtre-Dame in the foreground and the top of the Eiffel Tower in the background, the sky a perfect cornflower blue.

"It doesn't get any better than this," said Séb with a happy exhale.

I pushed the paranoia about Nicolas, which was infiltrating the deepest and darkest corners of my mind, to the side and tried my best to remain positive for Séb. "Wait until you try Berthillon ice cream," I said. "It's supposedly the best in the world. I saw a shop nearby. Ice cream after lunch?"

"Sounds like a plan," said Séb, and I swallowed hard, my throat constricting.

A plan. Nicolas had a plan. I was sure of it. I just didn't know what it was. Every hair on my body bristled. But it was too late to turn back now. And, as Jane had warned, nobody said no to the de la Barguelonnes.

15

somebody has a plan

SÉB AND I explored the beautiful neighborhood of l'Île Saint-Louis, eating savory crêpes made of buckwheat and filled with creamy goat cheese, crunchy arugula, and juicy tomatoes at one of the cafés, me doing my best to savor the textures. Lunch was followed by the famed Berthillon sorbets and ice creams, the latter of which we ate on the banks of the Seine, Séb drooling over the richness of the flavors. Considering they had over seventy *parfums*, we'd both found it hard to settle on one. Séb, the adventurer, took *café au whisky* with another scoop of tiramisu. I'd ended up taking *abricot* and *framboise*, always loving how apricot mixed with raspberries, and wanting something cool on this scorcher of a day. Paris was in the midst of a *canicule*, or heat wave, and sweat coated both of our necks, almost as sticky as the goodness melting in our paper cups. At least I could enjoy the reprieve from the heat, the sorbet soothing on my tongue.

"Are we on the *rive gauche*? Or *rive droite*?" he asked.

"I think we're somewhere in the middle," I said, watching couples walk hand in hand or tourists clicking photos. For me, this was a true escape. I'd never been on a vacation, taken a break from anything. "On an island."

"Do you want to see more of Paris?" he asked, pointing at a *bateau-mouche*. "Maybe take one of those boats on the river?"

As fun as that sounded, I wanted to explore more of Grand-mère's Parisian life, see if there was anything more I could find out about her, maybe make a different kind of connection. "Nah," I said. "I'm going to take it easy. But you go. Have fun. I'll meet you back at the apartment."

"You sure?"

"I am," I said. "I'll always have Paris."

"And a killer place," he said.

"One you can use anytime you want," I said. "A perk of working at the château."

"Really?" he said, his hazel eyes wide with delight. "My girlfriend would love it."

"You have a girlfriend?" I asked, realizing I didn't know much about him and feeling like a jerk. I'd been so absorbed in my own life, many things escaped me. Apart from Phillipa, Jane, and Rémi, I'd never really talked with the rest of the staff. Then again, prior to Walter and Robert, I never really opened up to anybody. Still, little by little, I was letting people in. And now it was Séb's turn, whether he liked it or not. "Tell me about her."

"She's beautiful, has blond hair, the cutest smile, and she's really funny. We've been together for five years. I'm thinking of asking her to marry me."

"But you're only nineteen," I said.

He popped his lips. "When you know you're in love, you know," he said. "And I know she's the one for me."

"You're right," I said, missing Rémi with all of my heart.

Séb threw our containers into a trash can and sauntered down the riverbank. "See you later, Chef," he said over his shoulder.

For a minute, I didn't move, just took in my surroundings, thinking of Rémi and Lola and how they both would have loved the ice cream. Lola, for sure, would have chosen chocolate. Rémi would have chosen a fruity flavor like strawberry or peach. I wished they were here to share Paris with me. My heart sprinted as I thought of his lips, his muscled body. And then it raced because exploring more of Grand-mère's Parisian life could give me the answers I needed to fully commit to life in Champvert. I needed to know if she was truly chained to the château or if she ever had an opportunity to leave.

FILLED WITH INSPIRED curiosity, I raced up the stairs to the apartment, breathless. I started in the kitchen, opening up drawers and cabinets, finding every tool a chef would need, everything organized. Like Grand-mère. I ran my hand across the Lacanche stove, pristine and white, wondering what kind of meals she'd prepared here. Bœuf bourguignon? Exotic dishes?

She'd opened up my taste buds to whole new worlds, gastronomic voyages of the best kind. And I was her little foodie adventuress. I closed my eyes, remembering the time she introduced me to a mango curry dish when I was twelve and how I'd been a lover of curry ever since. She'd added raisins, cumin, and ginger to the chicken dish. More fond memories flooded my core. How she could chop, dice, or julienne like the best of them. How everything came so easy to her, the sheer grace in how she did everything. Mostly, I thought about how much she inspired me. I was so proud of her.

After I took a culinary trip down memory lane, practically tasting every dish she'd ever made for me, I wandered into the dining room, the table set with white linens and roses. I felt her presence, right next to me. She would have said, "No paper napkins. Ever," and I stifled a laugh. I opened up the armoire to find crystal glasses for every drinking occasion—wine, water, cocktails, champagne, digestif—and at least six sets of plates, some porcelain, some faience, decorated with beautiful designs. One pattern jumped out at me: les coquelicots, wild French poppies, like Grand-mère's apron, and my favorite flower and French word.

In the living room, among the impressionist strokes of flowers, an abstract painting of blues and blacks caught my eye—so unlike my grand-mère. I thought she stuck to the classics. I stepped over to take a closer look at the portrait. As I squinted to read the name, shock took over. Picasso. I sucked in a breath. It was an original, because Grand-mère would never acquire anything fake. Not her style.

As I explored Grand-mère's apartment, finding pictures like the one where she was wearing a sari, the more I felt she'd lived a double life—a Mata Hari of sorts, except that she wasn't a rumored courtesan and executed in France for being a German spy, but a woman with desires that went beyond cooking. It was odd thinking of her in this way. I'd always seen her as just my grandmother, the one who taught me to savor food and nourished me with her recipes, the woman who inspired me, strict and sturdy in her practical shoes. Thinking of her in a different light like this blew my mind, mostly because she was more like me than I ever imagined.

I picked up a photo from when she was younger, around twelve, with the great-grandmother I never knew. The edges were frayed, and a gold-yellowish hue mottled the paper. There were so many things I didn't know about my roots. Sure, Grand-mère had shared a watered-down version with me. I knew she had married not for love but out of obligation, and grew to love my grandfather over time. I knew she loved me. I knew she said she'd created the legacy of the château for me.

But did she? Really?

A loud mew distracted my ocular reconnaissance, and the cat rubbed her little head on my ankles. Marianne had been right; this cat had ninja stealth qualities. I hadn't seen her follow me into the apartment.

"Did my grand-mère send you here?" I asked. The cat purred so loud my heart almost burst. It was as if she understood my life, me, and what I was about to do. She may have been damaged, but weren't we all? Didn't every creature large or small need a second chance at life and at love? I sat down on the sisal-covered flooring to pet her.

"I want to keep you. What do you think of that? Of course, I'll ask Marianne if Claude will be okay with that. But I think we have a bond. I'm kind of a stray too."

Her paw gripped my finger. She'd claimed me, and I realized it wasn't the other way around.

"I'm going to name you Étoile. It means 'star' in French," I said, stroking her fuzzy head. "You're moving to the countryside. What do you think of that?"

Yes, I was talking to a cat, and she seemed to be listening. Her one good eye closed in a slow blink. I think she was giving me the go-ahead to catnap her.

"Can I tell you something?" I asked, and she let out a mew. "I can't smell or taste anything. And I'm a chef."

Wow, did it feel good to finally say this out loud.

Étoile settled on my lap, nestling in between my sweaty legs, her purrs roar-like. I texted Marianne to ask if it was okay if I took the cat back to Champvert. She immediately got back to me with her and Claude's approval with an offer to purchase cat supplies—namely a litter box, litter, toys, croquettes, and, of course, tuna.

"Yep," I said, nodding my head. "You're moving to Champvert."

After setting Étoile down, I perused more of the photos, one in particular catching my eye. It was of Grand-mère, wearing the Chanel skirt suit she'd given to me to wear at the soft opening, cream tweed with a bit of green and slightly iridescent threads. She wore a white toque on her head, and her arm was latched on to a very attractive man's, her smile full of love and admiration. He regarded her with the same kind of adoring respect. Another woman stood behind Grand-mère, her blue eyes colder and icier than a Siberian winter. Her gaze was directed at Grand-mère, like a target on her back, and with one false move Grand-mère would be down for the count.

I sucked in my breath. I knew this woman. I had every one of her cookbooks. Aside from being a bit older, she hadn't changed, not one bit. Straight posture. Stick thin. Amélie.

Putain de bordel de merde. I set the photo down, my mind reeling. Amélie knew my grandmother? I shook my head to clear it and sauntered downstairs, the cat trailing at my feet. Séb was fumbling around in the kitchen, his shirt soaked with perspiration.

"You're back early," I said.

"It's too hot outside," he replied. "I couldn't take the canicule. And the crowds. So many people. And the lines." He let out a beleaguered sigh as he sliced a couple of lemons. "I'm making some lemonade. American-style, like you usually do. Want some?"

"Sure," I said. "Merci."

I wanted to blurt out that something sinister was up with Nicolas, or that I wasn't the chef he thought I was and the event could be a disaster but clamped my mouth shut before I could do so. I didn't want to shock or scare him. But something did. Étoile hopped on the counter and let out a mew, startling Séb.

He jumped backward, dropping a lemon on the floor. "Sophie, where did this ugly cat come from?"

"She followed me into the apartment," I said. "I'm adopting her. And she isn't ugly."

He grimaced. "*Sì*, she is."

I picked up Étoile and she snuggled into my neck, purring like a little motor. "No, she's adorable. Her name is Étoile. She's coming back to the château. Marianne is picking up all her supplies, and she's taking her to the vet tomorrow."

Séb set my lemonade on the counter. "What about Rémi's dogs? They're hunters."

Right. I'd forgotten about D'Artagnan and Aramis. Maybe I hadn't thought this crazed idea of mine through. But I couldn't help it, not when I gazed into her one good green eye and she blinked. "Étoile will live in my room. She wants to be an indoor cat," I said.

"Whatever you say, Chef," he said, fighting back a laugh.

"Are you ready for the next few days?" I asked.

He flashed a wide smile. "I'm excited and a bit nervous. You?"

I took a sip of my lemonade, a coolness filling my throat. What in the world was Nicolas up to? Setting me up for failure? For what? I sat down on a stool, paranoia pounding on my brain. I hugged Étoile closer to my chest.

"Séb?" I asked.

"Yes, Chef?"

"I am nervous. I hope you bring a healthy appetite to the event," I said. "And that you have the vision of a hawk."

"I'm always hungry," he said. "But I don't get the hawk reference."

I let out a huff and took in a breath. I needed to let him know what may or may not go down—for him, for the château, for me and my sanity. After I saw the way Amélie, one of my idols, glared at Grand-mère, I knew, from my experience at Cendrillon, some people could not be trusted. But I knew I could count on Séb.

"We're going to be working with a team of chefs we don't know. Nothing—not one plate, not one bowl, not one tray of appetizers—

can leave the kitchen without us tasting it, smelling it," I said, the "us" meaning "you." "And you need to keep your eyes open so wide they'll hurt. Don't even blink."

Séb set his lemonade down. His jaw went slack. "Are you worried about sabotage?"

I nodded. "Sadly, I am. I've gone through it before. And I don't want to go through it again."

But the potential threat of sabotage wasn't the only thing that had me on edge.

ALTHOUGH SLEEP ELUDED me, I had to pull myself together and face the day. I needed to find the fearless woman in me again; she'd taken the night off, tossing and turning in a state filled with sweat-inducing nightmares.

The car picked up Séb and me at nine a.m. sharp, and we whipped through the Paris streets, passing beautiful Haussmannian buildings with iron balconies. We drove by the Louvre and the Jardin des Tuileries and got an up-close view of the Eiffel Tower. Soon, we pulled up to the staff entrance at the Musée d'Orsay, housed in a Beaux-Arts railway station and built in the late 1800s.

"I've always wanted to visit this museum," said Séb. "I love the impressionists. Sometimes I paint in my spare time."

"When do you have spare time?" I asked with a forced laugh. "I sure as hell don't."

The driver opened our doors, and we stepped out of the car into the haze of a hot day. Nicolas made a beeline for us, or rather me. Granted, his looks rivaled male models, but he was just way too slick or, as I liked to say, cheesy. He kissed me on the cheeks, ignoring Séb.

Wiping the wetness off my cheeks, I nodded toward Séb. "This is my sous chef, Séb."

"We're thrilled to be a part of the gala," began Séb. "I—"

"I'm sure you are," said Nicolas, cutting him off. He placed an arm around my shoulders, and his hand inched his way down my spine. "I'll escort you in. The others are waiting. I have a good feeling about this, Sophie."

I picked up my pace, shrugging Nicolas's hand off my back. He didn't seem to notice. We followed him into the rear of the museum and then made our way to an elevator. In the confined quarters, Nicolas pressed his body into mine and I cringed. I took a step forward, putting much-needed space in between us.

"*Desolé*," he said, perhaps picking up on my discomfort. "The elevator is small."

Not like your giant ego, I thought. I couldn't stand him. And I couldn't wait for the doors to open; it felt like an eternity. Finally, escape was in sight.

"This way," he said, stopping midstep, and I bumped into him. His arms shot out to steady me. "Pull yourself together. You're about to meet my evil stepmother. I hear her slithering down the hall."

I was not expecting this statement or the hate in his eyes when he'd said it. My palm shot to my forehead and I took a step back. Nicolas ushered Séb to walk with him, and Séb shot me a worried look as they sauntered down the hallway, leaving me alone. Amélie made a slow approach. She wore a slashed black suit with cutouts in the arms. I remained solid, standing up straight in my blue shirtdress, eager to meet the famous Amélie.

"Mademoiselle Valroux," she said flatly, scanning me up and down with cold, laser blue eyes. "I was surprised my stepson invited you to cook at this event, but here you are."

Not the welcome I'd anticipated. Severe disappointment set in.

"I-i-it's nice to meet you, Amélie," I stuttered, and held my hand out. She ignored the greeting, staring at me like I had a contagious disease. Shaken with disbelief, I babbled. "I'm one of your biggest fans. I have every one of your cookbooks." I paused. "I believe you knew my grand-mère."

Her thin lips smashed together. Her eyes went wide and colder. She lifted her chin so high I could see right up into the nostrils of her pointy noise. "I am Madame de la Barguelonne when we're out of the kitchen and Chef when we are in it. Do you understand?"

Not really.

My breath froze in my chest. I needed to figure out what Nicolas's agenda was, what he had in store for me. Nothing about this situation sat right. Why did he invite me to cook at this event? All the other chefs were more famous than I was, all of them starred. There were plenty of other female chefs he could have had his pick of. Why me? My cooking idol clearly hated my guts.

Amélie turned on her heel and clicked down the hall, leaving me stunned. She stopped and looked over her thin shoulder. "Follow me. The other chefs are already here." She sniffed. "You were the last to arrive."

As I followed her into the salon, I clenched my teeth together, wanting to be the first to leave. But I had to stick it out.

16

an indecent proposal

BARREL-CHESTED AND BROAD shouldered, O'Shea hadn't changed, not one bit—his appearance was still more similar to a redheaded street boxer from Southie than that of a two-starred chef—although he should have had three stars by now. Semantics. And not my fault he lost one. Thankfully, he now knew this and wouldn't burn me alive with a kitchen torch. The moment I entered the room, I raced up to him, and his enormous baseball-glove-sized hands clasped my shoulders.

"Sophie, you look absolutely amazing," he said, spinning me around. "France has done wonders for you."

"Chef, you know me. I'm not just a pretty cooking face," I said, glaring at Nicolas.

"Oh, I know," he said. "What did the brigade call you?"

"Scary Spice," I answered, and he let out a roar of a laugh.

"Never mess with a woman wielding an oyster knife," he said, chuckling and shaking his head. "I remember you saying that."

"What can I say? I held my own," I said.

"You did. And you've done good," he said, nodding his big head. "Real good."

"I learned a lot from you, Chef," I said.

"Damn it, Sophie, I think you've surpassed me. I'm so proud of you. And just look at this place."

My eyes swept the room, from the parquet floors to the ornate chandeliers and lights dripping like magic from the painted ceiling, to the bronzed and blue decorated archways, to the sculptures. I felt like I was in a beautiful church, and it wouldn't have surprised me if the angels carved in relief flew off their pedestals and sang a chorus of sweet hallelujahs.

But this vision of heaven was cut short when Amélie made her approach with Jean-Jacques Gaston. I recognized him immediately. He wore the same wire-rimmed glasses, had the same kind look in his eyes I'd seen in the photo at Grand-mère's flat.

"Sophie, this is Jean-Jacques Gaston, a dear friend of your grand-mère's," said Amélie, putting way too much emphasis on "friend."

Jean-Jacques cleared his throat and his eyes glazed over. He clasped his hands onto mine. "I was your grand-mère's mentor at Le Cordon Bleu. I'm so sorry for your loss."

"Thank you," I said, my voice barely above a whisper.

"I loved Odette, such a talented chef," he said. "And I've been doing my best to help you from afar. I'm so very happy to finally meet you. You have my sincerest condolences." He paused and wiped a tear from his cheek. "You remind me so much of her. I see her spirit living and breathing through you."

I remembered finding out Jean-Jacques had written a letter of recommendation for me to get into the Culinary Institute of America. At first, I was mad my grandmother had gone behind my back and pulled some strings. But I'd proven my worth in the end, graduating at the top of my class, and then I'd secured a position at O'Shea's restaurant, Cendrillon NY—all on my own.

Grand-mère had also helped me from afar. I really hoped her spirit lived on in me and she'd help me get through this event. A long silence filled the air, punctuated by Jean-Jacques's and my heavy breaths.

O'Shea cleared his throat. "Sophie, why don't the three of us have dinner tonight before the madness of preparing for this event sets in? We can catch up."

"I'd love to," I said.

Amélie let out an irritated huff. "I can't. I have things to prepare for the gala."

Nicolas's lips twisted into a wicked smile. "Darling stepmother, I don't think *you* were invited."

Amélie's eyes blazed with a ferocity so intense I thought her head would instantaneously combust. Before she could utter a response to Nicolas, twenty chefs dressed in toques entered the room. She clasped her hands together. "Our brigade has arrived," said Amélie. "Sophie, you'll choose seven. After all, most of the guests have chosen your plat principal. I do hope you can handle it."

I winced.

"Stepmother," said Nicolas. "I'm sure Mademoiselle Valroux will be quite fine. The question of the day is: Will you be?"

My eyes locked onto his, and he shot me a surreptitious wink. Maybe I'd judged him wrong. Maybe he wasn't after me at all, but after her. He clearly detested her. And she knew it.

"Pick the members of your team. Prep them," said Amélie, straightening her posture in her ridiculously constructed outfit. "Then, let's head into the kitchen to get you acclimated."

She clicked out of the room, me feeling like I'd been thrown into the lioness's den.

Séb and I interviewed an unknown and eager-eyed team from Le Cordon Bleu. After we'd chosen our brigade, I pulled Séb to the side. "Don't forget what we discussed."

"I already have my hawk eye on two of them," he said.

"Good," I said, my heart beating furiously. "Because sabotage isn't just a threat; I think it's a reality."

"I know," said Séb, shuffling his feet. "I may have accidentally eavesdropped on the conversation."

"Which one?" I asked.

"All of them," he said. "I was worried about you." He puffed out his chest. "These people aren't going to screw with us. I've got your back."

When I'd first met him, I'd thought he was too shy and sensitive and that the tough testosterone-filled brigade at my former restaurant, Cendrillon NY, would have chewed him up and spit him out. But Séb was fierce, and I was glad I'd promoted him from the waitstaff to the kitchen a few months prior, where the only threat was the clucking of the granny brigade. I gave him a quick hug and then pulled away. "We've got this."

Séb held out his fist for a knuckle bump and I met it. He huffed out a surprised laugh. "I thought you didn't do that."

"I'm all for knuckle bumps, just not high fives," I said, and we cracked up. "Okay, take the team upstairs. Introduce them to the recipes. And I'll be there in a minute."

An impatient cough came from the doorway. "Sophie, you're needed in the kitchen," said Amélie, her smile tight. Gritting my teeth, I followed Amélie.

And then I saw him: Eric. My jaw unhinged, and I straightened my posture. My body, the tremors, found a life of their own. I couldn't control the shaking. I wasn't nervous anymore, not with the anger boiling in my veins. I couldn't believe it. Eric had eviscerated my career and cost O'Shea's restaurant a star. This was not only a personal affront to me, it was such a vindictive thing to do to O'Shea. Bile rose up in my throat.

Eric rolled up the sleeves of his chef's coat, revealing his tattoos. I used to find him bad-boy sexy with his dark hair and bedroom eyes; now he just repulsed me—even more than Nicolas did. Amélie shot me a closed-mouthed and satisfied grin.

O'Shea entered the kitchen with Jean-Jacques. Eric turned, his smile so smug I wanted to punch him.

"Why the fuck is this asshole here?" O'Shea bellowed the instant he took in Eric's presence. His face turned beet red and he gripped his hands into balls—ones he'd surely pound Eric into oblivion with.

"Language," said Amélie with a malevolent smile.

"How's this for language? I'm not cooking with that talentless, disloyal motherfucker," screamed O'Shea, his hand shaking. "And you didn't answer my question. Why is he here?"

Amélie lifted her skinny shoulders, her rigid outfit rising like a cardboard cutout. "He's here because I just hired him at Durand Paris. You're looking at my new chef de cuisine."

"I'm outta here," said O'Shea, turning on his heel.

"Oh, Dan, you are cooking at this event if you want my family to invest in Cendrillon Paris," said Amélie. "Do not test me."

"I'm going to get some air," he said with a growl, and then he stormed out of the kitchen, Jean-Jacques following. I wondered if he was leaving or just needed time to cool off; probably the latter, considering opening a Cendrillon in Paris was his dream, offering validation that a Southie from the docks had made it. But I wasn't about to let Eric get under my skin, not when I could slither up his.

"Eric," I said sweetly. "Whose recipes did you steal this time?"

"It's always a pleasure to see you, Sophie," he said, eyeing me up and down. "You've changed."

"You haven't. You're still a conniving dickhead," I said with a sneer.

"Language like that won't be tolerated in this kitchen," said Amélie. "You should go talk with your brigade."

"Yes, *Chef*," I said with sarcasm.

As I turned on my heel, seething, Nicolas pulled me to the side. He whispered in my ear, his breath hot and cringeworthy. "This is going to be so much more fun than I realized."

"This is *not* fun," I said, my shoulders tensing so tight I thought they'd snap. "It's a nightmare, and I know."

"I'm sorry. I don't understand," he said. "You know what?"

"I know Amélie and my grand-mère knew one another. And I don't think they liked one another very much. Did you know this?"

He chortled. "Of course. That's what private investigators are for," he said with an obnoxious snort. "The moment I found out she was jealous of your grand-mère and the fact that she didn't have her life but always wanted it, probably the reason she married my father, I knew you were the key to taking her down." He paused and raised his shoulders into a nonchalant shrug. "I know you can cook, but I hope you have sharp claws, kitten."

"I'm not a fucking kitten," I said, wanting to claw his eyes out. I clenched my fists.

He was pitting me against one of my cooking idols. He'd known this all along, and he hadn't told me when he'd had the chance to do so at the château. Whatever kind of twisted game he was playing, I didn't want to be a pawn in it. I pursed my lips, thinking about bolting. I could face the repercussions. I'd have Jane send out a press release. But I'd committed to the event and I wasn't going to run.

My gut told me Nicolas had it out for Amélie, and my instincts told me that he didn't think with his head. I could play with his obvious attraction to me, the way his eyes scanned my body. From fearless chef to femme fatale. Grand-mère would be proud. Or maybe not.

His lips pursed and he grabbed my hands. "Do you want your stars, Sophie?"

My eyelids fluttered involuntarily. My throat constricted. My words caught in my throat. "Yes, I think about them all the time."

"That's what I thought. And I'm going to bring them to you," said Nicolas. "Don't let Eric or anything else throw you off your game. That's what Amélie wants."

"I get it," I said, straightening my posture. The cutthroat culinary world. The competition. The jealousy. "I don't like it at all, but I get it."

He laced his arm with mine. "Come, I want to show you something." He walked us into the main salon, right up to a structure hidden under a piece of velvet. He swept the fabric off, and Van Gogh's *The Starry Night* swirled in front of my eyes—wisps of streaky blues, whites, and yellows rolling with energy, passion, and vigor. My hands flew to my heart—the stars, the maddening stars. My god, I wanted them. But would striving for them drive me crazy?

As I turned to head back into the kitchen, Amélie's eyes blazed into mine.

Determination set in.

O'SHEA AND JEAN-JACQUES arrived at Grand-mère's flat at eight. Séb had left to explore more of Paris without the heat, leaving me to prepare a meal for my former boss and his mentor while struggling with a tornado of angry emotions. I was keeping it simple tonight—a salad with toasted bread and panko-encrusted goat cheese, sprinkled with pomegranate and a variety of sausages. Wine—a rosé. Champagne for the apéro served with fresh veggies and a salmon tartare. Even chefs knew how to chill, focusing on good food and fresh ingredients without the fuss.

Jean-Jacques's eyes filled with tears as he entered the sprawling pied-à-terre. "I had so many wonderful memories here with Odette. Thank you, Sophie, for hosting us."

"It's my pleasure," I said, ushering them to sit at the dining room table.

"What a place," said O'Shea. "You lucky gal."

Jean-Jacques twiddled his fingers as I set the meal down. His eyes glazed over and he choked back a sob, his shoulders slumping. Odd behavior. After a few minutes of idle chatter about the cooking world and my grand-mère, something hit me. I didn't beat around the bush.

"I get a feeling there is something you're not telling me, Jean-Jacques," I said, placing a hand on his shoulder. "Is there something I should know?"

He let out the air in his lungs in one big whoosh. He nodded. "There is. I was more than your grand-mère's mentor. I was her lover."

I spat out my sip of wine. A laugh escaped my lips. Granted, I knew Grand-mère was a woman with a beating heart, but I never, ever expected she'd taken a lover. And that lover was Jean-Jacques Gaston. She'd really led a double life in Paris.

"What? For real?"

"I was mad for her, cut off my relations with Amélie the moment I met her. Such a force in the kitchen, a passionate woman."

I coughed. "You were involved with Amélie too?"

His chest puffed out as he took in a breath. "I was, and I broke things up with her for your grand-mère. She hated Odette. Call it jilted lover's syndrome."

Things were clicking into place one messed-up piece at a time, save for one thing. "What happened between you and Grand-mère?"

Jean-Jacques sighed. "She didn't want to leave her life in France for Boston. I'll always love her. And I knew she loved me." Tears filled his eyes. "She wanted to create a world for you. And nothing is more important than family."

We went silent for a moment, eating and drinking wine, a sadness burning my throat and making it tough to swallow. Grand-mère had denied herself a second chance at love for the château. Was I in the same position she'd put herself in? Granted, my grandmother was happy before she died, or she'd been excellent at faking it. Like I was doing, pretending I could cook without my senses. With my mind reeling, I wanted to change the subject and not push Jean-Jacques to share more, not with his quivering shoulders, and not with the waves of unexpected emotions.

"So what do we do about Amélie and Eric?" I finally asked, looking up.

"Skewer them," said O'Shea. "And then roast them on a grill. I can't believe Eric had the audacity to show his face."

Jean-Jacques leaned forward, his gaze intense. "It's obvious. Nicolas wanted to throw Amélie off by engaging the three of us. Amélie wanted to get under your skin by hiring Eric." He shook his head in thought. "As for me, she never liked being second best. Maybe she thought me seeing her with Eric would make me jealous." He laughed. "It didn't, quite the opposite. At any rate, I've always had a feeling that she was the one who talked your grand-mère into staying in Champvert. The farther away your grand-mère was from Paris, the closer Amélie could get to me. But I denied her advances."

I wanted to stay as far away from her as possible. This was insane. I shuddered. At least I knew what I was up against.

"Sophie, I'm afraid I can't beat around the bush," said O'Shea. "There's something important you need to know."

What now?

"Cendrillon Paris is a go—with or without Amélie—and we want you to spearhead it," he said, his large hands gripping his glass. "That's why I'm sticking around."

"We?" I questioned.

"Amélie is not the investor and neither is her husband—Nicolas is. Monsieur de la Barguelonne handed over the reins—everything—to Nicolas this year. I'm pretty sure Amélie doesn't know this."

So many secrets. So many backhanded moves. I felt played. How was I going to stay ahead of the game when I was just learning the rules?

O'Shea popped open the bubbly, serving us in the *coupe de champagne* glasses. We lifted them for a toast, meeting each other's eyes. "Do me a favor, don't answer right away. Just think about our offer. Aside from some standard dishes, you'd have complete control over the rest of the menu," said O'Shea. "As you know, things can change when you least expect them to."

I took my glass of champagne and drank it in one gulp, my mind swirling with maddening confusion.

I NEEDED ADVICE. I needed answers. There had to be another journal hidden somewhere. The moment O'Shea and Jean-Jacques left the apartment, I raced to Grand-mère's closet, jumping on the wooden floor like an overly caffeinated kangaroo. As I'd hoped, a plank with a knot lifted. I sat, placing it to the side. There it rested: a leather-bound journal with a red ribbon. My hands shook as I lifted out this diary from its hiding spot. Before I opened it, the cat crept into the room.

"Are you ready?" I asked Étoile, in her good eye. She blinked. "I don't know what I'm going to find in this book."

Étoile curled up into my legs, and I read.

Grand-mère's beautiful and loopy handwriting shook my core. The entries were short and, to say the least, mind-blowing. My breath came hard as I read her words.

Céleste has taken Sophie to New York. She won't even speak to me. I've tried, how I've tried, but she just shuts me out. Doesn't she know that I love her and that I forgive her for leaving with my darling Sophie? Am I a horrible mother?

Pierre died from a heart attack. My heart aches. I finally realized that I did love him, even though our marriage was arranged. I have nothing left except for the château.

With nobody in my life except for Clothilde and Bernard, I've decided at the old age of sixty to follow my dreams. I will be attending Le Cordon Bleu for two years, becoming a master chef. My world revolves and rotates around the thought of nourishing people's souls, cooking with love. I just bought a magnificent pied-à-terre in l'Île Saint-Louis. One day, this place will be part of my darling Sophie's heritage. I do hope to see her again. And soon.

Le Cordon Bleu is a dream come true. I adore our professor, Chef Gaston. Mais, I despise one of my classmates, Amélie Durand. She's jealous of my talent and the attention I receive from our esteemed chef.

I've taken on a lover. He makes me feel like a woman, like a blushing bride, and not the pile of old bones I see myself as. He's ten years younger than I am. I'm embarrassed to say that I never really enjoyed relations with Pierre. I'm a Catholic woman and we went through all the rigmarole to procreate. Jean-Jacques pleasures

*me to the point where I think I'm going to lose my head. I shouldn't
be doing this. But I can't help it. I've never felt more alive.*

*Jean-Jacques wants me to leave France for Boston to start a
restaurant with him. He wants to bring his fine cooking to
America, to live out his dreams, to reach for the Michelin stars.
Although his offer, indeed, is tempting, I cannot go, no matter his
constant pleas. I have to get back to Champvert. I have to build a
future for my family and all of the other people who depend on
me. I will miss him fiercely. And I will keep the two years we spent
together tucked in my memories like precious jewels. But I'm
following my dream, not his.*

I took a moment to catch my breath and then slammed the journal to a close. The cat jumped off my lap, letting out a surprised
meow. Merde! This was a lot to digest. I placed the book back in its
hiding place and paced, finally heading up to the roof deck, tears
streaming down my cheeks. If I'd thought life had been complicated
at the château, nothing had prepared me for Paris—the events I'd
experienced and the words I'd just read.

Why was I still so obsessed with the promise of stars? Because I
didn't have them? I wasn't so sure I wanted them anymore, not if it
meant dealing with people like Amélie and Nicolas de la Barguelonne, their moral compasses so out of whack and completely opposite to what I'd learned from Grand-mère.

My grand-mère loved to entertain, and it was through food that
she expressed her love. With this crowd, there was no love, only
backstabbing. I fingered the stars on the necklace Rémi had given
me for my birthday. Nobody could purchase me. I wasn't for sale.
And if I achieved the stars, if they were meant for me, they would
fall on my restaurant in Champvert.

Grand-mère's journal entries detailed her passion for Jean-Jacques, but she'd ignored them. Perhaps, with me finding her most private thoughts, she didn't want me to make the same mistakes. But I'd been directionless, and I didn't have a map to guide me. GPS doesn't tell the heart where to go, and I was finally going to listen to mine. I felt a deeper love, and more connected to my grand-mère, than ever before.

When Rémi had asked me what I wanted, I'd told him I wanted love. I wanted success. And I didn't want anybody to come in between me and my dreams. I'd also told him I was going to Paris and didn't listen to him when he said it wasn't a good idea. When I returned to Champvert, I'd tell him he'd been right—about everything, not just about Paris but about taking me to the doctor when I fell.

Although a shock of epic proportions, Paris had been a good idea; it had taken only a few hours of being away from the château to figure my feelings out. I had my answer. I wasn't going to turn my back on love, like Grand-mère had. And I certainly didn't feel chained to the château. In fact, I wanted to get back there as quickly as possible.

I was going to marry Rémi Dupont, my childhood sweetheart. I was going to be a good stepmom to Lola. I was going to write my own culinary narrative and not follow somebody else's story when I could create my own. And I was going to reach for the stars in Champvert.

This was my life, and I was in it one hundred percent.

Before I fell into a sleep filled with twisted nightmares of Amélie's glares, Nicolas's sexual innuendos, and worries of not being able to taste or smell, I texted Rémi.

Tu me manques.

(I miss you.)

Then, I curled up on the bed with Étoile and Grand-mère's apron, hoping her spirit truly lived on in me, because I'd need a lot of it to survive the next few torturous days.

17

the gala surprises

FRIDAY MORNING ARRIVED with an unexpected bonus: Amélie would be preparing her dishes in one of the Musée d'Orsay's other kitchens with Jean-Jacques Gaston, leaving me to cook side by side with O'Shea. I let out a sigh of relief. I didn't have to deal with douchebag Eric or walk on eggshells around psychopath Amélie. I could focus. I primed our eager-eyed brigade of Le Cordon Bleu chefs, introducing them to all the ingredients for the plat principal. Although Séb and I would take care of the main course together, him working the plancha grill for the seafood, me taking care of the base for the pot-au-feu de la mer, we still needed to train our group of seven on how to prepare the apéro courses, including the garnishes. Séb led our team into the walk-in. A half hour later, he walked out.

"Don't be mad at me, Chef," he said, grimacing with guilt, "but three members of our brigade just left."

"Why?" I asked.

His head dropped and he shuffled his feet. "I may have threatened them."

"Again, why?"

"Well, I noticed them whispering. And I heard one say they could oversalt the crab cakes. And then they were sharing other ideas—mostly regarding your plat principal. I may not have the eyes of a hawk, but my hearing is like a bat's. You were right, Chef."

I didn't want to be right. Anger coursed in my veins. For sure, Amélie was behind this. She probably paid them off. With a shaky hand, I motioned for Séb to continue.

"I exploded. And I screamed: 'If anybody on this team is even thinking about tampering with our dishes, I'll hang them up by their ankles, slit their throats, and then feed them to the wild boars.'" He paused, his breath heavy. "I pointed to the two culprits and I told them to get the fuck out. Then, I said if anybody else wants to mess with us or if they were on somebody's payroll, to get the fuck out too."

"Three left?" I asked, not exactly surprised.

"Oui," he said, his nose scrunching. "I'm sorry."

I slapped his back. "Don't be. You did the right thing. We can manage. And I'm thinking you'll get a huge Christmas bonus."

"Thank you, Chef," he said, blowing out a breath of relief.

"No, thank you," I said, and his posture straightened. "And we still have to keep our eyes on the others."

Séb flexed his muscles. He was built like a tank. Something I hadn't noticed before. "Yeah, I know. But I think they might be a bit scared of me." He handed me a spiny lobster tail. "At least the seafood is looking good. They didn't order crap."

"Séb?"

"Yeah?"

"Merci," I said. "You are so loyal. I don't know what I'd do without you."

He shrugged. "We're all loyal to you, Chef," he said. "And we've got work to do. More now that we have half a brigade."

"We can do it," I said, and he winked.

As I inspected the lobster tail, O'Shea barreled up to me. He let out a chortle. "Ah, Sophie, you're the reason I was downgraded to *bœuf en croûte* and Jean-Jacques the lamb," he said. "Your pot-au-feu de la mer sounds extremely interesting. I can't wait to see what you've planned."

"Sorry, Chef," I said with smile and a shrug. "But you're the one who turned me into a seafood expert. And the recipe just came to me."

Thankfully, Phillipa and I had tested the recipe before I lost my senses.

He placed his hands on my shoulders, squeezing them in a fatherly manner. "Call me Dan. We're equals now."

"Right," I said with a snort. "You're a starred chef, a master."

"If you come to Paris, the stars will fall right into your lap." His eyes crinkled when he smiled. "Have you thought about our offer?"

I had. And I didn't want to tell him my answer was no way in hell, not with his temper. The last thing I needed was an explosion. "I'm thinking about it," I said, "but I need more time to mull over the logistics."

"Don't take too long," he said. "We've already found a location in the *seizième* arrondissement. We'd like your answer sooner rather than later."

"I understand," I said. "Just let me get through this event and then I'll give you my decision."

A whisper brushed my ears. "How's my favorite cooking star?"

I turned around abruptly to find Nicolas wearing a sheepish smile and another expensive designer suit with a crisp white shirt. He shook hands with O'Shea. "Did she give you an answer?"

"Not yet," I said, my temper rising. "And please don't talk about me in the third person when I'm standing right in front of you."

Nicolas's eyes widened. "She's a feisty one. That's why I like her," he said.

"That she is," said O'Shea.

I slammed my hand on the prep table. "I'm right here."

O'Shea let out a boisterous laugh. "Sophie, we were both messing with you. Where's your sense of humor?"

In Champvert, I thought, with Rémi, Jane, and Phillipa. Nicolas's eyes swept over my face and down to my body. I felt violated. Naked. "We'll need an answer by Sunday," he said, brushing a finger down my arm.

"Sunday it is," I said sharply. "But, right now, I've got to train my team for your gala."

"Then I'm looking forward to Sunday," he said. "And tomorrow night. I can't wait to taste you."

No, he didn't just say that.

"You mean my meals?" I said with indignation.

"Bien sûr," he said. "What else could I have meant?" He turned to leave but stopped midstep. "If I were you, I'd dash into the other kitchen to see what Amélie and Eric are up to."

"Why?"

"You'll see," he said, and left the room.

I looked O'Shea squarely in the eyes. "You coming?"

"No, not unless you want me to kill that motherfucker with my bare hands," he said with a scowl. "I'm staying as far away from the sabotaging scumbag as I can."

"Yeah, you're probably right," I said. "But I'm going. Maybe I'll kick him in the balls."

"Better to cut them off," muttered O'Shea. "If he has any."

Before I stormed off to face my nemesis, I made my way into the walk-in and instructed Séb to show our team how to prepare the figs. Then, slowly, I trudged out the door to the steps leading upstairs to the other kitchen. A bit lost, I found myself standing in one of the museum's cafés. A large iron clock with glass windows, about thirty feet in circumference, summoned me with its views. The sky was devoid of clouds, and Paris spread out before me—the Seine, the Louvre, the Ferris wheel, the Jardin des Tuileries, and, in the far distance, the cake-like basilica of Sacré-Cœur.

I should have been awestruck by the beauty, by the architecture, by the history. I wasn't. My mind reeled with thoughts of Eric's conniving ways, Amélie's backhanded threats, and Nicolas's blatant sexual innuendos. All of them held one thing in common: they were all out to get what they wanted no matter if they hurt people along the way and regardless of any consequences. Of course, I thought about running as far away from Paris as I could, but I couldn't let these people win. I was Sophie Valroux. And I knew *exactly* what I wanted.

I was also lost. I walked up to a worker, an older man with kind eyes. "Bonjour. I'm looking for Amélie Durand, one of the chefs for the gala?"

"Yes, I'm afraid you're on the wrong floor. You're on the fifth. The kitchen she's working in is on the first," he said.

"Merci," I said. "Bonne journée."

"*De même*," he said.

The journey to the first floor took a lifetime, because I slunk down the stairs, placing one foot hesitantly in front of the other so I wouldn't risk a fall. The dread of finding out what Amélie and Eric were up to, since I was positive it had to do with me, made my heart stutter and race. Finally, I made it there without killing myself. It was as if an invisible force drew me straight to their kitchen.

Jean-Jacques meandered over to me and we swapped les bises.

"I'm so glad to see you, Sophie," he said, holding up a knife. "But

I'm in the process of teaching my loner brigade to prep. And let's just say I have a lot of training to do. Can we catch up later?"

"I'd love that," I said, my eyes scanning the kitchen as he went back to work.

Amélie and Eric's daurade dish sat on a prep table, complete with a sweet potato purée and braised cabbage, and garnished with edible flowers. Only thing was, this wasn't their recipe; it was mine. Last year, Eric had sent a foodie spy to the château to poach my recipes because he was a talentless cretin, a waste of space, with no creativity of his own.

Amélie took in my presence, and my fists clenched when she lifted up her pointy nose with arrogance. "Sophie, what do we owe this pleasure to?" she asked. "Shouldn't you be in your kitchen training your brigade?"

My blood boiled. I pointed to the plate, my finger shaking. "Why are you making *my* recipe for the gala?"

Amélie shot me a twisted smile. "But this isn't your recipe. It's Eric's, and it's quite phenomenal. One of the reasons I hired him as my chef de cuisine."

"Then you hired the wrong chef," I said.

Eric crossed his arms over his chest. "Sophie, you've got to get over your jealousy. I paved my own way. Didn't go to that fancy cooking school people pulled strings to get me into." He bared his teeth. "And this isn't your recipe, it's mine."

I wanted to slap the smug expressions off both of their faces. Or cut off Eric's balls. It took great restraint to keep myself from retorting. But I had another idea.

"No?" I said, words spilling from my mouth. "Let me taste it."

I immediately regretted this very bad idea.

Amélie held out a fork and I gripped it. "Go ahead," she said.

Rather than stabbing her in the head, I sank into the three layers of ingredients and brought a healthy-sized serving to my mouth. As I chewed, a triumphant smile curved across my lips. Eric's re-creation of my recipe was so off and so dreadful on my tongue, I couldn't believe they'd even think about serving this mess of slimy textures to anybody. Maybe Étoile would like it; she was a street cat. I knew in my cooking gut that this disaster wasn't fit for human consumption. I met their eyes and I said, "You are so very right. This isn't anything like my recipe. At all."

"It's better," said Eric, sliding his arm around Amélie. "I knew it."

She kissed him on the cheek. "Of course it is, ma chérie."

Call it a sixth sense, like Phillipa's, but I now knew what Nicolas's plan was for Amélie; he was setting her up for self-destruction. Bad food. And a bad-boy chef. But, aside from Nicolas trying to sway me to cook at Cendrillon Paris, I still didn't know what his true intentions were for me.

SATURDAY WAS HECTIC and more than crazy. The two brigades in the kitchen, O'Shea's and mine, chopped and sliced and sautéed like methodical, hyperactive robots as we prepared for the gala— preparing the base for our plat principal and all of the other dishes.

Séb wiped the sweat off his brow as he fired up the plancha. "I wish we were back at the château so we could jump in the lake."

"Me too," I said. "Believe me. I'm looking forward to Monday. I can't wait to get the hell out of here."

He nodded in agreement. "Paris was not what I expected."

I laughed. "That's an understatement if I've ever heard one."

Five o'clock rolled around, and it was time for the family meal— six on my team, five on O'Shea's. Jean-Jacques walked into our kitchen followed by two surprising and very unwelcome guests: Eric and Amélie.

Amélie shrugged when I raised my eyebrows at her. "What? You tasted ours. We want to taste yours, Sophie. It's only fair," she said, her eyes narrowed into little slits. She let out a low cackle. "Of course, you're probably scared your dish won't measure up to ours. And I wouldn't blame you. There's a reason I have three stars."

I refrained from laughing. She probably paid everybody off. "Have a seat, Chef. I do hope my dish is as good as yours was," I said, sarcasm dripping from my every word.

"I'm swooning with anticipation," said Amélie. "You've stirred my curiosity."

We all gathered around the prep table. I noticed Eric's hand sliding up Amélie's skinny ass. Gross. I nodded to Séb, letting him do the honors. He plated the dishes, setting them in front of Eric, Amélie, Jean-Jacques, and O'Shea first.

"Sophie, this is absolute art," said O'Shea. "I think I truly underestimated your talents."

"I concur," said Jean-Jacques. "I've never seen anything more creative and beautiful."

Eric let out a sarcastic grunt. O'Shea slammed his fork and spoon down and cornered Eric, his hands wrapped around his neck. Eric gagged and coughed as the brigades from Le Cordon Bleu tried peeling O'Shea off him. They finally succeeded. Eric sank to the floor, wheezing.

O'Shea's eyes went wild with anger. He panted, his hands braced on his knees. "Get. The. Hell. Out of this kitchen. Now. Or I will fucking kill you. I mean it."

Eric stood and backed up, his hands raised in surrender. All of us watched in disbelief as Amélie disregarded Eric and placed her spoon into the bowl of my pot-au-feu de la mer. She raised a morsel to her mouth. Tasted it. Her eyes rolled back into her head as if she were drowning in complete ecstasy. She brought a napkin to her thin lips, dabbing them.

"It's not what I expected," she said, her voice catching.

Her face paled, and she scrambled out of the kitchen, Eric in tow. Our brigades stood in shock, whispering. O'Shea's face lost its severely overboiled red lobster color. He said, "I'm sorry about that, Sophie. You know what a hothead I am."

I did. I'd dealt with his blowups before; he'd threatened to gut me open like a pig.

"It's okay," I said, placing my hands on my hips. "I kind of enjoyed it. This time it was completely called for. And your anger wasn't directed at me. Now, try my dish."

"I can't wait," said Jean-Jacques, raising a spoon to his lips. He closed his eyes, threw his head back, and sighed. "It tastes even more beautiful than it looks."

As Séb served the rest of the shaky staff, O'Shea didn't say a word, just kept shoveling the meal in his mouth like a starved animal. He closed his eyes and let out a groan. "Fuck, Sophie, you have surpassed me. Sweet. Tart. Bitter. Savory. Salty. How do you bring all these flavors together without them overpowering one another?"

Praise the cooking gods! I smiled. I had done it. I wanted to high-five myself, but that would look odd, so I did it in my mind.

"I don't know," I said, letting out a breath. "I suppose it's because I cook with love and with my emotions."

"You didn't learn how to do this with me or your fancy cooking school," he said. "Where?"

I wrapped my arms around myself in a hug. "Ma grand-mère."

"She taught you well. Those edible flowers? What are they? They have a cucumber-like bite, the perfect addition," said Jean-Jacques.

"Borage," I said. "We grow them at the château because they attract bees."

O'Shea embraced me, showing a warmth I'd never experienced from him. "Ready to get this night over and done with so you can go home?"

"Home?"

"I'm not blind, Sophie. You have what it takes to do everything on your own. You don't need me. And you don't need Paris." He cleared his throat. "I know your answer to our proposal is no. Just do me a favor and don't tell Nicolas yet."

I met his proud eyes. "I won't. I heard nobody says no to a de la Barguelonne."

O'Shea tilted his head back and let out a boisterous howl. "Good thing that old skinny bitch Amélie isn't *really* one of them."

18

sous les étoiles

SOMEHOW, EVEN WITH all the stress, with everything that had transpired, I pulled the event off with Séb and the assistance from our loaner brigade—all eighty meals sent out and plated perfectly, all the apéros circulating without one threat of sabotage. I wanted to curl up into a little ball, but the night wasn't over. Not yet. I still had to make my appearance after the dessert service or face the wrath of the de la Barguelonnes.

How classy—changing out of my chef's clothes and into a ball gown in a public bathroom. At least this one was private tonight and off-limits to the guests. I grabbed my wardrobe bag and purse. Before I donned my green ball gown and became a person that wasn't me, I thanked my brigade.

"You all did amazing tonight. Everything ran perfectly, something I wasn't expecting from a brigade I'd never worked with before. But we did it," I said. "Merci. Merci beaucoup. I hope I wasn't too tough on you."

My team's appreciative smiles shone brightly. "No, thank you, Chef," somebody said. "This was an incredible experience, and we were cooking with the best. I believe we've all learned a lot, more than we hoped for."

"Sorry about those other chefs," said another.

"Don't worry about it," I said with a grin. "We caught them red-handed. I'm reporting them to Le Cordon Bleu, and they'll be lucky if they find jobs flipping burgers."

"Don't mess with Chef Sophie," said Séb.

I placed my hands on my hips and raised an eyebrow. "That's right. My knives are always sharp," I said, this statement followed by boisterous laughter. "Now, go on, get out of here. Have a drink. You deserve it."

I exchanged les bises with everyone, and, save for Séb and O'Shea, one by one they left.

"Séb," I said. "You rocked it tonight. Thank you for having my back. I've got to go flit around like a trained dancing monkey. But I'll see you in the morning." I kissed him on the cheek and then handed him the keys to Grand-mère's. "À *demain*. And I was serious about the bonus."

Séb hopped out of the kitchen, a wide smile on his face.

O'Shea meandered up to me. "I can't wait for this night to be over."

"You and me both," I said. "Why did you do this event? You don't need the acclaim. Was it for Nicolas?"

"Nah," he said, his large shoulders lifting. "I did it for Olivier, his father. He and I go way back."

"Really?" I asked.

"Yes," said O'Shea. "And he knows what loyalty is." O'Shea placed a hand on my shoulder. "Sophie, you have nothing to worry about."

ALL DOLLED UP and feeling extremely uncomfortable in my gown and heels, one of my grand-mère's emerald necklaces weighing down on my chest like an anchor, more than anything I wished I was wearing jeans and a ponytail, not a tight French twist that gave me a headache, and that I was in the comfort of Champvert, surrounded by people I truly loved.

I didn't want to enter the party straightaway. I needed some me time to catch my breath in one of the stairwells. To my surprise, a man sat down on the stoop next to me. He was portly, dressed in the finest suit money could buy, and had a half-chewed cigar hanging out of his mouth.

"Do you mind if I puff on one of my cigars?" he asked.

"Go crazy," I said, slouching on the step. "I am."

He laughed and lit up. "I'm sure this night has been incredibly crazy. And so was your meal. Amélie was quite angry with me, as I ordered yours. And it exceeded all my expectations."

"Merci beaucoup," I said, my shoulders tensing so tightly I thought they'd snap off. "Are you Monsieur de la Barguelonne?"

"That's what they tell me."

"I'm Sophie," I said.

"I know exactly who you are. And please call me Olivier. You're a very talented chef. I see bright things in the future for you. Just do me a favor and stick to your guns. Don't let anybody force you into something you don't want to do. I heard my son has been pressuring you to move to Paris. If it's something you desire, by all means, go for it." He puffed on his cigar, exhaling a chestnut-scented smoke. "But if it isn't, follow your heart."

One flight above us, a wicked laugh interrupted our conversation, echoing in the stairwell. A cackle. A moan. Olivier snubbed out his cigar and put his fingers up to his lips. "Quiet. I know that laugh," he said, his voice just above whisper.

"Eric, not here, we'll get caught," came Amélie's affected voice.

"But I can't keep my hands off you," he said.

Olivier's face reddened. I sat rigid.

Another moan. Panting. Slamming. Sucking sounds. I stood up to leave. Olivier grabbed my hand and his eyes met mine. "I'm sending her papers for divorce first thing Monday morning."

"They're already prepared?" I asked, the words tumbling out of my mouth. None of my business.

"They are. Thankfully, she signed an ironclad prenup. She won't be getting a dime." He puffed on his cigar as I sat shocked. "I've had doubts about her faithfulness for quite some time but didn't want to believe it. But now I have the proof I need to follow through with what was a really hard decision. She's made it easy. God damn it, Nicolas warned me. I didn't listen."

Well, we were both listening now.

"I don't know what to say," I said.

"I do," said Olivier. "I'll have the plane take you back to Champvert tomorrow. There will be no dinner at Durand tomorrow night. Or any night after that. I'm closing the place down."

"You can do that?"

"I can," he said wearily. "Who do you think her investor was?" He paused and patted my hand. "You should go to the party."

The sound of footsteps clicked. The slam of a door closing shut. The tryst, thankfully, was over. Olivier shook his head with disgust. "Are you okay?" I asked, not wanting to leave him alone.

"Maybe I should think long and hard about wife number four," he said. "But yes, I'll be fine." He let out a sad laugh. "Sophie, go. Don't worry about me, ma chérie. The world is waiting for you. Paris is waiting for you."

A bit shaken up, I stood and smoothed out my dress. "Can I be honest?" I asked.

"After what we've just heard and talked about, I would want nothing but honesty."

"I'm really not into Paris. All this cutthroat business," I said with a shudder. "Honestly, I can't wait to get back to Champvert. My life is there with the people who support and love me."

"I don't blame you," he said. "My family is also from the south—but from Provence. I miss my birth home every day."

"Why don't you go back?" I asked.

"Because I can't. Not right now. I still have a business to run, people counting on me."

I got that. "I thought you handed everything over to Nicolas?"

"Who told you that?"

"O'Shea," I said.

"Sophie, I may be old, but I'm not dead yet. I'm only sixty. It's true that I gave Nicolas a little more leeway, but mostly to see what he'd do. It's a test period. Whether he passes or fails is up to him." Olivier straightened up. "Let me walk you into the salon. You, my dear, have passed your test."

This night was getting intense.

WITH MY HEAD held high, I entered the *salle des fêtes*, Olivier by my side. Nicolas, oblivious to his father's arm steadying my walk, ran up and then ushered me to a makeshift stage. The room glittered, filled with stars and magic. Unfortunately, Nicolas placed me next to Amélie.

Amélie whispered, "I didn't think you were the type to be a prima donna." She lifted up her chin so high I could see into her nostrils. "But I guess I was wrong. We've been waiting for you for five minutes."

Nicolas wrapped his arm around my waist. He whispered, "Step-mother, she is worth the wait. Maybe you should have taken more time to get ready? Your lipstick is a bit smeared."

Amélie brought a shaky, wrinkled finger to her thin lips. I turned my head, wishing I had supernatural powers so I could zap Amélie right into the starry night.

Somebody handed Nicolas a microphone. Amélie pasted on an uninspired smile, her eyes dead and expressionless. I didn't realize Nicolas's sweaty hand was gripping mine until it was too late, and he wasn't letting go of it. *"Merci, tout le monde,* for joining us on this spectacular evening filled with magic, art, and culinary delicacies. I hope you've all had a good look at Van Gogh's *The Starry Night."* He pointed with his microphone-laden hand. "And, more importantly, I hope you've enjoyed your dinners."

Applause.

"As you know, we had four of the world's master chefs cooking for you tonight. All but one of them Michelin starred." He let go of my hand. Finally. "You know what we're about to do here, right?"

Applause.

"I hope the offerings for the apéro dînatoire met your expectations," he said.

Wild applause.

"For those of you who enjoyed Chef O'Shea's bœuf en croûte, let me hear it."

Wild applause. O'Shea bowed.

"And what did you think of Chef Gaston's lamb?"

Wild applause.

"What about my stepmother's filet de daurade?"

Polite applause.

What was this? *The Hunger Games?* But with chefs killing one another off? I focused on the crowd, searching for Olivier and finding him among Paris's elite. He wasn't smiling, and I didn't blame him, not after what he'd heard. My eyes scanned the room, landing on Eric. He was chatting up a beautiful Japanese woman wearing a red kimono. I recognized her—Ayasa Watanabe, famed chef from Tokyo known for French fusion. Even I felt the chill creeping up Amélie's back.

"*Tant pis*" (too bad), continued Nicolas. He gripped my hand again. "And what did you think about Chef Valroux's extremely creative version of pot-au-feu de la mer?"

Thunderous applause. People, at least the ones who were sitting, leapt out of their seats. My hands flew to my heart. The room vibrated with shouts of praise.

"A pure work of art. Genius."

"I don't know how she tamed all those flavors into submission."

"It was the best meal I'd ever had in my life. And I'm seventy."

"She's the one who isn't starred? This is a travesty."

Amélie's eyes blazed into mine. Hatred emanated from every skinny bone in her body. I supposed that might happen when your plans to destroy somebody blew up in your face. And you'd also been caught with your skirt up. But she didn't know Olivier's plans for her just yet.

Game over, Amélie.

Nicolas cleared his throat. "My fellow Parisians, I have some stellar news. Chef Valroux, excuse me, Chef Valroux de la Tour de Champvert, will soon be joining us in Paris at the restaurant I'm investing in." He nodded to O'Shea. "She'll be spearheading Cendrillon Paris."

Wild applause.

What the hell? How dare he? I hadn't given him an answer. He was trying to take my life from me in front of an audience. Did he really think I'd say yes? My blood boiled, raging, about to spill over. My jaw completely unhinged.

Before I could scramble away, Nicolas grabbed me by the waist and planted his slippery and moist lips onto mine. As I struggled to get free from his grip, he pulled my body in tighter, dipping me. Clicks of cameras. Flashes. Finally, he let go of me and he said into the microphone, "I've fallen in love with this beautiful chef. And I believe you have too."

Applause.

O'Shea shot me a look and mouthed, "Sophie, I didn't have anything to do with this."

I angrily wiped the wetness from Nicolas's sloppy, sucking kiss away with the back of my hand. How dare he. I wished I had my knives. He'd violated me in front of five hundred people. And they'd actually applauded his actions.

"I can't believe you just did that," I said with a hiss.

More flashes from the cameras. Nicolas's eyes crinkled and he handed me the microphone. I gathered the one ounce of composure I had left, and I said, "Merci. I'm glad everybody enjoyed what we prepared for your gastronomic pleasures. But it's time for me to go. I'm one tired chef. Enjoy the rest of the evening. Merci. Merci beaucoup."

Nicolas latched onto my wrist. "The night is only beginning," he said, the tone in his voice menacing. "You can't leave now."

"Oh yes, I can," I said, shaking his hand off. "And if you touch me again, I'll—"

"You'll what?" he asked, sniggering.

I crossed my arms over my chest and glared at him. I wasn't afraid of this pompous jerk or the repercussions that might come from defying him. My life was at the château, not in Paris. He had no hold over me. And, obviously, I'd proven my worth to Parisian high society. "If you don't want me to make a scene, get the hell out of my way."

He stepped to the side and grinned wickedly. "As you wish," he said, with an over-the-top bow.

With unshakable intent, I walked through the crowd with a

clenched smile plastered on my face, shaking hands, saying "merci" to the accolades, and trying to avoid the cameras. Once I reached the exit, I bolted, eager to get out of there, just like Cinderella leaving the ball before the clock struck midnight. Unfortunately, there was no Prince Charming to save me, and I didn't lose a shoe; I lost my footing, my dress catching in my heel, and I tumbled down the stairs.

The stars Nicolas had assured he could give to me?

I saw them—zipping in and out in a blinding light, swirling and whirling like Van Gogh's painting. And then I saw nothing. Just blackness.

III

fall

SOUR GRAPES

*Cooking is like love. It should be entered
into with abandon or not at all.*

—HARRIET VAN HORNE, SYNDICATED COLUMNIST
FOR THE *NEW YORK POST*

19

❧

no taste, no confusion

I CAME TO IN a white room, a large, red-bearded face hovering over mine—O'Shea's. It took me a moment to get my bearings, with visions of the gala flashing in my mind like a nightmarish slideshow—preparing the food, catching Amélie in the stairwell with Eric, Nicolas's disgusting kiss and him setting me up in front of Paris's elite so I wouldn't have an out. I rubbed my eyes, confused as to why I was sprawled out in a hospital bed.

"What happened?" I asked. "Did I get mugged?"

"You had a fall. You've got a concussion," said O'Shea.

Maybe I'd always had a brain injury. That would explain why I dealt with Nicolas de la Barguelonne and his psychopath stepmother. I took in my surroundings, the light beaming into the windows. "What time is it?"

"Seven in the morning," said O'Shea.

"Have you been here all night?" I asked, taking in his disheveled tuxedo.

"Yep," he said, pointing to a chair in the corner. "I wanted to be here for you when you woke up. You're like family to me. And I was worried."

My stomach growled, making crazy animal noises and squeaks. "I'm absolutely starving. I didn't eat anything last night."

"I'll go grab you something," he said, scrambling to his feet. "The nurse's station is right outside."

"Thanks, Dan," I said, sitting up straighter and thinking it so strange to call my former boss by his first name.

My dress hung on the doorway. I wore a light blue hospital gown with little white bunnies on it. I shuddered. I hated everything about hospitals—the sterility and the fact that sometimes people never left them alive. I wanted to get out of here as soon as I could. Maybe I'd pull a Grand-mère and discharge myself. Unfortunately, with the open back of the snazzy sick bay duds, I wasn't exactly dressed for the occasion.

As I waited for his return, I hoped this second fall might cure me of my ailment. I drummed my fingers on my thighs, thinking of flavors.

A few moments passed and O'Shea returned to the room with a croissant and a juice. He pulled out the tray and placed the goods in front of me. "This is as gourmet as it gets. Sorry."

I dug into the croissant and then spit my bite out. "Ugh. It's so bland. It tastes like nothing—maybe cardboard." I washed back the crumbs with the juice. "And this orange juice? There is no flavor. It might as well be water."

My mouth twisted into a tight grimace. My stomach sank. I met O'Shea's eyes, wanting to tell him what had happened, but my words wouldn't form. He'd seen me as an equal at the event, and I didn't want him to lose respect for me.

O'Shea lifted his shoulders into a shrug. "It's hospital food. It's supposed to be bland," he said, and hope surged in my heart. "We'll get you something more substantial when you're released. Maybe I'll cook for you?"

My heart sparked. "Thanks. I've got to get out of here, and the sooner the better. But I can't wear that," I said, pointing to the ball gown.

"Don't worry," said O'Shea. "I found your phone and called Séb. He's bringing you something."

He'd been here for me. I wanted to give Dan something too. Chefs—we stuck together, thick as thieves.

"Thanks," I said, rubbing my throbbing temples. "And since you already know I'm saying a hard no to your offer to spearhead Cendrillon Paris, I may know somebody who would want to take on the challenge."

"If you say Eric, you won't leave this hospital alive," he said with a fake growl.

"God no, not Eric. My friend Monica. We went to the CIA together and she's a starred chef looking for new opportunities. She's completely brilliant—came up with that fig recipe."

O'Shea licked his lips. "Along with your magical dish, I dreamt about those figs all night." He sighed. "I'll seriously consider any candidate when the recommendation comes from you."

AN HOUR LATER, a doctor gave me the okay to leave the hospital, telling me to take one thousand milligrams of ibuprofen for the pain, never exceeding three times a day. Séb escorted me back to Grand-mère's so we could gather our things before the flight home. The rest of our kitchen goods would be taken care of by the museum's staff, and a van would drop them off at the aerodrome. Séb and I sat in the living room, decompressing. My stomach let out a roar of a growl.

"Hungry, Chef?" asked Séb with a snigger.

"Starving," I said. "Hospital food sucks."

"What do you want? I'll make you something."

"Honestly, anything."

As Séb hopped up from the couch, Étoile jumped up on my lap, snuggling in between my legs, her purrs so loud and forceful they vibrated on my legs. I stroked her little body, excited to get back home. I also hoped the fall I'd had had snapped my senses back.

"Are you really bringing the cat back to Champvert?" asked Séb.

"Does it look like I have a choice?" I asked. "We have a connection, a bond. No way would I leave her behind. She also told me that she doesn't want to live in Paris, so there's that."

"Whatever you say. And I'll be right back." He wiggled his butt. "In two shakes of a lamb's tail."

"Did you get that expression from Marie?"

"I did," he said. "I watched *Pulp Fiction* with her and Phillipa. Cool movie."

As Séb worked in the kitchen, the sounds of pots and pans banging brought me to attention. A whisk. The click of the burner. Chopping. I sniffed the air but couldn't figure out the aroma. Nothing. I couldn't smell anything. Maybe he'd put the exhaust fan on? I settled onto the couch with Étoile, closing my eyes in concentration. Still nothing.

Ten minutes later, Séb appeared with a plate of dill scrambled eggs and freshly sliced fruit. "Dig in," he said, placing the dish on the coffee table.

"Aren't you eating?"

"I already did. This is for you," he said. "Did you want to chow down in the dining room?"

"Nah," I said, sinking into the comfort of the cushy couch, hopeful this second fall might have awakened my senses. "I'm comfortable here and don't want to move."

I picked up the fork and brought a mouthful of eggs to my nose. No smell. I took a bite, chewed. No taste. These eggs were as bland as the hospital's croissants. But how could that be? I saw the dill, the fresh ground pepper.

"Is something wrong, Chef?" asked Séb, eyeing me warily. "I can make something else if you'd like."

"No, it's perfect," I lied, taking another bite of the eggs. "Delicious."

I shoved an orange wedge into my mouth. The juice slid down my tongue, but there were no citrus flavors tickling my taste buds. I ate a kiwi slice. An apple. Nothing tasted sweet; a tin taste filled my mouth. I inhaled deeply through my nostrils but could only come up with burnt or the scent of eggs gone bad. Severe disappointment set in. The fall hadn't cured me. I was still completely senseless.

I jumped up from my seat. "Séb, thank you for breakfast. It was delish," I said, my voice rising higher than I wanted it to.

"The expression on your face says otherwise," he said, worry creasing his brows. "You didn't like it."

"I did," I said. "I'm just tired. Spent. And can't wait to get back home. I have to get my things together."

I stumbled up to Grand-mère's suite in a daze, placing my hands on the walls so I wouldn't tumble down the stairs. My heart beat so fiercely I thought it might burst out of my chest. My brain was simply fried. And so was I. I just wanted to get back to Champvert and tell Rémi the truth. Living this lie was exhausting, especially if this was how I'd be for the rest of my life.

As I packed, I tucked a few photos of Grand-mère from her youth and her journal into my bag, nestling them in between my clothes. At least I'd have her with me.

SÉB AND I said goodbye to Marianne, thanking her for her service and kindness. I slipped her an envelope with eight hundred euros, reimbursements for Étoile's supplies and some extra moola to show my appreciation.

"I hope to see you again," said Marianne. She tucked the envelope into her purse without looking at it.

I didn't have the heart to tell her I'd be avoiding Paris for a long while and that the thought of selling the apartment crossed my mind. Paris had left a bad taste in my mouth—no, I couldn't taste anything. I straightened my posture. Still, I was holding on to the memories of Grand-mère, and a part of me wanted to come back here on my own terms.

"Merci, Marianne," I said. *"Pour tout."*

"You are very welcome," she said.

The driver pulled up and loaded our bags into the trunk. It was only a matter of time before I'd be home, where I belonged. I was looking forward to unwinding in the hammam spa, seeing Rémi and Lola. The Eiffel Tower disappeared from view. I let out a sigh and patted Séb's hand.

"Sorry to have put you through all of this bullshit," I said. "It wasn't exactly what I'd envisioned."

"Ah, it wasn't all bad. Just hot and crazy," he said. "I think I'm a country boy."

"Me too," I said. "City life is overrated."

"So you're not moving to Paris like that guy said? I overheard him talking to O'Shea."

"Are you kidding me?" I said. "No way in hell."

Séb settled in his seat. "Thank god. I was scared there for a minute."

Nadeem greeted Séb and me as our car pulled up to the aerodrome. "Bonjour, Sophie, Séb. The other two passengers are here," he said. "We're just waiting on one more."

I shuddered. If Amélie or Eric were on this plane, I'd have an instant heart attack.

"Other passengers?" I questioned.

"The East Coast chefs," he said. "We're dropping you off first, then heading for New York and Boston."

"Oh, oh, oh," I said, breathing out a sigh of relief. People I trusted were on this flight.

"Please make yourself comfortable," said Nadeem. "I'll take care of your bags."

He reached out for the cat-carrying case.

"No, this is special cargo," I said. "It's my cat. I can handle her."

"I don't recall you bringing a cat to Paris," said Nadeem, puzzled.

"I didn't," I said, making my way up the stairs. "But I am taking one back to Champvert."

O'Shea and Jean-Jacques leapt out of their seats upon my entrance, barraging me with questions and statements of worry. "Are you feeling okay?" "Does your head hurt?" "Can we get you anything?" "You're looking a little pale."

"Whoa, whoa, whoa," I said. "I'm fine. And I'm always pale."

"True," said O'Shea.

Étoile let out a strange mew.

"What's in your carry-on?" asked Jean-Jacques.

"Sophie found an ugly cat," said Séb.

"Don't listen to him," I said, whispering to Étoile. I looked up to Séb. "You should hear what she says about you."

We settled into our seats, either on the couch or the plush chairs. I didn't want to get in trouble for taking Étoile, so I kept her in the soft case, unzipping it a bit so I could stick my hand in and pet her sweet little head—her loud purrs were calming.

Jean-Jacques clasped my free hand. "I'm so very proud of you. And I know your grand-mère would be even prouder. The dish you made was incredible." His hand went to his heart. "I now know why she didn't leave Champvert to come with me. She told me she wanted to create a world for you." He sniffled, and his eyes welled up with tears. "I hope you know how much she loved you."

I couldn't meet his gaze. I didn't want to cry. My heart beat with so much pride for the dynasty my grand-mère had created. For me. She'd told me this before. And that it was also for her, the means by which she'd claimed her dreams. Through her spirit, I knew I could achieve mine. I had to.

"I do know how much she loved me," I said with a gulp.

Jean-Jacques let out a laugh. "Do you know how hard she worked at Le Cordon Bleu? How she didn't take crap from anybody? That woman stuck to her guns, which is why I fell in love with her." He placed his hands around my free hand, holding it tightly. "I see so much of her spirit in you. Please, stick to your beliefs."

"I am," I said. "I'm more like her than I ever realized."

We sat quiet for a moment.

A shadow loomed over us. Nicolas. He must have been the extra passenger we'd been waiting for. "And what are you all talking about? I hope it's about Amélie's demise." He let out a wicked laugh. "Sophie, you played the game perfectly."

So he really thought playing with people's life was a game. Well, he wasn't playing with mine.

"My father is filing for divorce tomorrow. And he's closing her restaurant down. I don't know how you got him to see her for the vicious, cheating *salope* she is."

"Your father and I caught her in the stairwell. It wasn't planned," I said.

"What were you doing in the stairwell with my father?" he asked, eyes narrowed. "Are you looking to be wife number four?"

I wanted to slap him but refrained. I realized I didn't owe him an explanation but ended up spouting one off anyway. "No, I was taking a break. He was sneaking a cigar. Nothing unsavory about that."

He reached into his pocket and slammed a box on the coffee table. "This is for you."

"Believe me, I don't want anything from you," I said.

"It's not from me, it's from my father," he said. "And what does that mean? I'm offering you the world." Nicolas sat down next to me, too close. I sniffed the air. I should have smelled his pungent cologne; I didn't. His knees touched mine. I swiveled my body away from his. "Shall I have the flight attendant pop open a bottle of bubbly so we can celebrate?"

"No thanks," I said. "There is absolutely nothing to celebrate." I stood up to change seats.

"Sit down," he said. "Buckle up and enjoy the ride. I believe you owe me an answer. Think of it. We could be a power couple."

"No," I said, crossing my arms over my chest. "That's my answer."

Nicolas recoiled. "What do you mean, non? I'm offering you the opportunity of a lifetime."

Clearly, he was used to getting everything he wanted. Well, that didn't include me.

"It means I'm not moving to Paris. I'm not working for you or your family. I'm staying in Champvert, where I'll create my *own* opportunities." I wanted to throw in "you misogynistic, spoiled brat" for good measure, but kept my cool.

"Then I'm pulling out of Cendrillon Paris," he said, his eyes blazing onto O'Shea's. "You promised me she'd be a part of the deal. And she isn't."

"I'm still here," I said, my blood boiling. "Stop talking about me in the third person or I'll gouge your eyes out."

O'Shea shrugged his giant shoulders. He leaned forward, meeting Nicolas's glare. "Good thing your father is backing my restaurant."

"What are you talking about? I'm in charge of the family estate now."

"Not anymore," said O'Shea. "He called me this morning. You've lost all control, so he's taking it away from you."

Nicolas punched the television screen, smashing it. I'd never seen a temper tantrum like the one Nicolas was having. He needed to be sedated, and quickly, before he destroyed the plane. To think I'd once referred to Rémi as a man-child. Compared to this creep, Rémi was all man. Nicolas was toxic and manipulative and took no responsibilities for his actions.

He made a move toward me, but Séb stepped in between us, puffing out his chest like a peacock defending its territory. "I'm a black belt and a mixed martial arts kickboxer," said Séb, flexing his muscles. "Back off. Or else."

Another detail I hadn't known about Séb. And, not only was he fierce, he was fiercely loyal. Pride swelled in my heart. He could cook like a pro, and he had my back.

"You're really messing with the wrong person," said Nicolas.

"No, you are," said Séb. "Sophie doesn't want you. And she doesn't want Paris. I don't think there's anything else left to say."

Nicolas stormed toward the door, stopped, and braced his hands on the frame, panting.

"You're leaving?" I asked, blowing out a sigh of relief. I couldn't imagine sitting in close quarters with him for a minute, let alone the forty-five-minute plane ride. "What about your business in New York?"

He turned, spittle flying out of his mouth. "It's over, and so are you."

I straightened my posture, not wanting to back down and give him the upper hand by acting intimidated and threatened by his wealth and power. But I was wealthy and becoming more powerful too—at least in the culinary circles. "I wouldn't be so sure about that," I said. "I'm just beginning."

"*Petite salope*" (little bitch), he said. "I will not forget this."

As Nicolas clomped down the steps, O'Shea whispered, "Who the holy fuck are you?"

My body shook. My head hurt. My hair hurt. But, in that moment, I knew who I was. "Well, I'm not a little bitch, I'm a fearless woman," I said, lifting my shoulders. "I'm just missing my cape."

Jean-Jacques let out a soft laugh. "I don't think Nicolas has ever met the likes of the stubborn and fiery women from the Valroux de la Tour de Champvert family."

After we settled down from the drama, O'Shea pointed to the small box on the table. "Aren't you going to open it?"

And with trembling hands I did. The note, which I read aloud, said:

Mademoiselle Valroux,

These are small tokens of my appreciation. Thank you for being you—for your honesty. Please, do me a favor and follow your dreams. Soar with the dragonflies and butterflies. Swing from the stars. (Yes, I've done my research.) And don't worry about Nicolas. I've already spoken with O'Shea. Everything is being handled and on track.

Cordialement,
Olivier de la Barguelonne

My eyes locked onto O'Shea's. "You knew?"

"I did," said O'Shea. "I called Olivier after I left the hospital. We've been doing business with him for years. I told you that he knows what loyalty is."

"We?" I asked.

"He was also the main investor for Le Homard," said Jean-Jacques. "Your grand-mère knew him, too, through me. He loved her spirit . . . and her cooking. Don't worry about that spoiled brat son of his. He's always stirring up trouble."

"Well, open the box," said O'Shea, pointing.

My fingers fumbled through thick tissue paper. Three diamond, ruby, and sapphire brooches rested inside—one a dragonfly, one a butterfly, and the other three stars—each piece more amazing and intricate than the next, the colored facets sparkling in the sunlight and bouncing on the walls like a crazy kaleidoscope. "Wow," I said. "I can't accept these."

O'Shea laughed. "In this case, I think it's okay to say yes to a de la Barguelonne."

He was right. I tucked the box into my purse.

Nadeem entered the cabin. "Please fasten your seat belts. We're about to take off." Like a ninja, he disappeared. Honestly, I didn't know where he went—the plane was so big.

"Do the two of you want to come to the château?" I asked. "I can hook you up. I know the owner. And, Chef—I mean, Dan—you can meet Monica."

O'Shea settled in his seat and clasped his giant hands together. "As much as I would love to, I can't. As you know, it's only a few more months until Michelin releases its red guide. I have to keep Cendrillon NY on track. I'll fly Monica to New York and put her up in a hotel if she's interested in meeting."

"You're hoping for the third star," I said, and he nodded. I didn't blame him. It was what he had been working toward for his entire life. "Jean-Jacques, what about you?"

He hung his head. "I've spent so many years trying to forget Odette," he said. "Seeing you brought all those lost feelings back.

I'm sorry, Sophie, I can't right now. But one day, when I'm ready, I would love to see the side of her that I didn't know."

"I understand," I said. "I've been dealing with the same roller coaster of emotions myself."

O'Shea belted out a laugh as the plane took off. "And then you had to deal with Nicolas and Amélie." He patted my hand. "You really are incredible, Sophie."

"Maybe," I said, my voice catching.

I tried to convince myself I was fearless, everything I'd just said I was. But, at the moment, I was scared shitless. Maybe Nicolas had been right. Maybe I was over.

20

knocked senseless

I'D EXPECTED TO see Rémi awaiting my arrival, for him to swing me in his arms, to kiss me and tell me how much he missed me. I was excited to tell him of my decision that I wanted to set a date, and soon. I was ready to tell him everything, ask him for his help. Instead, my father waited for me on the front steps.

"The Sunday lunch just started," said Jean-Marc. "Did you want to go?"

Completely spent, I just wanted to decompress from the nightmare of Paris. "No," I said. "I think I'm going to have to miss out on this one."

He helped me take my bags to my room as the driver and Séb unloaded the van.

"Thanks, Papa," I said.

His bottom lip quivered. "You don't know how proud it makes me when I hear you say that." Jean-Marc kissed me on the forehead and then turned for the door. "I can't wait to hear about Paris. But get some sleep first."

I did need that. Once settled in my room, I crawled into bed, noticing that bouquets of red roses filled my room. Rémi must have been anticipating my answer. Oh, sweet Rémi. I wanted to see him, but I couldn't move. My head got heavier. My eyes closed. Étoile curled up by my side, and as I stroked her, I passed out, happy to be home in Champvert, to see Rémi and my friends.

A hand swept through my hair. Two. Three. Four. I sat up, under the watchful gazes of Phillipa, Marie, Monica, and Jane.

"Séb told us what happened," said Jane, sitting down on the side of my bed.

"Merde, Sophie," said Phillipa. "This is royally messed up. But you have to tell us the whole story so we can help you."

Étoile jumped onto Marie's lap. "I didn't know you had a cat," she said.

"I didn't," I said. "She's the only good thing that came out of Paris."

"Did you catnap her?" asked Marie.

I wiped the sleep out of my eyes. "Kind of," I said. "But she people-napped my heart."

Jane grimaced at Étoile. "Enough about the cat. Tell us what happened. We'll set it straight."

I told them everything—how Amélie had a vendetta against Grand-mère because she'd captured the heart of a man Amélie wanted; how she was jealous of our family; how Nicolas acted like a bratty kid because he wasn't going to get what he wanted, which was me; how Olivier stepped up, along with O'Shea and Jean-Jacques; and how Eric was back in the picture. The only thing I left out was the fact that I couldn't smell or taste. Nobody needed to know that. Not until I knew what was going on and I spoke with Rémi.

"The douchebag was there? In Paris? And you didn't text us?" screeched Phillipa. "Holy merde! What were you thinking?"

"I was thinking to avoid him, especially after he and Amélie presented my daurade dish to the public." I put my finger in my throat, pretending to vomit. "Obviously, it wasn't my recipe. And she was screwing him."

"No," said Monica with a gasp.

"Yes," I said with a shudder. "Monsieur de la Barguelonne and I caught them, or, technically, overheard them in the stairwell. He's filing divorce papers and closing Durand down, and Amélie is probably now gunning for me. I'm pretty sure Eric will leave her high and dry, now that he doesn't need her. I saw him chatting up Ayasa Watanabe at the event. Hopefully, she'll be smart enough to steer clear of him."

Jane leaned forward, her eyes filled with curiosity. "Wait. What's this about Grand-mère having a love life?"

As I explained her relationship with Jean-Jacques, Jane's hands flew to her cheeks and she flopped down on my bed, giggling. "Oh my goodness. I can't believe it. Good for her."

Exactly my thoughts on the subject. Knowing she had a life outside of the kitchen made me smile from ear to ear. But then I frowned, my head pounding.

"Are you okay?" asked Phillipa. "Séb told us you had a serious fall."

"Just a minor concussion. I may have tripped on the stairs. You know me and my klutzy feet," I said glumly. "But, other than a few bruises, I'm perfectly fine."

A major lie. I was far from okay. We all went silent.

"Putain," said Jane. She got up and paced. "The de la Barguelonnes are very powerful. I'd hate to be on the receiving end of their firing line. Are we?"

I shook my head no and pointed to my purse. "Look inside. There are gifts and a note from Olivier. He's taking his company back, getting rid of Amélie, and cutting off Nicolas's power for now."

Jane scrambled to my purse and pulled out the box. Marie and Phillipa peered over her shoulder as she read the note and then lifted the lid. "Wow," said Jane, eyeing the brooches. "I think you have a fan, And phew. I couldn't imagine going head-to-head with them."

"You're not moving to Paris?" asked Phillipa. "I don't think I can go through that again. First O'Shea tempted you with New York, now this."

I bolted upright, my breath ragged.

"Are you freaking kidding me? That asshole put words in my mouth in front of everybody. I declined the offer." Once my heartbeat settled down, my gaze leapt to Monica's. "I told O'Shea, however, that you might be interested in the opportunity if he gives you a little creative license."

Monica's chin lifted. "Really?"

"Yep."

"Is this Nicolas asshole involved?"

"Nope. Not anymore," I said. "But his father is. And he's a nice guy. O'Shea? Well, he's O'Shea. He does have an explosive temper, but he also has the heart of a kitten."

"I don't know, Sophie," she said, shuffling her feet. "That would mean I wouldn't be here. And Champvert is growing on me."

I knew Monica needed something different. I could tell she was itching to get back to city life. I didn't want her to leave, especially since I needed her now more than ever, but the facts were the facts. We were cut from the same cookie mold, had the same dreams. Mine were here in Champvert; hers were elsewhere. She needed to spread her culinary wings and fly.

"It would also mean you'd have your own kitchen," I said. "Well, sort of. You'd have to follow a few of O'Shea's recipes to the letter. But, after tasting your figs, he'd probably give you carte blanche to create a couple of signature dishes. Are you interested?"

She swallowed hard. "Is it horrible if I say yes?"

I hugged her. "No."

"Then yes," she said with a laugh. "But if things don't work out—"

"You'd be welcome back here in a heartbeat," I said, and patted her back. "I'll let O'Shea know. He'll buy you a ticket for New York and put you up in a hotel to test you out."

We all flopped on my bed, toes pointed to the ceiling. Marie spoke up first. "Hey," she said, her eyebrows knitted together. "What did they think of my desserts?"

Shit. I didn't know. "I kind of pulled my Cinderella-falling-down-the-stairs act before the subject came up. I'm sure we'll find out in the press, though. And I'm sure everybody thought they were phenomenal. How could they not?"

Jane pulled out her phone, propped herself up against a pillow, and tapped away. "Found it," she said. "'Aside from Sophie Valroux's inspired dish, another highlight of the evening came when the desserts from her pastry chef, Marie Moreau, were presented. In line with the Sous les étoiles theme, these mirrored galaxy cakes were from out of this world, tasting as magical as they looked. This picky food critic expects amazing things from Château de Champvert and its flagship restaurant, Les Libellules.'" Jane slammed her phone on the bed. "This makes everything. We are golden."

I gulped. Golden—if I could find my senses. I sneezed—a good sign. The cause: the bouquets upon bouquets of roses. I pointed. "Where did those come from? Did Rémi do this?"

Jane pursed her lips. "I don't know. They must have arrived this morning. Housekeeping probably brought them up to your room."

I hopped off the bed and grabbed a card tucked into one of the bouquets. It was from Nicolas, and it read: *I can't wait to do business with you, my beautiful chef. We'll set the world on fire. I'm still thinking about our kiss. ~Nicolas*

He had to bring up that repulsive, stomach-turning assault. And he'd obviously sent the roses before his tantrum on the plane. I dropped the card and it fell to the floor. "Ugh, it's from the Parisian douchebag. Who is going to help me rip these up?"

Soon, the five of us danced in a flurry of red petals. They floated in the air like little devilish clouds. We tore those bouquets up like maniacs. Apparently, I wasn't the only person in need of a little stress relief.

Phillipa grabbed me by the shoulders, her eyes tearing with laughter. "Housekeeping is going to be pissed."

"I don't have them clean my room," I said. "I do it."

"On that, you look spent. Where's the dress?" asked Jane, and I nodded toward the suitcase. She unzipped the bag and grabbed the dress, which was rolled up in a ball. She smoothed out the fabric and hung it up. "You really should take better care of this."

"And of yourself," said Phillipa, nodding her head with concern.

Understatement of the year.

Jane continued to unpack for me, setting clothes aside for the laundry service—a bonus when you had a housekeeping staff and didn't know how to iron. Her eyes widened when she pulled out Grand-mère's poppy-print apron. She held it to her nose, breathing in the scent. "She had another one?"

"She did," I said. "And this apron will stay in my room."

Jane winked at me and hung the apron on the back of my door. "Will this do?"

"Yes," I said. "It's perfect."

"Speaking of perfect, I have an idea. Girls' night out," said Phillipa. "Just us. And a bunch of martinis."

Marie, Jane, and Monica let out whoops of agreement.

I didn't want to go anywhere. I picked up Étoile. "What about a girls' night in? Tomorrow night? I really should spend time with Rémi first."

"Oh," said Phillipa. "You're turning into one of *those* girls."

"No, I'm just one of those girls who really need a nap right about now," I said with a yawn. "You gals should probably head back down to the Sunday lunch."

"True," said Jane, shrugging. "Appearances must be kept up. And since you're obviously not going, it's on us."

A SLAM. MY bedroom door crashed in its frame, waking me with a jolt. Étoile let out a mew. Rémi pointed. "What the hell is that?" he asked.

"My cat," I said groggily.

"If you say so," he said. *"Il est moche."* (It's ugly.) "And I cannot believe you, Sophie."

"It's just a cat."

His face flushed redder than the scattered rose petals on the floor. He clenched his hands. "Non, non, non, I'm not talking about your stupid cat. I'm talking about Paris and what you did."

"I didn't do anything," I said, bolting upright. "I cooked, and I couldn't wait to get back here to you. To tell you my answer." I paused. "Rémi Dupont, *je t'aime avec tout mon cœur.* I want to set a date. More than anything, I want to marry you, and soon. When were you thinking?"

I jumped out of bed, expecting him to wrap me in his arms, to kiss me. Instead, he backed away from me, glaring. "Well, my answer is *non.* I do not want to marry you."

His eyes held so much fire in them I thought I would burn. My legs were about to go out from under me. What was his problem? Why the change of heart? My answer came when he pulled his cell phone out from his pocket, tapped a few keys, and then shoved the screen in my face. "Explain this."

I took his phone and sat down on my bed. The headline of the article was NICOLAS DE LA BARGUELONNE IS LEAVING HIS MODELIZING LIFE FOR HOT CHEF SOPHIE VALROUX. The photo accompanying the text was of Nicolas and me in a lip-lock. I cringed, thinking about how disgusting and repulsive his wet lips were.

"Jesus Christ, Rémi," I said. "I didn't kiss him. He kissed me."

"Photos speak a thousand words," he said. "Merde. You're only gone for a few days and you fall into the arms of another man. I told you this was going to happen. And I was right. Did you sleep with him?"

"No," I said, flinching. How could Rémi accuse me of this when I hadn't even slept with *him*? And I loved Rémi. "I hate that sniveling brat. He *forced* that kiss on me."

His cheeks flamed red. He snorted. "The kiss doesn't look forced."

"It was. And I didn't fall into his embrace. I fell down the stairs. I ran out of the room after he did what he did."

Rémi went silent, glaring at me, taking my words in. "Are you okay? Did you break anything?"

"No," I said, my eyes tearing up.

"You did, Sophie," he said, his eyes darting to the floor. "You broke my heart." He gripped his hair with his hands. "What's this about you moving to Paris and taking over Cendrillon?"

My shoulders went rigid. I spit out the words: "For your information, I declined their offer."

"That's not what it says in the article."

I couldn't believe he was taking the word of a tabloid press over mine. I thought we were over this kind of confrontation. I guessed I was wrong.

"Then you shouldn't believe everything you read," I said. Something didn't sit right. Rémi didn't keep up with the gossip pages. I wouldn't put anything past Nicolas. That coldhearted asshole was trying to take me down, get the last word in. Anger raged in my bones. "Who sent you the article?"

"Nobody. I have your name and the château's on Google Alerts," he said. "Your father set it up."

"Nicolas didn't send it to you?"

"Why would he send me anything?"

"Because he's a conniving, calculating brat who is used to getting what he wants," I said, panting out my words. "He set me up. Amélie hired Eric. They presented my daurade dish, the one he stole, at the gala. You were right: Paris was a really bad idea. You can't be mad at me," I said, my bottom lip quivering. "You have to believe me. Give me a chance to explain."

Rémi paced, his shoes scuffing up the Aubusson carpet, his fists clenched into tight balls. "Explain? I can't even look at you, let alone listen to you. I need to calm down and process everything you just told me. Because it's insane."

"I know it's insane, Rémi," I said with a sob. "And I'm sorry. I'm so, so sorry."

I'd never seen a man look so angry. But, with his attitude and disbelief in me, I sucked back my tears, my own anger starting to take over. I crossed my arms over my chest and glared at him. He turned on his heel and left my room, slamming the door on his way out. I ripped the ring off my finger and threw it against the wall.

For a moment, I sat in the window seat, hugging my knees to my chest while looking down at the guests still enjoying the Sunday lunch festivities, my mind spinning. I bit down on the inside of my cheek so hard I drew blood. I'd lost my grand-mère. I'd lost my senses. And now I'd lost Rémi. I didn't have anything else to lose.

After washing my face and tying my hair into a ponytail, I quickly dressed in one of Grand-mère's Chanel suits. Then I raced down the stairs, out of the kitchen, and ran straight up to Gustave. Although still banged up, he'd *never* miss a Sunday lunch.

"Gustave," I said, forgetting about doctor's orders. "Hand over the pastis."

21

stumble and fall

THE WORST OF hangovers rattled my brain.

I woke up the next morning not quite remembering the events of the day before until they flashed in front of my eyes one by one, particularly my fight with Rémi, and oh, the pastis—the goddamn pastis. Apparently, I'd had way too much of it, considering, with the exception of Jane's martinis, I rarely drank hard alcohol. Had I danced with the guests? Slurred my words? Stumbled? Maybe even fallen? I was sure I had. I wondered who had brought me up to my room, undressed me, and put me in my nightgown.

The sound of snoring emanated from my salon. Tentatively, I slunk out of bed and, in stealth mode, entered the room to find both Phillipa and Jane sleeping on the pullout couch. Jane was the snorer, gasping in and blowing out air in strange puffs. I bumped into a nightstand, waking them both.

Phillipa mumbled, "Oh, good. You're alive. We were so worried about you."

Jane glared at me with one eye open. "No, *we* were not. Maybe

Phillipa was, but I wasn't. What the hell is bloody wrong with you? You can't act that way in front of the guests."

The flashbacks I'd had in my head were real. Merde.

"I had a meltdown?" I said. "And please, don't tell me what I did."

"Oh, I'm telling you," said Jane, sitting up. "Because it can never, ever happen again. So don't drop it like it's hot in a Chanel skirt. Because you fell down. Multiple times."

I eyed my scraped knees. The proof was undeniable. I couldn't argue with her.

"Your knees will heal, but your skirt is ruined," said Jane. "But I'll see if I can get it fixed."

"Thanks," I said, poking my knee and wincing at the pain.

Phillipa slapped my hand lightly. "Don't do that. And are you ready to tell us what happened? Because you can't go on like this."

"Can we just blame Gustave and his pastis?" I asked, my head throbbing.

The twins raised their brows in unison.

"Fine," I said, and I told them about my argument with Rémi. I told them about my wavering grief. I told them Paris had rattled my bones. But I left out the part about me losing my senses.

"I get that you're upset with Rémi. I would be too. And I would have broken up with him," said Jane with a shudder. "Paris may have been a bad trip, but you got completely loaded in front of the guests. Don't get me wrong—I like to get pissed every now and again, but never when guests are at the château. Never."

"When you need to let your hair down, we're here for you," said Phillipa. "Girls' night out." She sighed. "On a Sunday or a Monday."

I felt terrible. Embarrassed. Guilty. "Do you think I ruined things for us?"

"No," said Jane. "I think the guests actually enjoyed your odd moves. Half of them made repeat bookings for next year."

"Really?"

"Yes," said Jane with a laugh. "Imagine that. Hopefully, the press won't get wind of this. If they do, I'll do my best to quash it. Or, who knows? Maybe it would be good for the château. As they say, any press is good press."

"What would I do without you?" I asked.

"Well, you'd be sleeping in a torn Chanel skirt," she said, eyeing me. "So, what's on the agenda?"

"Let's head down to the kitchen," I said. "I'm making us breakfast."

THE CHÂTEAU HAD this state-of-the-art coffee maker. I didn't know how to work it. I stood in front of the machine pressing buttons until Phillipa nudged me to the side.

"I've got this," said Phillipa. "I need the jolt. And seriously, this baby cost twenty thousand, so if you don't know what you're doing, don't touch it. You break it, you buy it." She hunched over in laughter. "Oh, right, it's yours, you can do whatever you want."

"Phillipa," I said, "just help me out and show me what to do."

A few minutes later: bingo. I wished I could have smelled the aroma. I didn't. I took a sip and almost spit it back out. Pure sludge.

Coffees in hand, Jane and Phillipa sat on stools at the prep table while I gathered the ingredients to prepare our breakfast. I was going to prepare the exact menu I'd created for Walter and Robert, right after I'd completely lost my shit in New York. When I'd last cooked the meal, it was a titanic disaster. I needed to prove to myself I could do it, or I would lose it.

"What's on the menu, Chef?" asked Phillipa.

"We're friends, not coworkers now. And I really need a friend," I said, wincing. What kind of chef was I? A damaged one. With an ache in my back, I bent down to get a pan from one of the shelves. "Please don't call me 'Chef' unless we're working."

"Okay, then. What's on the menu, Dancing Queen?" she replied.

I stood up, pan in hand. "Very funny."

"And?" said Phillipa.

I gave a perfunctory nod, hoping I could pull this meal off with my two friends looking over my shoulder. "Today's menu, for your gastronomic delight, will be comprised of *œufs cocotte* with fresh herbs and accompanied by crunchy potatoes."

"Sounds delish," said Phillipa. "Do you need my help?"

"No," I said. "I need to do this to make my amends, to you gals for acting like an idiot, and to the cooking gods."

"Cooking gods?" asked Phillipa.

I winked at her. "And goddesses. Believe me, they exist."

"I'm thinking a mimosa would be in order," said Jane with an unexpected snort. "Sophie looks as if she needs one. A little hair of the dog?"

I looked over my shoulder. "Then make yourself useful and pour us one."

"Oh, I'm on it," she said. "With fresh orange juice."

Jane got up and headed to the orange press, and in less than two minutes the room should have been enveloped in a sugary citrus haze. But I smelled nothing. As I chopped up herbs—mostly tarragon with a bit of thyme—and potatoes, the aroma in the kitchen should have become richer, sweet and pungent.

Phillipa sniffed the air. "It smells divine," she said.

"Right," I said, worry coursing through my veins like acid.

As Jane and Phillipa filled me in on what had happened at the château while I was stuck in a Parisian nightmare, I cooked. Twenty minutes later, breakfast was ready, the potatoes perfectly golden, the eggs the right consistency. We sat down with our mimosas and we ate, no words exchanged. I was happy to say I didn't make a mess of it. I knew this because Jane and Phillipa scarfed down their meals.

When we were finished eating, Jane said, "Look, if you need to cry, you can ugly cry in front of us. If you need to throw things, throw them. Just don't dance or lose it in front of the guests."

I shot Jane a sideways glance. "It was that bad?"

Phillipa nodded her head. "Sorry, but yes. Did you ever see that old *Seinfeld* episode when Elaine looked like she was having some kind of seizure?"

"Yeah," I said, slumping over.

"Imagine something worse," she said, scrunching her nose. "Hopefully there isn't a YouTube video of it."

Yeah, and hopefully my senses would come back.

UNFORTUNATELY, SOME RANDOM guest had captured my drunken state from the day I'd lost my mind, and had posted the photos on Twitter. I found myself in another media storm, this one called "The Many Faces of Grand Chef Sophie Valroux." Pictures of me with a constipated smile. Pictures of me dropping it like it was hot in a shredded Chanel skirt. Pictures of me doing God knew what. Although it was full-on embarrassing, and there were some mean comments that had me cringing and wanting to hide under my sheets for an eternity, the public ate it up and came to my defense. The bad press ended up doing us a favor.

"Give Chef Sophie a break. She's human and not a diva, asshole chef with an attitude."

"If you haven't had one of Chef Sophie's meals, you haven't lived."

"She let loose. So what? I'm a chef and I know life in the kitchen can be like a pressure cooker."

Everybody had their breaking point, but, even with all the support, mine had left me completely shattered.

A WEEK HAD passed since my return from Paris. Rémi avoided me like the plague and didn't attend the family dinners. I missed him so much my heart ached. Every night I prayed to Grand-mère, to the cooking gods and goddesses, to any higher power listening: *If anything, please give me my sense of taste back. And while you're at it—help me patch things up with Rémi.*

I escaped to the kitchen, trying to piece my life back together.

Phillipa and I were in the process of testing a new recipe composed of caramelized brussels sprouts, walnuts, and crispy lardons (cubed pieces of pancetta-like pork) when all of a sudden she turned, smoldering pan in hand, hot duck fat spilling onto the floor. I slipped on the grease, and, to bring more drama to the moment, I snapped.

"What the hell, Phillipa?" I screamed. "I thought you knew your way around the kitchen. I thought you knew how to work *around* me."

Phillipa just stood there, head down, shaking from side to side, and stuttered. "I-I-I-I'm so sorry, Sophie. It was an accident."

I couldn't control the rage in my voice. And I felt terrible. I'd made myself a personal promise, a pinkie swear, to treat the people who worked under me with respect and with kindness. But there I was acting like an abominable monster toward my closest friend, my sous chef, and the only person I'd ever truly confided in.

Phillipa's pale-blue-hydrangea-colored eyes darkened as if stormy clouds were rolling into a once sun-filled sky. By her expression, I knew she felt bad. But I felt worse.

"I'm so sorry, Sophie," said Phillipa, her strong English accent

oozing with pained worry. "I'm doing my best. Really, I am. I'm trying to keep up, but sometimes I feel like I can't. But you? There's
something going on that you're not telling me about. It's not grief.
And it's not Rémi. Who are you *now*? Because I've met many of you."

"Are you calling me nuts?"

She had every right to think I was insane.

"Look, I'm always here for you. Even when you're a complete
arse," said Phillipa. "You know that, right?"

"I'm sorry. You're right. I'm a complete arse," I said, and then
tried to make light of the situation. "At least they fixed the septic
system. I can throw myself into it."

Phillipa burst into laughter. "Please don't do that. Just another
mess we'd have to clean up."

"I'm sorry," I said again.

"Stop apologizing and tell me what's going on," she said with
concern. "You really haven't been acting like yourself since you've
come back. And, if I'm being honest with you, you were acting really
strange before that. Tell me. I can take it."

Clearly, I had a lot of things I needed to work out. I rubbed my
eyes with my fingertips. The juices from the onion I'd just chopped
burnt them.

I had to tell somebody the disastrous truth or I'd spontaneously
combust. She was going to be so disappointed in me, maybe even
lose all respect. How could she admire a chef who couldn't really
cook anymore? But she'd seen me through trials in the past, even
when she didn't really know me. I trusted her. I had to open my
heart. This was a risk I was willing to take. I met Phillipa's wide
eyes. "You have to promise me you won't share what I'm about to tell
you with anybody—especially your sister and Rémi."

She made the motion to zip her lips.

I bit down on my inner cheek and then took in a deep breath.

"After my fall a few months ago when I was picking cherries with Rémi and Lola, I haven't been able to taste or smell anything. And I think my fall in Paris has made it worse."

Phillipa's eyes relayed her shock. Her mouth dropped open wide. She threw her hands palms up. "What do you mean, you can't taste or smell? You're a chef, of course you can."

"Nope," I said. "Nothing."

She held up a finger. "Wait a second. You've been cooking for months? Like this? And you didn't tell anybody?"

"For months," I said, my head hanging low. "Not that you don't totally deserve it, because I was planning to do this anyway, but that's why I was giving you more responsibilities all of a sudden. And I'm so glad I did, because you're killing it."

She sucked in a breath. "Have you seen a doctor?"

"Aside from my stay in the hospital, no."

"Why?"

"I figured the problem would take care of itself," I said. "But it didn't."

Phillipa hopped off her stool. "Wait here. I'll be right back."

She scrambled around dry storage, dropping things, and returned with a few items Monica had brought to the château, namely a few different hot sauces and a jar of preserved habanero peppers, along with a variety of the château's confitures.

"Taste this," she said, handing me the hot sauce.

I took a giant swig. "Nothing."

She grabbed the bottle from me and took a little sip. Her eyes watered. She panted. Then she wiped off her tongue with her fingers and raced to the sink, drinking water straight from the tap. "My mouth is on fire. On fire. Merde, that stuff is hot. You really tasted nothing?"

I couldn't meet her eyes, so I looked at the floor. "Nope, nada."

"This is bad, Sophie," she said, her voice wavering. She placed a tender hand on my back. "But we'll figure something out. I promise."

But sometimes people broke their promises. Like the one Rémi had made to me when he said we'd talk about anything. No, Rémi couldn't even look at me. And, along with losing my senses, my heart was broken.

22

⟨ ✦ ⟩

where there's grease,
there's fire

FOR THE NEXT few evenings, dinner service was beyond stressful and bordering on catastrophic. No orchestrated dance, the brigade crashed into one another. Duck fat splattered on the floor. The flames of our flambéed dishes fired so high the kitchen could have burnt down.

One night, Séb slipped, banging his head on a countertop. But being Séb, he just wiped the blood off his forehead, bandaged the wound, and kept on cooking. Somehow we faced disaster and pulled through it. But on one particular night, the servers kept dashing back into the kitchen, returning meals, and we had to cook them up again.

"The customer said the rabbit is oversalted."

"The duck is bland."

"The potatoes are undercooked."

The list of grievances went on and on. And it was all my fault. I couldn't lead my team, not with a broken heart, not with the complete loss of my cooking mojo. They all sensed something was amiss.

I could tell by the odd stares, especially from Clothilde and the granny brigade. When one person was off, the whole ship sank with it.

Clothilde tapped me on the shoulder. "Maybe you should get some rest, ma puce," she said. "Paris seems to have taken its toll on you. And you still have your fall to recover from. We can handle things for a bit."

My eyes snapped onto Clothilde's. "I'm fine," I said with too much force. "I'm just getting back into the swing of things. That's all. You don't have to worry about me."

She pinched my cheek. "I know, dear. But I am."

As Clothilde shuffled back to her station, I caught Phillipa's eye and whispered, "You have to be my taste buds. I'm trying to cook from memory. But I can't."

My heart raced with panic. My body trembled.

"I've got you covered," she said. "Look what you've done for me."

"Made your life hell?"

She nudged me with her hip. "You've given me everything, the dream of becoming a chef like you. Oh, and that awesome necklace. I don't know when I'll be able to wear it, but I love it." She dipped a spoon into the tomato drizzle I'd been in the process of preparing, tasted it, and grimaced. "Too much ginger. I'll remake it. Tell me the exact measurements."

"Oh god," I said, squeezing my eyes shut. "This is worse than a nightmare."

"I'll wake you up from it." She shook my shoulders lightly. "Let's go through all the courses. And you're not getting out of this. I'm here for you."

Side by side, Phillipa and I worked methodically next to another, me prepping and trying to cook from the heart, Phillipa tasting. Marie wandered over from her station. "Chef, I'm so sorry this is happening. I can't imagine what you're going through."

I clenched my teeth and Phillipa grimaced. "What? Don't look at me like that," she said defensively. "You didn't say I couldn't tell Marie. And we talk about everything. That's what couples in a relationship do."

I let out a huff. I hadn't spoken with Rémi in over a week, and the thought of this stabbed at my heart. "At least we haven't had any complaints about the desserts. Merci, Marie. But not a word to anybody else, please, especially Jane. If people find out I'm not the chef that they say I am, that I can't even taste, this could destroy the château."

"My lips are sealed," said Phillipa.

"Mine too," said Marie.

Right then, Jane barreled into the kitchen, storming right up to us. "What in the bloody hell is going on? In all of my years here, we've never had complaints from the guests. I've had to comp at least twenty meals. And the château isn't a charity." Her hands shook like a blender set to high, and her eyes met mine. "Are you trying to sabotage us, Sophie?"

I hung my head. I couldn't even look Jane in the eyes. I hated lying. But I had to. "No," I started. "I've—"

"Been giving me more leeway and responsibilities," interrupted Phillipa. "It's my fault. Part of my training. And how dare you talk to your boss like that. This is not your château. You're just an employee."

I'd never seen Phillipa stand up to Jane. Things were definitely changing around here. And it didn't feel like it was for the better. The buzzing stress permeating the kitchen, the mistakes, intensified like a Category 5 hurricane, and I was caught in the eye of the storm.

"You clearly need more training, sister. Enough is enough," said Jane, and she raised her index finger, shaking it with fury. "Not another meal mishap."

As Jane turned on her heel, my eyes filled with tears. "Phillipa, you didn't have to do that," I said.

She placed her hand on my back. "Yes, I did. And remember rule number one—no crying in the kitchen."

"I've been breaking that rule all the time," I said, racing to the servants' entry and sinking to the floor.

Phillipa followed my every step.

"For very good reasons." She stroked my hair. "Sophie, I don't know how I would have dealt with half the crap you've gone through. But you did. You're a survivor. You *are* fearless. And honestly, and not to get too sappy, you're my idol."

I looked up, my tear-filled eyes meeting hers. "Some idol. I'm a mess."

"We are all messes in one way or the other. And all messes can be cleaned up," she said. "Do you know how long it took me to tell Jane and my parents that I was queer? I'll tell you. It took forever. Because I knew I was different at the age of twelve. And when I finally told them, I expected them to boot me out of the door. But they didn't. I finally talked to them—openly and honestly—when I was eighteen. I kept everything bottled up inside for far too long, and it killed me. And I found acceptance. You need to share your feelings with us."

"You realize I don't like relying on people," I said with shame, my shoulders caving in.

"I know. But you can rely on me, tell me anything," she said. "And we'll figure this out."

"Jane's really mad at you," I said.

"She'll get over it," she said with a shrug. "We're sisters. And she's mad at you too."

I wiped the snot dripping off my nose with my sleeve. "Honestly, Phillipa, I don't know. I feel like I've lost everything."

"No," she said. "You have me—if you trust me."

"I do," I said.

"That's the spirit." She held out her hand. "Now, get up. I know your senses will come back to you."

"How can you be so sure?"

She tapped her head twice with the index finger of her free hand. "Did you forget? I have a sixth sense."

I took her hand and she pulled me to my feet, fear racing through my veins.

A HESITANT KNOCK came on my door. I eyed the clock on my dresser. It was a little past midnight. I huffed. What problem did I have to overcome now? A septic issue? A missing dessert chef? A sanglier attack? Just feed me to the wild boars, I thought. A more forceful knock resounded.

"Come in," I said, and then let out a surprised gasp as Rémi walked into my room.

I wanted to race up to him and wrap myself in his arms, yet I stayed put in the window seat, hugging my knees to my chest. Since I couldn't sleep, I'd been staring at the stars, wishing on all of them.

Rémi sat on my bed. "We need to talk," he said.

"We do," I said, nodding my head. "We really do. You've been avoiding me."

"I haven't been avoiding you," he said, his eyes not meeting mine. "I just needed time to cool down. I was really angry, Sophie. I still am."

"Well, you shouldn't be angry with *me*," I said, my body quivering. "I didn't do anything."

His shoulders slumped. "You really didn't kiss that guy?"

"I told you that Nicolas forced that kiss on me," I said, wringing my hands. "And you were right: Paris was a really bad idea. I wish I'd never gone."

His eyes brightened as his gaze met mine. He tilted his head. "Did you just tell me I was right?"

"I did," I said. "Because you were. Paris was a nightmare."

"Tell me everything that happened," he said. He got up from the bed and sat down next to me on the window seat. He grasped my hands. "And by everything, I mean everything."

So I did. I told him about Amélie's vengeance. I told him Grand-mère had another side of her that we didn't know. I told him about O'Shea's offer and how it didn't even tempt me. His arm curled around my body and he drew me in close. I nestled into his neck, trying to breathe in his scent. Nothing. I told him everything—except for the fact that I couldn't smell or taste. I couldn't find the courage to do it. A tear slid down my cheek. With his free hand, Rémi wiped it away.

"So, no Paris?" he asked.

"Are you kidding? My life is here. And I was so excited to get back to Champvert so I could tell you I want to share everything with you," I said, my bottom lip finding a life of its own.

He placed his hand on his heart. "You were serious when you said you loved me and were ready to set the date?"

I twisted my body and crawled onto his lap, meeting his eyes. "Dead serious."

"I'm sorry for doubting you, Sophie. And if I ever see this Nicolas de la Barguelonne, I'm going to punch him in the face. A big part of me feels guilty because I wasn't there to protect you."

"I don't need protection," I said.

"Yes," he said. "Sometimes we all do. Even me. But a man isn't supposed to admit fear. We're always supposed to be strong. And, Sophie, you bring out every one of my weaknesses, because I love you so damned much."

"Je t'aime aussi, Rémi. Most of the time," I said. "But you can't just run away and get angry or lash out."

"Neither can you," he said. "Unless you're running away from an asshole like that de la Barguelonne."

"Touché."

"I'm sorry, Sophie," he said, closing his eyes. "I just love you so much."

My hands stroked his stubbled jaw, relief washing over me. "I love you too."

His arms wrapped around my waist, and he pulled me in for a kiss. First, our lips brushed softly against each other's, and then our mouths became hungrier—like we were starving, a fervent and urgent need. Our hands explored each other's backs, clinging. I yielded to his embrace, falling into his chest. Shivers made my whole body tremble, and he let out a moan. My breath came in gasps. Our kisses were usually delicious, but I couldn't taste the peppermint on his breath or smell his clean citrus scent. I pulled away.

Rémi eyed me curiously as I sat back on his thighs and gripped his shoulders. "Is something wrong?" he asked, concern knitting his eyebrows.

"Yes," I said, and he frowned, shaking his head in disbelief. "It's not what you think." My chin quivered. "Remember when I fell when we were picking cherries? Something . . . something happened to me." I took in a shaky breath. "Now I can't smell or taste anything— not even your kisses. It's my biggest nightmare come true. And my fall in Paris might have made it worse."

"And you didn't tell me?" he asked, his jaw dropped. "We're supposed to be a couple, to talk about everything."

I broke down into ragged sobs, and Rémi put his arms around me, holding me tight. I snuggled into his neck, trying to breathe him in, but couldn't. Tears rolled down my cheeks. "I can't even smell you," I said, my chest clamping up as if a tight vise squeezed it. "And I love your smell—clean with a bit of citrus, and woodsy."

Rémi stroked my chin. "I'm taking you to the doctor first thing tomorrow morning. We'll figure this out. Until then, try to sleep." He wiped away my tears with kisses.

"Are you staying?"

"Of course I am," he said.

Rémi lifted me up off the window seat and gingerly placed me in bed. He pulled me in close to his chest and rubbed my hair with a gentle hand until I stopped crying and fell asleep in his arms.

THE DOCTOR ASKED me some questions, checked my blood pressure, and sent me in for an MRI. The prognosis: a possible traumatic brain injury. The treatment: aside from monitoring my blood pressure, there was nothing he could do, no instant cure to this heart-pounding, nausea-inducing dilemma. The solution: wait.

On the ride home, Rémi gripped my hand as I stared vacantly out the window.

"I can't believe it could take up to a year for my senses to come back—if they come back at all," I said. "This is such a nightmare."

"Be positive. You'll be tasting and smelling in no time," he said.

I wasn't so sure about that. And I could kiss any dreams I had of cooking goodbye. I slumped in my seat, my knee on the dashboard, and rubbed the back of my neck. "At least you have your senses. How am I going to cook without tasting?"

"Until they come back, you have me," he said, and I grimaced. "Who else have you told?"

"Only Phillipa," I said.

"Before me?"

"We weren't exactly speaking," I said, my nose crinkling. "You were avoiding me, practically running away."

His shoulders caved. He gripped the steering wheel with one hand, the other squeezing mine. "I was wrong to be so hotheaded. And I'm never running away from you again."

"Good," I said, rocking my body. "Because I really need you. Now more than ever."

A grin lit up his face, his eyes. "Did you just say you needed me?"

"I did," I said, expecting a sexual comeback, like the one he'd said when Gustave went missing.

Instead Rémi said, "Wow, Sophie, this is a milestone for you. Part of me thought you didn't need anything from anyone, and it's nice to feel needed. I need you too."

I blurted out a laugh. "You need a hot mess?"

"Oui," he said, "the hottest mess I've ever loved."

I regarded Rémi's sweet, adoring gaze and remembered his words at the restaurant: dreams change. I hoped so.

23

this makes sense

M ONICA WAS ABOUT to take off for New York to show
O'Shea what she could do. The girls and I met her in the
driveway. After working at the château and seeing how busy we
were, she insisted on taking a taxi so we could enjoy our supposed
day off. Her eyes scanned the château, the grounds.

"I really hate goodbyes," Monica said, choking up. "No tears.
Rule number one. And, I know, we're not in the kitchen. I, uh, just
wanted to say thank you for welcoming me to Champvert."

I grasped Monica's shaky hands. "Soon, you'll be wearing glass
slippers at Cendrillon."

"I don't understand."

"Cendrillon means Cinderella in French. The glass slipper will
be yours."

Monica's eyes filled with tears. "My former restaurant was called
El Colibrí, which means 'hummingbird' in Spanish." Her lips quivered. "I named the restaurant after the animal I connected with
spiritually. My ex took that away from me."

"And now you're starting over again," I said. "I know it's tough. I've been through it too. And you can do this."

There I stood giving a pep talk, when I was still in the dumps, wondering if I'd ever be able to really cook again. For now, instead of Grand Chef, I was a senseless zombie. Monica didn't know about any of the turmoil spinning around in my head. I was going to keep it that way. If she knew what deep water I was in, she'd probably stay. At least she could follow her dreams, and I wasn't about to hold her back from doing just that.

"I'm so sorry we were so tough on you in the beginning," said Phillipa.

"I don't blame you," said Monica. "You were only protecting Sophie." She took in a deep breath, exhaled. "And being here has shown me what true friendship is all about. It's a lesson I'll never forget."

All of our lips pursed together like we were sucking on lemons. Not that I'd know the sensation now. My eyes landed on her one suitcase. "Wait, you brought three suitcases here. What about the others? Don't you want your ingredients?"

"They're yours now," she said. "So is the fig recipe. I'll send you more chipotle peppers, if you need them. My gift to you."

"You don't need to do that," I said.

"But I do," she said. "You've given me a second chance at life when I needed it. You've given me everything, Sophie. I'm really going to miss you. Thank you for everything."

"If things don't work out with O'Shea, come back here," I said, gulping and thinking, *Because I may need you to take over.* "And if they do and you need a place to stay in Paris, you can kick up your heels at my grand-mère's place."

"That is such a generous offer, but I kind of want to make it on my own," she said.

"Well, stay there until you find your own place," I said. "Marianne will hook you up with one of the guest rooms. I'd like to keep Grand-mère's suite clear. And you may have to occasionally deal with some of the staff from here. I kind of promised the apartment as a bonus."

She smiled. "Not a bad idea. I might take you up on that."

"When you see it, you're not going to want to leave," said Jane. "It's simply gorgeous."

The taxi pulled up. "I've got to bolt before I break down," she said, giving me a tight hug. "Again, thank you for everything."

"No, thank you, *babe*," I said, and we grinned.

Monica jumped into the back seat, tears streaming down her cheeks. The taxi rumbled down the long driveway. Marie, Phillipa, Jane, and I waved and blew air-kisses until she was out of sight.

"Well, that was sad," said Marie, snapping her pink bubble gum. "So, what do we do now?"

I thought about it. I wanted to stay away from the kitchen, and there was something I'd been longing to experience that would also keep my mind off my problems.

"Harvest grapes," I said, shifting my weight from one foot to the other.

"But that's hard work," said Jane.

"I know," I said. "But I've never been here this time of year. And shouldn't I know everything about the château?"

"You win," said Jane. "Let's go."

THE CHÂTEAU'S HARVEST was in full swing, the evenly spaced vines glistening with plump purple and green grapes. In addition to seasonal workers, some of the guests also picked these beauties by hand as part of the château experience. And they also got to indulge in a never-ending supply of free wine while learning about the vinification process—a win-win for everyone.

When he saw our approach, Bernard raced up to us, clippers in hand. He wore a floppy straw hat, a gray T-shirt, dirt-covered overalls, and a huge smile. "Are you beautiful ladies joining in?"

Jane pointed at me, her mouth twisted into a mock scowl. "Her idea."

Bernard beamed. "Wonderful! Wonderful! Follow me so I can set you up with baskets and clippers."

With our tools in hand and baskets latched onto our bodies like donkeys wielding twig backpacks, Bernard walked us into a row of vines, showing us how to cut. "Hold one cluster of grapes in your hand and carefully snip the whole cluster off the vine. Be careful not to damage the vine or the cluster. Once your baskets are full, take them to the sorting table. And don't pick any bad clusters with bruises. Got it?"

"Got it," we said.

Before walking away, Bernard kissed me on the cheek. "Your grand-père would be so proud."

I'd never met my grand-père and only knew stories of him. He'd died shortly after my mother had taken me to New York. I only knew that he was widely respected and helped out all of the villagers of Champvert. He'd started this world, and my grand-mère had improved upon it. And what a wonderful life it was. My grand-mère had, indeed, lived out her dreams.

The four of us set to clipping, the sun beating down on our heads. It was a good hour before the baskets were full. Jane wiped the sweat off her brow. "Well, that wasn't exactly what I had in mind for the few hours I had off. I suggest we bring these grapes to the sorting table. And then jump into the pool."

Marie whooped in agreement. "My underboobs are so sweaty.

And I hate that kind of sweat. They're sticking to my body, even when I bend over. And my back hurts in three million ways."

I looked down at my nonexistent chest. "Can you loan me a bit of yours? I'm as flat as a crêpe."

"You can have them," said Marie with a snort. "And then you'll be cursed."

Phillipa picked a grape off one of the clusters and shoved it in my mouth. I chewed. My eyes popped open wide. I reveled in the experience of the juices running down my tongue, all sticky and sweet. My heart sparked. For a moment, I stood completely motionless, and then I ran around in circles, leaping in the air. "Oh my god. Oh my god. Sweet, sweet, sweet! This is amazing. Sweet!"

I stopped twirling and faced my friends, smiling like a fool, and then I shoved another grape into my mouth.

Jane placed her hands on her hips and eyed me curiously. "What? You're acting strange. It's like you've never tasted a grape before."

"It's not just any grape," I said with unbridled enthusiasm. "It's the best damn grape I've ever had."

"Really?" said Phillipa with a squeal. "Really?"

"Yes!" I screamed.

She hugged me and then tapped her forehead twice. "I told you so."

Phillipa leapt with me and we twirled and whirled. An elderly couple wearing straw hats peeked over the next row of vines, curious and confused. Jane narrowed her eyes into a glare. She placed her hands on her hips. "Okay, you two are as mad as a box of frogs. What in the world is going on? This reaction isn't normal. It's downright bizarre. And, Sophie, you have to stop dancing before you fall down."

She was right on that account. The last thing I needed was another head injury.

"Well, I'm waiting for an explanation," said Jane.

Phillipa and I exchanged a nervous glance. Jane tapped her foot.

Marie popped her bubble gum. "Fine," I said with a guilty grin. I couldn't help but smile a little bit. "After my fall, I completely lost my senses of smell and taste. And I didn't tell anybody except for Phillipa. But now I have them back!"

"What?" said Jane, her mouth dropping in stunned horror. "That's terrifying. I can't even imagine what you've been going through. You must have been flipping out."

"I was," I said.

Jane glowered at me. "It's not just terrifying; it's very serious. And you should have told me. I've been noticing some of the meals have been off. As I recall, a few guests sent their meals back for being overly salted." She raised her voice. "And that's never happened. Not here."

"I'm sorry, Jane," I said. "I wanted to tell you. But I didn't want anybody to know. I hoped everything would work out. And it did."

"You told Phillipa," she said.

"She needed to be my taste buds, my nose, especially after the catastrophe with the meals being sent back."

"You should have told *me*," screamed Jane, storming out of the vineyard. She stopped, turned, and said, "Well, what are you waiting for? Get your butt in gear. Follow me. We're heading to the kitchen. You may know sweet, but what about other flavors?"

PHILLIPA, MARIE, AND I sat at the table as Jane slammed down ingredients one after the other, including Monica's hot sauce. She unscrewed the lid of the apricot confiture, stuck in a spoon, gathering a healthy serving, and shoved it in front of my mouth like a mother feeding a small infant.

"Eat it," she said, and I did. "And?"

"Sweet," I said, licking my lips.

"No sour?"

"No. Just sweet."

"It should be sour too. Or at least tart," she said. She opened up a jar of cornichons, small French pickles, and set it in front of me. "Well, don't just look at me. Dig in."

I dunked my fingers into the jar, pulling one out, and ate it. Nothing. No flavor. Shit. My face crumbled. Jane set one ingredient down in front of me, one right after the other. Fleur de sel was next. Nothing. Lemon peel, which was supposed to be bitter, but I tasted nothing. Finally, Jane handed me a fig. I bit into it, reveling in the texture and flavor.

"Sweet," I said glumly. I could only discern sugary tastes, when I was more of a savory girl.

Phillipa placed a hand on my shoulder. "I'm sure your other taste sensations will come back one at a time."

"They better," said Jane. "Or you can't be executive chef of this kitchen. You realize that, right?"

Of course I did. I'd been leaning on Phillipa way too hard. And it wasn't fair to her. But it finally seemed like my life was getting back on track—one small win following another. Rémi and I had made up. I could taste—at least sweet. I tilted my head back, thanking the cooking gods for answering my prayers.

"I know," I said. "Just give me a little time."

"Of course, it's your château, not mine," she said. "Until we figure out what's going on and your senses come back, we can't tell anybody. Not a word. If this gets out, we'd be destroyed."

"Exactly," said Phillipa with defiance. "Which was Sophie's plan to begin with. So you can't be mad at us."

"I'm not telling anybody anything," said Marie.

"Sophie, Phillipa," said Jane. "I hope you both realize that keeping secrets is just as bad as lying. I'm not happy with either one of you right now, but I'll get over it. In the future, keep me in the loop. We're all in this life together." She smoothed back her hair. "I have to check some guests out, then I'm off for a date with Loïc." Jane turned on her heel and ran straight into Rémi. "Sorry, I didn't see you there," she said.

Rémi excused himself from Jane and made a swift approach. He stood in front of me, blinking back his astonishment. "What's this about secrets?" he asked.

Phillipa and Marie shot me a concerned look and scrambled out of the kitchen.

"And?" questioned Rémi. His eyes blazed onto mine.

"Jane is mad that I didn't tell her about losing my senses of smell and taste. Nothing to worry about." I smiled. "I tasted sweet today, but not much else."

He flashed his brilliant smile and his dimple puckered. "Look, I'll help you find your senses, Sophie," he said, his eyes sparking mischievously. Our eyes locked and we kissed, our tongues exploring one another's. His hand ran down my back, and my legs quivered.

"How did that taste?" he asked, and pulled away from me, his hand stroking my chin.

"Sweet," I said, running my hands down his back. "Very sweet."

"I have to head over to Le Papillon Sauvage for lunch service," he said, pulling away. "And we have to stop this before I throw you on the counter. You're not working tonight. Can I come by your room? Around seven?"

"Sure," I said.

He shot me a sexy wink. "Wear something nice but practical," he said. "I have something planned."

As he bolted out of the kitchen, I yelled after him, "Rémi, you may recall, I'm not a fan of surprises."

As he left, his words echoed in the corridor. "You'll like this one."

What did he mean by practical? And what did he have planned?

24

love knots

A T SEVEN ON the nose, Rémi knocked on the door before entering my room. Per his request of wearing something practical, I wore my navy-blue shirtdress and ballet flats. Rémi smiled at me, his long eyelashes fluttering. He didn't say a word but just stood there, staring. I was beginning to get a complex.

"Is this outfit okay? I mean, you can't get any more practical than this," I asked hesitantly. "Or should I throw on a pair of jeans?"

"It's perfect. And you're perfect," he said, drumming his fingers on his thighs.

"Even with all my imperfections?" I asked, feeling nervous. What in the world was he up to? He was acting so strange and a bit jittery.

"Every single one of them, including your self-deprecating humor," he said. "Come, I want to show you something."

"What? Did you rearrange the kitchen without asking me?" I said, setting my book down and hopping off the window seat.

"No, nothing like that. I wouldn't want to suffer the fires of Sophie's wrath."

"Then what's your surprise?"

"If I told you, it wouldn't be a surprise," he said, clasping my hand. His fingers shook. In silence he led me up to the fourth floor and stopped. He pulled down a ladder from the ceiling. "Climb," he said.

"Up there?"

"Don't worry, Mademoiselle Maladroit," he said, referring to the fact that I was a klutz. "I'll be right behind you. You won't fall."

"Where does it go?" I asked nervously. "To the attic?"

"To the roof."

"The roof?" I parroted.

"Stop asking questions, Sophie, just go."

"You just want to look up my dress," I said in a lame attempt at a joke.

"I didn't think about that. But now that you've mentioned it, it's a bonus."

I fake scowled at him. He motioned for me to climb. To be safe, I kicked off my shoes, and placed a shaky hand on one of the rungs. "Go," said Rémi.

When I got to the top, I wasn't sure where I was. Tiny Christmas lights twinkled all around me, and there was a blanket spread out on a flat portion of the roof. A bottle of the château's *méthode ancestrale* chilled in a bucket. A silver bowl was filled with fruit. Wild French poppies were strewn everywhere. Rémi guided me to the blanket. We sat together for a moment, looking up at the sky.

"What are you up to?" I asked, not realizing he could be so romantic. "Seriously. What is all this?"

"I know you still think about your stars, Sophie." He smiled his fantastic smile and pointed to the sky. "This is me bringing you closer to them again. With me."

He pulled me in for a kiss, and we settled on the blanket, holding hands and looking up at the stars, my head resting on his chest as I listened to his heart beat.

"We're making a go of this, right?" he asked, and we both propped ourselves up.

I was ready to throw myself into this relationship one thousand percent. I puffed out my bottom lip into what I hoped was a sexy pout. "What do you think?"

His eyes narrowed mischievously. From his pocket, he pulled out a small velvet box. He opened it, revealing a beautiful two-carat emerald-cut diamond ring inset with pavé diamonds.

"Um, that's not Grand-mère's ring," I said with a gasp.

He let out a soft laugh. "I couldn't find it. And I noticed it wasn't on your finger."

My head dropped in shame. "I'm so sorry. I may have thrown it when we had our fight," I said. "It's in my room somewhere. I can't find it either. Believe me, I looked." I met his amused eyes. "You didn't have to get me another one."

He took my hand. "What are you saying? Are you disappointed with this one?"

"No," I said, backtracking. "Grand-mère's ring is kind of ridiculous. My tastes are a bit simpler."

"I know. I know you. Every beautiful inch of you. Plus, this ring was my mother's. I wanted for you to have a piece of her," he said, his eyes clouding up. "Well, Sophie Valroux, my sexy and beautiful chef from Château de Champvert, the love of my life, the woman keeping me on my toes, and who drives me absolutely crazy sometimes, can we finally make this official?"

I went silent.

"Sophie, I'm proposing to you for a third time. And you're not saying anything."

I tilted my head to the side. "Are you sure you want to do this? Want me?"

"I've never been more sure of anything in my entire life," he said. "Let's build the rest of our lives together, one brick at a time."

"If you put it that way," I said, tears streaming down my cheeks. "My answer is yes. Putain. Yes, yes, yes, you are my heart, Rémi Dupont."

After he slipped the ring on my finger, I gazed at it under the moonlight, an idea striking. "How do you feel about a double wedding?" I asked. "On Christmas Eve? With Walter and Robert?"

"They're getting married here?" he questioned.

"I didn't tell you?"

He laughed. "No, no you didn't," he said. "But you're telling me now."

"But wait," I said, another idea coming to mind. "We should ask Lola for her permission," I said. "I'm marrying her, too, you know."

"I can't wait to start this new chapter with you." He kissed my knuckles, his eyes lighting up. "Can I still call you 'boss'?"

I narrowed my eyes into a mock glare, my eyes glinting. I was ready. I wanted him. I wanted to fall into him. I wanted everything. I was ready to lose control. I was a woman with needs, too, and he brought the animal out in me; it was time to unleash her. "Only in bed," I said, getting up and smoothing out my dress. "Let's go."

Rémi let out a surprised gasp. "Are you serious, Sophie? Isn't that moving too fast for you?"

"I'm tired of moving slow," I said, shrugging. "Life is too short."

"Sophie," he said. "I'm going to take my time." He let out a heavy sigh. "But not tonight."

My heart jolted. I'd just offered myself to him, fully and completely, and he said no? "What? Why?"

"Believe me, I really want you right now, but I don't have protection," he said, breathing heavily.

"I do. In the drawer of my nightstand," I said while regarding his shocked expression. "Don't look so surprised. I've been thinking about ravaging you too. For quite some time. And I may have bought a box at a pharmacy in Paris when I'd realized how much I loved and wanted to be with you." I smiled and gripped his hands. "I want you so much right now."

"Oh, *mon Dieu*, I want you too," he said, his hands running through my hair. "So much."

After I managed to climb down the ladder, we headed back to my room hand in hand. We closed the door and he pulled me toward him, his woodsy scent calming me at first. It dawned on me.

"Rémi, I can smell you," I said, letting out my breath in a whoosh.

"I told you I'd help you find your senses," he said.

He kissed my neck, grasping my hair, and then kissed me so passionately it was like I hadn't seen him in years. "I've been wanting to do this all day, all year, all of my life," he said, his fingers running up and down my back as if the grooves of my spine were keys on a piano.

He pulled me down onto the bed, straddling me. As he unbuttoned my dress, he kissed my body, starting at my shoulder, then trailing down to my chest, and finally landing on my inner thighs. I let out a moan as he removed my underwear. With a skilled hand, he unhooked my bra and ran his hands over my bare breasts. The air filled with my soft sighs.

"Mon Dieu," he said with a low groan, his hands exploring every inch of me. "You are so damn beautiful."

"Don't stop," I said, my body throbbing with desire.

He kissed my neck. "I need to get undressed."

"Let me help you," I said, loosening his belt. I threw it on the floor and set to unbuttoning his shirt, running my fingers across his chest, breathing in his scent. His torso, everything about him, was rock hard, my skin tingling with want.

As Rémi wiggled out of his jeans and boxers, I fumbled through the drawer, and, once I got the package open, I slipped a condom on him. My legs wrapped around his waist, and I gripped his muscled back as he entered me, my thighs quivering, my nails digging into him. His caramel-colored eyes didn't leave mine, and I let out another moan. He was slow and methodical, passionate and deep, hitting my sweet spot. My hands moved up to his hair, and I pulled him in for a spine-tingling kiss. My body undulated, my back arched, and I met his every thrust, hungry for the fervor. And then I saw the stars again, swirling and whirling, but this time it wasn't from a fall, but from utter ecstasy. My whole body convulsed with an orgasm. I'd never had one, and, damn, the sensations snaking through my core left me close to hyperventilation.

Fifteen minutes later, we lay wrapped up in the sheets, panting, my orgasm hitting me in waves. As my heartbeat slowed down to a normal rate, Rémi's eyes locked onto mine in true adoration.

"Wow," I said, trying to catch my breath. "I can't believe I waited so long."

He grunted out a laugh. "I hope it was worth it."

Admittedly, it was the best sex of my life. Rémi took his time, kissed every inch of my body, made my legs quiver, and asked me what I wanted. Just like he was doing now. His hand ran up my thigh, and he kissed my neck. "Do you like this?"

I did.

"Je t'aime, Sophie," he said. "I can't wait to start a real life with you."

"Je t'aime aussi," I said, eyeing the ring on my finger. It sparkled in the moonlight, almost as bright as my heart.

BEFORE THE ALARM went off, I was wide-awake. I sat up in bed and inspected Rémi as if he were a slide under a microscope—his skin tanned the color of golden honey, his stubbled chin and masculine jawline, his beautiful bow-shaped lips. His breath came soft, the white sheet on my bed draped over his perfect frame, hugging his muscles in all the right places.

When he slept, he looked like a teenager, sweet, soft, and void of stress. His long eyelashes fluttered open and he gazed into my eyes. He pulled me toward him, wrapping me in his muscled arms. His skin smelled so good, like citrus combined with clean-cut grass, and so refreshing. I breathed him in, savoring his scent.

He shot me a sheepish grin. "You're so damn beautiful."

I was sure my long black hair was a tangled mess. I also wondered about morning breath. "Even in the morning?"

"Especially in the morning," he said, his hardness pressing into my thigh. "Your skin looks so beautiful shimmering in the sunlight. Come to think of it, you should never wear clothes."

"I think I'd scare the guests away with my pasty skin," I said with an insecure laugh.

"Not with those gorgeous green eyes," he said, gazing at my face. He looked at his watch. "As much as I'd like a repeat of last night, I've got to get back to Lola."

"I understand," I said, puffing my lip out in mock disappointment.

"Well, as much as I don't want you to, you should get dressed too." Rémi scrambled out of bed, standing before me wearing nothing but his tight-fitting boxers, revealing his cut body and his perfect V-shaped torso. He turned to face me as he buttoned his jeans. "Do you remember our first kiss?"

"How could I forget it?" I said. "It was damn awkward."

He huffed out a chuckle. "Was it your first?"

"Unless you count *Bear*nard," I said.

"Should I be jealous of this Bernard?"

I pointed to the stuffed animal sitting on one of the brocade chairs. "Who, him? The bear? And it's not Bernard. It's *Bear*nard. And I'm going to give him to Lola."

WHEN WE ENTERED Rémi's home, Laetitia was strapping Lola into her high chair and about to feed her a croissant slathered with strawberry jam. Jean-Marc scurried over to grab paper towels. He and Laetitia had been inseparable unless he was maintaining the grounds. Love wafted in the air, and I floated along right with it.

"Papa," said Lola with a big smile. "Tatie Sophie!"

"Bonjour, *mon petit chou*," said Rémi, bending over to kiss her. She put her strawberry hands on Rémi's face.

"You two look like you're back on track," said Laetitia, glancing at me. "I'm glad."

"Me too," I said.

"That makes three of us," said Rémi. "And we have some very exciting news to share."

Rémi crouched down to eye level and pointed to me. "Lola," he said. "How would you feel if Sophie becomes your *maman*?"

Laetitia clasped her hands over her mouth.

"Maman?" Lola questioned. "Ma maman?"

"Oui," said Rémi. "I want to marry Sophie. And she would become your *belle-mère*" (stepmother). His eyes turned toward Jean-Marc's. "Of course, if that's okay with everybody. Jean-Marc, I'd like to ask for your blessing to marry Sophie."

"Of course," he said, choking up.

I smiled. "Papa, I was wondering if you'd give away my hand in marriage."

Jean-Marc's eyes welled up with tears, as did Laetitia's. "I—I—I couldn't be a prouder father," he said, trying to find his words. "Nothing would make me happier."

I kissed him on the cheek. "Me too," I said with a laugh. "Well, apart from marrying Rémi."

All eyes shot to Lola and her strawberry-splattered face. She lifted her chin and spread out her arms to me. "*Maman* Sophie, *pas tatie*," said Lola with a smile. I scooped her up, breathing in her strawberry-scented hair as she wrapped her arms around my neck. "Un chocolat chaud, s'il te plaît, Maman."

Rémi closed his eyes, his lips twisting into a satisfied and happy smile.

Lola looked up at me with her eyes crinkled, her nose scrunched. Maybe motherhood wasn't going to be as hard as I thought it would be, because this feeling of contentment rocked my world.

"I think I can manage that," I said, smiling like a fool. In fact, I could manage a lot of things, including this wonderful life. "If it's not too early."

Rémi wrapped his arms around us. "It's never too early for a celebration."

I grinned. "Should I call Walter?"

25

unwanted guests

ONE BY ONE, flavors tickled my palate—sparking up my cooking soul. The granny brigade would jump in surprise as I shouted, "Salty!" "Sweet!" "Savory!" or "Bitter!" and they'd look around in supreme confusion as Phillipa wrapped me in a tight hug.

October turned into November, cool breezes swirling through the trees, a nice reprieve from the heat and stress of the summer, and we were still busier than ever—nonstop. We were all looking forward to when the château would close its doors and to the celebration of the double weddings—Rémi's and mine, and Walter and Robert's. The one thing I didn't think of, among a slew of other details: Who was going to cook for this occasion when I had been supposed to? I called Jane and Phillipa into Grand-mère's office to brainstorm.

"I can't cook the dishes on Christmas Eve," I said. "Along with Walter and Robert's guests, we have the entire village for the party. How much would a caterer cost?"

Jane sat up straight and leaned forward. "You mean the servers I already hired? Like last year?"

"Yes, but I had to prepare the food. They just served," I said. "And you made me shuck oysters in a black sheath when we ran out."

"We weren't exactly getting along back then," said Jane. "But we are now. You're my other demented sister."

"Mine too. Which is why Clothilde, Séb, Marie, and yours truly are handling everything," said Phillipa.

"But you're supposed to be guests," I said.

"We will be. We'll prepare whatever we can in advance," said Phillipa. "And this is our wedding gift to you. I mean, what do you give a girl who has everything? We're going to cook our hearts out with love. Saying no to us is not an option."

I flopped back on the settee, placing my feet on the coffee table. "Ugh. There's so much to plan. Walter and Robert have twenty-five guests coming, more than half of them couples, and then Nicole, Walter's mother, with her ladies who lunch. They'll need eighteen rooms. I've invited O'Shea, Monica, and Jean-Jacques Gaston. We'll have a full house." Alarm set in. "And I don't even know what I'll be wearing. Chanel?"

"Uh, no," said Jane, her face flushing. "This is your big day. You need to dress for it."

I knew Jane. "What did you do?"

"I may have designed your dress. And it may be here. It's my wedding gift to you, no arguments." She held up a finger. "Hold on. I'll be right back."

I sat motionless, thankful for my friends, for my life. Phillipa grasped my hand. She whispered, "You are going to die when you see it."

A few moments later, Jane returned with the dress, holding it out so I could step into it. The gown was made of ivory silk with an organza overlay, embellished with silver stitching cascading down to a smattering of embroidered stars. The bust of the dress crossed along my chest, thin straps with two stars resting on my collarbone, the waist tying with a silk bow, the open back dipping down, also encrusted with two stars. I glanced at my reflection in the mirror, and the woman staring back at me wasn't quite me; she was fierce, maybe even beautiful. I'd never felt that way before, but I did in this moment. This dress was perfect.

"Jane, I don't know what to say," I said, bursting into tears. "Thank you so much. Why did you do this for me?"

"No need to thank me. And you're family. Plus, I really like designing clothes." Jane tilted her head to the side. "What are you wearing to the civil ceremony?"

I hadn't even thought about it. "I'm not sure," I said, my hands fluttering to my neck.

"That's what I thought," she said. "Phillipa?"

I stood speechless as Phillipa held out a white dress with three-quarter-length sleeves, the length hitting right above the knee. The front of the dress had a boat collar, the back plunging into a deep V. Simple. Elegant. "This is going to look incredible on you, Sophie."

Jane helped me step out of the wedding dress. My body trembled with so much emotion I could barely stand. As she hung the gown up, Phillipa zipped me into the new dress.

"Like the other dress, it's like it was made for you, which they were. You look gorgeous. This dress fits you like a glove," said Jane, looking over her shoulder.

"I think she'd look amazing in a potato sack," said Phillipa.

"I concur," said Jane.

"Well," I said, biting down on my lip. "I guess we're good. I'm all set."

"Not really," said Jane. "We haven't shown you our dresses. We realize you don't think of such things and didn't ask us, but you are looking at your maids of honor. Marie is one too. Well, that and I also designed a dress for Lola. She's your flower girl."

Feeling faint from all the love, I sank down onto a settee. I sobbed, "I love you girls."

"Yeah, we know," said Phillipa. "And we love you too."

NOVEMBER WAS MY favorite time of the year because so many of the foods that stirred my cooking spirit burst into the season—mussels, oysters, and a variety of squashes exploding in yellows and oranges, including my former nemesis: the potimarron. I'd made amends with this chestnut-flavored squash, the one I'd used in the velouté that Eric had tricked me into overspicing and had gotten me fired from O'Shea's kitchen. All those struggles were in the past, and Eric was far removed from my life. Rumor had it he was living in Japan, cooking for and dating Ayasa Watanabe. A part of me wished I'd warned her about him at the Sous les étoiles gala, but I was sure Eric would show his true colors sooner rather than later. The guy didn't know how to be loyal.

But the most exciting thing happening at the château was that two of my favorite ingredients—cèpe mushrooms and truffles—were abundant this year. So were the guests. We were at ninety-five percent occupancy, amazing for the end of fall. The pool may have been closed down, but guests had new activities to choose from: skeet shooting or hunting down truffles with Rémi and his dogs, D'Artagnan and Aramis, or foraging cèpes in the forest with Phillipa and me.

Phillipa and I had just returned to the kitchen with a full basket of these beautiful mushrooms. I held a dirt-encrusted one up to my nose, breathing in its earthy aromas, happy to have all of my senses back.

"What do you want to do with these?" asked Phillipa.

"Something traditional and simple so the flavor of the mushrooms isn't lost," I said. "*Poêlée de cèpes à la bordelaise?*"

"Perfectly delicious," said Phillipa. "I'll scrub the beauties down and then grab the ingredients."

"You remember what they are?"

"Of course. Olive oil, butter, garlic, thyme, bay leaves, flat parsley, salt, and pepper," she said. "And I'm already drooling."

Phillipa set to work scraping off the mushrooms, and I pulled on some gloves, ready to shuck oysters. I had the knife in the first shell when Jane flew into the kitchen, sliding across the floor. She braced her hands on her knees. "Don't flip out, Sophie," she said.

"What now? Please don't tell me it's the septic system again."

"Worse," she said, breathless. "We had a last-minute check-in. A couple. She checked them in with her card. It's that French model Camille Charpentier."

"And what's the problem?" I asked. "I'm sure she's harmless and will only request vegetarian meals if she eats at all."

"That's not the issue. The man she checked in with is Nicolas de la Barguelonne. I'm so sorry. I didn't recognize him. He was wearing dark sunglasses."

I could feel the blood rush from my face. The oyster knife dropped from my hand, clattering on the floor. My heart pitched. "Can we ask them to leave the château?"

"That would be like poking a hornet's nest with bare hands," said Jane. "He may be ousted from his father's company, but he's still rich and powerful. Good news—they're only staying one night."

"But Rémi might shoot him," I pointed out. "He might not leave the château alive."

Per his usual habit of coming into the kitchen at the most inopportune of times, Rémi busted in on our conversation. He set a sack of truffles on the scale. "Who am I going to shoot? And why?"

"Nicolas de la Barguelonne is staying at the château," I said, cringing. "Jane didn't realize who he was when she checked him in."

Rémi's chest visibly rose and fell. He slammed his fist on the prep table. "If he takes one step toward you, says one word to you, you're right, I will kill him, and then I'll feed his scrawny, rich ass to the sangliers." He placed his hands on my shoulders. "I'm serious, Sophie. Stay clear of him."

"Believe me, Rémi, I don't want to see his smug face ever again," I said.

"Somebody needs to be with you at all times," he said. "After what he did to you in Paris, I don't trust his intentions."

Neither did I. I wondered what game Nicolas was playing now. Knowing Nicolas and his calculating methods, the slimy snake of a man was up to something.

"I'm here for Sophie," said Phillipa.

"Me too," said Jane.

"That makes three of us," said Rémi, giving me a peck on the cheek. "Promise me you'll find me if he gives you any trouble. Phillipa, Jane, you too."

"I promise," I said.

I picked up my oyster knife and washed it off, hoping Nicolas wouldn't slam it into my back when nobody was looking. When Rémi and Jane left the kitchen, Phillipa and I went back to prepping and planning the evening's meal. I thought about finding out what table Nicolas would be sitting at and adding laxatives to his dish, because nothing put someone out of commission like explosive diarrhea. But if anybody found out, the château would suffer. No, I had to keep calm, cook on, and stay out of his path.

JANE CAME INTO the kitchen at seven thirty. "It's time for you to speak to the guests," she said. "Nicolas and Camille are seated at the table by the fireplace. I'd highly suggest not making eye contact. Those two are all over one another and making some of the guests extremely uncomfortable. I heard they were practically humping in the hammam spa."

Just the thought of Nicolas and his forced kiss churned my stomach. No, for my sanity and health, I had to get out of the speech.

"Have any new guests checked in?"

"Besides them, no," said Jane. "There are those two diners, those men, I pointed out to you last night, though. They're a bit strange. Do you think they could be from Michelin?"

"Your guess is as good as mine," I said.

Although the inspectors didn't drop a fork or knife on the floor like they did in the movies, their behavior was slightly different than regular diners. Often well-dressed men in their midthirties or early forties, although there were women as well if they were dining in pairs, one usually went up to the bar and ordered a drink while waiting for the other one to arrive. When seated, one would order the tasting menu, the other à la carte and, if available, a half bottle of wine.

"Anyway, what do you want to do?" asked Jane.

I thought about it. I was going to avoid it.

"You and my chef de cuisine will do the honors and make up some excuse for why I'm not doing it tonight. Maybe that I reserve the honors for the chief member of my brigade and like sharing the joy."

"Ah, Sophie, I'm not good with those s-s-speeches," said Phillipa, stuttering a bit. "I love you. I do. But I don't think it's a good idea. I like being on the sidelines—"

"Phillipa, tonight you're on the front line," said Jane. "It's the only solution. And I'll stand beside you, help you out when you lose your focus."

Phillipa huffed and puffed. "Fine, I'll do it. But, Sophie, you owe me one."

"I owe you more than one," I said with a wink. "Jane, what time are they checking out?" After Nicolas left, I wanted to have house-keeping disinfect the room the snake was staying in—if he didn't trash it in one of his spoiled brat temper tantrums.

"I believe noon," she said.

"So they won't be at the Sunday lunch?"

"I don't think so," she said. "But you never know. Plans can change."

I MADE IT through the evening without running into Nicolas by keeping my head down in the kitchen. After service, Rémi escorted me to my room, his arm linked with mine as we headed up the servants' stairwell.

"So far, so good?" he asked. "No problems with our special guest?"

"Nope," I said. "The kitchen is off-limits. Séb guarded the door like a vicious dog. How about you?"

"I've been staying clear of everybody too," he said. "And, just so you know, I've locked up my shotguns."

We stopped in the middle of the stairwell. Rémi pressed his fore-head against mine. I inhaled his scent and wrapped my arms around his waist. "Are you staying the night with me?"

"I am," he said, batting his long eyelashes. "Laetitia and Jean-Marc are watching after Lola. I just have to head back in the morning before she wakes up."

In this aspect we were all lucky. Rémi usually put Lola down for bed at around six thirty p.m., just before the wine tasting, which gave everybody plenty of private time. Lola didn't usually wake up until seven in the morning. I didn't mind the early hours, not when I could spend my nights wrapped in Rémi's arms. Sometimes we made passionate, lift-me-to-the-heavens love. But tonight was a fall-asleep-from-stress kind of night.

IN THE MORNING, Rémi kissed me lightly on the lips, and I rubbed the sleep from my eyes.

"I'll see you later," he said. "If you're coming to the lunch."

"I am, but I'll be a bit late," I said. "Jane said the asshole is checking out at noon. I'll hunker down in here until the coast is clear."

"Good idea. I'll be happy when this weekend is over and he's gone. Je t'aime," he said, blowing me a kiss.

"Je t'aime aussi," I said, my eyes fluttering back to a close.

A few hours later, I woke up to get ready for the day. It was the end of November, and this was the last Sunday lunch of the season before the weather got too cold. After taking a shower and my time, I sat in the window stroking Étoile and watching the staff set up while keeping an eagle eye out for Nicolas. Rémi manned the méchoui, Gustave sipping from his bottle of pastis by his side. The plan? Jane was going to shoot me the okay sign once Nicolas and his supermodel of the day checked out.

Around twelve thirty, Jane and Phillipa waved their arms, alerting me that the coast was clear. I set Étoile down on the cushion of the window seat, brushed her fur off my Chanel skirt suit, and, breathing a sigh of relief, practically skipped downstairs. The moment I set foot on the terrace, a rough finger tapped me on the back.

"There's my favorite chef," said a man's voice. "We've been wondering where you were."

With dread, I turned to face Nicolas and Camille. She wore a dress so sheer you could see her nipples. He wore a designer suit, a smug-ass smile, and his nauseating cologne, which was so strong I wished I didn't have my sense of smell back.

"I thought you checked out," I said.

"What? And not see you before we left? Our car is waiting in the driveway," said Nicolas.

"Why the hell are you here?" I asked.

He popped his lips, shrugged nonchalantly. "I wanted to see why somebody would be so stupid as to say non to me." He eyed the grounds, the château. "Don't get me wrong, this country life isn't what I expected, but you could have more in Paris."

Camille eyed me up and down, then turned to Nicolas. "You were right. Her meals are delectable."

"Thank you," I said, turning to leave. "I'm sorry. I have to go mingle with the other guests."

Nicolas latched a sweaty hand onto my wrist. "Just hear me out. I want to invest in the château," he said. "And you. In the end, I always get what I want."

No, this guy was too much.

"The château is a family business," I said, ripping my arm from his grasp. "Do not manhandle me. My answer is no. I'm not for sale."

"But you don't have any family left," said Nicolas, raising an eyebrow.

The next few moments blurred together into one messed-up vision. A fist flying into Nicolas's nose. A loud crack. Blood splattering on Camille's dress. Rémi putting his arm around me. Jane, Phillipa, and Marie racing up to see what the commotion was all about. The clicks of cameras. A nightmare.

"This is private property. You're no longer guests of the château. Leave now," said Rémi as Nicolas scrambled up from the ground. "And stay away, far away from my fiancée, or I'll hunt you down."

Jane, Marie, and Phillipa flanked my sides, supporting my shaky body. Phillipa hissed to Nicolas, "You're wrong. Sophie has a family. She has all of us. And her dad."

I couldn't help but smile. What Phillipa said was true. I had everything.

"He broke my nose," said Nicolas, holding his hand up to his face, blood pouring down like a waterfall. "I'm going to press charges against you, all of you, you pieces of merde."

"Go ahead," said Rémi. "We may not be as wealthy as you are, but we're not doing so bad. You can try to destroy us, but if you know Sophie as well as I do, you know she fights back. And hard. Believe me. Nothing, not you, not me, will stand in her way. You're the only one with a reputation to lose—and from what I've read, most people think you're the scum of the earth."

Camille walked up the steps. "I'm out of here." She stopped and looked over her shoulder. "I'm sorry, Sophie. I should have known. Small dick, small mind."

"I do not have a small dick," screamed Nicolas, his face turning red.

The guests from the Sunday lunch clasped their hands over their mouths. I felt like I was the star of a B movie. Who were these people? Cartoon characters?

"Oh yes, you have a small penis. The smallest one I've ever seen," said Camille, winking at me. "And you think with it. Now, take me back to Paris so I can get rid of you. That is, unless you want my Instagram to blow up. Don't forget. I have pictures of your cornichon."

Nicolas raced after Camille. "You salope, those pictures are private."

Camille placed her hands on her skinny hips. "For now," she said.

I had to give Camille credit when it was due; she wasn't a brain-dead model, she was fierce. As they left the château, Nicolas screaming obscenities at Camille, the five of us stood immobile for a few minutes, jaws dropped, the chatter of the guests and villagers ringing in our ears.

Rémi was the first to speak. "Mon Dieu, punching him in the face felt so good."

"I wish I'd done it," I said.

Rémi rubbed his knuckles. "No, you're not that kind of fighter," he said. "I know you don't need me to protect you. But I'd do that all over again."

I kissed him on the temples. "You're right. And I didn't have my knife to cut off his balls."

Phillipa snorted. "I don't think he has any."

"Do you think we're done with that messed-up family?" I asked.

Jane grinned. "I'm thinking a big, fat yes and that we should celebrate. Some sparkling wine?"

I needed something stronger after that crazy scene.

"No," I said. "Monica left a stellar bottle of tequila here."

Phillipa and Marie launched into the famed arm-pumping dance, similar to the horrid flossing dance phase, while singing the Champs. "Dah-dah-dah-dah duh. Tequila."

Jane met my eyes. "No dancing, Sophie—"

Rémi cut her off. "Don't worry, Jane. This time, if Sophie falls, I'll catch her. And she deserves a stiff drink." He pulled me in for a kiss. "I don't care if people are watching. Je t'aime, Sophie Valroux."

At that moment, I was surrounded by the people who saw me for what I was, who accepted me for what I was, even when I vacillated with self-doubt. Grand-mère would have been proud. I felt her spirit growing stronger inside me every day. And then . . . a dragonfly flew over my head, circled, and landed on my shoulder.

IV

winter

PERFECT PEAR-INGS

The only real stumbling block is fear of failure. In cooking you've got to have a what-the-hell attitude.

—JULIA CHILD, PIONEERING AMERICAN CHEF, TELEVISION PERSONALITY, AND AUTHOR CELEBRATED FOR BRINGING FRENCH COOKING TO THE AMERICAN PUBLIC

hark hear the
marriage bells

IN MID-DECEMBER, THE château finally closed its doors to the public, which meant no guests, no cooking—just freedom; long, sexy naps with Rémi; hanging out with my friends; and making last-minute plans for the Christmas Eve double wedding. There hadn't been a word from Nicolas de la Barguelonne and his intimidation tactics. And, save for a tabloid picking up on her divorce and the closing of her restaurant, no news on Amélie. Life was grand.

Technically, Walter and Robert were just celebrating their nuptials at the château, but they wanted to bring a bit of magic to their union, transforming it from a bland ceremony at the unimpressive and sterile city clerk's office in New York to a wonderful party here. They couldn't tie the knot officially in France due to laws and never-ending blue, white, and red tape—unless one of them moved here and became French. So yeah, not an option for either one of them. Alas, Walter and Robert were not allowed to have their relationship legitimized at the mairie of Champvert, a ceremony necessary for the marriage of Rémi and me to be recognized by the French government. We were going to keep this event, which took around fifteen minutes, along with a religious ceremony at Champvert's local church, limited to a small crowd of our closest friends, and set the event for the day before the big celebration.

Snow dusted the grounds of the château, making it all magical like the prettiest of snow globes. In a way, it was an oxymoron—most people came alive in spring or summer, but apparently winter floated my boat. The leaves crumbled and cracked underneath my feet, and with each step I took, my soul awakened. I was a savory kind of girl. And I was going to savor every moment.

The fireplaces in the château roared, flickering with orange flames, and I flickered, too, happy to have my senses back, to smell and taste everything, this life, and, most of all, happy to have Rémi by my side and to curl up to him. I watched Lola coloring in her books on the floor. I kissed Rémi on his cheek.

"I'm heading out," I said, brushing off my hands on my jeans. "You coming?"

"Where? You don't know how to drive," he said.

"To the Christmas market, of course, and you're taking me," I said. "I need to pick up the ingredients for the thirteen desserts. And I thought Lola could visit with le Père Noël."

Lola's eyes went wide. She whispered, "Le Père Noël," and then she hopped up and danced.

"Let's go," said Rémi with a laugh. "I'll grab our coats."

Phillipa and Marie interrupted, followed by Jane. "We're coming too," they said.

"It's a family event," I said with a smile. "But, Jane, I thought you didn't like the market."

She popped her lips. "What can I say? I'm a changed woman." She grinned. "Thanks to you. And thanks to Loïc."

"Change is good," I said. "Believe me, I know."

AFTER THE MARKET, I was unwinding with Phillipa, Jane, and Marie. We all sank into the warm water of the Jacuzzi, letting the jets massage our backs. Grand-mère had renovated the entire downstairs into a hammam spa decorated with intricate blue, green, and ivory Moroccan tiles, complete with two small pools, the bubbling Jacuzzi, and private rooms overflowing with orchids and set up with massage tables. Palm trees gave the space a tropical vibe. Out of season, the staff could enjoy a slice of blissful heaven.

"Oh my god," said Marie. "This break is just what I needed. When do we start up service after Christmas?"

"April," said Jane.

"What do I do until then?" she asked.

"Whatever you want," I said.

"Can I still stay in the clock tower?" asked Marie.

"Of course," I said. "You're a full-time employee with a contract."

Marie blew out a sigh of relief. "Thank god, because I don't have anywhere else to go."

"I'm staying with you," said Phillipa. "As much as I love my parents, I see them enough. I'll stick around too. Maybe we can take a few road trips, see more of France?"

Marie gripped Phillipa's hand. "That would be fantastic."

"Sophie, did you want to have a bachelorette party?" asked Jane, wiggling her brows. "Could be fun."

"Only if you invite the granny brigade," I said, and Jane splashed me. "Seriously, I don't want a wild night. Or penis straws.

Or a cheesy male stripper. Why don't we consider this my bachelorette party?"

"Like right now?" asked Phillipa.

"Yes," I said.

The three gals scrambled out of the Jacuzzi, grabbing towels.
"Wait here," said Jane. "We'll be right back."

They disappeared, leaving me wondering what they were up to.
I closed my eyes and let the jets wash away the past eight and a half
months of tension, completely oblivious when Rémi slipped down
next to me. He pulled me onto his lap, nibbled on my ear. "I was
hoping to find you here," he said, planting a delicious kiss on my lips.

"Did you just eat an orange?" I asked.

"I did," he said. "I forgot how keen your sense of taste is."

"I'm so glad to have it back. Because you taste divine," I said, and
then our lips locked together.

Before things got too hot and heavy, Phillipa, Jane, and Marie
returned, holding a wrapped gift box and a few bottles of the château's sparkling wine. Jane set the box down and placed her hands
on her hips. "Rémi, you have to leave," she said, pointing to the door.

He frowned. "Why? I want to spend time with my future wife."

"She'll be yours after the wedding. Right now, she's ours. We're
celebrating her *enterrement de vie de jeune fille*. No future husbands or
men allowed."

Burial of the life of a young girl. How poetic. I crawled off Rémi's
lap, laughing. "Well, you heard Jane. Go," I said, shrugging. "It's my
burial."

His chest rose and fell. "Fine," he said. He kissed me on the lips
and hopped out of the Jacuzzi. "Just don't get too crazy."

"I'll see you tomorrow," I said.

As he left, Marie hopped over to the Bose sound system and
cranked up the volume, playing Britney Spears's "Till the World

Ends." "We made you a playlist," she said, wiggling her hips. "Now hop out and open our gift."

"Don't hop. And don't dance," said Jane. "The last thing we need is for you to fall and break something before your wedding."

I was never going to live my klutziness down. Or the day I'd dropped it like it was hot. "What if I just move my shoulders?" I asked as I carefully exited the water. I shimmied awkwardly. "Like this."

Phillipa spit out a laugh as I grabbed a towel and dried off. She handed me a card. "Good thing the housekeeping staff chipped in and bought you dance lessons."

In less than two seconds, Phillipa placed a veil with the words "Bride to Be" encrusted with rhinestones on my head, along with a ridiculous sash she threw over my body. Jane popped open a bottle of sparkling wine and poured. Marie ushered me to sit down on one of the loungers. The music changed from Britney to R.E.M.'s "It's the End of the World as We Know It." The playlist's theme was transparent.

"Well, don't just sit there grinning like a fool," said Jane, plopping a box on my lap. "Open your present."

I tore the wrapping paper off the package to reveal a box with the Aubade logo, the finest French lingerie manufacturer, along with the word "*Tentations*." I set the lid to the side to discover a white lace bodysuit, a white lace matching bra and panties with garter belt set, and a sexy black baby doll, or *nuisette*, with pink embroidered flowers.

"You're going to be one sexy bride," said Jane. "The bodysuit is for the civil ceremony. The others, well, for the celebration. Rémi can't see these beforehand. Hide them."

In silence, I ran my fingers across the delicate lace, tears of happiness streaming down my cheeks.

"Don't you like them?" asked Phillipa.

"I love them. They're beautiful," I said, kissing each of them on the cheeks. "You've all done way too much for me."

Marie wiggled her brows and raised her glass. "Here's to sexily-ever-after."

"But wait. There's more," said Jane. "Something old, something new, something borrowed, something blue."

Phillipa handed me the sapphire necklace I'd given her, pushing it in my palm. "You have the something new now. This is the old, borrowed, and blue."

I took a step back, my eyebrows furrowed with confusion. "But I gave that to you."

"Yeah, I know. I didn't say I was giving it *back* to you. It's a loaner," said Phillipa with a smirk. "I think it's time for that group hug."

The four of us stood up and brought it in. "Merci," I said. "For everything."

Madonna's "Lucky Star" blared from the speakers and we all sang along. The last time I'd heard this tune, my life had exploded like an overcooked soufflé with a bomb hidden in it. We'd been waiting to hear about O'Shea's third star coming in. But we hadn't gained one; we'd lost one, the brigade placing the blame on me, and I'd been sent packing.

This time, I knew things would work out. They already had. I wasn't waiting for the other shoe to drop; I was barefoot, and it couldn't. The only thing troubling me was that I'd never even been to a wedding, let alone planned one. The music changed to a slower song I didn't know. We sat down, and Jane poured us shots of tequila.

"Let's keep this party going," she said.

"On parties, I don't know what to do for a wedding," I said. "What about flowers?"

"Already taken care of," said Jane.

"Favors for the guests? And villagers? And the staff?"

"I found these beautiful silver dragonfly paperweights." Jane pulled one from out of nowhere, placing it in my hand. "What do you think about this? They're seventy euros each. And we'll need over two hundred of them. Should I order them?"

"They are perfect," I said. "And I seriously don't know what I'd do without you."

"We don't know what we'd do without you," said Phillipa.

FOR THE NEXT week, everybody pitched in to prepare the château for the Christmas Eve wedding celebration. Rémi set up the thirty-foot-tall tree and hung all the lights, me eyeing his ass when he was on the ladder. We'd been sharing dinners together but not our bed, me wanting to build up the anticipation for the big night when we were husband and wife. He wasn't too happy about this but agreed. He pulled me to the side one day.

"Where did you want to go on our *voyage de noces*?" he asked.

Our honeymoon. I hadn't really thought about it. "Anywhere you'd like," I said.

I was looking forward to an actual vacation, maybe somewhere tropical. In my mind, Paris most definitely didn't count.

"I have a few ideas. Somewhere warm. A place where we don't have to wear clothes," he said.

"Great minds think alike," I said.

"You know this idea of yours? Not sleeping together again until our wedding night? It's driving me nuts." He held up a spherical blue Christmas ornament. "This is me."

"It's only six more days," I said, batting my eyelashes. "And then I'm all yours."

"It's going to be the longest six days of my life."

Lola scrambled up to us, followed by Laetitia and Jean-Marc. Lola tugged on my skirt. "After you and Papa get married, you will really be ma maman?"

I swooped Lola up. "Yes, I'll be your belle-mère."

Her head bobbed up and down with confused happiness. She wrapped her little arms around my neck, squeezing it. I breathed in her baby powder fragrance and her strawberry-scented hair. "Maman," she said. "Je t'aime."

"Je t'aime aussi, ma petite puce," I said.

Laetitia's eyes clouded with tears, her smile thankful and big. It meant a lot for her to know her granddaughter was in good hands. Before she broke down, she cleared her throat. "Rémi, Sophie," she said, "our wedding gift to you is your voyage de noces. We just overheard you talking about it and had to step in before you did anything. I hope the Seychelles will work out for you, because the trip is already booked."

Both of our mouths unhinged. The lyrics to Julien Doré's "Paris-Seychelles" ran through my head, but replacing Paris with Champvert. I envisioned myself swimming with giant sea turtles, skinny-dipping with Rémi, and making love on the beach under a palm tree with ocean breezes blowing through our hair, the aroma of coconut oil. I was already looking forward to dipping my toes into crystal-clear waters.

"It's too much, Laetitia," said Rémi. "I'll pay you back."

Jean-Marc slugged him on the arm. "No, you won't. Don't forget, Sophie is my daughter. And I want to do this for both of you."

I set Lola down and kissed my father on the cheek. "Thank you, Papa."

His eyes welled up. "You are a wonderful daughter. And you make me so proud. So beautiful, kind, and talented."

"Don't forget you created me," I said, squeezing his shoulder. I turned to Laetitia and we exchanged les bises.

Lola clasped one chubby hand over mine. She pointed to the tree and then to the boxes of ornaments with the other one. I picked up on the hint. "Do you want to help decorate?" I asked.

"Mm-hmm," she said.

"Hold on," I said, and I walked into the salon to put on Christmas carols, feeling holly jolly myself.

Soon, the magic of the season resounded, the château sparkling with beautiful decorations and lights. Outside, a light dusting of snow covered the grounds. All of this magic—this château, this family, this life, and this love—was mine. As I hung a blown-glass dragonfly on the tree, I felt my grand-mère's strength coursing through my veins, and I knew her legacy, everything she taught me, would live on. I once thought I didn't deserve any of this, feelings of unworthiness rocking my mind. But the truth was, we all deserved love, even me.

27

the stars are falling

ON DECEMBER 23, Jane wandered into my bedroom at around nine a.m. "Sophie, you have a call," she said.

I'd slept in, nice and comfortable, with Étoile curled up in my arms. Cooking at the château for the season had been beyond exhausting, and I could have slept for weeks. Phillipa said I could hibernate in the winter; that was exactly what I wanted to do, at least for a few more hours. I wanted to be refreshed, alive, and awake on my wedding day. "Can you take a message? I'll call whoever it is back."

Jane nodded her head with a slow no, her eyes wider than I'd ever seen them. She covered the mouthpiece and whispered, "I think you might want to take this. It's Michelin."

I bolted upright, no longer sleepy. "What?"

Étoile let out a mew and jumped off the bed. I didn't want to get my hopes up. This could either be good news for Les Libellules or bad news for Le Papillon Sauvage. Probably bad news, I thought. I gripped the sheets in my hands.

"You heard me," she said, thrusting the phone in my hand. She sat down on the edge of my bed as I tried to find my voice.

"Bonjour," I said, trying to remember my full name and not drop the phone. "This is Sophie Valroux de la Tour de Champvert."

"Bonjour, madame, this is Pierre-Louis Dubois, and I'm calling from Michelin."

My heart pounded. My throat constricted. I managed to squeak out, "Oui."

"I'm sorry to disturb you during the holiday season, but you may know that France's red guide releases in January."

"Oui," I said, being a one-word wonder. I regained my composure, sitting up straighter, hoping I wasn't breathing too loud. "Does this have to do with Le Papillon Sauvage and its Bib Gourmand status?"

Jane leaned into me, eavesdropping on the conversation. I gripped the phone in one hand, her hand in the other.

"Non," he said. "This is a courtesy call for your other restaurant, Les Libellules." He paused, and I almost had a heart attack. "I'm pleased to inform you that you are on the rising stars list. I'm thrilled to welcome you to the Michelin family. Les Libellules has achieved its first star."

Oh my god. I was part of the one percent of female chefs to be starred. I'd achieved my dream. I let go of Jane's fingers to cover the scream that was about to escape my mouth. Grand-mère had been right. The stars were falling right into my lap. Jane muffled her excitement by pushing her face into one of my pillows.

"Madame, are you there?" he asked.

"Yes, I'm here," I said, my voice quivering. "Merci. I'm beyond thankful. Achieving stars has always been a dream of mine."

Monsieur Dubois chuckled. "Dreams do come true sometimes. Merry Christmas, and have a safe and joy-filled holiday season."

"*Merci,*" I said. "*De même et bonnes fêtes.*"

The line clicked to a close. Jane flopped down onto my bed, kicking her feet with excitement. And we screamed so loud Étoile nearly jumped out of her orange-and-cream fur. She hid under the bed as Jane and I rolled around on it, yelping out obscenities.

"Putain! Putain! Putain," I said. "I can't believe it. I can't believe it."

"Believe it," said Jane.

Phillipa and Marie skidded into my room. "What's going on?" asked Phillipa. "Is something wrong? We heard screaming. Are you okay? Did somebody die?"

"Nobody died," said Jane. "Sophie just found out she received her first Michelin star."

More window-rattling screams.

We jumped on my bed in circles, holding hands, until we were breathless.

"One down, two to go," I said. "And I achieved this crazy dream of mine with you gals by my side."

WALTER, ROBERT, WALTER'S mom, Nicole, and her ladies who lunch arrived at the château, followed by O'Shea, Jean-Jacques Gaston, and Monica. As the drivers unloaded the luggage, Rémi led everybody into the salon, where Jane, Phillipa, Marie, and I waited for a glass of sparkling wine and appetizers.

When Nicole walked in, she linked her arm with mine and whispered, "I really wish Walter had married you. But, alas, he didn't. At the very least, Robert is growing on me. He has great fashion sense if you ignore his silly ascot."

She and her ladies who lunch were not only dressed the same way in cashmere sweaters, knee-length skirts, kitten heels, and pearls, they all wore their hair the same way, bobbed and polished. Save for the varying hair colors, they could have been over-fifty quintuplets.

"I heard that, Mother," said Walter with a grin. "The château looks outstanding, Sophie. And so do you. I've missed you so much."

Walter had donned his conservative yet fashionable attorney style, wearing a Brioni suit with suspenders and his trademark Façonnable shirt. My eyes darted to Robert. He was dressed exactly the same way, save for an ascot with a Christmas print. I missed my Sunday movie days with Walter, when we'd go to a theater to watch French films or chill out with a glass of red wine while listening to Édith Piaf and Nina Simone. After I'd accepted his proposal to be his fake fiancée to throw his mother off and moved in with him, we'd just gotten closer. And now things had changed. We were both living our lives out in the open.

I smiled. "Right back at you."

"Ready to get hitched?" he asked.

"I am," I said. "And sorry to have hijacked your celebration."

"It just makes the day so much better," said Robert, sneaking up on us.

"I can't believe everything that's happened," I said. "It's crazy."

"But it's a good crazy," said Robert, kissing me on the cheeks. "And we all deserve it."

As one of our servers opened a bottle and served the guests, Monica wandered over to us, and I introduced her to my friends, explaining we'd settled our differences and how she'd pulled through for me.

I grinned. "Happy with O'Shea?"

"We've had our moments, and he's flipped out a few times, but it's all under control and we've come to a mutual understanding," she said, embracing me. "Thanks again. For everything. And I'm moving to Paris in a few months. We'll be closer."

Before we toasted, O'Shea and Jean-Jacques joined us for the lovefest.

"I feel like a proud father, Sophie," said O'Shea, his voice catching.

"Thank you for inviting me," said Jean-Jacques with a gulp. "I feel Odette's spirit, and coming here just reminds me that it was better to have loved once than never at all."

"She loved you too," I said, taking his hand in mine.

He smiled wistfully. "I know," he said. "She brought you into my life. I'm so very happy for you and your stars. Santé," he said, and we all clinked glasses.

After making the rounds, I looked at my watch. "Excuse me, everybody. I have to get ready for the civil ceremony. The housekeeping staff will get you situated in your rooms. The cars for the mairie will leave here promptly at four p.m. Merci."

Phillipa and Jane followed me out of the salon. Jane let out a squeak. "This is so exciting. I love weddings," she said as we entered the elevator.

IN ADDITION TO the crowd from the salon, Laetitia, Lola, Clothilde, Bernard, Séb, the granny brigade, and, of course, Rémi awaited my arrival at the mairie. Apparently, even Gustave and Ines sat in attendance, as I learned from Phillipa's text. Oddly, he didn't have his bottle of pastis in hand. Along with Phillipa's loaner necklace, I'd decided to embellish my white dress with the diamond pin with the three stars that Olivier had given to me. Because *pourquoi pas?* Jane put the final changes on my hair, which was styled into a loose chignon, and makeup—another bonus of having a fashionista friend.

Nerves set in as the car approached the mairie. I was really doing this. I was marrying Rémi, my childhood sweetheart.

Jean-Marc clasped my hand. "You look beautiful, Sophie," he said.

"I'm feeling a bit nervous," I said, my heart pounding.

"That's understandable. It's a big life-changing day," he said. "Just breathe."

We stood in the doorway, me peeking over my father's shoulder. Our portly mayor wore a navy-blue suit with a blue, white, and red sash and his trademark walrus-like mustache. He stood behind a large wooden table, facing Rémi, who sat in a chair on the other side. I made my grand entrance, led by my father, and took my place beside Rémi. Rémi looked extraordinarily handsome in his crisp white shirt and black tailored suit. He smiled his dimpled smile, flashing those beautiful white teeth, his eyes sparking with happiness. We gripped each other's hands as the guests, my adoptive family, took photo after photo and the mayor read the French civil code. Soon after, Rémi and I signed the *livret de famille*, or marriage booklet, which our witnesses, my father and Laetitia, also signed. I glanced over my shoulder. Tears of happiness slid down Phillipa's, Jane's, Marie's, and Clothilde's cheeks.

"*Les bagues?*" asked the mayor.

My eyes widened. Rings? I hadn't thought of getting rings. Of course we needed them. We were in the process of getting married. I shot Rémi a panicked look. He winked and pulled out a box from his coat pocket. He opened it and placed it on the table. Two platinum bands were nestled in black velvet. Rémi nodded. I slid my engagement ring off and held out my left hand. Rémi slipped a wedding band onto my finger, and I did the same for him.

"*Vous pouvez embrasser la mariée,*" said the mayor, and Rémi pulled me in for a passionate kiss. The crowd cheered.

Lola ran up to us. "Maman, Papa," she said, and my heart soared. "*J'ai faim.*"

Everybody laughed.

"Ma puce," said Rémi, swooping up Lola. "We'll get you something to eat after the other ceremony."

Rémi, being the good Catholic boy he was (save for being a sinner in bed, which I often teased him about), wanted our marriage to be recognized not only by the state but also in the eyes of God. Our crowd of around twenty-five headed across the street, where Father Toussaint waited in front of the small stone church, the bells ringing. The moment I stepped into the church I felt my grand-mère's presence. Something told me she was very, very happy. And so was I.

I WOKE UP early, tucked into Rémi's arms.

Last night's celebration was going to be tame compared to what we had in store on this joyful Christmas Eve. The mayor and Father Toussaint would perform a short ceremony for over two hundred guests, followed by the buffet, cocktails, and dancing. We were starting earlier this year—at six p.m. I should have fallen back asleep, but, all wired up, I couldn't.

Rémi pulled me in closer. "*Bonjour, ma femme*," he said, his voice a lazy whisper. "Je t'aime."

I snuggled into his embrace. "Good morning, husband."

"We need to talk about something important," he said.

Oh no, I thought. What was he going to drop on me now? I sat up, my spine tingling with fear. "What?"

"Where do you want to live? At my place or the château?"

As I blew out a sigh of relief, the answer came easily. I felt more comfortable at Rémi's charming home, and it would give me time away from the workplace. "Your house," I said.

"Good," he said. "I was hoping you'd say that. I talked to Laetitia and she'd be willing to move out, giving us our space. Of course, she'd still take care of Lola."

"Where would she go?"

"She'd move in with your father," he said.

"The clock tower is too small. That wouldn't be fair to either of them, especially with Jane, Phillipa, and Marie breathing down their necks," I said, a thought coming to mind. "What if they move into Grand-mère's suite? I mean, nobody is using it. We could keep my room for us, if needed."

"Are you sure?" he asked. "I thought you wanted to preserve her memories and keep her room like a shrine."

I bit down on my bottom lip.

"I want to focus on the future," I said. "She's living on in my memories and photographs, not a stuffy room." I curled into his embrace. "We'll move her things to my room, though—at least the meaningful stuff."

"You're right. And good idea," he said just as Étoile jumped on the bed, settling on my legs. Rémi pointed. "But what do we do with your cat? D'Artagnan and Aramis—"

"We'll figure something out," I said.

I was about to scramble out of bed when Rémi pulled me back down, rolling on top of me. "Not so fast, my beautiful wife."

getting into the spirit

A S THE STAFF set up for the evening, the château rolled in waves of madness and mirth. Walter and Robert's guests had taken over the hammam spa, giving Nicole and her ladies who lunch an eyeful. Around eleven in the morning, I wandered into the kitchen. Phillipa and the rest of the brigade moved like clockwork, chopping, slicing, and shucking. I felt useless.

"What can I do?" I asked.

"Nothing," said Phillipa, pointing. "Out of this kitchen."

"Please give me something to do," I said.

"Relax," she said. "That's an order. I'm the chef of the day."

My eyes scanned the Christmas Eve menu, written on the chalkboard in Phillipa's handwriting.

CHRISTMAS EVE MENU

Foie Gras with Caramelized Apples

*Salmon with Lemon, Cucumber, and Dill, served on
Small Rounds of Toasted Bread*

Escargots de Bourgogne

Oysters Three Ways

Oysters with a Mignonette Sauce

Oysters with Pimento Peppers and Apple Cider Vinegar

*Oysters Rockefeller, deglazed with Pernod, served with Spinach,
Pimento Peppers, and Lardons*

Sophie's Spiced Langoustes (Spiny Lobster) à l'Armoricaine

AND

*Crayfish and Shrimp with a Saffron-Infused Aioli
Dipping Sauce*

AND

Moules à la Plancha with Chorizo

LA SALADE ET LE FROMAGE
Selection of the château's cheeses

LE DESSERT
Three varieties of les Bûches de Noël
AND
Marie's Wedding Cake

Phillipa had kept up with the traditional menu, only adding Marie's cake. Surely I could help with my spiced *langoustes à l'armoricaine*.

Ignoring Phillipa's order, I made my way to the walk-in, bumping into Monica. "What are you doing here? You're a guest."

"I'm helping out, babe," said Monica, ushering me back into the kitchen. "I'm not the one celebrating her marriage tonight."

Monica linked her arm with mine, and we made our way back into the kitchen, laughing.

Marie positioned herself in front of her station, hiding her creation. "Really, Sophie, it's super-bad luck to see the wedding cake before it's presented."

I held back a laugh. "You've got it all wrong. It's bad luck for the groom to see the bride in her wedding dress."

She shrugged. "Mine must be a French superstition. Yours is American. We've got everything covered. Go to the spa or something."

"I can't," I said. "Walter and his tribe took it over, and they're singing at the top of their lungs. It's not exactly relaxing."

My three friends pointed to the doorway. "Go," they said.

"Fine," I huffed.

I shuffled out of the kitchen, wondering what I was going to do with myself for the next six hours. With a sigh, I climbed up the steps, making my way to my room, and I flopped on my bed. Étoile joined me. I stared at the ceiling, thinking about my grand-mère, my mother, and love, and then I drifted off to sleep.

Jane, Phillipa, and Marie barged into my room at around four, wearing emerald-green silk dresses in varying cuts. As my eyes focused, Phillipa shook my shoulder. "Get up, sleepyhead. You have two hours to get ready, and we'd like to get some shots in."

"Shots?" I asked. "I don't want to drink. I just woke up."

"No, you silly girl. The shots with the photographer I hired," said Jane. "Oh, and meet your hairdresser."

"I really passed out hard," I said, sitting up, pieces of my hair sticking to my lips.

"No wonder. This place is a volcanic center of activity," said the photographer, eyeing the Aubade box on the dresser. "Okay, princess, get up and get into your sexy lingerie. We'll do some boudoir shots."

The hairdresser rubbed her hands together with glee. "I can't wait to make you gorgeous. Just look at her hair."

For a good hour, the hairdresser poked, prodded, and preened me. She twisted my hair into a loose updo, sticking white roses and baby's breath into my locks, the photographer capturing each step with her camera. Finally, Jane helped me into the dress.

"Wow," said Phillipa with a gasp, staring at me. "You look absolutely gorgeous. Like you've fallen from the stars."

"She does," said Marie, and everybody nodded in agreement.

I hooked the necklace Rémi had given me around my neck. And then I took a good look at myself in the full-length mirror. What I saw shocked me. In this glorious dress, the way the silver threads sparkled, I felt like I was sparkling, too, like I had metamorphosed from a caterpillar into a wild butterfly. It was then that I found my own spirit insect—probably Grand-mère's plan all along. Le Papillon Sauvage. Me.

"You've come a long way, baby," said Phillipa.

"You know what?" I said. "I have."

Jane popped open a bottle of the sparkling wine, handing me a glass. "Cheers to you," she said.

Before my father arrived to escort me downstairs, the photographer took a slew of shots of the girls and me, along with a few close-ups of all the details, like my shoes. A knock came at the door. Jane dashed for it, opened it, and retrieved a large box. "Your bouquet is here. And ours."

Another detail I'd overlooked.

"I hope you like it," said Jane.

I peeked into the box, stunned by glorious beauty—a huge bouquet of white roses and calla lilies, adorned with shimmering pine cones and flowing with earthy greenery for me, and smaller versions for my friends. My hands fluttered to my heart.

"What?" said Jane. "Every bride needs a bouquet. So do her bridesmaids. I know you didn't ask us because you don't think of such things. We kind of volunteered on our own. And, like I told you, Lola is your flower girl. She'll be throwing white rose petals from a silver basket."

"Were you a wedding planner in a past life?" asked Marie.

Jane grinned. "Actually, I was. It's the reason Sophie's grand-mère hired me."

"She's a woman of many talents," said Phillipa.

"That she is," I said, giving Jane a hug. "Thank you. You've just made this night all the more special."

"Just part of the château experience," said Jane with a sly wink, and I bit down on my lip.

Phillipa nudged my shoulder. "Don't get all weepy on us. You'll mess up your makeup."

Lola scrambled into the room, followed by my father. She wore a white dress adorned with silk flowers on the top, a few layers of tulle on the bottom. My father looked dapper in his black tuxedo, with his salt-and-pepper hair styled. Lola raced over to me and grabbed my hand, staring up at me in awe. "Maman," she said, holding the hem of her dress out and swinging her little hips from side to side. "I'm a princess, just like you."

I crouched so I could get down to eye level with her. Nope, the thought of motherhood didn't intimidate me anymore; she was an angel. And I was going to be a good mom to her. I kissed her on the cheek. "You are ma princesse."

The photographer's camera clicked away.

My father placed his hand on his heart. "Sophie, ma chérie, you look so beautiful. I really can't find the words to describe how I feel." He swallowed hard, his Adam's apple bobbing up and down. "I promised myself I wouldn't cry."

A tear slid down his cheek. I walked up to him and wiped it away. For a moment, we just gazed into one another's eyes, smiling and gulping.

"Are you ready for your big entrance?" he asked, and I nodded.

"So, I'm taking Lola down," said Jane, handing Lola a basket of rose petals. "Phillipa and Marie will follow us. Then it's you and your dad. Sound good?"

"Yes," I said.

A harp played Pachelbel's Canon in D, the beautiful sound echoing throughout the halls of the château.

"Where is that music coming from?" I asked.

"I hired a string quartet and a harpist," said Jane.

Of course she had. Jane never overlooked a single detail.

"It's go time," said Phillipa, handing over my bouquet.

We all headed to the stairs, my father's arm hooked with mine. With Jane's guidance, Lola threw the flower petals; they floated to the ground, Marie and Phillipa following. My father nodded. A collective gasp filled the château when I made my grand entrance. Rémi's mouth dropped open, and then he smiled his delicious smile, his dimple showing. Walter and Robert both mouthed, "Whoa," as my father placed my hand into Rémi's.

"You take care of her," said Jean-Marc.

"I will," said Rémi with a proud nod of his head.

My eyes met his. Boy, did he look sexy in a tux.

On the landing of the château's main double staircase, the ceremony began, Rémi and me in front of Father Toussaint, and Walter and Robert in front of the mayor. Time passed by so quickly, with me staring into Rémi's adoring eyes, that it seemed like it was over before it began. A cheer erupted from the crowd.

"Kiss, kiss, kiss!" they chanted, and so Rémi dipped me down and locked his lips on mine.

I believe Walter did the same with Robert.

Walter caught my eye. "My friends are in a choir," he said. "We chose this song for you. Here's to your stars, Sophie."

Once the applause died down, music started up—first the harpist, then the violins and the cellist. Walter and Robert's friends clustered together and sang in harmony: the song, Coldplay's "A Sky Full of Stars," had an effect so beautiful and mesmerizing it sent shivers down my spine. Rémi set my bouquet on the ground, twirled me around, pressing his body into mine, and, after I kicked my heels off, afraid of falling, we danced for the first time as husband and wife.

The château glittered with Christmas lights, the tree flickering. The servers popped open the sparkling wine and served the two hundred guests. Somebody placed a glass in my hand. Jane handed me a microphone. I hadn't thought of preparing a speech, but I wasn't nervous; as I did when I cooked, I was going to go with my heart. "Thank you all for coming here to celebrate two marriages and Christmas Eve," I said, clearing my throat.

"Tonight's celebration is all about love," I continued. "And I'm blessed to have so many friends here—old and new—to experience all of this magic with us. As you know it's a very special evening. So cheers to my best friends, Walter and Robert. Congratulations on your nuptials. May life bring the two of you everything you've ever wanted."

I waited for the applause to die down. The last time I'd given a speech in front of such a large audience was at Grand-mère's funeral.

"On love, there is somebody important missing tonight. But I do believe she's here in spirit, living on through me." I raised my glass. "Here's to Grand-mère Odette. I hope I've made you proud. Your teachings opened my heart to love. And I thank you. Without you and your meddling, I wouldn't have anything I have today, including the loves of my life, Rémi and cooking."

A few people sniffled. Some wiped tears from their eyes.

"It's time to swing from the stars, to eat, to drink, and to be merry and bright," I said. "But, before I go on, there's something I need to do. All the single ladies, please step forward to the bottom of the staircase." I handed Rémi my glass of sparkling wine, picked up the bouquet, and turned, my back facing the audience. "Are you ready?"

"Oui!"

I launched the bouquet over my shoulder and snapped my shoulders forward just in time to see the ladies jump up and Laetitia catch it, as I'd hoped. Before I'd turned, I'd seen where she stood, and my intention was planned. I smiled at Laetitia and threw her a surreptitious wink. "Well, I hope we'll have another marriage at the château in the near future." Rémi handed me my glass, and I lifted it. I surveyed the smiling crowd, locking eyes with all the important people in my world. "Please enjoy yourselves. The buffet is open. Merry Christmas Eve."

Applause. The clinking of champagne glasses. Rémi pulled me in for another kiss.

"Je t'aime, Sophie," he said. "You really are an incredible woman."

I smiled and batted my eyelashes. "I'm really looking forward to our honeymoon."

Before he could respond, my attention was drawn to Marie. She wheeled out a flower-and-linen-decorated trolley with her masterpiece. Rémi and I stepped down the stairs to get a closer look. I was blown away. Five tiers of white-frosted exquisiteness, the cake was a replica of my dress, with silver threads of icing flowing down the sides to a smattering of stars, and white roses decorating the top, just like my hair.

Marie grinned. "You can have your cake and wear it too," she said. "And, before you correct me, I know that's not the expression."

Rémi whispered in my ear, "I'd love to see you wearing nothing but cake."

I kissed him on the cheek and turned toward Marie. "I've never seen anything more beautiful."

"I have," said Marie. "You."

"I'll agree with that sentiment," said Rémi.

I smiled. "Come on, let's go get something to eat."

With all the guests vying for our attention and kissing our cheeks, it took a good hour for Rémi and me to make it to the buffet. Everybody wanted a piece of us, and I was okay with that, because the spirit of the season was giving, and I was swinging-from-the-stars-and-jumping-over-the-moon happy.

My eyes latched on to the dragonfly ornament sparkling on the tree. "Thank you, Grand-mère, thank you, Rémi, and thank you, friends," I whispered, "for opening up my eyes to bigger and better dreams."

EPILOGUE

so this is life

TWO DAYS AFTER Christmas, Rémi and I took off for the Seychelles. Although it did rain a bit, the trip was a dream come to reality. I'd been silly to think Rémi and I needed to take a vacation together before our marriage. I guess it was true: when you know you are in love . . . you know. And, just like the crystal-clear waters I swam in, I was falling deeper into it every day. We returned to the château a few days after New Year's, settling in and moving my things over to Rémi's, and moving Laetitia's and Jean Marc's into Grand-mère's suite, which took a few weeks of organization. But we got it done. As for Étoile, she was moving in with them, where she'd have a new window seat, and I'd have visitation rights. Aside from that, everybody was taking advantage of having time off.

Sometime before Valentine's Day, Phillipa and Jane entered the kitchen as I was preparing lunch for everybody, Lola by my side.

"Now that you're married, I feel like I never see you," said Phillipa, placing a basket of lavender on the prep table. She handed Lola a few sprigs.

"What? I see you practically every day!" I responded.

"I know. It's just different now. We don't cook together as much. Hug?" she asked, and I complied. "Oh, you're so good at this now."

"What can I say? I had an excellent teacher," I said, before bolting to the garbage can and vomiting.

Phillipa rubbed my back. Lola toddled over and held the lavender to my face, which made me retch even more.

"Are you sick?" asked Jane.

"No, I think it's just stress and fatigue finally catching up to me."

Jane ushered me over to a stool and handed me a glass of water. "I noticed your nose pinch when Lola put the lavender to your nose. You were sniffing like a dog. Are you allergic to lavender?"

"No, not at all," I said.

"I don't think she's stressed or sick. I'm thinking it's something else," said Phillipa. "I didn't want to say anything, but your mood has been swinging back and forth for about a week. Do you remember when you burst into tears for no reason at all? And then you threw up after tasting your own dish, which was absolutely perfect."

"What are you driving at?"

"I think you may be pregnant," she said.

"Impossible," I said.

"Is it?" asked the twins in unison.

I bit down on my bottom lip in thought. I couldn't remember the last time Aunt Flow had visited. Had it been over a month? I didn't exactly keep track. Rémi and I had been extremely careful, using protection. My eyes snapped open wide. All except for that one night in the Seychelles when we'd ripped each other's clothes off and made love like wild animals on the beach under a full moon.

"Merde, merde, merde," I said. "I think you may be right. What do I do?"

"I'll run to the pharmacy and grab a test," said Jane. She bolted out the door.

Phillipa blathered on and on about how exciting this was. I sat numb, wondering how I could have let this happen. What was I going to do? How would I handle taking care of a baby and a Michelin-starred restaurant? I barely had time for myself. Plus, I was such a klutz, I'd probably drop the baby on its head. And how would Lola feel about being a big sister?

A half hour later, Phillipa, Jane, and I stared down at two bright pink lines. As they screeched with excitement, I was flipping out. I should have been ecstatic, but I wasn't. "Jane, can you watch, Lola? I need air," I said. Before she could answer, I bolted out the back door and ran toward the river.

I must have been sitting by the banks for at least a half hour when I heard footsteps crunching in the leaves. Red-eyed from crying, I turned. Jean-Marc walked toward me, carrying a basket. "Sophie, what's wrong? Have you been crying?"

"I have," I said. There was no point in trying to cover it up.

"Is everything okay between you and Rémi?"

I shrugged. "He's fine, Papa. But the timing isn't right."

"For what?"

"To be pregnant." I rubbed my hand across my still-flat belly. "And I am. Pregnant."

"Oh, I see," he said. "The timing is always a surprise when it comes to that. When would it be right?"

"I don't know."

Jean-Marc scooted down to the ground and sat next to me. He wrapped his arm around my shoulders. "Sophie, my advice to you is to focus on the good in your life. Your eyes light up when you're in the kitchen . . . and when you see Rémi and Lola. My eyes light up when I see you. I'm the proudest father in the world."

"I still don't know if I'll be a good mother." There. I said it and I broke down again, hugging my knees to my chest.

"You've done pretty well with Lola. She adores you," he said. "And just take a look at what's going on at the château. You took over the helm from the word go. You're the apple of the media's eyes, and things are only getting better for you. A child won't make it worse."

"Yes, but what if I can't take all of the pressure?"

"You'll be able to, if you focus on taking things one step at a time. Life happens when we least expect it. You have so many people around you, willing and wanting to help. You're not alone in this," he said, sweeping his hand out. "You, ma chérie, deserve every ounce of happiness coming your way."

I lowered my head. "I'm supposed to be fearless," I said. "But I'm not, really. I'm just me."

"Which proves you're human with a beating heart. It's okay to feel vulnerable when it comes to affairs of the heart and motherhood, and you have every right to be scared," he said. "Do you know how scary it was for me to come here and meet you that first day?" Jean-Marc's hands shot to his eyes, covering them. "And now you call me Papa. In the past, I was never there for you. Perhaps I don't deserve the title."

"Yes, you do, Papa," I said, wiping away my tears. "You didn't know where I was. And you're here for me now."

"And you'll be there for Rémi, Lola, and your new baby, especially if you show them the love, kindness, and forgiveness you've given me."

I CLOSED MY eyes as Rémi whipped us to the doctor, the car twisting and turning on the winding country roads. We parked, and I couldn't force my legs to move. Rémi held out his hand, helping me from the passenger seat. "Sophie, I'm nervous too."

He escorted me to the waiting room, and Dr. Marchand ushered us into the examination room after a harrowing thirty-minute wait. After asking us a few questions and taking my health card, she motioned me toward the exam table. I splayed out on the bed and pulled up my shirt, my fingers drumming by my sides and taking on a life of their own. Dr. Marchand rubbed in the blue gel and placed the scanner on my belly. Rémi gripped my hand and I closed my eyes. We both held our breath.

"Well, well, well," said the doctor, "there it is, the fetal pole. You're measuring five weeks and two days." My eyes shot to the screen. Dr. Marchand turned a knob on the ultrasound machine. *Thump, thump. Boom.* "And we already have a fetal heartbeat." She set the scanner down and picked up a paper wheel. "By my calculations, the baby was conceived in the beginning of January. With that said, she or he will be born in October."

A feeling of overwhelming joy replaced my fear. I was going to be a real *mother* to both Lola and this baby. I'd do everything in my power to protect my children, to teach them everything I'd learned about love and life. And cooking.

"I'm going to be a papa," said Rémi, gripping my hand.

"Again," I said. "And I'm thinking I should adopt Lola before the baby is born so there is no jealousy between them when they're older." I paused. "If that's okay with you."

Rémi's eyes sparkled with tears, proving, once and for all, he was human and full of love, sensitive and kind, and mine. "You've made me the happiest man in the world."

Dr. Marchand handed me a printout. "No shellfish. Wash your vegetables, maybe even peel them. No raw or undercooked meats. Which means no foie gras. And stay away from cats."

"Cats?" I questioned.

She nodded. "Most Frenchwomen are immune to toxoplasmosis, an infection from a parasite found in cats' feces that can spread with something as simple as a scratch, but as an American, you need to be all the more careful."

I rubbed my hand across my belly. Poor Étoile. My fur baby wasn't going to see me for eight more months. But at least she'd be surrounded with love.

Rémi gripped my hand. "I can't believe we're doing this," he said. "I can't believe this has happened."

"We are, and we did it," I said. "Here's to the next chapter of our lives."

"One brick at a time," he said.

"Let's have one more look and we can get photos for you," said Dr. Marchand. She placed the scanner on my belly again. And then she gasped. "Well, what do we have here? I'm so sorry. I missed the other one. He or she must have been hiding." She smiled. "Twins."

Oh. My. Stars. My life was going to change—big-time. And, after everything I'd gone through, I told myself I was ready for it.

Be fearless, I chanted in my head, even though I knew I could do this.

In the past, I'd gone through so much. I'd lost my mother. I'd lost my job. I'd lost my grandmother. But I'd gained everything, including a Michelin star. Funny, this dream didn't matter to me as much when I had so much more, a dream I'd never thought possible or even imagined. I had a big family and friends and they loved me. Happiness gripped me in a tight vise, and I wasn't going to let the feeling go. I met Rémi's tear-filled eyes. "You know what?" I asked.

"What?"

"You were right," I said.

"Sophie, please don't give me a heart attack."

I kissed his knuckles. "You were right about dreams."

"Are you thinking about your stars?" he asked. "And how this pregnancy might mess up your plans?"

"No, I couldn't care less about the stars. Been there, done that, got one," I said with a grin. "I'm thinking about what you said, how dreams can change. I'm thinking about our family, a very bright future, and us."

For a moment, my gaze left Rémi's and locked on to the breathtaking view outside of the window. A swarm of wild butterflies danced in the sky, floating and dipping. Spring, the season of renewal, had sprung early, and I was ready for this new, wildly wonderful life.

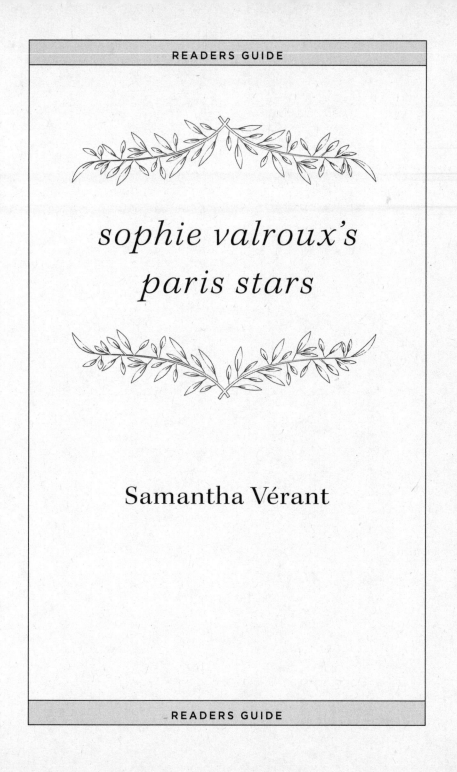

sophie valroux's paris stars

Samantha Vérant

discussion questions

—◦◦◦◦◦—

1. In the beginning of the novel, we learn that Sophie still wants to go after the one and only dream she had before arriving to Champvert—achieving Michelin stars—and she thinks Rémi might stand in her way because he doesn't seem all that supportive. Have you ever given up on a dream? Have you ever had somebody not show support?

2. Sophie still feels as though everything has just been handed to her, that she truly didn't work for this new life at the château. Do you think her pride stands in her way? Or is it fear? How would you feel if you inherited a château and all of the responsibilities that come with running an estate of this magnitude?

3. Rémi invites Sophie's father, Jean-Marc—a man she'd met only two weeks prior—to help tend the grounds. Do you think Rémi overstepped boundaries, or was he looking after Sophie's best interests?

4. Sophie's grief wavers from the recent loss of her grand-mère. When she sees items or smells scents that remind her of Odette, she loses focus and wishes she still had her grand-mère's guidance. Thankfully, she has the friendships of Phillipa and Jane. When you're going through a tough time, are your friends there for you? What is a real, tried-and-true friendship?

5. Rémi wants to get married to Sophie sooner rather than later and puts pressure on her to do just that. Do you think his reasons about loss are justified? Do you think that Sophie needs more time to adjust to everything, including becoming a mother to Rémi's daughter, Lola?

6. When Rémi finds out that Nicolas de la Barguelonne asked Sophie to cook at the Sous les étoiles event in Paris and Sophie agrees, Rémi loses his cool. He feels she might be taken from him by high society because she was born of noble blood and he's just the farm boy from next door. What did you think of his statement and Sophie's reaction?

7. After Sophie falls and loses her senses of smell and taste—the worst thing that could happen to a chef—she doesn't tell anybody. She doesn't want to believe it's happened, and she cooks blindly in the kitchen for a few months, giving Phillipa more responsibilities. Has something similar happened to you to impede your work or aspirations? Do you think Sophie's pride and stubbornness get in her way?

8. There is a large cast of characters at the château, all of whom become family to Sophie. Which character do you gravitate toward the most?

9. At the event, Sophie feels set up for failure. She still can't smell or taste. Her cooking idol seems to hate her on sight. The threat of sabotage in the kitchen runs rampant. Would you have cracked under the pressure or run away?

10. What do you think of Rémi's reaction to the photo of Sophie and Nicolas kissing? If the scenarios were reversed and it was Sophie who saw Rémi kissing another woman in a photo, how do you think she'd react? What would you do?

11. As Sophie hides her condition, her kitchen is out of sorts, and she finally breaks down and confides in Phillipa, who takes the brunt of the blame. Have any of your friends gone to bat for you even though the problem was you?

12. When Rémi and Sophie finally make up, everything in Sophie's world changes and her senses return. Do you think stress, pressure, sadness, and grief contributed to her condition? How would you have handled everything Sophie struggled with on this journey?

sophie's recipes

❦

Dear Reader,

As Jacques Pépin has said: "Cooking is about the art of adjustment."
Please remember every stove or oven has different cooking temperatures,
and to season to your taste.

 I hope you enjoy the recipes I've chosen to share with you. To all the
vegetarians and vegans in the world, some of these dishes can be modified
to your dietary restrictions—ignore the meats, replace chicken stock with
vegetable, or use more olive oil instead of butter (etc.). Remember, recipes
are only guidelines, and you can make them your own.

 To everyone, if having company over, prepare whatever you can in
advance—chop, slice, dice, and store. I've learned this lesson from the
best—ma grand-mère. Also, if you buy pre-chopped vegetables, like
onions and peppers, that will save you time, although this is not an
option in France or my kitchen.

 Finally, as a reminder, a French meal or dinner party is comprised
of five courses—the amuse-bouche at a restaurant or an apéro at home,
the entrée (small plate), the plat principal (main course), the cheese or
salad course, and dessert.

Best wishes, bon appétit, and bisous,
Chef Sophie

L'Amuse-Bouche *(Apéro)*

Monica's Stuffed Chipotle Figs, wrapped in Jambon Sec and served with a Cocoa–Chili Powder Balsamic Glaze

SERVES 8 TO 16

PREP TIME: 10 MINUTES

COOK TIME: 3 TO 4 MINUTES FOR THE FIGS,
   7 MINUTES FOR THE GLAZE

REST TIME: 10 MINUTES FOR THE GLAZE

EQUIPMENT: SMALL POT, TOOTHPICKS, FRYING PAN

INGREDIENTS

1 cup balsamic vinegar

8 fresh figs

1 (7-oz.) can chipotle peppers

3 or 4 slices jambon sec or other dry-cured ham like prosciutto

Extra-virgin olive oil

1 tablespoon unsalted butter

½ tablespoon cocoa powder

1 to 2 teaspoons chili powder

Fresh ground black pepper

TECHNIQUE

Pour the vinegar into a small pot and cook over high heat until it reduces to a syrup-like consistency, 5 to 7 minutes. Lower the heat to keep it warm.

Cut the stems off the figs and then cut them in half. Lightly score the centers with a knife. Slice small knobs, about ½ inch, of the chipotle peppers and stuff them into each fig. Slice the dry-cured ham in quarters lengthwise. Wrap each stuffed fig half with a strip of the ham, securing it with a toothpick.

Combine a dash of olive oil and the butter in a large frying pan over medium-high heat. Once the pan is hot, add the wrapped figs and cook, about 2 to 3 minutes per side, until the ham is golden. Remove from the pan and place on a plate.

Once the balsamic glaze has cooled to room temperature, add the cocoa and chili powder. Mix well and taste. If you want more chili or cocoa powder, add it in. Using a small spoon, drizzle the wrapped figs with the glaze. Garnish with fresh ground black pepper and serve.

L'Entrée

Velouté d'Artichaut (Creamy Artichoke Soup)

SERVES 6

PREP TIME: 30 TO 60 MINUTES
(LONGER IF USING FRESH ARTICHOKES)

COOK TIME: 50 MINUTES

EQUIPMENT: LARGE POT, IMMERSION BLENDER (PREFERRED) OR
FOOD PROCESSOR

INGREDIENTS

2 lemons

Salt

6 large globe artichokes or 1 (14-oz.) can artichoke bottoms
(7 to 9 count)

Extra-virgin olive oil

1 teaspoon finely minced garlic

1 teaspoon finely minced ginger

3 shallots, peeled and sliced into rounds

1 carrot, peeled and sliced into rounds

1 celery stalk, diced

1 leek, green and ends cut off, sliced into rounds

Fresh ground black pepper

2 bouquets garnis (bay leaves and sprigs of dried thyme,
tied together)

¼ cup dry white wine

4½ to 5 cups vegetable stock

¾ cup crème fraîche or heavy cream

½ teaspoon saffron (optional)

½ to 1 tablespoon unsalted butter (optional), softened to room
   temperature

½ to 1 tablespoon flour (optional)

1 (14-oz.) can baby artichoke hearts packed in water

Paprika

1 small bunch fresh tarragon, roughly chopped

TECHNIQUE

Fill a large bowl with cold water. Add in the juice of one lemon and
two dashes of salt. If using fresh artichokes, cut off the stems and place
them in the bowl, bottom side down. One by one, press your thumbs
in the center of each artichoke and pull outward to remove the hard
leaves, setting them aside.* Pull the softer leaves out and then remove
the hairy choke using a small spoon. Discard. Carefully trim any ex-
cess hard leaves off the artichoke bottom. Slice into strips and place in
the water.

Pour 2 to 3 tablespoons of olive oil into the pot, enough to coat
the bottom, and set the burner to medium-high. Once heated, add
the garlic and the ginger, cooking until golden and fragrant, about 1
minute. Add in the shallots, cooking until slightly transparent (about
2 minutes), followed by the carrots and celery. Stir and cook for another 3 to 4 minutes, until softened. Add in the leeks, pushing the
rounds apart. Lower the heat to medium-low and cook for another 10
minutes, stirring occasionally and adding in a dash or two of salt,
fresh ground black pepper, and the two bouquets garnis.

Pour in the wine, the remaining lemon juice, and the vegetable
stock. Bring to a boil and then lower the heat. Simmer for 25 minutes.

Remove the pot from the heat. Carefully remove the two bouquets garnis with kitchen tongs. Purée the mixture with an immersion blender, or in small batches using a food processor, until there

are no chunks left. Return the pot to the stove and mix in the crème fraîche and saffron (if using), setting the burner to low. If you want a thicker velouté, mix the butter and flour (a quick and easy beurre manié) in a small bowl, then add it to the pot, stirring until the butter is melted.

Serve in small bowls. Set a baby artichoke in the middle of each bowl. Garnish with a pinch of paprika, fresh ground black pepper, and the tarragon.

> *Chef's note: This is also a nice meal for four. Serve with a baguette and a crisp salad with a lemon–Dijon mustard vinaigrette.*

> **If keeping the leaves from the fresh artichokes, steam them for about 20 minutes (until the bottoms are tender) and serve with a dipping sauce of your choice.*

Prune, Apricot, and Preserved Lemon Couscous Royale aux Legumes garnished with Toasted Slivered Almonds

SERVES 6

PREP TIME: 35 MINUTES

COOK TIME: 1 HOUR

EQUIPMENT: LARGE POT OR DUTCH OVEN, FRYING PAN

INGREDIENTS

Extra-virgin olive oil

1 tablespoon finely minced garlic

1 tablespoon finely minced ginger

1 red or yellow onion, roughly chopped

3 carrots, peeled and quartered

2 medium red potatoes (optional), peeled and chopped into ½-inch cubes

1 medium turnip, peeled and chopped into ½-inch cubes

1 small eggplant, diced into ½-inch cubes

1 red pepper, deseeded and diced

1 yellow pepper, deseeded and diced

¾ cup diced celery

6 to 8 artichoke bottoms, quartered

1 tablespoon ras el hanout (if available)

1 tablespoon cocoa powder

1 tablespoon ground ginger

½ tablespoon ground cinnamon

½ tablespoon ground turmeric

½ tablespoon ground cumin

2 teaspoons chili powder

1 tablespoon tomato paste

8 plum tomatoes, peeled and roughly chopped, or 1 (14-oz.)
    can crushed tomatoes

3½ to 4 cups vegetable stock, plus more for the couscous

1 medium zucchini, halved lengthwise then chopped into
    ¼-inch half circles

1 cup fresh haricots verts (thin French green beans) or green
    beans, ends trimmed and sliced in half

1 to 1½ cups chickpeas or garbanzo beans

1 cup oil-cured black and/or green olives, pits removed

1 cup prunes

1 cup dried apricots

¾ cup golden raisins

2 tablespoons unsalted butter

1 cup slivered almonds

3 cups fine or medium couscous grains (½ cup per person)

1 cup chopped parsley or cilantro

½ cup preserved lemons, chopped into small chunks (quick
    and easy recipe follows)

Harissa (if available)

Salt

Fresh ground black pepper

TECHNIQUE

Heat up 2 to 3 tablespoons of olive oil (enough to coat the bottom) in a large pot. Once heated, add in the garlic and ginger, cooking until fragrant, about 1 minute. Add in the onion, cooking until slightly transparent, followed by the carrots, potato (if using), turnip, eggplant, red and yellow peppers, celery, and artichoke bottoms. Add a dash or two of olive oil, stir, and cook for 10 to 15 minutes, until the vegetables soften.

Add in all the spices, coating the vegetables, and cook for 3 to 5 minutes, until fragrant. Then add in the tomato paste, the plum tomatoes, and the 3½ to 4 cups vegetable stock. Stir and bring to a boil. Add in the zucchini, haricots verts, chickpeas, and olives, followed by the prunes, apricots, and raisins. Lower heat to a simmer, cover the pot with a lid, and simmer for 35 minutes.

Melt the butter in a small pan over medium-high heat. Once heated, add in the almonds, tossing them slightly. Cook for 1 to 2 minutes, or until slightly golden. Set aside.

Prepare the couscous according to the package instructions, but instead of bringing water to a boil, use vegetable stock. Place individual servings of the prepared couscous in shallow bowls or on plates. Stir the veggie mixture and ladle 1 or 2 scoops onto each serving. Garnish with the toasted slivered almonds, chopped parsley, and preserved lemon chunks. Place a small bowl of the broth on the table with the harissa and a small ladle (the harissa is mixed into the broth), as well as salt and pepper. Your guests, your family, and you can season to taste.

> *Chef's note: Leftover vegetables are wonderful on pasta and rice. Just store them in the refrigerator in a plastic container, using them within three days, or in the freezer, thawing and reheating when needed. Also, the vegetables are a perfect healthy side dish for a main course, such as lamb or chicken.*

Preserved Lemons

If you are unable to find preserved lemons at your local grocery store and you don't want to wait a month to make them from scratch, here's a quick and easy recipe that gives off the same flavors. The lemons should be prepared the day before you want to use them. Note: They are also great in salads. They can be stored for two weeks in the refrigerator.

MAKES AROUND 1½ CUPS

PREP TIME: 10 MINUTES

REST TIME: 12 TO 24 HOURS

EQUIPMENT: 1 MEDIUM-SIZED MASON JAR

INGREDIENTS

    8 to 10 Meyer lemons, sliced into thin rounds and
        then quartered
    Juice of 1 lemon
    2½ tablespoons coarse sea or kosher salt
    5 tablespoons sugar
    1 sprig fresh rosemary (optional)

TECHNIQUE

Wash the lemons thoroughly, then prepare as instructed. In a bowl, toss the lemon slices with the lemon juice, salt, and sugar. Place the mixture in a mason jar with a sprig of rosemary, if using. Place the jar in the refrigerator for a minimum of 12 hours.

Gigot d'Agneau (Leg of Lamb) served with a Red-Wine Shallot Reduction (served with Mille-Feuille potatoes; recipe follows)

SERVES 6

PREP TIME: 10 MINUTES

COOK TIME: 45 TO 55 MINUTES

REST TIME: 15 MINUTES

EQUIPMENT: ROASTING PAN, MEAT THERMOMETER, CUTTING BOARD, MEDIUM-SIZED SAUCEPOT

INGREDIENTS

3 large red onions, peeled, halved, and ends leveled flat

4 large carrots, peeled and halved

13 cloves garlic, peeled: 5 sliced into ¼-inch slices lengthwise, 7 kept whole, 1 minced

1 (3½ to 4-pound) bone-in leg of lamb

Extra-virgin olive oil

10 to 12 dried cloves

1 to 1½ tablespoons fleur de sel or kosher salt

Fresh ground black pepper

½ tablespoon brown sugar

1 handful rosemary needles, a little over ¼ cup

1 or 2 bay leaves

1¾ cups red wine

½ beef bouillon cube (if necessary)

3 or 4 shallots, peeled and sliced into rounds

½ to 1 tablespoon unsalted butter (optional), softened to room
   temperature

½ to 1 tablespoon flour (optional)

TECHNIQUE

Preheat the oven to 350°F. Place the onions, carrots, and whole garlic cloves in your roasting pan. (This serves as an edible baking rack.) Place the leg of lamb on the vegetables, and then, with a knife, make small incisions every 1 to 2 inches into the meat. Rub the lamb with a dash or two of olive oil and the brown sugar, then stuff the garlic slices into the incisions. Sprinkle the salt and pepper onto the lamb to taste, rubbing it in slightly. Then, sprinkle the rosemary onto the lamb and push the dried cloves into the meat. Submerge the vegetables (not the meat) with about 3½ cups of water, then add the bay leaves to the liquid. Place the pan in the oven and bake for 45 to 55 minutes. The lamb is ready when the temperature reads 135°F for medium rare on the inside, medium on the ends. Transfer the lamb to a cutting board to rest while you prepare the red wine–shallot sauce. Cover the lamb with aluminum foil to keep it warm.

Remove the vegetables and garlic from the roasting pan and set aside. In a frying pan, add a dash of oil, setting the burner to medium-low. Place the vegetables in the pan to keep them warm. Pour any drippings and rosemary from the roasting pan into a measuring cup. Hopefully, 1½ cups of liquid remain. If not, add water to reach 1½ cups, plus the beef bouillon cube.

Place 3 tablespoons of olive oil in a saucepan at medium-high heat. Add the shallots and cook until softened, about 3 minutes. Add in the minced garlic, stirring often, and cook for another 3 to 4 minutes. Add in the stock and then the wine, bring the mixture to a boil, then lower the heat and simmer for 15 to 20 minutes, until the mixture reduces by approximately half. The sauce is done when the wine reduces. If the sauce isn't as thick as you'd like it, mix the butter and flour together, add it to the sauce, and stir until dissolved. Once finished, place the sauce in a gravy boat and the vegetables on a serving platter.

You're ready to carve up the lamb tableside and serve!

SIDE DISH

Mille-Feuilles de Pommes de Terre with Greens

SERVES 6

PREP TIME: 20 MINUTES

COOK TIME: 25 TO 30 MINUTES

EQUIPMENT: MANDOLINE, SILICONE MUFFIN PAN FOR SIX
    (MOLDS 2¾-INCH WIDTH, 1½-INCH HEIGHT),
    PASTRY BRUSH

INGREDIENTS

    10 to 12 medium-sized red potatoes, peeled and halved

    1 stick salted butter, melted (divided)

    1 tablespoon herbes de Provence

    ¾ cup grated Gruyère (or similar cheese)

    1 teaspoon ground nutmeg

    1 tablespoon crushed garlic (optional)

    ½ tablespoon salt

    Fresh ground black pepper

    ¼ cup crème fraîche or heavy cream

    6 cups arugula (or other greens)

    12 cherry tomatoes, halved

    6 to 8 chives for garnish, cut into 2-inch pieces

Lemon/Garlic/Mustard Vinaigrette

    Juice of 1 lemon

    1 tablespoon Dijon mustard

    1 large shallot, peeled and finely diced

1 clove garlic, peeled and finely minced

½ cup extra-virgin olive oil (or more, if needed)

1 or 2 pinches fleur de sel or kosher salt

TECHNIQUE

Preheat the oven to 350°F. While it's heating, slice your peeled and halved potatoes with the smallest setting on your mandoline. We want these slices thin! Place the sliced potatoes in the muffin molds as you slice, as you may need more or fewer potatoes depending on their size. Transfer the potatoes to a bowl. Add in half of the melted butter and the herbes de Provence, cheese, nutmeg, garlic (if using), and salt and fresh ground pepper to taste, followed by the crème fraîche. Mix well. Using a pastry brush, butter the muffin molds. Divide the potatoes among the molds, lightly pushing them down. Bake for 25 to 30 minutes, or until golden.

Prepare the dressing. Mix all ingredients and whisk until creamy. If it isn't, add in olive oil until you've reached the desired consistency. Season with salt and pepper to taste.

Take the potatoes out of the oven and let them cool for 5 minutes. Using a large soup spoon, take them out of the molds, placing them on the bed of arugula and cherry tomatoes. Brush a bit of the remaining melted butter onto the potatoes. Drizzle the salad with the dressing. Garnish with the chives.

> *Chef's note: As most of us don't have two ovens, I suggest preparing the potatoes 1 day in advance, leaving them in the muffin pan and refrigerating. After the lamb (or whatever meal you're preparing) has finished cooking, lower the heat to around 200°F and reheat the potatoes for 10 to 15 minutes. Also, these potatoes are great for any holiday meal!*

During a traditional French meal, the cheese course is served between the plat principal (main dish) and the dessert. Because it comes quite late in the meal, the focus should be on the quality of the cheeses, not the quantity (especially if you're saving room for dessert), so pay a visit to your local cheese shop, if you're so lucky as to have one nearby, for the best selection and recommendations.

The French cheese course is usually very streamlined and elegant, with four to five cheeses arranged simply on a cutting board and served with fresh bread, bien sûr. If you want, you can also serve a simple salad of greens and vinaigrette, which helps balance the richness of the cheeses, or (and this is my preference) garnish the board with seasonal fruit such as grapes, apple slices, currants, or pomegranate seeds.

When cutting your cheeses, focus on leaving an equal portion of the rind for everyone. No one wants to be left with a lot of rind and very little of the paste (the interior of the cheese)! The following are my and Sophie's favorite cheeses from southwestern France that you might find during your cheese course at the Château de Champvert:

The Chèvre: Rocamadour AOP

These small rounds of goat's milk cheese are known for their velvety-soft rind, melt-in-your-mouth texture, and fresh, nutty taste. They are made primarily in the *département* of the Lot (where the town of Rocamadour is located), just north of Tarn-et-Garonne, where production of this cheese dates back more than six hundred years. The Rocamadour is part of a family of cheeses in southwest France called the *cabécous*, meaning "little goat cheeses" in Occitan, which was once the dominant language in this part of France. This delicate, young cheese is not often exported, so look for any other soft, creamy goat cheese or ask your local cheese shop what they would recommend.

The Tomme de Brebis: Ossau-Iraty AOP

In French, *tomme* is a catchall term for round, flat wheels, so a *tomme de brebis* is a wheel of sheep's milk cheese. This style of semi-firm cheese is prevalent south and southwest of Toulouse in the Pyrénées mountains, which form the dividing line between France and Spain. The most famous of these cheeses is Ossau-Iraty (pronounced "oh-so ear-ah-tee"), named after the Ossau Valley in Béarn and the Iraty beech forest of the Basque region. This cheese comes in several varieties, with differentiating symbols stamped into the rind. The most exclusive is called *fermier* (made on the farm with milk coming only from animals on that farm) and is stamped with a front-facing ram's head with an "F." Ossau-Iraty made in cheese-making factories with milk pooled from many farms is stamped with a ram's head in profile. Whichever kind you are lucky enough to find is guaranteed to be a crowd-pleaser, with a silky-smooth, semi-firm paste and sweet, nutty taste that is beloved by both cheese connoisseurs and *débutants* alike.

The Vache: Cantal AOP

More than two thousand years ago, when the Romans marched through the mountainous Auvergne region, northeast of modern-day Toulouse, they found the Gauls making the cheese that would come to be called Cantal, after the département in which it is made. In fact, some say that the Romans then passed the technique for making

Cantal on to the inhabitants of the British Isles, where it eventually (over a thousand years or so) developed into the technique used to make cheddar cheese! The tall, cylindrical wheels of Cantal can weigh up to one hundred pounds, so they are usually cut in half horizontally before being cut into smaller *morceaux* (morsels). Cantal, with its beautiful buttery-yellow paste, comes in different ages: *jeune* ("young," aged 1 to 2 months with a mild, buttery flavor), *entre-doux* ("between-sweet," aged 3 to 7 months and becoming stronger, with a more complex, sharp, nutty flavor), and *vieux* ("old," aged at least 8 months, the strongest).

The Bleu: Roquefort AOP

This salty, creamy sheep's milk blue cheese has been called the King of Cheeses, and it has been reigning over cheese plates for centuries. One of the things that sets this cheese apart is that in order for it to legally bear the name Roquefort, it must be aged in caves beneath the rocky hillsides around the town of Roquefort-sur-Soulzon in southwest France. These caves, legend has it, are where a shepherd boy left a bit of his lunch—bread and some fresh sheep's milk cheese—after being distracted by a shepherdess. He came back weeks later to find that the bread had grown mold, which had spread to the cheese! And the ambience of these caves has lent itself to this cheese ever since. If you think this pungent, salty blue is too strong for you, try it on some bread slathered with butter to cut the strength of the cheese, or paired with honey for an addictive sweet-salty combination.

A NOTE ON AOPS: When you see a cheese name followed by the letters "AOP," that means the cheese has been awarded a protected designation called *appellation d'origine protégée* (protected name of origin). This system protects traditional cheeses (and other agricultural products, like wine) by setting out requirements that must be met in order to be able to call a cheese by a specific name. Regulations include the geographical boundaries for milk and cheese production, the breed of animal allowed to produce the milk, what they are fed, how much pasture space and grazing time is required, cheese-making techniques and standards—sometimes even the time of the year the cheese is allowed to be made. All of these factors contribute to the French philosophy of *terroir*, the notion that the place where something is produced and the traditions and techniques for making that product are intimately linked with taste. Hopefully these cheeses will help you to experience Sophie's beloved terroir of southwest France from wherever you are in the world!

Amitiés,
Jessica Hammer, Taste of Toulouse
tasteoftoulouse.com

DESSERT

Gustave's Flambéed Cognac Strawberry Crêpes served with Whipped Cream and Chocolate Sauce

SERVES 12

PREP TIME: 40 MINUTES

COOK TIME: 30 MINUTES

REST TIME: 30 TO 45 MINUTES

EQUIPMENT: MIXING BOWL, HAND MIXER, WHISK, DOUBLE
   BOILER, NONSTICK 12-INCH FRYING OR CRÊPE PAN, LARGE
   FRYING PAN, KITCHEN MATCHES OR LONG LIGHTER

INGREDIENTS

For the whipped cream:

   2 cups cold heavy cream

   1 cup mascarpone

   Seeds of 1 vanilla bean pod or ½ tablespoon vanilla extract

   ¼ cup granulated sugar or vanilla sugar, plus more if needed

For the crêpe batter:

   2 cups flour

   3½ cups milk, plus extra if needed

   ¼ teaspoon salt

   3 large eggs

   4 tablespoons unsalted butter, melted

   Seeds of 1 vanilla bean pod or ½ tablespoon vanilla extract

   Vegetable oil

For the chocolate sauce:

1¼ cups dark baker's or dessert chocolate (70% cacao)

¾ cup milk

2 tablespoons heavy cream

¼ cup sugar

Seeds of 1 vanilla bean pod

1 tablespoon Grand Marnier or Armagnac (optional)

1 teaspoon chili powder (optional but highly recommended)

2½ tablespoons unsalted butter, sliced

For the flambéed strawberries:

2 pounds fresh strawberries, ends trimmed, halved

¼ cup Armagnac or cognac, plus more if needed

TECHNIQUE

Combine all the ingredients for the whipped cream in a mixing bowl. Whisk together using a hand mixer on high speed until stiff peaks form, about 3 minutes. Taste and mix in more sugar until your desired sweetness is achieved. Cover the bowl and transfer to the refrigerator until ready to use. The whipped cream will keep for up to 24 hours.

Crêpes: Step one. Combine the flour, milk, and salt in a medium mixing bowl. In a separate bowl, whisk the eggs until foamy. Little by little, fold the eggs into the flour mixture. Add the butter and the vanilla. Mix well. Get rid of all those clumps! The batter shouldn't be thick but fluid. Place the bowl in the refrigerator, letting the mixture set for 30 to 45 minutes.

Chocolate sauce: Break up the chocolate and crush it with a rubber mallet or rolling pin. Fill the bottom of your double boiler with water, bring to a simmer, and place the chocolate in the upper container. If you don't have a double boiler, set a heatproof bowl over a pot of gently simmering water, careful not to submerge the bowl or chocolate. In both cases, allow the chocolate to melt slowly, stirring until creamy. Remove from the heat. Combine the milk, cream, sugar, and vanilla (as well as the Grand Marnier or Armagnac and chili powder, if using) in a medium saucepan. Whisk together and bring to a boil. Lower the heat to a simmer. Gradually pour the melted chocolate into the mixture, whisking away until thoroughly blended. Turn off the heat and whisk in the butter, one chunk at a time. Once the butter is melted, set the sauce to the side.

Crêpes: Step two. Once rested, take the batter out of the refrigerator and whisk again. If the batter is too thick, add a tad more milk. When ready, coat the bottom of 12-inch nonstick pan lightly with vegetable oil and heat the pan on a medium-high burner. Once the pan is hot, pour in one ladleful of the batter. Quickly swirl the pan so the batter spreads evenly. Place the pan back on the burner. Once the edges are slightly browned (1 to 2 minutes), loosen them with a spatula and use it to flip the crêpe—unless you've mastered the pan flip. Cook for about 1 minute more. Place the crêpe on a plate, cover with a kitchen towel or paper towel, and continue stacking the crêpes under the towel until all the batter is gone.

Reheat your chocolate sauce, setting the burner to low, until warm. Mix well.

Flambé the strawberries: Heat a large nonstick frying pan on medium-high heat. Pat your strawberries down with a paper towel and place them in the pan, warming for 1 to 2 minutes. Do not turn on the evacuation, as fire rises toward grease. Keep a large lid by you in case the flames don't settle down and rise too high. Pour the cognac over the strawberries and immediately dip the lighter or the lit match into the cognac. The flames will rise and settle down after 5 to 10 seconds. If flambéing makes you uncomfortable, just warm up the strawberries in the cognac.

To serve, place one crêpe on your serving dish. Take a large spoon full of strawberries, setting them in the center lengthwise. Roll the sides of the crêpe toward the center, covering the strawberries. Using a small spoon, drizzle the chocolate sauce over the crêpe. Top with a dollop of whipped cream. Serve immediately and repeat.

Chef's note:

Flambé at your own risk.

If making the chocolate sauce in advance, store in a glass container with a lid. To reheat, place the glass container in a bowl (microwave) or pot (stove) filled with enough water to submerge it about 1 inch. Heat until warm and melted! This recipe should keep for about 1 week in the refrigerator.

acknowledgments

———◦◦◦———

Once again, it took a "brigade" to write this book. I'm so very thankful for all of the people who helped carve this story into what it is today.

Thank you to my agents: Kimberly Witherspoon for her guidance, and Jessica Mileo for her supremely detailed editorial feedback. Thank you for your kindness, advice, and patience.

Thank you to my fabulous and kindhearted editor, Cindy Hwang. Working with her and the Berkley family has been an incredible experience and a dream come true. On this family, thank you to Cindy's incredible assistant Angela Kim, copy editor extraordinaire Angelina Krahn, the fabulous publicity and marketing team made up of Tara O'Connor and Jessica Plummer, page designer Alison Cnockaert, and wonderful cover designer Eileen Carey. You've all gone above and beyond. The entire process of getting this book to market has been amazing.

A huge merci goes out to my army of sous chefs, my beta readers: Lainey Cameron, Valerie Hilal, Leslie Ficcaglia, Jo Maeder, Emily Monaco, Elizabeth Penney, and Barbara Conrey. Your feedback was invaluable. And thank you to the 2020s Debut Group for all of your support and love. Thank you to friend and cheese connoisseur Jessica Hammer from Taste of Toulouse for supplying the cheese tasting notes. And thank you to all of my friends who have supported this writing journey, especially chef Mary O'Leary, Susy Barrat, Lisa Anselmo, Tracey Biesterfeldt, Oksana Ritchie, and Jennifer Kincaid.

Merci to Dominique Crenn—the first woman in the United States to receive three Michelin stars. I applaud you. You truly are formidable and an inspiration.

I'd like to thank my family—my parents, Anne and Tony; my sister, Jessica; my stepkids, Max and Elvire; and my French husband, Jean-Luc. Thank you for eating all of the meals I tested. (I believe we ate well!) Thank you for being there for me—always. *Je vous aime. Beaucoup! Beaucoup! Beaucoup!*

Finally, I'd like to thank you, dear reader, for choosing this book. *Merci! Merci beaucoup! Merci mille fois!*

Author photo by Susy Barrat

Samantha Vérant is a travel addict, a self-professed oenophile, and a determined, if occasionally unconventional, at-home French chef. She lives in southwestern France, where she's married to a sexy French rocket scientist she met in 1989 (but ignored for twenty years), a step-mom to two incredible kids, and the adoptive mother to a ridiculously adorable French cat. When she's not trekking from Provence to the Pyrénées or embracing her inner Julia Child, Sam is making her best effort to relearn those dreaded conjugations.

Connect Online

SamanthaVerant.com

f AuthorSamanthaVerant

☐ Samantha_Verant

🐦 Samantha_Verant

Ready to find
your next great read?

Let us help.

Visit prh.com/nextread